Fellow Creatures

Fellow Creatures

EMMA LOWTHER

QUERCUS

First published in Great Britain in 2026 by Quercus
Part of John Murray Group

1

A CIP catalogue record for this book is available from the British Library

HB ISBN 978 1 52944 405 6
TPB ISBN 978 1 52944 406 3
EBOOK ISBN 978 1 52944 407 0

Typeset in 12.5/18pt Fournier MT Std by Six Red Marbles UK, Thetford, Norfolk
Printed and bound in Great Britain by Clays Ltd, Elcograf S.p.A.

MIX
Paper | Supporting responsible forestry
FSC www.fsc.org FSC® C104740

Papers used by Quercus are from well-managed forests and other responsible sources.

Quercus
Carmelite House
50 Victoria Embankment
London EC4Y 0DZ

John Murray Group
Part of Hodder & Stoughton Limited
An Hachette UK company

The authorised representative in the EEA is Hachette Ireland,
8 Castlecourt Centre, Dublin 15, D15 XTP3, Ireland (email: info@hbgi.ie)

For my parents, Colin and Dawn

'The time onstage is easier than the rest of one's existence. At least for those two and a half hours, you can be quite sure who you are.'

Dame Maggie Smith

PROLOGUE

OF COURSE, I'VE ALWAYS known there's something wrong with me. As far back as I can remember, there has been this wall, this two-inch-thick pane of glass that no one else seems to have. When I'm behind the glass, I see the world, I interact with it in a vague sort of way, but I never really come close to touching it. Except occasionally, when I get these bursts of feeling, where something takes over, some madness descends, and for a moment everything appears in vivid technicolour. It's in those moments that I'm afraid, those moments when I don't know what I might do.

One time I killed a bird. The neighbour's cat had got to it first. Its wing was hanging on by a single sinewy thread. My parents were late back from work. I was hungry and tired. My uniform stank. I hadn't yet worked out how to ask my mum for deodorant, too embarrassed to alert her to her little girl's leaking, pubescent body. Kids picked on me for the smell. One boy worse than others. That afternoon I'd been forced to sit next to him. I was always being asked to sit next to the naughty kids, as if my 'goodness' might rub off on them. Whenever the teacher's back was turned, the boy would lean in and whisper obscenities in my ear, informing me of all the ways he'd like to defile me, the stinky weirdo bitch. These aren't excuses. I don't know why I even mention them at all. But that day, standing alone in the garden, seeing the bird's oily feathers, its pleading bead of an eye, something inside me cracked. I took a brick, lifted it high in the air, and bashed the bird's skull in . . .

But then the feeling goes.

Punctured by shame, the madness drains away.

Life flattens into 2D. It becomes a movie reel, something everyone else takes part in while I just watch. I follow the plot, laughing and crying at all the right moments; I eat my popcorn, but really, it doesn't matter who lives or dies. When the credits roll, it's still just me, sitting alone inside a dark theatre.

I don't know why I'm telling you all this. It doesn't change anything. It doesn't absolve me of what comes next.

Victoria died twelve years ago, and even now I think about her every single day.

Forgive me. I'm getting ahead of myself. These things have an order. A beginning, a middle and an end. But you know that. You've had stories bred into you since your mother first peered into your crib and whispered songs of grizzly picnics and twinkling stars, blind mice and carving knives. I'll return to our beginning. Act One.

Lights.

Act One

ONE

MY LIFE IS A clerical error. The simple truth is that I'm only here, writing this, because of some mix-up at school with the GCSE classes; too many kids for Art, not enough for Drama.

Every Friday afternoon, in the small black classroom they called a theatre, we – the show-offs, the skivers and me – plodded through the syllabus: *Blood Brothers*, *Shakers*, *A Taste of Honey*, *Two*. And, much to near everyone's surprise, not least my own, I did well. It wasn't long before people wanted to partner with me, and the popular girls wanted me in their scenes. Offstage, I was a mess of hormones and insecurity. But onstage, there was this calm. Onstage, I made sense.

When I moved up to sixth form, my new teacher took me aside after class. She put her arm around my shoulder and told me I was *watchable*, that I had *a spark*.

'Do you have plans for uni, Shannon?'

She told me I ought to think about drama school. I said I didn't know what that was. She laughed like I was telling a joke.

That night I went home and typed *drama school* into my laptop, and waited for the screen to load.

>*LAMDA*

>*RADA*

I scrolled through page after page of the stuff.

>*Bristol Old Vic*

>*Italia Conti*

>*Central*

Each establishment gloated with ever more bloated pride about their successes; each repeated their commitment to only the finest tutors, the most state-of-the-art facilities, the brightest and best students.

I stared at the screen, transfixed. Suddenly the life I'd pictured for myself – living ten minutes from home, a safe, comfortable job, circling the same bunch of people I'd known since primary school – didn't seem so certain.

But Mum was calling. Tea was ready. I went and had my chips, egg and beans, and when my parents asked me how school was that day I said *fine*. I didn't tell them what the teacher had said. I didn't tell them about those impressive buildings down south with their acronymic names and blessings from the Queen. Or that my thoughts were distended with that new world, that bright, brilliant world that someone actually thought I had a chance of entering. I didn't tell them about the pilot light that was tick, tick, ticking inside my belly.

IN SECRET I ORDERED prospectuses. When they arrived, I stowed them in a plastic carrier bag beneath my bed. At night I took them out and ran my fingers over the stiff glossy covers. I touched the faces of lovelorn heroines, their nubile bodies contorted in grief. I stroked the chiselled jawline of the second-year clutching a weathered skull. I read the words of crusty principals, listing the merits of their revered establishments. I absorbed the course descriptions, memorizing the minutiae of each semester, learning by rote the names of graduates who'd gone on to success in the West End, Broadway, Hollywood.

I continued with my studies, with rehearsals. I perfected how I walked, how I spoke, the way I held myself, shoulders back, neck long, *pretending.* I watched my teacher's eyes light up from across the room at my final performance and allowed myself a small smile when the A* was slid across the desk two weeks later. A little bit of praise is a dangerous thing. Tick, tick, tick. That weak blue flame again.

AND THEN THE LETTER arrived: creamy, thick, weighted with expectation.

Dear Shannon Bell, I am delighted to confirm—

'Mum!' I yelled up the stairs. 'Dad?'

—an unconditional offer of acceptance.

It didn't feel real. The audition process had been gruelling, and – to my parents' dismay – expensive. Fifty quid a pop for the privilege of delivering a two-minute Portia or Juliet to a panel of indifferent tutors, not to mention the small fortune spent on train fares and hotels. I auditioned at five drama schools over four months. At each place, the people there already seemed to know one another. The waiting rooms were crammed to bursting with Tillys and Xanders, Hugos and Veritys, sharing tips, titbits and gossip.

Did you hear that Kitty got accepted at RADA?

I've got my second round at LAMDA next week.

They say the head of movement's a real ballbreaker.

What's your classical?

What's your modern?

My final audition was at the Royal London School of Dramatic Arts. I'd been rejected everywhere else, so this was my last shot before an enforced year of waiting tables.

Three rounds; one day. Three rounds doing the same classical and modern speeches to a rotation of different faces; three rounds of wondering if I was too fat, too wiry, too ugly, too plain; three rounds of waiting to be called out; three rounds of asking myself if this was it, if this was the moment they'd realize there'd been a mistake, that this girl shouldn't be here, that she shouldn't have made it this far.

But here it was.

—we look forward to welcoming you in the new academic year.

Proof of . . . something. A spark, maybe.

LOOKING BACK, MAYBE THAT was the perfect moment. The letter trembling in my hand. Or maybe it was before then, that teacher's arm around my shoulder, her hot mid-morning coffee breath in my ear, telling me I had *something*. I keep looking back for it, the moment, keep fumbling my way through memories to find it. When the future was held, a suspended thing, humming with possibility. I could've stopped it all then, before I met her . . . before she—

I could've taken that teacher's kernel of praise and nurtured it, let it grow into something private and perfect. Something no one else needed to know about. Something just for me. I could've done English at uni, gone to Durham or Warwick or wherever. I could've joined the drama society, performed in some poorly attended *Pygmalion* and enjoyed the secret knowledge that someone, somewhere once thought I had talent. I could've met somebody – some untroubled boy with scruffy hair and a battered pair of Converse who thought he was an artist but was happy to work in marketing. We could've dated for three years, got married, had 2.5 children and lived happily ever after, or something like that. I could've been normal, a normal person with a family, a job, and an unending cache of blameless days and dreamless nights.

But I didn't do that.

If I had, maybe she would still be alive.

TWO

THE ROYAL LONDON SCHOOL of Dramatic Arts. Although we called it the White Elephant. A mighty beast felled between two tower blocks, a strip club and Marylebone Road. It had been constructed two hundred years earlier as a refuge for performers, a safehouse to cosset their craft. Four towers (the legs) contained the beast, while the theatre huddled in its belly. Over time, more and more sections had been added to its hulking facade: a red-brick building tacked to the left, a Modernist cube dumped to the right. With each century the creature had grown and grown, a hodgepodge of fashions, an ungainly chimera.

I stood before it, awed by its ugliness, cowed by its majesty.

The ground shuddered below me. Later I came to recognize the sound as a train hurtling beneath my feet, but just then, I could've sworn it came from the beast, a low rumble, a warning.

I LAY ON MY unmade bed in the halls of residence. The room was small. A bed, a desk, three drawers and a closet. A bluebottle climbed the window. In the courtyard below me was a circle of weatherworn benches. In the bedroom above me was the cast of *STOMP*.

I knew I should unpack, but the task seemed too arduous to contemplate. I couldn't be bothered sliding the cardboard out from never-slept-in sheets or clipping the plastic ties off the many utensils

Mum – going overboard as usual – had got me from the homewares section of Wilko. But then I felt the familiar sting of guilt my parents always seemed to inspire in me. She'd tried, bless her. They both had. I mean, they'd said yes when I begged them to drive down and move me in the first day my room became available. They'd wanted to make a moment of it; go for coffee, tour the area with me, and size up the school's grand exterior. But, impatient to begin my new life, I'd made excuses – a headache, exhaustion – bundled them into the car and waved them off.

I got up and pulled back the sheer curtain. It was nearly seven o'clock. The chimney tops were bathed in an orange glow. Rose-coloured clouds daubed the sky. I opened the window its regulation six centimetres (to prevent overwrought freshmen from hurling themselves to their deaths), sat at the desk and opened my laptop. Facebook pinged. Someone had left a comment beneath my Leavers' Day photo.

Laura Stead

Haha good times. Keep in touch Shannon u star ★

I selected her profile and clicked Unfriend. We wouldn't keep in touch. I didn't want to. I wanted to discard the girl I'd been and build someone new.

I then clicked onto the group I'd been invited to a few weeks before, *>RLSDA Actors 09*. Although I knew them by memory, I read through the comments again.

Obi Njoku posted 1 hour ago

Did anyone get their books second-hand?

2 comments

Jolly McAndrew posted 2 days ago

OMG this reading list is KILLING ME

18 comments

Stefano Bianchi posted 5 days ago

Have any of the guys actually bought a dance belt?

3 comments

Archie Melling posted 7 days ago

Me and my band are doing a gig in Reading this weekend if anyone wants to meet up before term starts? X

No one has commented yet

Maddy McAuley posted 9 days ago

Which audition speech did you guys do to get in btw? ;) xx

12 comments

Hettie Walker-Grant posted 14 days ago

Just got my leotard home aaaaaaand it doesn't fit . . . X

No one has commented yet

I scrolled down to the bottom of the page.

Jolly McAndrew posted 3 weeks ago

Hey gang, allow me to introduce myself. I'm Jacob McAndrew but PLEASE PLEASE PLEASE just call me Jolly. I've set up this group so we can chat/meet/get to know each other before term begins. So excited to get started and meet y'all in the flesh! Wooo! Xxx

12 comments

I hadn't posted anything yet; I hadn't commented. Instead, I hovered like a ghost, absorbing what the others were up to, gathering information, plotting how I would present myself before them. These people were vibrant; they were interesting. I wasn't. Not yet.

My laptop pinged again. A new notification winked in the corner.

Victoria Parker-Tilley posted just now

I'm bored. Anyone in London yet – drink?

Victoria, like me, hadn't posted or commented before.

I clicked on her profile. It was private. Her picture was black and white, her face turned away from the camera. Beneath the image lay a single word. *Actor.*

She looked like the sort of girl I'd never dare to approach back home, the sort of girl who knew how to find and wear vintage clothing without looking stupid, the sort of girl who didn't need makeup to look pretty, the sort of girl who was bound to ignore me.

I gazed out at the pink-orange sky.

But maybe things were different now. Perhaps here, in London, we'd be friends. Perhaps I could be someone else.

I began typing.

Shannon Bell commented just now

I'm here. Tell me when and where. X

THREE

THE CITY WAS IN heat. The pub, busy. I'd forgotten it was a bank holiday weekend. Outside, the tables were full. I lurked by the railings for a few minutes, watching a couple pick through the last salty remains of their crisps and drain their pints while a poodle whined hungrily by their ankles.

The Thames lay in front of me. A lazy river, parched and unwieldly. It hadn't rained in weeks, and the smell of hot sewage filled the air.

The couple left and I grabbed their place.

I waited ten minutes. Then another twenty. The landlord came out and circled my bench, eyeing up my drink-less hand. Finally, just when I was starting to think this whole excursion had been some sort of joke, she appeared.

The first thing you noticed about Victoria was the way she moved. She didn't clomp through space, a victim of gravity like the rest of us, but seemed to glide effortlessly, like reeds waving in water, changing the density of the air around her. Every rise and footfall seemed to land exactly where it was meant to, her feet blindly confident they'd be lifted, carried – nay, exalted – by the earth.

She approached. I shielded my eyes against the sun.

She had her hands in her pockets. She was wearing creamy denim overalls with the sleeves rolled up to the elbows. On anyone else the clothes would've looked ridiculous – shapeless, rough and dry as they were – but she filled them out with an assumed elegance that made me yearn for a pair of my own.

She spoke first.

'I recognized you from your picture.'

Her voice surprised me. She was posh, yes, but there was something else there.

'Thanks for meeting me.' A deliberate slackening of her vowels, but veiled, like she was trying to hide the fact.

'No problem,' I said, trying to mirror the easy smile that spread across her lips.

'I'm Victoria,' she said, tilting her head. A rust-coloured curl slid from her shoulder.

'Shannon,' I replied, extending a hand.

She looked at my outstretched palm. A momentary crease formed in the freckled space between her eyebrows, but just as quickly disappeared. It was then that I knew I'd made a mistake, that I'd broken some impenetrable social code, that I might as well have handed her a banana as have performed this outdated greeting. But it was too late. I waited, my palm hovering in the space between us. Mercifully, she extracted a hand from her pocket and grazed the tips of my fingers with her own.

'A pleasure,' she said.

I offered to buy her a drink. At the bar, the landlord eyeballed me as I fumbled for my ID. 'What do you want?'

I looked at the row of taps, the neat shelves of bottles beyond the counter. He crossed his arms and stared past my forehead. I pointed at the pump nearest to me. Stout. I took the milky black thick-quid back to the bench and handed Victoria her slim-line vodka and tonic.

'Thanks,' she said, placing the drink on the table. 'I'll get the next one. I love your jacket by the way,' she added, waving her fingers towards where it had fallen to the floor.

'Thanks,' I said, retrieving the limp garment.

'It looks vintage?'

'Oh no, my mum got it from the supermarket, I think.'

'Cute.'

She unfurled herself from the bench and stretched. A moment of eye contact. That easy smile again. She turned her back on me and, grasping the railings, stared out at the river. In profile I noticed her carved cheekbones, the equine structure of her jaw. She leaned forwards. Hair fell about her face. She turned and picked up her drink. As she did so, a dewdrop of condensation dribbled onto her wrist and escaped down the cuff of her sleeve. She wiped her forearm on her thigh and tossed her hair behind her shoulders. Victoria liked touching her hair.

'How long have you been in London?' I asked.

She thought for a moment. 'Oh, I'd say about fourteen years.'

'Really?' I said, surprised to learn that anyone actually got to live here for real.

'Well, my dad has a place in north London.' She hesitated for a moment. 'Hampstead. I split my time between there and Mum's. I've been at Dad's all summer.'

'What does he do?'

'Finance.' She leaned against the railings. 'He's abroad mostly, in the US. It's just me and my brother, Rupert, in the house at the moment. Sometimes his girlfriend. We all just come and go really.'

I nodded. It all sounded so grown up.

'How old's your brother?'

'Thirty-one.'

'What does he do?'

'Corporate PR.'

I didn't know what that was, but made noises like I did. I sipped my pint. It was slimy, warm, too heavy for the occasion. I wiped the white moustache from my lip, hoping she wouldn't notice.

'Then there's Henry, who's a lawyer, and Lawrence who's in advertising. They don't visit much though . . .' She trailed off. 'In fact, I've mostly been on my own this summer so, as you can imagine, I'm fucking bored out of my mind.' She laughed, revealing a perfectly formed gap between her two front teeth, and sat down again.

'Don't you have friends in London?' I asked.

'What? Oh, yeah,' she said, taken aback. 'Yeah, I have friends. It's just, you know, people are travelling, some are back at uni already, people have other things on, different priorities.' She took another sip of her drink. The ice rattled in the glass. 'Anyway, what about you?' she said. 'Do you have any brothers or sisters?'

'Erm . . .' I hesitated, wary of how much to disclose. 'It's just me. And my parents, of course.'

'Hmm.' She took another sip of her drink.

We both stared at the river and I grasped for something to say. 'Are you looking forward to the course?'

She thought again. 'I guess.' She shrugged. 'I mean, obviously RLSDA wasn't my first choice.'

'It wasn't?'

'No. It doesn't even compare to RADA or LAMDA. But it's fine, I suppose.'

'Yeah.'

'My agent's making me go.'

'You have an agent?'

'Yeah. She says if I go to drama school, I'll get more theatre. And theatre's the way into TV and films nowadays. I'm like, *whatever.* It's only three years. And I can still do auditions and stuff.'

'Oh, wow.' My hands felt clammy; I wiped them on my jeans.

'I've spoken to the tutors. They know about my situation. It's fine, they're cool with it.' She sipped her drink. 'To be honest, if I get a big job, I might not even finish the whole three years. We'll see.'

'Great,' I said, fixing a smile in place and reaching for my glass.

I already had a dim awareness that part of the course – the grand finale, if you will – was a showcase at the end of our third year, and that it was there that we'd be premiered like debutantes, there that the entire theatre and film industry would be invited to judge, pluck and anoint us. I knew that the holy grail was signing with a big agent. But here was Victoria, one of my apparent equals, already signed, already dismissing the course, already on her way out of the door. Her clear-sighted indifference suddenly made my excitement seem faintly embarrassing. I felt like a child caught playing dress-up in my mother's lipstick and bras, a fantasist in sagging elastic.

'Where are you from, by the way?' she asked.

'Meltham.'

'Where's that?'

'Up North.'

'*Ooop North*,' she said, her eyes shining wickedly.

'Yes.'

'So near Birmingham?'

'No, that's the Midlands.'

'Isn't that the North?

'No.'

'But it's north of London.'

'I suppose.'

'Hmm. Don't worry.' She crunched a shard of ice. 'I like your accent. It's cute.'

'Oh, thanks.'

'It means you'll be fine. You've got a *thing*.' She shifted and, reaching inside her back pocket, said to herself, 'I wish I had a *thing*.' She pulled out a crushed box of cigarettes, brought one to her lips, then paused. 'God, I'm so fucking rude, I'm sorry – do you want one?'

'Erm, yeah,' I said. 'Go on then.' Although half my family smoked, I'd never taken it up myself. I didn't like the smell, and the one time I tried it at a party, I coughed until I threw up.

Victoria placed two cigarettes between her lips and thumbed the purple lighter. It wouldn't take. She fumbled with the cog and I noticed that her nails, in contrast to the rest of her chic exterior, were bitten down to the nub, the skin around them dry and cracked. She shook the thing and tried again. A weak flame leapt in front of her face. She inhaled. The two ends glowed. She handed me one, and I saw her mouth had wet the thin ribbon of paper. I placed it between my lips.

'I only do this when I drink.' She took a drag. Smoke curled free with her words. 'It's a filthy habit otherwise.'

I nodded and inhaled. The space between my ears buzzed. The pads of my fingers tingled. I wanted to cough but managed to get away with just clearing my throat. She didn't seem to notice.

Just then, a shadow fell across the table. I turned around and came face to face with a great beast of a man. He had a map of patchy stubble across his chin and yellow, watery eyes. Stinking of piss and booze, he leaned across the two of us.

'Pretty girls,' he slurred, slapping his hand down beside Victoria's drink. 'Mind if I join you?'

Victoria, flinching, seemed to shrink beneath his gaze. Gone was the blasé confidence of a few moments earlier. Noticing this, I sat up straight and answered on her behalf.

'No. Go away, please. We're having a private conversation.'

'I didn't mean you,' the man answered, his eyes fixed on Victoria.

I rested my cigarette in the ashtray and stood up. It wasn't much of a gesture, but the man seemed to notice my existence then at least. 'Fuck off now or I'll go get the landlord,' I said, with as much dignified rage as I could muster.

Some of the other tables were starting to notice what was happening. A handful of people got up from their benches, ready to step in.

The man, slowly becoming aware of the watchful crowd, shrugged and removed his hand from the table.

'Ugly bitches anyway,' he grunted to himself, before disappearing inside the pub.

With my heart racing, I returned to my seat and sipped my pint. I glanced up to see Victoria looking at me curiously.

'What?' I asked, wiping my upper lip self-consciously.

She took another drag on her cigarette. I noted the slight tremor in her fingers. 'So, what shall we do tomorrow?' she asked.

'Tomorrow? What do you mean?'

'I mean, what shall we *do*? I'm bored. We've got a week until term starts. So?'

I felt my skin flush. I had to turn away to hide the inelegant grin that threatened to spread across my face.

'Whatever you want,' I said. I picked up my cigarette and took a deeper drag this time. 'I don't mind. I'll do whatever you want.'

FOUR

WE MET IN HEAVEN. I stood beneath the arches nursing a vodka and lemonade, and peered out at the gyrating mass of bodies. The DJ, shirtless, tipped his head back and spread his arms wide, Christ-like, while the crowd squirmed as one at his feet. I leaned back but then thought better of it. The brick wall was damp with other people's sweat and breath. Someone tapped me on the shoulder.

'You came!' Victoria yelled over the music. She was wearing a tartan mini skirt, Doc Martens and a faded Rolling Stones T-shirt. Her hair was loose, her eyelids heavy with glitter. She pulled me into a hug, then took a step back and looked me up and down. 'You look gorgeous.'

I smiled, relieved. I'd spent hours that afternoon deciding what to wear. I'd packed a few flimsy bodycon dresses and strappy heels in my suitcase, the sort of things girls wore on nights out back home, but, after meeting Victoria, I sensed a different look was required. I'd finally landed on a green check shirt, denim hotpants and Converse. 'Thanks,' I yelled back. 'So do you.'

'Sorry I'm late. The tubes were shit.'

I waved her apology away.

'Thanks for agreeing to come out,' she said. 'You know when you just *need* to dance?'

I nodded, although the urge had never taken me.

The song changed and a cheer went up. Victoria squealed and, taking my hand, dragged me into the crowd. 'I love this song!'

'What?'

'I said I love this song.'

I didn't recognize it. It sounded just like the last one and the one before that, but when we reached the centre, I jumped and threw my arms in the air like everyone else.

As we danced, I caught glimpses of the people around me. I'd never been to a club like this before, one where men embraced men, women embraced women, and the air felt charged with possibility. It was different from the clubs I'd sneaked into while at college, where two-for-one Apple Sourz and getting groped by some acne-scarred teenage boy to Usher's 'Yeah!' were the hallmarks of a Good Night Out.

The bass hummed in my teeth and one song blended into another. Sometimes I managed to catch Victoria's eye, at which point she'd smile or pout or beckon me closer. I saw a couple of guys glance over at her approvingly, a couple of girls. I felt proud then, that Victoria had chosen me.

The lights flipped, green to blue. The song changed and the crowd lurched forward, pushing us closer together. Victoria turned to face me.

'Are you having a good time?' she shouted in my ear.

'The best,' I said, dabbing my forehead with my sleeve.

She looped her arms around my neck. 'Are you drunk?' she asked. Her breath was both sweet and vinegary.

'Not really.'

'Do you want to be?' She pressed her hips against my own and swayed from side to side. I felt a dull ache in my pelvis. I laughed nervously and pulled away from her, ashamed.

'I brought my brother's credit card.' She felt inside her back pocket and re-looped her arms, so we were nose to nose. 'What do you want?'

'I can pay.'

She shook her head and pulled a face.

'I'll have the same as you, then.'

Her fingers lingered a moment on my neck before she removed her hands and disappeared into the darkness. I bopped on the spot, looking to see which direction she'd gone. But it was useless. The music continued and people danced around me. I tried to watch what they were doing, to move in time with the crowd, but without Victoria there to guide me, I felt ridiculous.

After ten minutes, I pushed my way towards the bar, where I saw Victoria talking to an impossibly tall and handsome man in a tight white T-shirt and brown chinos. An unpleasant, unnameable sensation flared up inside my chest. Victoria glanced over and motioned for me to join them.

'Double vodka and cranberry,' she said, thrusting a plastic cup into my hand so red liquid sloshed onto my wrist.

'Thanks,' I said, not meeting her eye.

'This is Angus,' she said, sliding her arm around the man's middle and resting her head on his chest.

'Hi.'

He nodded and gave me a bland, disinterested smile.

'We were at Trinity together,' Victoria said.

'Where?' I asked, unsure whether I'd heard her correctly.

'Oxford. I only managed two terms.' She took a slug of her drink. 'It was *not* for me. Angus is still on the academia treadmill though, aren't you?'

The man bent down and whispered something in her ear.

She flashed him a knowing grin. 'OK, see you later, hun.'

We watched him re-enter the crowd.

'Isn't he an absolute darling?'

'Yeah.'

'He's doing Classics.'

'Right.'

'Bless him, he came out to his parents last weekend. I don't think they were too happy about it, so he's hiding out with some friends in Clapham until term restarts.'

'Right,' I said. 'He's gay. Of course.'

'Well, yeah,' Victoria said, rolling her eyes and gesturing towards the Pride flag emblazoned on the wall. 'Obviously.' She took a sip of her drink. 'It's not a problem, is it?'

'What?'

'Being here.' Her eyes flicked towards a woman leaning against the wall with another pressed up against her, a hand disappearing beneath her top.

'No. No problem,' I said, looking at the floor, my drink, at anyone but her.

'We can leave if you're uncomfortable.'

'I'm not uncomfortable. I'm . . .' I grasped for the correct thing to say. 'Comfortable.'

Victoria looked sceptical. 'OK.' She brushed her hair behind her ear. 'Seen anyone you like?'

'What do you mean?' I wasn't sure what she was asking. Did she think I was—?

'Here – is there anyone you like the look of?'

'No,' I replied firmly. 'You?'

She pursed her lips, considering the question, then, grinning, laced her fingers with my own. 'Come on, let's dance.'

WE SAT ON THE floor of McDonald's, drunk and ravenous. The place was heaving despite the late hour. A gaggle of teenage girls stumbled past us in ankle-breaking stilettos; a homeless man lingered by the door asking for spare change or, *if it's not too much trouble*, a Diet Coke; a stag group, all wearing shirts the same shade of salmon, eyeballed us as they swaggered towards the counter. Victoria stuffed a handful of fries inside her mouth.

'It's so weird,' she slurred. 'My parents have been divorced for years, but there's still this flirtiness between them. When they see each other – which isn't very often, I should say – Mum's like a teenager again; she gets all giggly.'

'When did they split up?'

'God.' She thought for a moment, swaying lightly. 'I must've been six years old?'

'That's young.'

'Yeah.' She leaned over and swirled a fry in my barbecue sauce. 'Dad's a cad. He could never keep it in his trousers.'

'Do you see your stepmum?'

'Ugh, don't say it like that, *stepmum*. No, I can't stand her. Or the twins. Nasty little shits. But it's fine. Dad's in America mostly, and they almost never come over with him.'

'What does your mum do in Surrey?'

Victoria grimaced. 'Not a lot. The official line is, *she runs a wine-importing business*.' She slurped her milkshake. 'What about you? What do your parents do?'

'Dad sells garden awnings and Mum works as a teaching assistant in a high school.'

'Fun.'

'Special educational needs, you know, things like that.'

'Hmm.' She sniffed and rummaged in her bag for more chips.

I felt I'd disappointed her in some way, although I wasn't sure how.

'I'm probably closer to my grandma though.'

'Oh yeah?' she said, still rummaging.

'Yeah. She's cool; a bit odd. Mum and Dad . . . ever since I was a kid, I don't know, it's like there's been this distance between us—'

'My great-grandmother had an affair with a Nazi officer,' Victoria said, talking over me, her mouth filled with food.

'Seriously?' I said, trying to match her animated tone. It wasn't something I'd brag openly about, but I was starting to realize Victoria came from a different world entirely.

'Yep. There's pictures and everything. Dad keeps them locked away though, for obvious reasons.'

'You've had such an interesting life.'

She shrugged. 'Not really. It's just my family; they're a mad bunch.' She dipped another fry into my sauce. 'My great-aunt died in a plane crash in the Alps.'

'Wow.'

'Now, she *did* have an interesting life. I think she was involved with a Kennedy at one point. Bless her, the old slag.' She laughed and clambered unsteadily to her feet. She crushed the brown bag into a ball, then took my hand and pulled me up to standing. 'Where do you live?'

'I'm in halls.'

'Oh, weird.' She pulled down her top, which had ridden up. 'I thought everyone house shared at RLSDA.'

'They do. I just wanted my own space.'

'Whereabouts?' she asked, staggering towards the door.

'Near Baker Street.'

'Can I stay at yours? It'll be a pain getting back to mine at this time.'

I hesitated. As much as I'd enjoyed the evening, I wasn't sure if I could handle being alone with Victoria in my cramped little room. But then I pictured her standing on the kerb, shivering and off her face, desperately trying to hail a cab. 'Sure. Of course you can.'

I UNLOCKED THE DOOR.

'You've not unpacked much,' she said, stepping inside.

'No, sorry – I would've tidied up more if I'd known you were coming over.'

Her eyes roamed the blank walls. 'You should put posters up.'

'Yeah, no, I will. I'll get around to it soon,' I replied, chastened.

'You know what' – Victoria edged past my open suitcase – 'although it's small, it's actually kind of cute.' She placed her hands on the windowsill and peered down at the courtyard. 'I mean, for you. I don't think *I* could live here. But then I have *a lot* of stuff.' She reached for the photograph by my bedside – one of the few things I'd unpacked – and turned it over. '*Julie and Tom with Shannon, aged five*. Are these your parents?'

'Yes. That was taken at my auntie's wedding.'

'You look so cute.' She squinted at the picture, then me. 'Your hair was a bit redder back then. And your eyes looked bluer.'

I took the photo from her and stared at the girl in the frame, the hopeful expression on her face. 'Yeah, well, it was a long time ago.'

I let Victoria take the bed. She said she was happy to share, but I wasn't used to sharing my space with anyone and Victoria's presence, although flattering, made me feel uneasy. There was something about her manner that was too familiar, too intimate, like she was daring me to cross a line I wasn't sure I wanted to cross yet. I couldn't trust myself to lie so close to her, to feel her chest rise and fall beside mine, to have her hair spread across the pillow, mingling with my own.

I went to the bathroom to brush my teeth. When I returned, Victoria was in her bra and knickers, sitting on the bed. She had headphones in and was flicking through my MP3 player. I coughed and tapped on the door, *my* door.

'What are you doing?'

Victoria glanced up at me and smiled. 'What did you say?' she said, removing an earpiece.

'What are you doing?'

'Seeing what you're into.'

'Oh.'

She replaced the earpiece and returned to twiddling the dial.

I wanted her to stop, to stop touching and fiddling and looking through my things.

'I've got pyjamas you can borrow, if you want,' I said pointedly.

'Hmm?' she said, looking up.

'I said I've got pyjamas you can borrow,' more softly this time.

She pulled the headphones out and rolled up the wire. 'Nah. I'm like a furnace at night.'

'OK.' I stood, lingering by the door, trying to look anywhere else but at the porcelain line of her tummy.

'You're a dark horse,' she said, waving the MP3 player at me. 'Lots of classical music.' She slid it back inside the drawer. 'I wouldn't have expected that.'

I felt my cheeks redden. 'Yeah, no, it's dumb.'

'Babe, I'm not criticizing you. I think it's cool that you like your own thing.'

'Oh, OK.' I dumped the two cushions I'd nicked from the shared living area on the floor. 'Err yeah, well, it helps me relax.'

'Oh, absolutely. I get it. Me? I just *love* jazz,' she said, sitting forward.

'You do?' I kicked my suitcase under the desk and pulled my thickest bath towel from the closet. 'What kind?'

'Just like' – she thought for a moment – 'just like general jazz.'

There was a pause.

'Cool. Are you ready for bed?'

'God yeah, I'm exhausted.'

I flicked the light switch and arranged myself on the floor. Victoria hitched her knees up and scooted down under the covers. She plumped the pillow with her fist and lay on her side to face me.

'Well, this is *cosy*,' she said in a low purr.

'Yes,' I replied, shifting my weight to try and get comfortable.

'Are you sure you're OK down there?' she asked, dangling her arm from the bed and pawing at my shoulder.

'Don't worry about me.'

She lifted the covers a few inches. 'There's room, you know. If you're cold.'

'Honestly, I'm fine.'

'Suit yourself,' she said, curling into a ball. 'So . . .'

'So . . .'

'Do you think your boyfriend will come and visit you in halls?' she asked.

'I don't have a boyfriend.'

'You don't? I thought you said you did.'

'No.'

'A girlfriend?'

I buried my face in the cushion at the insinuation. 'No.'

'How come?'

I sighed. 'I don't know . . . I've just never really done all that.' I paused. 'What about you?'

'Are you asking if I'm single?'

'Yes.'

'I mean, I guess so, yeah . . . I've not been with anyone for a while.'

I waited for her to continue, but she didn't. I glanced over. She'd rolled away from me and was staring at the ceiling, her eyes glowing white in the darkness.

We lay in silence for a few minutes and I began to drift off.

'Shannon?'

'Yes,' I replied, half asleep.

'Can I ask you something?' She sounded different, vulnerable all of a sudden.

'Go on then.'

'Are you a virgin?' *Is that what she said?* Her voice was so quiet I could barely hear her.

I opened my eyes. There was only one answer, but I wasn't sure whether I wanted to give it to her. 'Yes,' I said eventually, shifting to face her. 'Are you?'

I watched her snuggle down deeper and then, after a moment, the imperceptible shake of her head.

I BOUGHT TWO COFFEES, two muffins and a fruit salad (in case that was her thing) from the cafeteria and climbed the stairs. I hadn't slept a wink. All night my mind had been racing, replaying every moment of the evening, wondering if I'd pitched myself right, if I'd given too much of myself away or not enough, whether she liked me. When I re-entered the room, Victoria was dressed in her clothes from last night and picking through one of my still-to-be-unpacked boxes of books.

'I didn't realize you were awake,' I said, placing the coffees on the desk.

'You read a lot,' she replied.

'Err, yeah.'

She lifted a book out. '*How to Win Friends and Influence People*.'

I grabbed it from her and laughed – self-deprecatingly, I hoped. 'There's a lot of old shit in there. I just brought everything I could pack.'

'I can see that,' she said, raising an eyebrow. She picked out another. '*Jane Eyre*.'

'Careful, there're a couple of loose pages,' I said, taking it from her. 'It's my favourite.'

'I've never read it.'

'I stole it from school. We had to do it in English,' I said, gazing at the worn cover. 'We had to read aloud for an assessment.' I paused. 'I was so shy. I don't think I'd ever read aloud to anyone before that point.'

'Ah, *the burgeoning actress*. Did you do well?'

I felt my cheeks go red. I placed the book back in the box. 'Yes and no. I liked it, reading aloud, having all those people watching me. I didn't expect to, but then, I don't know . . .'

'What happened?'

'I got some weird feedback.'

'What?'

'It's nothing.'

'Go on.'

I sighed. 'The teacher said I did really well, that I inhabited the character of Jane and everything, but at the bottom of the assessment page I could see he'd written something and then rubbed it out.'

'What did it say?'

'I've never told anyone this before.'

'Go on, what did he write?'

I hesitated. '*Face disappears.*'

Victoria gave a bark of laughter. '*Face disappears?* What does that even mean?'

I hadn't expected that response. It wasn't funny, not to me at least. 'I don't know,' I said. 'I don't know what it means.'

'That's some cryptic bullshit.'

'Yeah.'

'What a creep.'

'Yeah.'

Victoria picked up the book and flipped to a page where the corner had been folded down. '*There is no happiness like that of being loved by your fellow creatures, and feeling that your presence is an addition to their comfort.*' She closed it. 'Is that when you knew you wanted to act, reading *Jane Eyre* out loud to the class?'

I shrugged. 'I don't know. I don't remember making a choice.'

'Well, did you want to do it when you were a kid?'

'Maybe. I can't really remember. My childhood's a bit of a blur.' My hand shook as I prised the lid off my coffee. I didn't want to think about that, not now, not in this new life. I sat on the edge of the desk. 'What about you? When did you decide you wanted to be an actress?'

Victoria lay back on the bed and puffed out her cheeks. 'Now there's a question.' She narrowed her eyes. 'Well, I suppose I've always been a *performer.* I used to do dressage, ballet and piano. And then when I was eight, I was crowned May Queen in the nearby village. That was pretty cool.'

'Did you get to wear a crown?'

'I did!' She sat up on her elbows. 'And I had a sash and this big gold stick to wave around, which I enjoyed *very* much.' She smiled to herself. 'And then I think I was around eleven when I got my modelling agent.'

'You had a modelling agent?'

'Yes. I got scouted at a friend's birthday party, in Pizza Express of all places.' She rolled her eyes and grinned. 'Oh, the *glamour.* Anyway, she got me my acting agent after that.'

'Wait, you've had your agent since you were eleven?'

'Yeah,' she shrugged. 'Well, I've had *an* agent since then. I'm with an adult one now obviously. I didn't get much work when I was a kid. Although I did do this fizzy drink advert—'

'What for?'

'Believe me, you wouldn't have heard of it. I think it got banned in the EU or something. There was a whole lawsuit. I've looked for it online, but I can't find it anywhere. Anyway, then I played Marta in *The Sound of Music*, which was pretty cool.'

'Where?'

'Oh, everywhere. It was the national tour. I got to meet Julie Andrews after the show one evening, which was just *insane*. But then after that I didn't really act again for a while.' She grabbed both her tits. 'Alas, the awkward adolescent years.'

'Not a girl, not yet a woman.'

'You said it, Britney. Then I did some stuff at boarding school, a load of gender-bending because it was all girls and I was unlucky enough to have a *husky voice*, so I had to play all the old man parts.'

I smiled and scooped a piece of muffin into my mouth. I liked Victoria. I liked her stories.

'And then, when I was sixteen, I played Gwendolen Fairfax in *The Importance of Being Earnest*.' She stopped and her shoulders seemed to slump. She cleared her throat. 'Sorry, can you pass me that coffee?'

I handed it to her. She took a sip and stared at her lap for a moment. 'Anyway, it turns out there was this BBC casting assistant in the audience, some relative of one of the girls, and he invited me to audition for *Sense and Sensibility*. It was just a small role, a maid, but I got the part, and that was the last time I acted. So, I don't know when I decided to be an actress. I guess it just happened.'

'Wait, wait, hold on. You were in *Sense and Sensibility*? You were in a period drama on the BBC?'

She gave me a tight smile. 'Yep.'

'That's huge.'

'I guess.' She placed the coffee down and got up. 'You know what – sorry, Shannon – I've got a busy day. I should probably get back.'

'Do you want to shower?' I asked, crestfallen. I didn't want her to leave. 'You can shower if you want.'

'No, it's fine. Thanks. And thanks for letting me stay.' She grabbed her things and went towards the door. But then, thinking better of it, she stopped and turned around. 'Although, maybe we could hang out later?' All of a sudden she looked nervous, like a little girl. 'If you want to. Only if you want to though.'

'I do want to, yeah.'

'Cool.' Her eyes lit up. She smiled and, despite the hangover and the bed head and the makeup still smeared across her face from last night, just then, my new friend Victoria looked impossibly beautiful to me. 'I'll text you.'

*

WE ENDED UP SPENDING the whole week together. I visited her at her father's house in Hampstead. We climbed out of the poky attic window and onto the roof, where we settled ourselves on the lichen-covered slate. We drank whatever we could find in the house. We smoked. We stared out across sunsets on the Heath. She told me about the girls she'd been to school with, that they were all bitches, that they were all sweethearts, that she wished she'd been home-schooled, that boarding builds character, that she didn't want children, that she longed to be a mother. I listened to it all. I ummed and ahhed and cooed at all the right moments, lapping up her stories like a greedy cat, my whiskers covered in cream, enjoying every slick morsel of information, storing away each memory to be taken out and turned over, rattled and cherished.

We went to pubs, we visited bars. She took me to a rooftop in Dalston where we danced until 4 a.m. We caught night buses and rode on the top deck as dawn broke and the city's cleaners boarded, ready to scrape away the detritus of the previous day. We went to the theatre. We got groundling tickets for *Macbeth* at the Globe. We gazed up at the wide eye of the sky. My legs ached from standing. My cheeks ached from smiling. Red liquid sprayed the audience when the knife plunged into Duncan's heart. When we emerged onto the riverbank, she licked her thumb and wiped the blood from my forehead.

One week. That's how long it took for me to love Victoria completely.

I stopped checking the Facebook group. I didn't care about the others. I'd meet them when the time came. And until then, I had Victoria. We were going to conquer the school, the stage, the world – together.

REGISTRATION WAS ON MONDAY. On Sunday afternoon I called Victoria. It went straight to voicemail. I left a message. *Let's get a drink.*

Shall I come over? That evening I still hadn't heard from her. I called again. This time she picked up. *Hi*, she said stuffily. She said she was sorry for not calling but she felt like she was coming down with something. She said she thought she'd better rest, that she didn't want to turn up on the first day feeling ill. I said that was fine, it was fair enough. I offered to come over with a tin of chicken soup. She laughed and said I was sweet, but no. She said she was just going to take a bath and go to sleep, that she'd see me in the morning, *bright and early, Shirley*.

She said goodbye and hung up. *Love you, bye*. I lay on my bed. I hoped my friend would feel better by tomorrow. She was right, it *was* for the best that we didn't see each other. We'd catch up in the morning. We had a big day ahead of us. I put my phone on the floor and, within minutes, was asleep.

FIVE

'CALL ME REX,' THE third-year in the grey T-shirt said. 'I'll be your student liaison for the day. Any questions, just come and find me. We'll do a quick tour and then I'll drop you off back at reception, where you can get your ID cards. Sound good?'

The group murmured their assent. I looked around. Victoria wasn't here yet. Or maybe she was with another cohort. As Rex led us up the stairs, I typed out a quick message.

Monday, 7th September at 10:05

Shannon Bell

Hey, what group are you in? I'm with this Rex guy. Maybe I can meet you for the ID bit? Let me know xx

Rex ushered us through some security doors and down a long corridor. The excited chatter died away, replaced with hushed awe at the vaulted ceilings, the polished marble floor, the gilded portraits that peered down at us.

Rex stopped by a plinth. He reached a hand out and stroked the bronze bust that sat atop it.

'This is Ollie,' he announced. 'Oliver Hewlett-Smith – the founder of the school.' He smirked at us. 'All us students stroke his nose before doing a show. It's good luck.'

A ripple of excitement went through the group as we were let in on this nugget of theatrical lore.

'Honest to God, it's not even bollocks. A girl in my class, Annabelle, stroked him before she went on to do her Ophelia, and the next day she got a job at The Nash.'

The group cooed and chattered in response. I wasn't entirely sure what *The Nash* was, but it sounded impressive.

'Go ahead, give him a stroke.' He raised an eyebrow. 'You're at RLSDA now. You need all the luck you can get.'

Each member of the group stepped forward in turn and stroked the long nose, worn to a dull copper by years of fraught, ambitious fingers.

I went last. I pressed my thumb to the bust. The head toppled slightly. Rex stepped in front of me.

'Woah there. I think that's enough luck for today.'

Monday, 7th September at 10:56

Shannon Bell

Hey, I'm in the queue. You here yet? Xx

The person ahead of me moved.

Monday, 7th September at 10:57

Shannon Bell

The ID queue I mean, haha, just in case you were like, what queue?? Xx

I shuffled forwards. I glanced over my shoulder but didn't see anyone I recognized. Even Rex had abandoned us.

I looked at my phone. There were no new messages.

I sighed and rubbed my eye, whereupon some dust mote, some speck of dirt got stuck. I blinked a few times, trying to dislodge it, but the thing burrowed deeper.

'Ow, bastard.'

I wiped my hand on my jeans, pulled back my eyelid, and tried to dig it out with my finger.

The queue moved forward.

I tried again, pinning my eyelid back, rooting around for the lash or grit or demon that was causing my discomfort.

'Next!'

I looked to the side and caught my reflection in a glass display case. My eyes were streaming. A woman with a clipboard stopped beside me.

'Name?'

'Shannon Bell.'

'Are you OK, sweetheart?'

'Yes, no, I'm fine – I've just—'

'I know the first day is nerve-racking, but you'll be all right.' She squeezed my shoulder and continued moving down the line.

'Name?'

The queue moved forward again. Now there were only two people between me and the camera's unforgiving gaze. I dabbed at my face, wiping as much mascara from beneath my eyes as I could.

'Next!' the photographer yelled.

I sat down in front of the blue backdrop. My nose was running now too. I stared down the lens, holding my eye open as long as I dared.

The camera flashed.

'Next!'

One more blink and the grit, with virtuosic timing, dislodged itself.

'First-years, this way please!' someone yelled.

I was ushered through a different door and into a new crowd of people.

'Once you've had your photograph taken, please head to the Hewlett Theatre. The principal's address will start in five minutes.'

I walked through the padded velvet doors and into the crimson five-hundred-seat theatre. Another third-year was directing students to fill up from the front.

That's when I saw her.

She was sitting three rows from the stage, already hemmed in by students on all sides. She had her feet on the chair in front of her. To her left was a broad-shouldered boy. On his head sat a tight crop of black curls. A delicate silver chain glinted from around his dark-brown neck. To her right bounced a puckish boy with alabaster skin and a messy shock of white-yellow hair.

The skinny boy delivered the punchline to a joke and the three of them laughed. He stood up in his chair. Victoria, giggling, pulled him back down into his seat.

'Up here, please.' The third-year tapped me on the shoulder. 'There are places near the back.'

I climbed the stairs, sat down and pulled out my phone.

Nervous, excited chatter filled the room.

Monday, 7th September at 11:12

Shannon Bell

Look up ^^ I'm here! Xx

'Hi, I'm Lucy. What's your name?' the girl beside me said.

Victoria, still deep in conversation, reached for her phone.

'Shannon.'

She glanced at the screen and replaced it in her pocket.

'Oh, cool. I'm doing the set design course. What about you?'

I shifted in my seat to get a better look at the three of them.

'Did you hear what I said?'

Turn around, Victoria.

'I said I was doing the set design course, what about you?'

Notice me.

'Hello?'

See me.

'Hello?'

'EVERY ONE OF YOU is sitting here today because you have something special. Whether you call it talent or that maddeningly inscrutable "X factor", every one of you has it.' The principal stopped and gazed around the room. 'So use it.'

I stared at the back of Victoria's head.

'You are the storytellers. You are the witnesses. Use your voice. Tell the world what you have seen and heard and felt.'

Why hadn't she responded to any of my messages?

'Tell the world what matters, why it matters. Use your voice to make them laugh and cry and feel things, to experience everything that this world has to offer.'

Just a simple text?

'As performers and theatre makers, you have the power to reach inside people's heads, inside their very beings, and connect with them.'

Had I upset her somehow?

'You have the power to transport them across borders, continents, galaxies.'

I watched as she leaned her head on the arm of the guy to her right, watched as she was handed a tissue by the puckish boy. The small tight-knit group sat forwards in their seats, hanging on the principal's every word.

'You have the power to—'

She was wearing baggy paint-splattered jeans, a cropped white vest.

'Your time here won't be easy. There will be times when you'll struggle, when you'll falter. When you'll fall so low you won't know how to get back up again.'

The three of them turned and looked at one another, smiling, gushing and spilling over with pride at how demonstrably special they all were, how very chosen.

'But, as I believe Confucius once said: *Our greatest glory is not in never falling, but in rising every time we fall*—'

Her hair fell in waves across her shoulders.

'We expect a lot of our students. You are the creators of the future—'

She'd said I should grow my hair too, that then we could be twins.

'As students of the Royal London School of Dramatic Arts, we want to teach you how to thrive, to flourish—'

She said she'd never met anyone like me before, that she'd never felt such an instant connection.

'—like the bright butterflies you all are—'

That we were like sisters.

'We want you to learn lots of things. But above all, my dear first-years—'

We're sisters now, you and I. Don't ever forget that.

'—we want you to rise!'

Sisters.

The hall erupted in applause. Students leapt to their feet. Whoops and cheers filled the auditorium. Someone started stamping their feet, and soon the whole student body had joined in.

The principal touched his head, his heart, placing his hands in a mandala pose of humble grace, bowing, grinning, genuflecting; a deity, a rockstar.

Victoria was on her feet too, clapping her hands high above her head, the hem of her vest lifting with every slap of air.

SIX

'V. OVER HERE,' I said, grabbing her wrist as she exited the auditorium.

'What the—' She jerked her arm away like I'd burned her. 'Shannon, what are you doing? You gave me a fucking heart attack.'

'Sorry,' I said. 'I didn't mean to startle you.'

'Guys,' Victoria called out, bringing her companions to a stop. 'Wait a sec.'

'Are you OK? Do you still feel ill?'

She looked confused for a moment before rearranging her features. 'Oh yeah, no. I'm fine. It was just like one of those twenty-four-hour things.'

'Oh, cool. Did you get my texts? I was up near the back.'

'Oh, no, sorry. It's shit signal in there. That'll be why.'

'Yeah,' I said, swallowing the lie.

The two guys I'd seen her with wandered over.

'And who's this then?' the puckish boy said.

'Jolly, this is Shannon,' Victoria said, tossing her hair over one shoulder.

'Oh my God, *you're* Shannon! Hi!' He pulled me into a hug. 'I'm Jolly. I run the Facebook group.' He stepped back, still gripping my elbows. 'I'm sorry, I'm just so excited to like meet everyone, you know?'

'Jol, leave her alone,' Victoria said.

Jolly let go, but made a face as he did so. I liked him immediately.

Victoria's other companion extended a hand. 'Obi,' he said in a deep voice. I shook it, relieved at the straightforward gesture. 'It's lovely to meet you.'

His palm was warm. I met his eyes. They were grey and shining. I looked away.

'You too,' I stammered.

I glanced at Victoria. She was staring at me, her head cocked to one side. Her eyes narrowed momentarily, flicking between Obi and me.

Sensing I'd displeased her, I crossed my arms and stepped back from him. 'Are you guys going somewhere now?' I asked, giving her my most placatory smile.

Her mouth twitched into a smirk. She shrugged and slouched her weight onto one hip. 'We're going for lunch.'

'Oh, cool,' I said. I waited, praying for an invitation. 'Can – can I tag along too?'

She shrugged again. 'It's a free country.' She turned and started walking towards the main door. The boys followed close behind.

AT LUNCH, THE THREE of them chatted, parrying easy words back and forth across the Formica table. Meanwhile I sat quietly, picking through an egg and watercress sandwich and trying to make my latte last another ten minutes. I could feel myself disappearing, becoming just another tired piece of furniture in the dim little cafe. They talked about the school, their expectations of what was to come, rumours they'd heard, horror stories.

'Apparently in second year they tie you naked to a tree. It's like some sort of endurance thing.'

'Jolly, that's bollocks.'

'It's true! And the longer you're there, the longer you can stand it, the higher your final grade.'

'What's that got to do with acting though?' Obi interjected.

'Fucked if I know. Proves you're committed or something?'

'OK, well Jolly's clearly full of shit—'

'Am not—'

'But have you guys heard about the living history stuff?' Victoria asked.

'No, what's that?' Jolly said.

'OK, so apparently there's this one term where you study a period of history and then you like literally live through it.'

'So?'

'So, they don't pick any old period. Last year they had people in gulags building the road of bones, and before that they had prisoners working in concentration camps.'

'Surely not,' Obi said, playing with the cross on his chain.

Victoria grimaced. 'I wish I was lying. The worst part is they divide you into groups, like the oppressors and the oppressed, and then you just have to stay in character the whole time. Like if a commander feels you up or spits in your face or whatever, you just have to take it.'

'What if you break character?' Obi asked.

'Lower marks, *this student lacks commitment*, blah blah blah. Some people take it *really* seriously though, like *way too* seriously. My friend Nadia was living with a guy who did the course a few years ago, and he stayed in character *the whole time*. Like he was an SS officer *at home*.'

'That's fucked,' Jolly said.

I took another bite of my sandwich.

The conversation moved on. Soon Victoria was needling the boys for their life stories. Obi told us about his home in Peckham, that he'd caught the acting bug at his local church theatre group, that he was the only one from his family who was bothered about the arts, that he'd lucked out with a bursary for the first year.

She moved on to Jolly. Gay and bullied for it, then one day he joined the after-school drama club where he found his people. So still gay, but bullied a bit less. At drama club, he was allowed to dress up in feathers and corsets and fat suits and pantaloons, and no one could say shit.

'It's like, when I was performing, no one could take the piss any more. It's like suddenly I was untouchable.' Jolly beamed at Victoria, then turned to me. 'What about you, Shannon. What's your deal?'

I opened my mouth to say something, but Victoria cut in.

'She's from the *North*, aren't you, *luv*?'

I nodded. 'Yeah—'

'Her dad sells awnings, her mum's a teaching assistant, she's a virgin, and her favourite colour is green. That's about it, isn't it?' She looked at me, her eyebrows raised.

Pinned by her gaze, my cheeks burning, I nodded.

'So cute.' She smiled at me, the picture of innocence, before returning to Jolly. 'Have you ever done any modelling, Jol? You're so skinny, you probably could.'

'Oh, shush.'

'No, seriously! You've got great cheekbones and a jawline most guys would kill for. I bet I can hook you up.'

My insides still churning from Victoria's crude assessment, I took a sip of my latte. It seemed we were done with Shannon's story, for now.

SEVEN

Tuesday, 8th September at 01:51

V

are you awake

Tuesday, 8th September at 01:53

Shannon Bell

Was just going to sleep xx

Tuesday, 8th September at 01:53

Shannon Bell

Everything ok? Xx

Tuesday, 8th September at 01:57

V

sorry about earlier

Tuesday, 8th September at 01:57

Shannon Bell

What do you mean? Xx

Tuesday, 8th September at 01:59

V

I think I talked over you

Tuesday, 8th September at 01:59

Shannon Bell

Oh that's fine – don't worry! Xx

Tuesday, 8th September at 02:04

V

freaking out about tomorrow

Tuesday, 8th September at 02:05

Shannon Bell

Why? Xx

Tuesday, 8th September at 02:07

V

idk just nervous I guesss

Tuesday, 8th September at 02:07

Shannon Bell

You'll be fine! Xx

Tuesday, 8th September at 02:09

V

yeah

Tuesday, 8th September at 02:10

Shannon Bell

Do you want me to come over? Xx

Tuesday, 8th September at 02:11

V

haha no it's like 2am silly

Tuesday, 8th September at 02:11

Shannon Bell

I can get a taxi, if you need me xx

Tuesday, 8th September at 02:16

V

was nice seeing you today

Tuesday, 8th September at 02:16

Shannon Bell

You too xx

Tuesday, 8th September at 02:22

V

and the guys, they're cool

Tuesday, 8th September at 02:23

Shannon Bell

Yeah xx

Tuesday, 8th September at 02:24

V

it will be ok won't it

Tuesday, 8th September at 02:24

Shannon Bell

Of course!! Xx

Tuesday, 8th September at 02:27

Shannon Bell

I can come over if you need me xx

Tuesday, 8th September at 02:35

V

no don't worry about it

Tuesday, 8th September at 02:35

V

need my beauty sleep

Tuesday, 8th September at 02:36

V

night x

Tuesday, 8th September at 02:36

Shannon Bell

OK. See you tomorrow xx

Tuesday, 8th September at 02:37

Shannon Bell

Bright and early Shirley xx

Tuesday, 8th September at 02:38

Shannon Bell

Night xxxxxxx

EIGHT

'I EXPECT THREE THINGS from you: rigour, professionalism and commitment. If you cannot give me those, then my advice is for you to collect your bags and go. This is not the training for you.' She waited. 'No objections, I take it?' She raised an eyebrow and looked around the circle. No one moved an inch. 'Good.' She clasped her hands in front of her. 'As I'm sure you're aware, I am Frida Anselm.' She announced this with taut Scandinavian emphasis. 'I am a theatre director, movement practitioner, and head of the BA Acting course at this school. Of course, I already know some of you from the third round of auditions' – her steely eyes scanned the room before resting on my own – 'while some of you I've not yet had the pleasure of encountering.'

She placed her hands behind her back and began patrolling the perimeter of the circle. Although no taller than five foot, her presence crowded the room. Her neck was rigid and slender. Her gaze, steady and penetrating. I watched as her frizzy crown of silvery-blonde hair vanished then reappeared between my classmates' shoulders. The room was completely silent but for the slow pad of her feet on the polished sprung boards, the languid swish of her charcoal palazzo pants along the floor.

She passed what felt like a few centimetres behind me. I stared down at my toes, hardly daring to breathe.

'Your first lesson: the actor's body is a machine.' She stopped and picked a stray hair from Jolly's shoulder. He flinched.

'It is a tool which can be used to convey emotions and tell stories. If I am casting a play and I need an actor to serve the narrative, am I going to choose the actor with the purple highlights and colourful tattoos, or am I going to choose the actor who is prepared, focused, a blank canvas ready for me to paint my story upon?'

She returned to her place and gazed around the circle.

'I am not interested in who you think you are. I am interested only in what you can do. If you come to class with hairstyles I deem extreme, piercings or makeup, you will be asked to leave and not invited to return until you have rectified the situation. Do I make myself clear?'

People nodded.

'Tattoos will be covered with bandages. You will wear black every day of your first and second year. You will not test this rule. You will not complain about it. If you are late to class, you will be red lit. You will not be allowed to attend classes for the day and will be expected to catch up in your own time. If you are red lit three times, you will be given a warning. Four times, and you will be asked to leave the school.'

She narrowed her eyes and scanned the circle.

'And if you smoke, quit. If I see any of you smoking outside the school, I will take it as an attack on the values of this institution and proof that you do not take your studies, your craft or yourselves seriously as actors.'

My legs trembled. I tried to catch Victoria's eye, but she was staring dreamily into space, for all the world in a different place completely.

NINE

VICTORIA CLICKED THE LIGHTER.

We were gathered around her on a picnic table outside the pub. It was the end of our first week, and despite our exhaustion, Jolly had demanded we all go for an inaugural pint.

'I didn't think I could feel this tired,' he groaned, his forehead on the table.

'I think it only gets worse from here,' Obi said, slipping his large frame in beside Jolly.

Victoria passed Obi a rolled cigarette. He took it without looking at her, the movement already so practised, so natural, the twisted end gliding from her fingers to his.

Victoria had stopped offering me cigarettes.

The Masons was across the road from school. Everyone drank there, even the teachers. The place was heaving. First-, second- and third-years swarmed the courtyard like ants. I glanced over my shoulder.

Jolly rolled his head to one side. 'Who're you looking for, Shan?'

'No one.'

'She doesn't come here, you know,' Victoria said, blowing a plume of smoke from the corner of her mouth.

'Who?' Obi asked.

'She's worried about Frida,' Jolly replied.

'Don't. I doubt bitch robot even drinks,' Victoria said.

'Except maybe WD-40,' Jolly added.

Victoria and Obi laughed.

Stefano emerged from the pub carrying a tray of shots. 'What did I miss?' he yelled, striding across the yard.

Stefano was another of our classmates, an international student who'd joined us from Milan. He had hazel eyes and tied his hair in a top knot with a rubber band.

'Nothing,' Victoria said, lifting one from the tray. 'We were just discussing how fucking adorable you are.'

Stefano grinned and sat down beside her. Victoria inched closer to Obi. He put his arm around her shoulder.

'Shot?' Stefano said, raising his eyebrows and gesturing towards the tray.

I shook my head.

He slid one towards me. 'Come on,' he said with a wink. 'You scared you'll lose control?'

Heat prickled across my neck. 'No,' I laughed uncertainly. 'I'm OK, thanks.'

Stefano was the kind of man who hovered his arms out to the side to make them look thicker. He was the guy who liked to pick up girls until they giggled and squealed and begged to be put down. At 5'7", we were the same height. Sometimes, when I stood next to him in class, I noticed him rise up onto the balls of his feet.

'Sure I can't tempt you?'

'Fine, go on then,' I said, accepting the drink with a reluctant smile.

Ordinarily, Stefano was someone I'd avoid. But here, it was impossible. We'd only been around each other one week but already these people, my classmates, were beginning to coagulate into a sort of family.

Thrown together by circumstance from different corners of the country, of the world, we'd settled inside each other's pockets, a ragtag group of sisters, brothers, lovers.

'Well, I think we should toast,' Victoria said, lifting her glass.

'What are we toasting?' Obi asked.

'We're toasting . . . erm, oh God, I'm pissed already,' she giggled. 'We're toasting the first week of the rest of our lives.'

'Uh-oh, she's going to make a speech,' Jolly said, rolling his eyes.

'Maybe I am,' Victoria said. She clambered up onto the bench, and Obi grabbed hold of her legs to steady her. 'Would that be so terrible?'

'If you fall and smack your head on the concrete, we're not taking you to A&E, you know.'

Victoria gave Jolly a withering look and cleared her throat. 'Now, it's not often that you meet someone wonderful.' Her eyes travelled across Obi's face. 'But it's even rarer to meet several wonderful people at once.' She smiled. 'You, my darlings, are all wonderful people, and I feel truly blessed to count myself among your company.'

'Oh God, it's *Rent*. She'll start singing "La Vie Bohème" next,' Jolly said.

'Don't interrupt!'

'*Here she lies, no one knew her worth. The late great daughter of Mother Earth.*'

'Shut up!' she laughed. 'Shit, I've lost my place now.' She paused and thought for a moment, and we gazed up at her, content to wait.

'OK. Yes.' She tossed her hair back. 'Although but one week has passed, I can already tell that you're all disgustingly talented and we're going to have the best three fucking years of our lives here. So, comrades, here's to love, to art . . . and to us.'

'To *bohemia*!' Jolly yelled.

'To us,' I whispered, raising my glass.

ONE PINT TURNED INTO many and, when the last orders bell rang out, Victoria, eager to continue the night, invited the four of us back to hers. A black cab pulled up outside the pub. It had rained a few minutes earlier. A fine mist still hung beneath the streetlamps. As I climbed in behind Jolly, I saw a handful of our classmates, damp and forlorn, look over from their benches, craning their necks for an invitation. But V's was an exclusive club, closed to new members. She'd already decided who her people were. And I, clinging on against all odds, was one of them.

Victoria and Obi shifted closer together on the black leather to make room for me, while Jolly and Stefano took the flip seats opposite. The car pulled away and hurtled into the night. Streetlights whipped past our faces. The engine rattled beneath me, broiling my innards: the six pints, the two sambucas, the ill-advised platter of cheesy chips. I looked out of the window, fogged by the heat of us, at the slick, dark London streets.

I'd lived the last two weeks trying to be someone else, and Victoria, to my surprise, had decided she liked that person. It was a case of pacing. I just needed to hold on, to play the game a bit longer, to mould myself to her delight. It wasn't so difficult. It was just acting, just pretending. I'd done it my whole life.

I rested my head against the window and wrote on the glass.

SHANNON BELL

The car lurched over a pothole and fat droplets of water trickled down the window, erasing the letters one by one.

WE GATHERED IN WHAT Victoria called *the den*, a grandly furnished room bigger than the floorspace of my parents' entire kitchen and living room. Despite it still only being September, the rain had made us needy and so Victoria lit a fire. We huddled in a half-circle around the tiled Victorian hearth.

'Red wine,' Victoria said, getting up. 'A night like this calls for red.'

I wasn't sure I could manage any more alcohol, but the soft warmth of the lamps, the heat of the flames and the closeness of Obi's leg beside mine made me oblige. Victoria brought a bottle of something French and five crystal wine glasses over. She set them on the floor.

Jolly knelt forward. 'Shall I be mother?' he asked, uncorking the bottle and filling each glass.

We raised our drinks and, done with toasts for the evening, sipped in silence. For a moment the only sounds were the crackle of the flames and the rain beating against the window. I glanced around at the tall bookcases filled with leather-bound spines, at the plump plum-coloured Chesterfield sofas and wing-backed accent chair, at the tasteful gallery wall of art and carefully arranged curios placed around the room. My eyes met Victoria's. She smiled and blinked sleepily, then reached over her shoulder and retrieved a small wooden box from the nearest end table.

'What's that?' Jolly asked.

She shrugged. 'Just something to relax us.'

'V, come on. We're all practically fucking comatose as it is. How much more do we really need to relax?'

Victoria, bristling, pulled out a pre-rolled spliff. 'You don't have to partake if you don't want to, Jolly.'

'Yeah man, no one's forcing you,' Stefano added, handing her his lighter.

Jolly sat back, defeated, and twirled the contents of his glass.

Victoria lit the joint and took a long pull. She gave it to Obi, who did the same and passed it to me. I, not knowing what on earth I was meant to do with the thing, just bowed my head, took a short, sharp puff, and handed it to Stefano.

'Thanks.' He clicked his neck and shifted to get more comfortable. 'You know what, guys, I'm going to be honest with you. When I first came here, I thought you English drama kids would be boring as fuck. But you're not, you're actually kind of great.'

'Aaaw, Steffy,' Victoria cooed.

Obi gave him a gentle punch on the shoulder. 'Pleased to know you.'

Stefano inhaled and let out a long plume of smoke. 'V, this is good shit,' he said, his voice tight. 'Where did you get it?'

She gathered her hair over one shoulder. 'My brother. He keeps us well stocked.'

'He has good taste. Hey,' he said, as if the idea was just occurring to him then, 'you know what we should do, what might wake us up a bit? We should play spin the bottle.'

'Oh *Stefano*, I thought you'd never ask!' Jolly exclaimed, clambering on top of him and reaching for his face. 'Come here!'

'Argh no, fuck off,' Stefano said, pushing him away, his cheeks flushed.

'Zounds! You wound me!'

Obi and I laughed.

'We're not playing spin the bottle, Stef,' Victoria said, giggling.

'Why not?'

'Because we're not thirteen?'

'What about truth or dare, then?' Jolly said.

'Because we're not ten.'

'Seven minutes in heaven?' Stefano suggested.

'Because we're not perverts!' Victoria replied with mock outrage. She paused. 'OK, what about this: everyone has to say their absolute *dream* role.'

Stefano nodded appreciatively. 'Nice.'

Obi ran his hands across his head. 'I have no idea.'

'Of course you do,' Victoria said, shifting onto her knees. '*Everyone* has a dream role.'

'I want to play Hamlet,' Jolly said.

'I can see that,' Obi said. 'You'd make a good one.'

'Thanks.'

'Don't you think you're a bit . . .' Victoria screwed up her nose.

'A bit what?' Jolly asked.

'I don't know. I always sort of imagine Hamlet to be like really strong and intellectual.'

'So you're saying, what, I'm weedy and thick?'

'No, no,' Victoria laughed. 'That's not what I mean.'

'What do you mean then?' Jolly spat back.

'I'm fucked. Ignore me. You'd make a *great* Hamlet, Jol.'

Jolly chewed the inside of his cheek and stared into the flames.

'I like the Greeks,' Obi said. 'I guess I'd like to do Agamemnon or Oedipus, something like that.'

'So, you want to screw your mum then, yeah?' Stefano chimed in.

'Ha ha,' Obi replied sarcastically. 'Fine, who would you play, big man?'

'Stanley Kowalski. Straight up.'

'Ooh yeah,' Victoria said. 'I see that for you.'

'Why him?' I asked.

Stefano shrugged noncommittally. 'He's just a classic, a real man. Every guy wants to play Stanley at some point. He's just . . .' He thought for a moment, digging for a more complete answer. 'A classic.'

'You know, some scholars argue Stanley's a closeted homosexual,' Jolly drawled.

'Yeah, you wish,' Stefano said, giving him a shove.

'What about you, Shannon?' Obi asked, nudging my shoulder.

'Oh, I'd like to play Jane Eyre.'

'Nice.' He smiled, and I felt my belly flood with warmth. 'I mean, I *say* nice,' he continued. 'I've not actually read it.'

'I can lend it to you, if you want,' I said, perhaps a little too eagerly. I glanced at Victoria. She was looking at me strangely.

'I'd like that, yeah.' Obi shifted and crossed his legs. 'What do you like about her – the character, I mean?'

'She's unassuming.' I thought for a moment. 'But passionate too.' My eyes flicked to Victoria again. She was picking at her fingernails now, visibly bored. 'She's strong-willed and principled. I suppose – I don't know – I feel a sort of affinity towards—'

'Now I think about it,' Victoria said, talking over me, 'I don't know if I can choose just one. I mean, for Shakespeare, it would *have* to be Juliet. But then if I'm allowed another tragedy, maybe Hedda Gabler? Oh, but then I'd want to star in an American epic too. I've always liked the idea of playing Curley's wife in *Of Mice and Men* too. Yes, I think I'd have to choose that as my American.'

'So basically you want to play women who die at the end,' Jolly said.

Victoria pulled a face. 'I hadn't thought of it like that. Maybe I do.'

She swooned theatrically into Obi's lap. He shifted to accommodate her, and I inched away from the two of them. 'Maybe I want the whole audience weeping when I take my bow.'

'That's assuming they'll be upset,' Jolly muttered to himself.

Victoria's face darkened; she sat up. 'And why wouldn't they be?'

'No reason. Never mind. I didn't say anything.'

Victoria glowered at Jolly. 'I mean, I doubt I'll do much theatre anyway. My agent has her sights set on bigger things – TV, film. To be honest, I'll probably move to LA at some point.' She plucked the half-smouldering joint from Stefano's fingers and threw it into the fire. 'God, I'd *hate* to get stuck here, doing the same boring plays to the same boring audiences night after night.' Her mouth twitched. 'But that's just me.'

TEN

THOSE FIRST WEEKS PASSED in a blur. Our days were militarized. My classmates and I arrived at 8 a.m. outside the building just as the janitors were unlocking the front gate. Then, at 6 p.m. when the school day technically ended, it was off to an after-hours rehearsal, to study in the library, to read plays for discussion, to prepare for our end-of-term examinations or, if we found ourselves with a spare evening, to go to some tiny black-box theatre in the arse end of nowhere to catch some obscure play the teacher recommended we see. It wasn't compulsory, no, no, not compulsory *per se*, but if you chose not to, then you obviously weren't committed, you obviously didn't care, you obviously might not last the year.

They gave us homework, though we were never home. They asked us to learn lines, to rehearse scenes, to fit it all in, to cram every inch of our brains with *theatre theatre theatre*. And if you didn't, you were a bad person, or worse, a bad actor. You were letting the side down, letting yourself down, wasting your time, wasting a space at this revered institution, you might as well quit, might as well crawl back to your underwhelming life and give up on your dreams. If you couldn't make it fit, then you were a failure, and if you didn't leave of your own volition, then you faced the threat of being asked to leave by Frida.

I don't think I ate a proper meal in that time. I was always scarfing down a sandwich as I hurried through some corridor, sneaking a coffee into my five-minute break for a brief hit of energy or wolfing down a McDonald's at midnight just to get some hot food in my belly. There wasn't time to stop, to sleep, to unwind, to reply to loved ones. In that first term, three of my classmates broke up with their long-term partners. Occasionally I'd see a name flash up on my phone – *Mum, Dad, Grandma* – and, dripping with bone-weary shame, wait out the seconds until the screen went dark again. Sometimes I'd glimpse an unfamiliar city from the school windows and be reminded of the fact that I apparently lived in London now. Other times I caught sight of myself in the girls' bathroom and was jolted by my appearance, by the dark hollows beneath my eyes, the layers of adolescent puppy fat that had melted from my face.

Finally, at the end of each long day, I'd stumble into my dorm room and collapse on my bed. One night, despite my exhaustion, I couldn't sleep. I couldn't face catching up on the homework I needed to do for the next day, so I pulled out my laptop and opened Facebook. Updates and pictures filled the screen, news from old friends and acquaintances, the people I knew from sixth form, now at university, out partying, rolling in at 1 p.m. for their one lecture of the day, clutching their takeaway coffees and stickered MacBooks, gabbling about the Socialist Workers Party and freshers' foam parties, posting about some march they'd been to in London, a coachload of young hopefuls shouting at the sky, and then back on the coach for more pictures, their faces ruddy and complacent, winding their way back up the motorway towards more parties, more socializing, more sex.

I closed the laptop. My phone buzzed. A voicemail. I brought it to my ear.

'Hi Shannon, it's Dad. I hope you're all right and school's going well. Did you see that Mum sent you an email? We just wondered if writing might be a

bit easier than chatting, you know, if you're a bit tired and that. But no pressure. We know you must be busy . . . We can't wait to hear what you're up to. Anyway . . . we miss you . . . Your grandma's doing all right, by the way. She had an appointment last week for her knee. Nothing to worry about. Just routine stuff. But you'll see that if you read the email . . . Right then . . . I'll try you again at the weekend. Don't be a stranger, love . . . All right . . . Bye, chuck.'

The screen went dark. I drank a glass of water. I lay down on my bed and, finally defeated by exhaustion, I went to sleep.

I SAT ALONE WITH Victoria outside in the quad. *The quad*. It sounds rather grand for what was really just a scrappy patch of grass outside the main building. Green space was at a premium in that part of London though, so we often hung out there, sunbathing or eating or learning our lines. It was a bright September morning. Summer was still clinging on, despite the ochre leaves blowing from the sky. That day, we'd just been given our casting. Each term, we studied and performed a different play. This term was Chekhov's *The Seagull*.

'I'm *so* jealous you're playing Masha,' Victoria said, shielding her eyes from the sun.

'But you're the lead,' I shot back.

'Am I?' Victoria thought for a moment. 'I mean I *guess* you could argue Nina's the lead but like, *come on*, the ingénue? It's so predictable.'

I felt an unfamiliar flash of irritation towards her then. Victoria *knew* she had the better role. 'Nina's a great part.'

'Yeah, I mean, I guess it'll be fun. But *Masha*. You'll get to be like all dark and twisted and depressed and stuff. A proper weirdo.'

All the female roles had been divided up, there not being enough good parts for girls. Victoria and Lola were sharing the role of Nina, while Masha (a smaller role) had been divided between myself and Poppy.

'You're going to be fantastic,' Victoria said, lying back on the grass.

'Thanks. So are you.'

Jolly emerged from the building and came over.

'What are you guys up to?'

'Just making the most of the weather,' Victoria said, propping herself up on one elbow. 'Where've you been?'

Jolly puffed out his cheeks. 'I just had the pleasure of a meeting with Frida.'

'How come?' I asked.

'She wanted to talk about the play.'

Jolly had been given the role of Konstantin, the tragic hero. He would play him in the first half while Matt, a friendly, broad-chested Scot, would play him in the second.

'So apparently Frida's casting decision wasn't entirely benevolent.' Jolly picked at a tuft of grass. 'She told me that she wanted to see if I could "play anything other than gay".'

Victoria sat up and frowned. 'Really?'

He nodded, his expression guarded. 'Yeah, apparently she's worried. She said so far she's not seen anything in me that demonstrates versatility.'

'But it's like week three, how can she say that? Also, you're super versatile.'

'Thanks. I mean, *I* know that, but . . .' He shrugged and sprinkled grass over his shoes. 'Anyway, well done on getting Nina, V.'

'Thanks.'

'Who are you again, Shan?'

'Masha.'

'Ah, figures.'

I narrowed my eyes. 'Why does it figure?'

'Well, you know ... *I'm depressed. I'm in mourning for my life*,' Jolly intoned.

Victoria laughed.

'I don't get it,' I said, suddenly feeling self-conscious.

'Well, I mean, come on,' Jolly laughed. 'You're kind of serious.'

'Am I?'

I saw a glance pass between them. 'Well no, not all the time, obviously,' Jolly said, scrabbling for the right words.

'Sometimes you just look a bit stern,' Victoria explained matter-of-factly.

'Oh.'

'There, see,' Jolly said, pointing at me and grinning. 'You're doing it now.'

I turned away from them and tried rearranging my features into something more acceptable, but it was pointless. I felt another look pass between them, behind my back.

At that moment, Obi came through the front gate.

Jolly, all too happy to change the subject, called out to him, 'What about you, Obi? Who're you playing again?'

He came over. 'What's that?'

'Who are you playing?' Victoria repeated.

'Yakov,' he replied with a sigh.

'Remind me?' Victoria said.

'Oh my God, V, you have read the play, haven't you?' Jolly said.

'I skimmed it.'

'He's a workman on the estate,' Obi said. 'I've got like three lines.'

'Oh.'

There was an uncomfortable pause.

Obi, noticing this, shook his head. 'It's fine. I can take this term easy.' He smiled ruefully. 'I just hope they don't have me playing servants for the entire three years.'

ELEVEN

I ARRIVED IN THE rehearsal room with a minute to spare.

'You're cutting it a bit fine, aren't you,' Jolly whispered, as I lay down on the parquet beside him and began stretching out my aching hamstrings.

'My alarm didn't go off.'

'Even Victoria was here before you.'

I glanced over to where she stood stretching her arms above her head in front of the floor-to-ceiling mirrors.

At that moment, our teacher walked in.

Casper Drake was the head of voice at the school. He had a clipped South African accent and the guru-like intensity of a wellness instructor.

'Good morning, actors. Form a circle, please.'

I dragged myself up off the floor.

Casper disliked us. Well, most of us. He somehow found it in his heart to love any students who came from acting families of renown. His eyes twinkled whenever Tiff, for example, asked a question, her being some long-distant progeny of the Redgrave dynasty. Despite his obvious disdain for young people, the second- and third-years assured us he was an excellent voice coach. Casper had trained under Cicely Berry's guidance at the Royal Shakespeare Company, a fact he seemed at pains to remind us of whenever possible.

'Come on, chop, chop.' He clapped his hands.

We gathered around him.

'Good. Let's begin.' He stared around the room. His nostrils flared. 'Why do we scream?'

At first, no one spoke. Last week Poppy had given an incorrect answer about where the diaphragm was located, and Casper had berated her to the point of tears.

Finally, when no one else volunteered, Victoria raised her hand. 'Because we're afraid?'

'Excellent, Victoria. Yes. Anyone else?'

'We're shocked.'

'We're excited.'

'Good, yes.' He pushed his glasses up his nose. 'The world provides a stimulant, and the brain and body respond by making a noise.' He looked around the room. 'Tell me, can anyone remember the last time they screamed?'

After a few seconds, Maddy, a pale, orange-haired girl, raised her hand. 'I saw a spider the other week.'

'And did you scream?'

'Well, no. I think I sort of gasped.'

'Hmm.' Casper shook his head. 'That is because your voice is trapped. You've grown used to subduing your natural impulses and now your responses are dulled, your inner life is incomplete.' He addressed the rest of us. 'You're watchful and uncertain, disconnected from your basest impulses. Babies scream. Babies scream all the time. They cry and laugh freely too, but as we grow, these impulses are quashed. We're told to keep silent, to stop crying, to not be so afraid, to not laugh quite so loudly. And with each command, our emotional inner life is dulled ever further. The only way many people now access these emotions is through short-circuiting their secondary impulses by, for example, putting themselves in the way of extreme fear or ecstasy.'

Outside, the sun disappeared behind a cloud.

'Many of the characters you'll play in your careers will be people at the extremes of their emotional life. You might play the Dane contemplating taking his uncle's life, or Medea driven to murder her entire family. That is why freeing your caged voices is of the utmost importance.' He looked around the room at us. 'And we begin today. May I have a volunteer?'

He waited. No one raised their hand.

'Very well. Ms Madeleine, our arachnophobe.' Casper gestured towards the centre of the circle. 'If you please.'

Maddy stepped forward.

'When was the last time you were frightened? And I'm not talking about creepy crawlies.'

'Erm, I – I don't know.'

'Don't stammer, please. This is a voice class. I won't abide stammering.'

'Sorry.'

'When were you last frightened?'

Maddy stared down, searching the floor for an answer.

'I don't know, like maybe just over a year ago?'

'Good, go on.' Casper took a step forward.

'It was, well, I was walking home from school – erm, from college – sorry.'

'That's quite all right.' Casper came forward and placed one of his hands on her lower back, the other on her belly.

I saw her stiffen.

'Please continue.'

'I was walking home from college and I felt like I was being followed.'

'Yes?'

'And I looked behind me to see who it was, but I couldn't quite tell. It was dark. It was winter. There weren't many cars on the road.'

Maddy glanced sideways. Casper pressed his palms against her middle.

'Carry on,' he murmured in her ear, 'and think from your diaphragm.'

'And I don't know, I thought it might be my – my uncle.'

'Don't stammer.'

'Sorry – I thought it might be him. And we, well, we don't see him any more, my family, we don't talk to him any more ever since – sorry, no, this isn't about that – I, I wasn't sure who it was behind me, whether it was him or not, so I started running.'

We were all silent, frozen in place.

'I – I started running and I ran in the direction of home and – I don't know – I thought I could hear him running after me, I didn't know if it was my feet or his, but it was so loud, it was so loud, I thought he was right behind me. And – and I, I was fumbling for my keys—'

She began to cry.

'Good, good,' Casper whispered, his face inches from hers. 'Let it out.'

'And I – I dropped them and I bent down and picked them up and just kept running and running and I couldn't breathe and it felt like he was right behind me, like I could feel him behind me, he's a bad man, not a good man, and I knew I still had so far to run and I couldn't breathe, I couldn't breathe and – I can't breathe – sir, I can't breathe.'

'You can breathe. You're letting it all out. This is good.'

'No – no – please, I can't breathe.'

'You're connecting to your inner life. You're doing wonderfully.'

'Please – please, sir – please—'

'Sir' – Obi stepped forward – 'I think she's having a panic attack.'

Casper let go of Maddy and wheeled round to face him. 'She is *not* having a panic attack, she is having a natural vocal reaction to intense fear, she is learning to uncage her voice. Do not *ever* presume to tell me how to teach my lessons, young man.'

Obi replaced his hands in his pockets and took a step back.

Casper crossed his arms and waited. Maddy stood in the centre of the circle, bent at the waist. We watched in silence as her shoulders heaved up and down, hiccupping sobs escaping with every breath.

'That's it.' Casper pursed his lips. 'You're fine now.' He cleared his throat. 'Do you see what happened? What we just witnessed was Maddy *nearly* accessing her true voice. We short-circuited her impulse to hide her feelings away and accessed a more truthful place in her vocal range.' His lip curled into a smile. 'There now. Don't you feel better after that?' Casper gave Maddy a light pat on the back. 'Cathartic, yes?'

TWELVE

'IT'S YOU,' OBI SAID brightly as I pushed open the door.

'Hi,' I said. 'Are your rehearsing in here?'

'Yeah, I'm meeting Victoria in' – he glanced down at his watch – 'well, now apparently.'

'Oh, me too,' I said, confused. 'She said she wanted me to help her learn lines.'

Obi rolled his eyes. 'She's double-booked us.'

'Right.' I laughed nervously. 'Typical.' I stood half in, half out of the doorway.

Noticing this, Obi waved me inside. 'You might as well come in and wait with me. Then she can pick who she wants.' He smiled and I felt that swell of warmth again. 'Maybe one of us will get the evening off.'

I went over to the wall where he was slouched. I sat down and crossed my legs. I could feel his shoulder inches from mine. I pretended to stretch and, taking the opportunity, slid my rucksack into the space between us.

Although autumn had begun its slow creep through the building, I suddenly felt hot. I removed my black sweatshirt and put it to one side. Another line of defence.

'So . . . are you OK?' Obi asked.

'Yeah. Just a bit tired.'

'Yeah, me too.'

'Yeah.'

'Yeah.'

There was a pause.

'Have you learned all your lines?' he asked.

'Oh, yeah. I'm only in like two scenes, I've probably got twelve lines overall.'

'Cool.'

'Yeah.'

I searched for something to say. I liked Obi. There was a kind of sturdiness to him, a sureness. But we'd never been alone together, just the two of us. Without Victoria's marshalling gaze, I didn't know the protocol. Obi drummed his fingers on his knees, tapping out an agitated beat. Neither did he, apparently.

I sat forward for something to do and stared out of the floor-length window. I could see the winking dial of the BT Tower and, in the distance, the silvery dome of St Paul's Cathedral. A helicopter flew overhead, pedestrians scuttled down below, and somewhere, beyond my sight, the long spine of the Thames sliced the city in two.

Obi gave an exaggerated sigh and glanced at his watch again. 'Where the hell is she?'

I shrugged and brought my knees up under my chin.

The radiator gurgled. I heard shouts from the corridor. Obi shifted closer, and I felt a surge of nervous energy go through me.

'So, what do you think about all this?' Obi said, his hands finally stilling. 'Is it like how you imagined?'

'Is what like how I imagined?'

'Drama school.'

I turned the question over in my mind. 'I don't know.'

I paused, waiting for the inevitable interruption, the navigation on my behalf, but it never came. Obi just looked at me, his eyes shining, waiting to hear my thoughts.

'I guess I didn't have any expectations of what it would be like,' I managed. 'They call it a school, but it's nothing like any of the schools I've ever been to.' I paused and tucked a loose strand of hair behind my ear. 'I'm eighteen years old.' I screwed up my forehead. 'I thought maybe I'd be treated like a grown-up here, but half the time I feel like a naughty kid.'

Obi nodded.

'I thought I'd learn a bit more about myself, you know, experiment and things. But it doesn't feel like there's any time for that.' I scratched at a scab on my wrist. 'I don't think they want us to experiment anyway. I think they just want us to behave in a certain way, and if we're not like that, if it doesn't come naturally to behave like that, then they get angry.' I rested my head against the wall and stared at the ceiling. 'I didn't expect them to be so angry. Why are they angry at us?' I laughed. 'What have they got to be angry about?' I frowned. 'I thought there'd be more creative expression, maybe it would be a bit more . . .' I searched for the word. '*Hippy dippy*, liberal. I don't know. I mean, I say I didn't come with any expectations, but I guess I must've done. Everyone has expectations. We wouldn't *do* anything if we didn't think there'd be a good outcome, would we? I must've thought coming here would be a good thing or I wouldn't have done it, right?' I stared at the wall in front of me. 'So no, it's not like I imagined it. No. Not at all.'

Obi was silent. After a moment, he spoke. 'You know, I think that's the most I've ever heard you say, Shannon.'

I felt my cheeks redden. 'I'm sorry.'

'Don't apologize.' Obi was staring at me with a peculiar expression on his face. 'It's a good thing.' He was closer now, so close I could study the lines of his face.

The door was flung open and we sprang apart.

'Shannon, I'm so sorry I'm late. I was in the library and the fucking printer wouldn't work—' Victoria saw the two of us bunched together on the floor and came to a halt. 'Obi, what are you doing here?'

I got to my feet and, gabbling, answered for him: 'Nothing. We're not doing anything. It's just a mix-up. Obi thought you guys were rehearsing and I thought I was rehearsing with you too, so—'

'Oh.' Victoria dropped her bag against the wall. 'Shit. My mistake. Obi, I think maybe we were meant to see each other tomorrow evening instead.'

'No worries,' Obi said, jumping to his feet. 'Tomorrow it is.' He slung his rucksack over his shoulder and, without a backward glance, went towards the door. He squeezed Victoria's arm as he brushed past her.

'Bye, hun,' she said, not looking up from her satchel. The door closed behind him. She turned around, put her hands on her hips and smiled at me. 'Right. Let's get started.'

Victoria stood in the centre of the room, her hair fanned around her shoulders, her gaze fixed ahead.

Outside, the sky darkened.

I cradled the script in my lap. My eyes felt heavy. I traced her handwriting with my finger, the sentences and scribbles, ready to jump in with the line if she needed me. But she didn't need me, not really. The words, their soft repetition, dripped like honey from her lips.

'If my life can ever be of any use to you, come and take it.'

THIRTEEN

'MADDY'S GONE MISSING.'

'What do you mean?'

'She's gone missing,' Jolly whispered. 'She's not at home. Her housemates say they haven't seen her since Saturday.'

It was Monday morning. Jolly, Victoria and I were at the far end of Rehearsal Room Four, warming up. Our first class was due to start in ten minutes.

Jolly dropped his chin to his chest and rolled down to the floor. I did the same while Victoria sat, massaging the soles of her feet.

'Do the police know?' she asked.

'Yes. But I don't know if they've started searching yet.'

Stefano came over. 'Are you guys talking about Maddy?'

'Yes. Why? What do you know?' Jolly said.

Stefano crouched on his haunches beside Victoria. 'My friend knows one of the guys she lives with.' He shook his head. 'She's crazy.'

Victoria slapped his chest lightly and laughed – almost despite herself, I thought. 'Stefano! She's *not* crazy.'

'She is!' he replied, a little too loudly. Victoria and Jolly shushed him. 'Sorry, she is,' he whispered. 'All that stuff with Casper? Pretending to be all hard done by. I mean, come on.'

'The girl had a panic attack,' Jolly said.

'Yeah, but like it was kind of performative, no? Like Casper was just doing his job, and she had to go and get all dramatic about her uncle or whatever, then drag it out over weeks. She should've just let it go. That's what I would've done.'

Victoria lowered her voice conspiratorially. 'I was talking to Poppy, and apparently she reckons Maddy was abused or something, and that they cut the uncle out of the family because of that.'

Stefano shook his head and laughed. 'Nah. Maddy's just a drama queen. Her uncle probably just hugged her too tight one day or something.'

'Oh my God, Stefano. You can't say that,' Jolly replied with gossipy glee. He continued, 'I mean, I think Casper's a good teacher and everything, don't get me wrong, but it kind of seemed like he went too far.'

'Yeah,' Victoria said.

'Definitely,' I added.

'What? Are you guys kidding? He didn't go too far. He didn't go far enough. I don't know about you, but I came to drama school to be challenged. I don't give a damn if he touches me or asks hard questions or punches me in the face even. If it makes me a better actor then I'm here for it, I'm all in.'

Victoria, with a look of grudging admiration, was about to reply when the door opened, and Obi ushered a frail-looking Maddy into the room. She was wearing the same clothes she'd left school in on Friday. Her face was drawn, her hair frizzy and unkempt.

Victoria stood and went towards her. She whispered something in Maddy's ear and put an arm around her shoulder. Maddy smiled weakly and let the two of them lead her to a chair. She pulled a crumpled tissue from her sleeve and dabbed at her cheek. Her eyes looked red and sore.

Stefano got up and sauntered over to the scene, but Victoria shooed him away.

I saw other people in the class glance at Maddy, then look away. I looked away too. Here, sheltered within the White Elephant, weakness was a disease, one we couldn't risk catching.

Just then, Frida and Casper entered the room. They went towards Maddy and formed a tight huddle. Frida crouched in front of her while Casper stood by the chair with his hands on his hips. After a few moments, Victoria and Obi were dismissed, whereupon Frida helped Maddy to her feet and escorted her from the room.

The door slammed shut behind them.

'Right,' Casper said, clapping his hands. 'Let's begin today's session.'

MADDY DIDN'T RETURN THAT day. She wasn't there the next day either, or the one after that.

Six weeks she'd lasted, two weeks shy of an entire term.

Poppy said she'd chosen to defer. Archie said she was in hospital. Stefano, the loony bin. But, in the end, no one really knew. Looking back, I suppose one of us could've asked Frida. But no one ever did.

After a while, we stopped wondering where Maddy had gone. Soon, 'Maddy' became a noun separate from the person we once knew, a byword for weakness, for failure, a joke, just a harmless joke. *That scene was intense, are you OK? You're not going to do a Maddy on me, are you?* With time, the girl we'd known, albeit briefly, faded from our minds. Now, so many years later, I find it hard to picture her. All that remains is a shock of orange hair, a constellation of freckles, and those eyes, burning with hope for the future.

FOURTEEN

In week eight, Stefano's living situation broke down. He'd had a good deal, lodging on the cheap with a woman in Kilburn, but her new boyfriend didn't like Stefano's 'energy', so he was asked to leave. Meanwhile, one of Jolly's housemates, who was on the set design course, had dropped out two weeks prior. According to Jolly, she'd decided travelling around India on Daddy's Amex would be much more beneficial to her creative process than building miniature coat stands out of toothpicks and glue. And so, with one beat-up suitcase of black clothes and a rucksack of textbooks, Stefano rolled up the cement path, knocked on Jolly's front door, and stepped across the threshold of his new home.

While living in halls was the norm for most university students, at RLSDA students were strongly encouraged to *live with housemates who can empathize with the demand and intensity of the school's workload and expectations*. There was even a list of letting agents included in the welcome booklet. Every year, all across north London, RLSDA students squatted, studied and shagged within the same register of chipped suburban houses. But me? I wanted the sanitized version of university I'd been promised in sixth form, the glossy UCAS one with its new-build flats and brochure-friendly campus life. I wanted privacy, a room of my own, a cell with blank walls to paint myself upon.

The Saturday that Stefano moved in, it was the birthday of another of Jolly's housemates. Abigail was a first-year on the costume design and construction course. I don't know what it was like at other drama schools, but at RLSDA, costume girls were the good girls. They were polite and well dressed, wearing homemade tea-dresses or hand-crocheted jumpers. They didn't barge past you in the corridor. They didn't drag their egos around with them like the acting students did, expecting you to make way for their monumental talent. They just quietly got on with the job and grew into highly employable professionals. Jolly liked to joke that Abigail and his other housemates never made a sound at home, that the only reason he even knew they were there was because of the rhythmic chugging of sewing machines behind closed doors.

'At least, I think they're sewing machines,' he joked. 'Either that or they've got *a lot* of pent-up energy.'

When Jolly told the class Abigail was having a party, we weren't interested. Our final week loomed ahead of us with all the attendant assessments to prepare for and lines to drill. But Jolly begged us.

'Come on,' he said. 'The house will be crawling with techies and costume people. I need you there. Plus Stefano's moving in. We can make it a housewarming.'

And so, reluctantly, we agreed.

THE PARTY WAS DUE to start at nine, so I arrived at ten.

'Oh my God, Shannon, you're *so* early,' Jolly said, air-kissing my cheek. 'I've barely done my face.' His hair was scraped back from his forehead. He wore a mask of foundation, a navy dressing gown and pleather crimson stilettos. 'Come in, come in,' he said, ushering me inside. 'I've got gin somewhere.'

The hallway smelled of stir-fry and old trainers. As I followed Jolly through into the kitchen, I bumped into a plastic airer crammed with socks and faded pink polyester bras. The house was already filled with people. I looked around for someone I recognized, but it was mostly hairy young men wearing dark T-shirts and cargo shorts.

'Sorry about this lot,' Jolly whispered, as he slid the gin from the counter and led me upstairs. 'Abi invited a bunch of people from lighting and props.'

I peered over the banister. A guy with frizzy shoulder-length hair and a blurry Sonic the Hedgehog tattoo on his arm caught me staring. He raised his beer and winked at me. I hurried upstairs.

Jolly sat in front of the mirror and I settled myself on the bed. Jolly's room was a mess of sensuality. Despite the same tired IKEA furniture of every other student's bedroom – the paper globe lampshade, the BRIMNES wardrobe, the BILLY bookcase – Jolly had somehow made the space his own. He'd created a canopy over the bed with a slip of red taffeta. What should've been a study desk was instead a riot of bottles, creams and hair-styling products. Pinned to the mirror were ticket stubs, Polaroids and cut-outs of his favourite actors, singers and artists, while the dresser overflowed with satins, sequins, velvets and feathers. The only evidence of our strict day-to-day was a heap of black clothes on the floor, which he kicked aside as we entered.

'I don't know why I bother with all this,' Jolly said, applying a thin strip of eyeliner to his lid and addressing me through the mirror. 'It's not like there are any hot guys coming tonight.'

'What about Jonah?' I asked.

Jonah was on the Musical Theatre MA. He was 6'1", Canadian, and had never shown the slightest interest in Jolly. Despite this, Jolly had spent the first few weeks of term trailing him around school in the hopes of an organic meet-cute.

'Ugh, he's straight.'

'Really?'

'I know. Apparently V saw him making out with some Contemporary Theatre slut in the library. It's so annoying. I could've sworn he was gay.'

'Maybe he's bisexual.'

Jolly turned to me. 'Oh honey, bisexuals don't exist. They're just gays who can't commit or straights who want to play dress-up.'

'Oh, OK.'

'Anyway, what about you? Anyone on your horizon?' Jolly said, his eyes glinting mischievously.

Recently I'd begun to notice Jolly and Victoria do this; treat me like a sort of project, a doll they could dress up and parade around. In the last few weeks, their attention had turned towards trying to help me lose my virginity. I'd never asked them to do this, but whenever we talked it was always: what about this guy, or this guy, or this guy.

I fidgeted against the pillows. 'No, no. Not for me.'

'What about Stefano? He's pretty fit.'

I must've pulled a face. Jolly laughed. 'Not a fan of the bad boys, then?'

I scoffed. 'I don't know if he's a bad boy or just plain *bad*.'

'You're too hard on him. I reckon he's a big old softie deep down.'

'Maybe.'

'I was chatting with him this morning, you know, helping him unpack. He was talking about his sister getting engaged, how he's giving her away. It was quite sweet actually.'

'Hmm.'

'Fine, never mind then! You look cute by the way,' he said, pointing the eyeliner pen at the glass. 'I don't think I've seen you wear makeup before.'

'Oh it's just a bit of foundation and mascara,' I said, lowering my eyes. 'Unless Frida's invited, I think I'm safe.'

Jolly snorted. 'Yeah, what is it with her? I mean, I get that we shouldn't be focusing on what we look like and stuff, but we're *actors*. Of course we care how we look. And like, how is a bit of concealer going to harm anyone? What's me covering up a blackhead got to do with Bertolt Brecht, you know?'

I shrugged and let my eyes wander across the room. There was a book open down the side of Jolly's bed. *Freeing the Natural Voice* by Kristin Linklater. He'd stuck a blue Post-it note to the front page. *Must make myself heard!!!*

'Frida scares me,' I said.

'Me too,' Jolly said, tilting his chin in the mirror. 'But I also respect her. Like she's scary, but in a kind of diva way. Like Joan Crawford or something.'

'Yes,' I agreed, although I wasn't 100 per cent sure who Joan Crawford was.

'Bet she's into some *Mommie Dearest* shit.' He turned around and jabbed the eyeliner pen at me again. '*No wire hangers! No wire hangers!*'

I laughed. I found when people did impressions, even if I didn't recognize them, it was best to laugh.

Jolly stood up. 'Do you mind if I put some music on?' he asked.

'Go ahead.'

He fiddled with his iPod for a moment, then returned to the desk. A tinny drumbeat started up. 'Do you like Sparks?'

'Yes,' I replied, making a mental note to google them later on.

'I fucking adore Sparks. The guy on the piano?' He fanned himself. 'Oooft.'

'Yeah, they're great.'

He narrowed his eyes at me. 'OK, now don't get me wrong, but to be honest – and like absolutely no offence, Shannon – but I'm kind of surprised you know who they are?'

I dug my nails into the meat of my thigh. 'Oh yeah?' I said, trying to keep my voice even. 'Why's that?'

'Well, I don't know.' He laughed. 'Sometimes, I guess you just come across as a bit' – he thought for a moment – '*small town*. But like, I'm not saying that in a mean way.'

'Right.'

Jolly jumped up and came towards me. 'Oh no, no, no. God, I feel like I've offended you now.'

'No, not at all,' I said stiffly.

He pulled me into a hug. 'I just don't want you to pretend to be someone you're not, you know?' He held my head against his torso and stroked my hair. 'I mean, I spent *so* long pretending to be someone I wasn't, back when I was a teenager, and let me tell you, it's just not worth it.' He took a step back, still holding my shoulders. 'All I'm saying is just, like, *you do you*. Like no one cares who you are, as long as you're yourself.'

I cleared my throat. 'Yeah, no, of course. I get it.' I tossed my hair over one shoulder like I'd seen Victoria do countless times. Victoria, who would never find herself in a situation like this. Victoria, whose authenticity no one would ever dare question. 'I get your concern, but like, I'm totally just *me*.'

Jolly offered a tight smile. 'Good.'

Just then there was a knock at the door.

'Come in!' Jolly yelled.

It was Obi.

I sat up and smoothed my skirt.

'Hello ladies,' he said, brandishing a bottle of Jack Daniel's from his coat.

'Darling,' Jolly said, jumping to his feet. He kissed Obi on his cheek, grabbed the bottle, unscrewed it and took a large swig. 'Shan?' he said, wiping his mouth and waving it in my direction.

'No, you're all right.'

'Go on,' Obi said softly. 'I nicked it from my brother's room specially.'

'He won't notice?' Jolly asked.

'Nah, he spends most evenings round his fiancée's now anyway.'

'OK,' I said, returning Obi's smile and feeling the tension of the previous conversation melt from my shoulders. I took a sip. Fiery liquid burned the back of my throat. I coughed and passed it back to him.

'Is V coming?' Jolly asked him from the mirror.

'No idea,' Obi said, opening the window and feeling in his back pocket for filters. 'She never tells me anything. I'll just get a phone call out of the blue. *Oh, Obi, can you meet me in South Ken? Obi, darling, there's a party in Soho.*'

I stared at my pumps, at the white flesh bulging from the tops of them. She'd never told me about any parties in Soho.

'Yeah,' Jolly agreed. 'I was hoping she'd come tonight. But you know V. She probably wouldn't be seen dead at a dank little house party like this.'

I gestured for the bottle. 'Actually, can I have some more of that?'

IT WAS MIDNIGHT. NO one had heard from Victoria. I asked Obi to text her, hoping she'd reply to him, but when I found him smoking in the garden an hour later, he said she still hadn't responded. I went inside.

'Hey, Shannon.' Stefano was sitting on the kitchen counter. He beckoned me over. 'Are you having a good time?'

The music was loud. Bodies pressed in on me from all sides.

'What?'

He tried again, louder this time. 'I said, are you having a good time?'

The scrum pushed me closer. I shrugged and looked around for Jolly, Obi, anyone else I could speak to.

'You know this is my housewarming, right?' Stefano shouted in my ear.

'I thought it was Abigail's birthday?'

Stefano smirked. 'I mean, yeah, sure. But people get birthdays every year.'

I looked around. There was still no one I knew. I gave in. 'So what happened with your landlady, then?'

Stefano swigged his beer. 'I don't know. I mean, she was cool to begin with. It was a cheap room, although the house was kind of a dump – loads of hippy crap everywhere, incense, you know.' He laughed. 'To tell you the truth, I think she had a thing for me.'

'Really?' I said, trying to mask my disbelief.

'Yeah, she was always running into me just after I got out of the shower, asking why I was home late, stuff like that.'

'Right.'

'You know what it's like – some ladies, at a certain age . . .' He trailed off, seemingly unable to add any more substantiating details. 'Anyway, so she gets this boyfriend.' Stefano sat up straighter and puffed out his chest. 'I could've taken him, if it came to it. But then I thought, hey, if she wants to waste her time with a guy like that, then whatever. I can live wherever, you know?' He took another swig of his drink. 'You look nice, by the way.'

'Oh. Thank you,' I said, taken aback by the compliment.

'You should wear makeup more often. It brings out the blue of your eyes.'

My skin prickled, although not unpleasantly. 'Thanks.'

'And your hair, the redness.'

'I don't have red hair. Victoria has red hair.'

'You do, sort of, in some lights. It changes though.'

'Victoria's is prettier.'

He raised his eyebrows. 'Are you serious? She looks like a scarecrow!'

I gave him a playful shove, grinning despite myself. 'Shut up.'

'I'm serious. That girl's got some *Wizard of Oz* shit going on.'

'You're just trying to make me feel good.'

'And what's wrong with that?' Stefano asked, his eyes crinkling at the corners.

I didn't answer.

'You know, you and me, we should get a drink sometime.'

I rolled my eyes. 'All we do is drink.' It was true. Sometimes the musty carpets and sticky tables at The Masons felt more like home than my room in halls.

'Yes, but . . .' Stefano trailed off and reached for my wrist. For some reason I let him take it, whereupon he began running his index finger along my veins. 'I more meant a drink like *just the two of us*.'

'Maybe,' I said, suddenly wanting to leave, to unsnarl my arm. I pulled away from him. 'I should go. I think Jolly's looking for me.'

Stefano reached for his beer and grinned. 'Sure thing, Shannon. You go find your *friend*.'

I slipped into the crowd, feeling flushed and unsettled, rubbing at the place where he'd touched me, trying to erase the memory of his skin from my own.

Fairy lights twinkled from the living room ceiling. Smoke filled the air. There was a window open but no one was bothering to stand near it any more. La Roux's 'In For The Kill' boomed from an iPod dock in the corner. Hairy young men and indie-twee costume girls draped themselves across every available surface, limbs knotted, faces mashed into one another. *Good girls?* I picked at a bowl of crisps and poured a slug of vodka into a beaker of cloudy liquid.

Just then, Jolly made his entrance. He'd somehow convinced one of the burlier techies to haul him up on his shoulders and, after crouching momentarily beneath the door jamb, rode into the room like Aladdin on a great elephant. He cleared his throat theatrically until he had everyone's attention, then began an operatic rendition of 'Happy Birthday'. Everyone joined in, and Abigail extricated herself from the tech guy she'd been under. She climbed up onto the coffee table. Jolly took her hand and, with some manoeuvring from his ride, twirled her around in a circle. Everyone harmonized on the final note then broke out into applause, after which Jolly was dumped onto the sofa and the crowd returned to their sordid ministrations.

I went to the window. Someone had left a pack of cigarettes on the sill, which I helped myself to. I dangled my legs out of the window. I lit a cigarette and shuffled forward until I was more outside the room than in. My bare feet grazed wet heads of lavender. A car trundled down the street. Somewhere a siren bawled. In the house opposite, a string of lights flickered red, gold and green.

A fox, lured by the row of overflowing bins, trotted across the road. It stopped and watched me for a moment, ears twitching, snout nosing the air. I heard a car approach. A pair of headlamps swung around the corner. The fox, briefly illuminated, dropped to its haunches and loped into the shadows.

The car, a taxi, rolled to a stop. I saw a flash of rust-coloured hair. My heart leapt. The door opened. One long pale leg emerged, then another. Victoria.

She chucked some notes behind her, slammed the door shut and stumbled towards the gate. The lining of her dress was torn. A limp section of fabric hung down over her knee. She teetered down the path. She looked skinnier than usual. Her thin arms were bone-white against the dark shapes of the garden. When she came closer I saw that her hair was sticky and tangled, her eyes smudged and vacant. She staggered forwards, oblivious to my gaze.

'V,' I called out.

She stopped and squinted in my direction.

'Shannon, is that you?' she said, her voice little more than a croak.

I jumped down from the window. As I did, my skirt caught on some invisible thorn. 'We didn't think you were coming.' I tugged at it and felt the rip of cheap fabric. 'Are you all right?' I asked, picking my way across the wet grass.

'Mmm. Yeah, yeah,' she said, pulling absentmindedly at the hem of her dress. 'Who's here? Is it just you?'

'No,' I said, trying to ignore the implicit dismissal. 'There's Obi and Jolly and Stefano. I think Matt's around too, but he went off with some costume girl.'

Victoria, swaying, peered up at the house. I grabbed her arm to steady her.

'Take me inside, Shannon. Don't lose sight of me, OK?'

'V, what's happened?'

'Nothing, nothing,' she said. 'He was there – but it's nothing.'

'Who was there? Where were you?'

She closed her eyes and shook her head. 'A party, a film thing. It's nothing.' She jerked her arm away. 'It's nothing, I'm fine, really.' She opened her eyes and, like the sun coming out, something lifted. She was Victoria again. 'Nothing. I'm great, I'm perfect.' But then it was gone. Her eyes became hooded and distant. 'I just need you, Shannon. OK? Just – just don't let me go.'

'I won't,' I said, taking her hand and leading her up the step. 'I won't leave you.'

'IT WAS INSANE.'

'Who was there?' Jolly asked, resting his head against Victoria's shoulder.

We were in the conservatory. It was 2 a.m. and the party showed no signs of slowing. Everyone had perked up at Victoria's arrival. Jolly had kissed her face like a homesick dog, while Stefano had given her a fireman's lift and carried her though the house. As soon as we were inside, around people, Victoria returned to herself. With an audience, she seemed to make sense again.

'Erm, fuck. Who was there?' She glanced at the ceiling. Her eyes were glazed and faraway. I looked across at Obi to see if he'd noticed, but he was staring off into the garden. 'There were some casting director types, my agent, her team, some actors – Colin Firth, Jennifer Ehle.'

'Go on, who else?' Jolly said.

'Erm, Helena Bonham Carter was there and Eve Best, Tim Spall.'

'Oh my God, V. You have got to bring me next time as your plus-one,' Jolly said.

'Or me,' Stefano chimed in. 'Don't take him. You'll look much better with a big strong Italian on your arm.'

'Big?' Jolly said beneath his breath.

Something unpleasant flashed behind Stefano's eyes. But then he laughed and the moment was gone.

Obi got up. 'Do you want anything, V? A glass of water maybe?'

Victoria ignored him and drew her knees up onto the sofa. She wasn't wearing any underwear. I caught Jolly's eye and threw him a cushion, which he placed in front of her.

'I can't just – just . . .' Victoria hiccupped and examined a scrape on her leg. 'Bring everyone to these things, you know. Then they wouldn't be exclusive.'

'We're not just anyone. We're the hot young things,' Jolly said. 'We're like pre-acting royalty. People should be *begging* to have us at parties. Well, *I'm* a hot young thing anyway.'

'Aww Jol, it doesn't work like that,' Victoria said, ruffling his hair.

'And me. I'm a hot young thing too,' Stefano added.

'Yeah, sure,' Jolly said, glancing sideways at Victoria.

Victoria laughed and let out a snort.

'Why do you do that?' Stefano said, addressing Jolly.

'Do what?' he replied.

Stefano sat forward. I glimpsed a coldness behind his gaze. 'That thing with your face, with your eyes.'

'What do you mean?' Jolly laughed uncertainly. He looked at Victoria for support, but she was elsewhere, staring at her nails like they held the answer to something.

'You do that thing,' he said calmly. 'You roll your eyes at me.'

'I didn't do anything, hun.'

'Yes, you did. You do. You always do this thing, it's like you don't respect me. It's like, what?' A vein bulged in Stefano's neck. 'You think I shouldn't get invited to parties?'

'I never said that. I don't give a tiny little shit about whether or not you're invited to parties.'

'You think you're smarter than me?'

'Oh shut up, Stef.'

'You think, what, because you wear stupid girls' dresses and put makeup on your face that you're better than me?'

'Babe, you wear what you want and I'll wear what I want. I literally don't care.'

'Fuck you,' Stefano snarled.

'Woah,' Obi said, sitting forwards. He lowered his voice. 'Let's just calm down, yeah?'

'You act like you're so much better than me.' Stefano stood up. 'You think you're so fucking special.'

'I *am* fucking special.' Jolly sprang to his feet.

I glanced across at Victoria, who remained in her seat. She looked so tiny, so inconsequential, like if she wanted to, she could squeeze herself between the sofa cushions and disappear forever.

'And I'm not?'

'Well, to be honest, no.'

People were staring now. Someone was tapping at the speakers, trying to turn the music down.

'You're pathetic,' Jolly said. In heels he towered over Stefano. 'I've seen you perform in class. You're shit. You're like a knock-off Marlon Brando that's shrunk in the wash. You're boring and you're basic, and everyone thinks you're going to fail.'

'Who said that? Who thinks I'm going to fail?' Stefano glanced nervously between me and Victoria. 'Who fucking said that?'

Obi stood from his chair. 'Guys, just calm down.'

'Everyone thinks so,' Jolly said, gesturing in the direction of the rapidly swelling crowd. Some of the costume girls giggled. A techie whispered something and ushered them outside.

'Fuck you, you little gay boy,' Stefano growled.

'*Gay boy?* Oh yeah, real nice,' Jolly jeered.

'Guys, stop it,' Obi said firmly, putting himself between them.

'Good to know you're a homophobe as well as a short-arse—'

Stefano went to push him, but Jolly was quicker. He grabbed Stefano's hand between his manicured fingers and bit down hard on the heel of his palm.

'*Finocchio*,' Stefano yelped, before raising his fist and lunging towards him.

Jolly tumbled backwards into a lamp, which crashed against the window. One of the costume girls squealed. A pile of books toppled from the sill and a drink capsized, spilling its contents across the floor. Obi got in between the two of them again. He pushed Stefano down into the opposite chair and held Jolly against the window. There was shushing, giggles, excited whispers ricocheting down the hallway, a few lone voices chanting *fight, fight, fight*.

Just then, an odd mewling sound filled the room.

I looked around. Victoria's face was buried in her hands. Her shoulders were trembling.

'Just stop it, stop it, please,' she begged through muffled fingers. 'I can't bear it, please, please.'

Jolly was by her side in a flash. 'Oh babe. Oh hun,' he cooed. 'I'm sorry, I'm so *so* sorry.'

Stefano lay panting at the other end of the room. 'Yeah, fuck, I'm sorry, Victoria.'

'I j-just want everyone to get along,' she stuttered.

I gazed around the room, at all the people craning to get a look. All those eyes, fixed on Victoria.

'W-why can't we just be friends? I j-just want us to get along and be n-nice to each other. W-why does there have to be all this drama?'

And then I saw her: the birthday girl, Abigail.

She'd just come in. She smiled and tried to drape herself around the guy she'd been making out with earlier, but he frowned and shrugged her off. Abigail, downcast, looked from his face to Victoria's. Something hardened in her eyes. She crossed her arms and stormed from the room.

'They're sorry, V,' Obi said. 'Come on, let's get you that water.'

Victoria's sobs intensified. She still looked pretty, even when she cried. I hated her for that.

'Poor V, poor poor V,' Jolly whispered.

She'd arrived late, pissed and off her face on something, and still, *still*, it was all about her. It would always be all about her. She was magic. She was a witch.

Sick of being a spectator, I stood up. 'It's getting late,' I said, to no one in particular. And, as if hadn't breathed a word, no one in particular responded. 'I think I'm going to go.'

Jolly took Victoria's hand in his own and, stroking it like a fine piece of silk, whispered more apologies. Obi came and knelt down beside her, rearranging the cushion to guard her dignity. Stefano sat staring at her, breathing heavily, red-faced and contrite at the far end of the room. I picked up my bag and, with one last glance at the miserable tableau, disappeared into the crowd.

FIFTEEN

'IT'S A PASS FROM me for your independent movement piece this term, although not a strong one.'

A panel of faces stared at me. Critical feedback. 'Crits' for short. On the last day of term, when the assessments were over and the holidays were in touching distance, we were invited to receive 'constructive' feedback on whether we'd passed or not.

Frida continued, 'There is something odd about the way you move your limbs. It's as if your brain and body are disconnected. I could see you were trying and that you'd taken on the advice I gave you in week three, but really, Shannon, I think this is something you need to be aware of. You were like a broken-stringed puppet. It was quite uncomfortable to watch.'

I nodded and swallowed. I glanced across at Jolly who was bent low over his notebook, scribbling furiously. Jolly was my scribe that afternoon. Whoever was scheduled to go after you sat in and took notes. This was for our benefit, apparently. With a scribe, you could fully absorb your failings, truly take in the tsunami of shit that washed your way without distraction. We'd been asked to buy Dictaphones at the start of term, and mine sat blinking in front of me. I knew I wouldn't be able to read Jolly's spidery handwriting and that I'd simply listen back and transcribe the whole thing myself. He needn't have been there. But now I think about it, that wasn't the point. They didn't make up the scribe rule to help us, they did it to hold us accountable. Scribes were spies, inserted into this private, shaming moment to deny us the chance to lie about our successes. If, following Crits, you dared to bullshit about your achievements, there was always someone there to set the record straight in the pub after.

'Shannon, are you listening?' It was Casper. I nodded and he pursed his lips. 'I'd also like to add to Frida's comments on your performance in *The Seagull*. Ultimately, I have to agree. You didn't inhabit the role of Masha as much as you could've. I felt you were technically committed, but emotionally held back, slightly out of the frame, as it were, like you were hiding something, like there was something you didn't want the audience to see.' Casper shook his head. 'And that's a real problem if your aim is to build connection.' He scanned his notes. 'As far as your voice work goes this term,' he sniffed, 'vocally you're weak. Your voice lacks fullness, richness. Now, this is just term one, so there is still time to improve, but you've got a long way to go. I've given you a pass for your monologue, but again, it's not a strong pass, Shannon. You need to work a lot harder if you ever realistically hope to perform on a professional stage.'

I held my forearm, pressing the pads of my fingers into the doughy flesh. I smiled and nodded. I could already feel the bruises forming.

Next up was Malcolm Hurst, a gin-soaked man with a wandering eye who the school still kept around, I can only assume, for the prestige of him having once worked with Peter Brook.

Casper gave him a sharp kick under the table, and Malcolm woke with a snort.

'Ah, ah, ah, ah yes. It's Shannon, isn't it?'

'Yes,' I replied. He'd only taught me for the last eight weeks.

'Good, good, ah yes.' He shuffled his papers and leaned forward. His eyes twinkled from behind his spectacles. 'Yes, I'm afraid, Shannon, I have to agree with Frida and Casper.' He beamed at me, his crooked grin belying the barbs he was about to inflict. 'It's as if you weren't totally present. Masha is such a complicated, vital and engaging character, and I'm afraid you failed to live up to the richness of her inner life.' He paused and pushed his glasses up his nose. 'And in my lessons this term, well, I'm afraid I've found you to be, my dear, a little solemn. You never seem to take any joy in what's happening in the room. It's as if you wish to be absolutely anywhere else but here. But you're at the *Royal London School of Dramatic Arts*!' He gripped the table and shook it. 'You should feel like you've won the lottery! I often see you glowering in the corner of my lessons, and I'm sorry but that sort of attitude simply won't cut the mustard out in the real world. Directors want to work with women who are happy and cheerful and light. I think you need to work on your openness, and, dare I say it, your *likeability*. There are a million young actresses out there who are fun and amiable and, frankly, a delight to work with, and if you don't nip this *attitude problem* in the bud, then I'm afraid the industry will not be kind to you.' He shifted in his seat. A faint whiff of sulphur leaked across the room. 'I've given you a pass for your scene study presentation from last week. Again, not a strong pass. The research was there, but your actioning was a little underdeveloped. But you're on the right lines at least.' He glanced up. 'So work harder, and let's try and be a little cheerier next term, yes?'

I nodded and gripped the underside of my chair.

'And what about a smile, eh?'

I did something with my face, although I couldn't say what.

'There you go,' Malcolm said, grinning and folding his papers in half. 'You *can* be pretty when you try.'

'That will be all, Shannon,' Frida said, replacing the lid of her pen.

I reached for the Dictaphone, stuffed it inside my rucksack, and stood to leave.

'Oh, Shannon,' she continued. 'One more thing before you go.' She narrowed her eyes and pressed her hands into a fist. 'Why exactly are you here?'

I clutched the strap of my bag. It was a trick, surely.

'What do you mean?' I said. I could feel myself floating, lifting out of my body, out of the room.

'Why did you bother coming to this school? Why are you here?'

'I – I'm here because . . .' *An imposter, floating, doubling, slicing in two.* 'Because – because I . . .' *Face disappears.*

'Oh dear, Shannon.' Frida tsked. 'The fact you don't have an answer worries me. This is a top conservatoire and you are extremely lucky to be here.' She sighed. 'Passive: that's the word I'd use to describe you. And an actress needs to be anything but passive. This industry is tough, perhaps the toughest. If you're going to succeed, you need passion and, frankly, I've not seen that from you these last eight weeks.' She shook her head. 'I didn't adjudicate your initial audition. Had I done so, I'm not sure I would've put your name forward as a suitable candidate for this course. You have some of my more sympathetic colleagues to thank for this opportunity.' She glanced sideways at Malcolm. His eyes were closed, his chin on his chest. A wad of white spittle clung to the corner of his lips. 'Anyway, you're here now. And, I suppose, you do have some potential.' She sat forward. 'Potential is a rare and brilliant thing, but potential also so often disappoints. This is only your first term. Next term will be harder, and the one after that even more so. If you seriously hope to complete your three years here then you will have to make some huge improvements to your work. If you really want to be here then I would come prepared in January with an answer to my question.' She gave a tiny shrug. 'Or don't come at all.' She stood from her chair and went to the door. 'Thank you, Shannon. You're free to go.'

Jolly, not meeting my eye, handed me the notes.

'Next scribe, please,' Frida said.

She held the door open. I walked past her, my legs shaking.

Don't cry don't cry don't cry don't cry—

'Oh, and merry Christmas, Shannon.'

SIXTEEN

GRANDMA PICKED ME UP from the station.

'Your dad said to come and get you. He's on a late one at work and your mum's not feeling so well.'

I kissed her cheek through the open window and lifted my suitcase into the boot.

After spending ten minutes telling me about her electrician's cruise and the terrible food poisoning he and his wife had on the third night, she glanced over. 'You're awfully quiet, missus.'

'I'm just tired,' I said, resting my head against the window.

And I was – exhausted, in fact. I felt scooped out. Ever since Abigail's party, I'd been avoiding my classmates. As soon as that day's assessments were over, I'd scurried to the library, the supermarket, anywhere, home. I didn't want to see any of them. I was sick of the drama that seemed to circle our little clique and of Victoria, always seemingly at the centre of it.

And then there was Crits. I looked at the fingerprint bruises dotted up my arm. Apparently everyone had gone to the pub straight afterwards to discuss how it had gone. I went back to my halls and slept a fitful twelve hours. I only found out what had happened because Toby posted on Facebook.

Toby Grant posted 3 hours ago

Hi all, I didn't get to see everyone on Friday so I just wanted to let you know I won't be coming back next term. As most of you already know by now, during Crits I was asked to leave the course. Being an actor is all I've ever dreamed of so I was understandably upset. I'm still devastated. But you guys made me feel so loved and so supported and I just wanted to say thank you. I'm going to do some travelling then reapply to drama schools next year (although not RLSDA – fuck you, Frida) and I'm not going to give up on my dream. This place might not have seen my potential but I know somewhere else will. Anyway, just wanted to say goodbye and hope you all have a good Christmas/NY. Let's keep in touch, yeah? And I'll definitely try to see your final third-year shows.

Love you all. Toby x

'You should've called more, you know,' Grandma said, gently slapping my knee.

'Grandma, keep your eyes on the road.'

'Oh, live a little,' she said, chuckling and swerving the car towards the pavement.

'You'll kill someone someday, you know.'

'Still a drama queen then?'

People always described my grandma as a 'character'. She'd lived her entire life in the house she grew up in on Saddleworth Moor. Her mum had died when she was a baby, so she was raised by her father. Once, when I slept over as a kid, she told me how, as a girl, she'd stood in the doorway and watched torch beams comb the moorland, searching for the small, ruined bodies of children returned to the earth too soon. Grandma believed in ghosts. She said they walked among us until their dealings were done. When I asked her what the ghosts wanted, she said it was none of our business, but that we should be kind to them and let them pass on in their own time.

At age nineteen, Grandma married a man from Huddersfield. He died in the Falklands and she was left, like her father, to raise a child alone. She joined the CND and went on anti-war protests, making it her mission to stamp out hatred and violence in all its many forms. She had a monthly standing order to the Socialist Workers Party, weak eyesight, a suede jacket laden with badges and pins that clicked as she moved, two cats, skin like crepe paper, and the biggest heart of anyone I knew.

'I'm just saying, your mum and dad, they've barely heard a peep from you in weeks. What, your fancy school doesn't let you ring home? Did they confiscate your phone or something?'

'I've just been busy.'

'Too busy to call your mum and wish her happy birthday?'

'I sent a card,' I protested.

'*I sent a card, I sent a card*,' she repeated. 'Anyway, I've said my piece. I won't say another word.' She flicked the indicator and popped a Fruit Pastille in her mouth. 'It's just, I know your mum and dad. They won't say anything.'

'I thought you said you were done?'

Grandma held her palms up in surrender.

'Hands on the wheel, Grandma!'

She replaced them, her eyes twinkling. 'They'll be so happy to see you.'

'And you're not?'

She chuckled. 'Oh shush, of course I am. Anyway.' She twisted the dial on the radio. 'Last Christmas'. 'I'll say no more about it.'

We turned the corner and the cemetery gates reared into view. I looked away, averting my eyes like I'd trained myself to do since childhood.

Grandma noticed. 'I was there last week,' she said. 'We could just stop by if you wanted to, get some flowers—'

'No,' I said, cutting her off. 'Not today.'

WE DID ALL THE usual stuff that Christmas: we saw Dad's sister's brood in Halifax and went to the carol concert at the minster; we visited the German market in Leeds; we filled the cupboards with crisps and crackers, chocolates, nuts, and a shrink-wrapped platter of dried fruits we knew no one would touch. A week before Christmas, Mum tasked me with decorating the tree. It was a job I usually enjoyed. I liked unwrapping the glass nativity figures from their nests of tissue paper and arranging them in the manger: Mary, Joseph, the Christ Child, the ass – every actor knowing their part. I liked hanging the glitter-dusted candy canes I'd made in primary school and finally, placing the beautiful fiery-haired doll we used as an angel on top of the tree. But this year, looking at the looming six-foot structure of wire and plastic squashed behind the telly, I felt only a bone-deep tiredness.

Every night I lay awake in my room, staring at the dark shapes of my girlhood and contemplating the term ahead. We'd done Chekhov; Shakespeare's comedies were next. There was a stack of textbooks and plays by my bed which I knew I needed to get through before the first day back. But as each day passed, I found it harder and harder to even contemplate picking one of them up. What was the point? Frida had already confirmed my worst fear, that I was an imposter who should never have been accepted to the school. I wasn't like the Victorias of the world. My future wasn't written in the stars. It was scratched into the dirt. Another term would roll around, more difficult this time. I'd work my arse off and then, on the final day, they'd summon me like they had done Toby, and turn me out onto the street.

AS FAR BACK AS I could remember, I'd always spent New Year's Eve with Grandma. It was tradition. Mum and Dad would go to the big house down the road which laid on fireworks and karaoke, while Grandma and I would ring in the new year with a quiet night in front of the telly. Grandma liked the small man with the piano, and I liked sneaking snifters of brandy when her back was turned. I was watching the *Hootenanny* with my hand in a tube of Pringles when the doorbell went. I glanced across at Grandma. She was asleep, her head on one side, her mouth open. Marx, the grey cat, was curled up in her lap. I wiped my hand on my jeans and crept from the room.

'Surprise!'

I blinked rapidly, not believing my eyes. They were a mirage, an illusion, ghostly apparitions that had wandered down from the moor.

'God, it's freezing,' Jolly said, clapping his hands together and squeezing past me. 'Where's your loo? I'm busting for a piss.'

'Erm, top of the landing,' I stammered.

'We brought Bolly,' Victoria announced, holding the bottle aloft. 'Where's the fridge?'

'Far end of the corridor—'

Obi was next. 'Hello Shannon,' he said, pulling me into a bear hug. 'Happy New Year.'

Then, after throwing the butt of his still-glowing cigarette over the hedge, Stefano. '*Madame*,' he purred, lowering himself into a bow and planting a kiss on my hand.

'Hi.'

He brought himself up to his full height, winked and followed the others inside.

Stunned by the sudden materialization of my classmates, I shut the door and tiptoed down the hall. I pulled back the beaded curtain. Grandma was still asleep in her chair. On the television, a mute Jools Holland slammed his fingers against the keys of a piano. I let the beads fall and went to join the others in the kitchen.

'What are you all doing here?' I whispered. 'You could've called or something.'

'No time,' Jolly said, walking in behind me and zipping up his fly. 'It was a spur-of-the-moment thing. We're *carpe*-ing the *diem*, bitch.'

'But how did you know I'd be here?'

'Because I'm a regular Jessica Fletcher,' he replied with a sly smile. 'In the last week, when I was waiting in reception to sort that bloody student loan thing, I went through everyone's emergency contacts. I tried your dad. He said you'd be here.'

'But why?'

'Because no one had heard a thing from you in weeks.'

'We assumed you'd died,' Victoria said, tearing foil from the champagne.

'Really?' I said, alarmed.

'Yeah, V wanted to pick through your pockets. Find out where the family gold was hidden.'

'Fuck off, Jol,' Victoria said.

'But, it's New Year's Eve. Don't you all have plans?'

'Well, we *did*,' Victoria said, hoisting herself onto the countertop. 'I had *fabulous* plans until my brothers got pulled away to some bacchanal in fucking Berkshire, or something.'

'My flight to Milan got cancelled,' Stefano said.

'Terrence bailed on me,' Jolly said, then added, 'Oh, by the way, I'm seeing a guy called Terrence.'

'And I got fired from my weekend job,' Obi finished.

'You got fired?'

'Yeah, but it's OK.' He glanced uncertainly at Victoria. 'I'll make things work.'

'And besides,' Jolly said, slinging his arm around my shoulder, 'we thought you might need cheering up. You were a right little storm cloud in the last week of term.' He gave my arm a squeeze and I felt something unclench in my stomach. I knew then that he hadn't said a word to anyone about my Crits.

'Also, it's nice to be out in the country,' Victoria said.

'Yes,' Stefano agreed.

'Fucking awful journey though,' Jolly added, kneeling down and sliding a bottle of apricot wine from the back of Grandma's cupboard. 'V can't drive for shit.'

'Ha ha. You can get the train back then.'

'I misspoke. Victoria is an excellent driver. It was those bollards really, they shouldn't have got in her way.'

The four of them laughed.

'What's going on?' Grandma said nervously, appearing in the doorway. Her hair was all fluffy on one side and she was cradling the cat. 'Shannon, what's happening?'

'Grandma, I—'

Jolly swept in front of me. 'Hello, so sorry to barge in like this. It's Mary, isn't it?' He gave her a warm smile and scratched Marx under the chin. 'I'm Jolly, and this is Victoria, Obi and Stefano.'

'We're Shannon's friends from university,' Victoria added, jumping down from the counter.

I glanced around at them, at their beaming faces. *Shannon's friends.*

'Shannon, you didn't say anything to me about this, did you?'

I shrugged, at a loss for words. 'It was a surprise.'

'Well,' she said, the confusion thawing from her features. 'Shannon's *friends.*' Her face lit up. 'Where are my manners?' She dropped Marx to the floor. 'Does anyone fancy a brew?'

'I'm on it,' Obi said, lifting the kettle from the hob.

'Or something to eat?' Grandma went to the counter and began rummaging in the cupboard. 'We've got crisps. Does anyone want a bag of crisps? Or a sandwich. I can make up some sandwiches. We've got After Eights in here somewhere too. And biscuits. In fact, I think I've got some of those nice M&S ones, haven't I, Shannon?'

Victoria crouched down beside her. 'Here, Mary,' she said. 'I'll help you look.'

LATER THAT EVENING, AFTER snacks, chatter and a boozy countdown to midnight, Grandma fetched an assortment of pillows, blankets and towels from the airing cupboard and said her goodnights.

The light from the convector glowed amber. Jolly and I sat side by side on one sofa. Obi and Victoria were squeezed together on the other. Stefano sat across from us in the recliner. I turned the volume down on the TV; some New Year's concert, a roomful of partygoers having the time of their lives. We talked aimlessly for a short while, but the conversation soon turned to school.

'Tiff got her tits out in the individual dance assessment!'

'Stefano, you're so full of shit,' Jolly said, laughing.

'I'm telling you, she 100 per cent did. I was her scribe. Frida congratulated her on it in her Crits.'

'They actually congratulated her?' I asked, reaching for another biscuit.

'Yeah, they said it was really brave and moving and that she expressed herself authentically with beauty and grace, or some bullshit like that. Malcolm was practically salivating.'

'Well, watch out then, fellas,' Victoria said, laughing, 'cos next term I'm getting the girls out.'

'Hmm. Titties. An interesting development. Do you think I'd get better grades if I slung my knob out?' Jolly asked.

'I doubt Malcolm would be as amenable to that,' Obi answered.

We all laughed.

'Speaking of Malcolm,' Jolly continued, 'in *my* Crits, the old coot told me I was camper than ten tent pegs and grass.'

'Jeez.' Obi shook his head.

Victoria laughed incredulously. 'Oh, come on. I'm pretty sure they're not allowed to say stuff like that.'

'Ask Lola, she was my scribe. Anyway, allowed or not, that's what he said.'

'Yeah, they can say what they want,' Obi added. 'Casper told me I needed to soften my accent if I wanted to be taken seriously. He said my voice was intimidating and that I should try to *think a bit more like an upper-class gentleman*.'

'Ugh' – Jolly rolled his eyes – 'they're so fucking tone-deaf.'

'What's tone-deaf about that?' Victoria said. 'They're just trying to expand your casting.'

'What's tone-deaf?' Obi repeated. 'Come on, V. They might as well have said, *can you try being a bit less black?*'

Victoria frowned. 'Oh, well, I suppose you could take it that way, yes.'

'And Frida said she *still* didn't think I could play straight,' Jolly added, draining his glass.

'Straight people are boring to play anyway,' Victoria said. 'Believe me, I'm going to be playing straight fucking ingénues for the next ten years. But that's the way things are.' She smiled at Jolly. 'I'm actually jealous of you. I wish I got to play gay people. You're just so much more' – she thought for a moment – '*interesting*.'

'Well, thank you. I'll pass on your kind words at the next big meeting,' Jolly replied sarcastically.

Victoria bristled. 'I'm just saying.'

'I know. I'm only joking.' He tipped more champagne into his glass. 'I don't care. Fuck them. Queers before careers.'

'I was Hettie's scribe,' Obi said. 'They told her she had about as much grace as a baby rhino.'

'Oh, bless her,' Jolly said. 'The poor girl's one Ryvita away from developing an eating disorder as it is.'

'How was your Crits, Shannon?' Victoria asked, turning her attention on me.

'It was – erm.' I racked my brain for an answer. 'They said – they said—'

'They said,' Jolly cut in, 'that she had some things to work on, like all of us, but that generally things were moving in the right direction. *Potential*, isn't that right, Shan?'

I nodded and bit my lip. *Don't cry – don't cry.*

'Anyway, why do we have to talk about school all the time?' Jolly added. 'We're more interesting than that, aren't we? Obi, talk to me. Tell me about your *life*. How was your Christmas?'

Obi shrugged. 'It was OK. The usual. Church with my mum, then food at my auntie's. Everyone was there, the whole family. Lots of my little cousins running around, you know, same as last year and the one before that, and the one before that. Nice though.'

'You're so lucky. My family's a bin fire. There's always some fucking drama. I got into an awful argument with my brother on Christmas Eve,' Victoria said, shaking her head.

'Which one?'

'Lawrence. It's the same every year. It's like he's this little' – she scrunched up her nose – 'this little fucking ringleader who gets my other brothers on side and convinces them to bully me. They're grown men, for God's sake, but it's like they become kids—'

'Ah, they're just messing around,' Stefano said.

'And then I tell my mum they're all ganging up on me, and she says I'm old enough to fight my own battles, which I am, don't get me wrong, but it's just a bit mad when you've got three older brothers holding you down or attacking you with cushions, and their literal *girlfriends* and *wives* are sitting there watching the whole thing like it's a big fucking laugh and not doing a thing to stop them.' Victoria gestured at Jolly and me. 'You guys don't know how lucky you are, being an only child.'

Jolly raised his glass. 'Hear, hear.'

'I'm not an only child,' I said.

Everyone looked at me.

'What do you mean?' Victoria said, frowning.

I swallowed. They were all staring at me, waiting for an answer. 'Yeah, erm' – I cleared my throat – 'I have a sister – *had* a sister. She died when I was a kid.'

There was a pause.

Victoria sank against the sofa cushions. 'Shit.'

'Oh my God, Shannon. That's so sad,' Jolly said.

'I'm so sorry,' Obi added.

'It's OK. It was a long time ago.'

'God. What, like, *happened*?' Victoria said. 'If you don't mind me asking, that is.'

'Erm.' I looked at the ceiling. 'Well, we – me and my parents – don't really know. We were living at a different house, and in the garden there was a pond . . .'

'Oh God,' Jolly whispered.

'And yeah, one day she was playing in the garden and – we still don't know how it happened – she tripped over, cracked her head or something, and the next minute she was, well, she was face down in the water. I don't really remember it though. I don't remember much before it all happened actually – about her, or anything really.'

The room was silent.

'Sorry,' I laughed half-heartedly, 'mood-killer.'

'No, no.' Victoria smiled softly. 'Not at all, babe.'

'Yeah, no, it's fine,' Jolly added.

'Thanks for telling us,' Obi said.

'Yeah,' Stefano agreed. 'Thanks for sharing.'

I shrugged. 'It's fine. It is what it is.' Another uncomfortable silence followed. I settled my gaze on the convector's amber rods. 'These things happen.'

SEVENTEEN

THE NEXT MORNING, I pulled back the beaded curtain of the living room to find the four of them still asleep. Obi and Stefano were on the floor in sleeping bags. Jolly was sprawled beneath a beach towel on one sofa while Victoria was tucked beneath a patchwork quilt on the other. I dared myself to creep closer to her. The floorboard creaked beneath my weight. I froze. Her eyelashes fluttered and she turned her face away. I inched backwards and, letting the beads fall, went through into the kitchen.

Grandma was frying eggs. I gave her a kiss.

'You should take them for a walk later today. Shake off the cobwebs.'

I nodded and picked a slice of toast from the plate next to her. Engels, the black cat, slithered between my ankles.

She glanced up from the pan. 'You look well today.'

I covered my mouth. 'Do I?'

'You look like you slept.'

It was true; I had slept, better than I had done in weeks, in fact. My head felt clear, my body light. For the first time in a while, it felt like the day ahead held some kind of possibility.

'They're nice,' she continued.

'Who?'

'Your friends.'

'Yes.'

'It's not every day you make good friends, you know,' Grandma said, turning her cool blue eyes on me. 'Hold on to them, won't you?'

'I will,' I replied. And I meant it.

AFTER WOLFING DOWN A fry-up, we set out. In the end, my *soft southern* friends (as Grandma affectionately termed them) were entirely unprepared and had to borrow coats. Obi got Grandma's mauve rain mac, Victoria her rose quilted jacket; Stefano insisted he didn't feel the cold – but still tied a cagoule around his waist – and Jolly took great delight in a 1980s faux-fur number he found at the back of the wardrobe.

'I feel like Elizabeth Taylor,' he said, doing a twirl in the hallway mirror.

We set off up the hill. Toffee-coloured bracken lined the dry-stone walls. Tendrils of grey cloud fingered the sky. The wind slapped our skin. We chatted in pairs, sometimes keeping up, sometimes falling back. Occasionally the sun broke through, piercing the gloom with needles of light. We climbed higher and higher, tall heads of cotton grass urging us onward.

Stefano, Jolly and Victoria walked ahead, and I found myself next to Obi.

'I'm sorry about your job.'

'Thanks,' Obi said, his eyes fixed on the horizon. 'It's fine. I'm doing OK. It was kind of getting in the way of school anyway. They said in my Crits that I should think about quitting.'

'Really?'

'Oh yeah.' He laughed bitterly. '*Obi, do you want to be an actor or do you want to stack shelves in Tesco? You must decide.*'

'That's bullshit.'

'Yeah. I mean, I wasn't working there for the networking opportunities.'

'No.'

Up ahead, Stefano said something and Victoria cackled with delight.

'So' – I lowered my voice to avoid anyone overhearing – 'what will you do about money?'

'Um.' Obi cleared his throat. 'V's helped me out.'

'Oh. Cool.'

'Yeah – no – I mean, she's helped me find a new job.' He kicked a stone. It rolled into a ditch. 'She got in touch with the school, actually. Sorted me out a job at the student union. Just some bar stuff, but still. It'll help.'

'That's great,' I said.

Victoria was helping Obi out. This was good. So why did it feel like there was something stuck in my throat? Something sharp and difficult to dislodge.

'She's a really good person,' Obi said flatly, then, with more enthusiasm: 'Like, one of the best.'

I nodded and we continued in silence.

THE SEASONS CHANGED AROUND us. The sky turned like a roll of parchment, a spinning zoetrope. Light and dark. Wind and cold skin. Sun and sweat. We climbed higher and higher, eventually reaching the pinnacle, the plateau, a gritstone cliff from where the valley spread out below us. We stopped and caught our breath, staring at the great bowl of the land. Purples, browns and greens. A patchwork quilt of heather, crowberry and bog.

'I didn't know England could look like this,' Obi said.

'Yeah, it's bleak, man,' Stefano added.

'No.' Victoria shivered. 'It's beautiful.' She crossed her arms and pulled the pink jacket tight around herself. 'But it kind of scares me.'

'Yeah, it's creepy up here,' Jolly said.

As if on cue, the wind shushed and the ground rustled beneath our feet. A bank of cloud loomed in the distance. We huddled closer. Victoria took Obi's arm. Jolly rested his chin on her shoulder. Loath to forgo some imagined intimacy, Stefano put his arm around my waist. I flinched and pulled apart from him, stepping away from the group. I walked forwards, putting a hand to my chest, feeling the knock of my heart. I tipped my head back. A kestrel waited, suspended above us, then dived headfirst like a sycamore seed into the marsh. I continued forwards until my soles found the edge of the plateau. I curled my trainers over the boulder's lip and peered down into oblivion.

What would it be like, I wondered, to let go? To fall. Or leap? To dive, like a kestrel.

The drop wasn't so far. You might survive. Or you might not. There were always two ways, always two endings.

The wind picked up again. I shut my eyes. I could feel them behind me, the four of them. *Shannon's friends*. But then there was another, a fifth, some phantom self.

I felt a hand on my shoulder.

'All right, daredevil,' Victoria said. 'Don't get too close to the edge.'

She pulled me back and slipped her arm through my own.

We gazed out at the landscape for another few minutes, before Jolly, his teeth chattering, asked: 'Is anyone else fucking freezing?'

*

WE MADE OUR WAY down the hill. Victoria and I walked arm in arm at the head of the group while the boys wandered a few paces behind. She leaned into me.

'You know you can talk to me about anything, don't you?'

'I know.'

'Because, like, all that stuff about your sister, you could've told me. I would've understood.'

'I know you would, V.'

She pulled me closer and whispered sincerely. 'Like, you can trust me.'

'Of course,' I said, not quite knowing if I could.

'Good. Because no one should have to hold on to something like that.'

I shook my head. 'It's not like I was holding on to it. I just never found the right moment to tell you guys,' I said, my voice sounding artificially bright. 'Honestly, I don't even think about it most of the time. It doesn't really feel like something that happened to me. I was so young.'

'Sure, sure. But you know, like, if there's anything else you want to tell me, then you totally can.'

'I know.'

The path crunched unsteadily beneath our feet. Black clouds threatened overhead.

'You're such a closed book,' she said, sighing wistfully.

'I don't mean to be.'

'It's not a criticism. It's just that you know everything about me.'

I frowned. Was that true? It felt like, despite my dedication to studying Victoria, I still hadn't got past the first page.

She pulled me closer. 'Like, are there any guys you like in our class?'

I hesitated. 'No.'

'No?'

'No.'

Victoria pursed her lips. She glanced over her shoulder at the boys, then back at me. 'Are you sure about that?'

I laughed. 'What do you want me to say?'

'Nothing.' The hint of an eye-roll. 'You don't have to say anything. I just don't want you to feel like you have to keep secrets from me.'

'I don't, V,' I replied. My voice sounded small, insubstantial.

'OK.' She separated herself from me and put her hands in her pockets. 'We don't have to talk about it any more.'

Something in the set of her jaw told me I'd upset her. I racked my brain for what to say, how to make her like me again, to thaw her chilly demeanour. But I was interrupted. Behind us, Jolly let out a yelp of pain.

'FUCK!'

We turned around. Jolly lay on the ground, rubble skittering in his wake.

'My ankle, my fucking ankle!'

We rushed towards him.

'Oh fuckety-fuck, that hurts.'

'Stay calm. Can you move it?' Obi said, crouching beside him.

'Shit – ah – bollocks – no, I can't move it – shit.' He winced and pulled down his sock. I looked away.

'Here.' Stefano put Jolly's arm across his shoulder. Obi came around the other side of him, and together the two of them hoisted him up onto his feet.

The sky rumbled ominously.

'Can you make it down?' Victoria asked.

Jolly winced again. 'I don't know. Shit. Where the fuck are we anyway?'

*

OBI AND STEFANO CARRIED Jolly down the moor. Luckily for them, he weighed practically nothing, and luckily for Jolly, even if he had, neither one of them wanted to lose face in front of Victoria. Halfway down, the clouds burst. We made the rest of the journey beneath a thick blanket of rain. When we arrived back at the house, it was nearly dark and we were soaked.

We dragged Jolly inside and Grandma gave him the once-over. She pulled up the damp hem of his jeans and tssked at the purplish swollen flesh.

'I'm afraid it's A&E for you, lad.'

The boys hoisted him into the back of Grandma's car, and I said a silent prayer that she'd take the roads carefully. At the last moment Victoria offered to go too, but Jolly shooed her away.

'No, no. I've already ballsed up your New Year enough. You lot get the Monopoly out or something. Mary and I will be fine.'

We stood on the front step and waved them off. The car disappeared around the corner, its brake lights dimming from view, swallowed up by the bleak winter night.

EIGHTEEN

THE FOUR OF US sat in front of the television. There was a quiz on, some loud colourful thing that none of us were really watching. Jolly had sent Victoria a text when they'd arrived at A&E saying there was a huge wait. Then again at 11 p.m., moaning that they still hadn't been seen. Realizing they might not be back until the early hours of the morning, we abandoned our mugs of tea and instead began passing a bottle of champagne backwards and forwards between us.

Obi and Victoria sat beneath a blanket on one sofa while Stefano lounged beside me on the other, his hairy legs encroaching ever more boldly beyond the borders of our designated seat cushions. When we'd arrived back at the house earlier, Stefano had stretched his damp socks out along the radiator. His bare feet edged closer to me now. I glanced sideways at them, at the pale bumps and blue veins that snaked along the knuckles of flesh. I shifted imperceptibly; the feet slid closer.

'Does anyone want anything from the kitchen?' I said, getting up.

Victoria shook her head. 'No, thanks. I might turn in.'

'Me too,' Obi added.

Grandma had changed the sheets in my room earlier. She said I could share her bed – if she ever got back – so that one of my friends could take the single.

Victoria stretched her arms above her head and stood up. 'Mind if I take the bedroom?' she asked, to which the boys replied that they weren't bothered.

'Are you sure you want to go to bed so soon?' I asked her. The drama of the day, along with the copious amounts of champagne I'd consumed, had left me feeling jittery and awake. 'It's still early. We could play a board game or put a film on or something.'

Victoria knelt down in front of me. 'Goodnight, darling,' she said firmly, taking my hands and placing a kiss on my forehead. 'Go. To. Bed. And dream sweet dreams.'

'Fine,' I sighed. 'Goodnight, V.'

She went upstairs and Obi headed to the bathroom to clean his teeth, leaving Stefano and me alone.

'I'll stay up with you,' Stefano said.

I faked a yawn. 'No, V's right. We should probably get some sleep.'

'Your call.' He turned off the TV, and I grabbed the linens piled in the corner from the previous night. His phone buzzed.

'It's my brother.' He turned the phone around. His smiling family crowded the frame. 'He says they're all there and they miss me.'

I arranged my face into a smile and replaced some Christmas cards that had fallen from the mantelpiece. 'That's nice.'

'After I get married, I want a big family. Do you?'

'I don't know.' I hesitated. 'I don't even know if I want to get married.'

'What?' Stefano laughed. 'That's crazy. Every woman wants to get married.'

'Well, I don't.' I picked at my jumper, at a loose thread clawed free by the cats. 'I mean, I don't know if I want to yet.'

He laughed again. 'You'll change your mind. A woman's greatest gift is being a wife and mother. You'll want a family eventually.'

'I guess,' I mumbled. My cheeks reddened and something unnameable flared up inside my chest. I felt mortified but I couldn't say why. It was as if some part of me had been denied, as if my thoughts, the words that came from my mouth, were mere suggestions, raw ingredients not yet baked by more perceptive minds.

He came up behind me and began massaging my shoulders. 'You just need to relax, Shannon.'

'Maybe.' I slipped out from under him and went to turn off the convector.

'Hey, did you hear anything more from your grandma?' he asked.

I shook my head.

A coy smile spread across his face. 'Look, *you're* wide awake; *I'm* wide awake. Why don't we keep each other company, just the two of us?' he said. 'Until she gets back, of course.'

The radiator clicked. Warm air rose between the greyed fabric of Stefano's socks, making the room smell sour. I opened my mouth to answer, but just then Obi re-entered the room. 'I used a blue towel that I found in the airing cupboard, I hope you don't mind.'

'That's fine,' I said, relieved at the interruption. I edged past the two of them and into the hallway. 'I'll see you both in the morning. Goodnight.'

I LAY CURLED UP in Grandma's bed. I could hear the wind keening in the chimney, the walls and floors creaking and complaining with age. At what must've been around 4 a.m., I thought I heard footsteps in the hallway and then a door opening, whispers, something falling to the floor. I sat up and pressed my ear to the wall.

'I couldn't sleep.'

'Don't worry.'

It was Obi and Victoria, with just one thin membrane of plaster between us.

'*Come here.*'

I remained where I was, still and silent. My heart knocked against my chest. My eyes felt heavy. I waited, listening for more, listening for furtive gasps and metal springs, for him, for her, for words of love, for bodies pressed together, lips against torsos, legs twisted, the scrape of fingers through hair, for salt, for sweat, for wet, for hard, for soft, for soft, for falling, falling—

'Shannon?'

I stirred.

'Shannon?'

'Hmm.'

I opened my eyes to find Victoria staring down at me. She was wearing a long white T-shirt and little else.

'Come with me to the bathroom.'

She took my hand and pulled me out from beneath the covers.

We crept along the landing.

She led me inside the bathroom and carefully clicked shut the door. I stood awkwardly by the bath as she pulled her knickers down and sat on the toilet. The porcelain sink glowed like polished bone in the darkness. She dropped her head and pissed. I looked away.

'Are you embarrassed?' she asked.

I shook my head.

'I went to boarding school. No manners. Sorry.'

She flushed and padded towards the sink. I noticed she was wearing Obi's sports socks.

She leaned forwards and inspected her reflection. She brushed her fingers through her hair, pinched her cheek, sighed.

'What's wrong?' I asked.

'Hmm? Nothing. Just checking I'm still real.'

I came up beside her. The Victoria in the mirror leaned her head against my shoulder. I turned slightly and buried my nose in her hair, breathing her in. She smelled sweet, smoky, faintly bitter.

'Here we are,' she said.

'Here we are.'

She continued staring at her reflection, at mine.

'How's Obi?' I asked, immediately regretting the question. The words tasted wrong on my tongue. Victoria noticed. She raised one eyebrow.

'He's fine, I believe.' A smile tugged at the corners of her mouth. 'Why do you ask?'

'No reason.'

She laughed. 'You know I love you, Shannon, don't you?'

I nodded at the pale ghost in the glass.

'You know I'd do anything for you?'

I nodded again.

'We're sisters, you and I.'

I shivered.

Her hand brushed against mine and a bolt of electricity rippled through my skin.

She turned to face me. 'These boys,' she said, as if picking up the strands of some long-discarded conversation. She shook her head. 'These silly, silly boys.'

I waited for an explanation, but it never arrived.

She came closer.

I shut my eyes. And she kissed me.

Her lips were dry and chapped, but human and throbbing with life.

I didn't know what to do.

I felt frozen by the warmth of her.

But then something in my body replied.

An ache pooled in the curve of my belly. I pressed against her. My tongue found hers.

She grabbed a handful of my thigh. She pushed me up against the sink and slid her hand under my vest. She pulled down the elastic of my shorts. I gasped and arched my back involuntarily as her fingers slid inside me.

Fireworks.

Explosions.

Blindness and light.

Everything, everything leading to this, this moment, this bliss, this ecstasy.

But then she stopped.

'What is it?' I asked, my heart racing beneath her cupped hand.

'I—' She shook her head.

'Please, what is it?' I begged her. 'Tell me.'

She lifted her chin and looked at me. 'Don't send me away, Shannon,' she said, her eyes two damp ponds.

'You know I won't.'

'Let me pretend with you.'

'Why are you pretending?' I whispered. I searched her eyes for an answer. Not finding one, I kissed her again, running my tongue along her lips, pretending the wetted flesh beneath it were my own.

She pulled away and her face twisted into something different, a smirk.

'You know why I'm pretending.'

My heart, afraid. *Knock knock.*

'Come on, Shannon . . .'

'What?'

'This is silly.'

'I don't understand.'

I tried to pull away, but she held me fast.

'We're both pretending.' She released her fingers and brought her mouth to my ear. 'I'm pretending to be real. But I'm not, Shannon. I live in your imagination. I'm a collection of lines, a smattering of remarks, of sinewy memories. I'm someone you once knew, your half-baked remembrances. I'm a slight and an insult, a careless word. I'm jealousy and violence and the chaos that spreads. I'm a lie, a character. I'm not real, Shannon. None of this is real.'

She pulled away and looked at me. And then she laughed in that familiar Victoria way, whooping and careless. And so I laughed as well, and we cackled in the darkness like two witches, finally cracking beneath the burden of ourselves. Because why not. Why not laugh and enjoy the whole damn performance of it.

And then I gripped her wrist, lowering her hand again, stretching her fingers back – beckoning her to – begging her to—

Knock knock.

No, let me stay.

Knock knock knock.

Jolly.

Knock knock knock.

Let me dream.

'Shannon, we're back. Your grandma wants to know if you want eggs?'

I wake up.

Act Two

ONE

IN JANUARY WE BEGAN a new term, our second. When we'd started there had been seventeen of us. Now we were down to fourteen. No one had heard from Maddy. Toby occasionally sent pictures of his travels around Thailand or Vietnam or wherever, riding elephants, posing with tigers, petite young women hanging from his arm and a pair of wraparound sunglasses glued to his forehead. Another classmate, Felix, had dropped out in the first week back. On his final day we sat around in the pub while he explained that university or, holding up his fingers, 'drama school', was meant to be fun, how he'd expected to be drunk each night and that he was tired of working his arse off day after day, only to be told he was a shit actor and destined to fail.

We all sipped our drinks in silence at that. It was hard to disagree with him. Most of us were fresh from visits home, from catch-ups with old school friends who were having the time of their lives at uni, shagging, drinking, making mistakes, discovering who they were. Meanwhile, what had we discovered? That we had limited casting, weak voices and bad attitudes.

That term we studied *Twelfth Night* in amongst the usual voice, movement, accent and dance classes. As rain fell in icy sheets against the windows of Rehearsal Room Three, we paraded back and forth in practice skirts and billowing shirts, parrying clever witticisms, *de-dum-de-dum-de-dumming* iambic verse, and repeating archaic jokes we didn't understand and which never once raised a smile from Frida, our director. First-years weren't usually directed by Frida – that pleasure being reserved for second- and third-years – but on the first day back in January, she marched into the room where we were warming up and announced that we'd made a poor start, and that from now on she'd be personally intervening in our development. The news she'd be directing us divided opinion. Frida was Marmite. A brave few openly expressed their dislike, calling her a has-been, a harpy and a thwarted, ageing nobody with sadomasochistic tendencies. But for the most part, the majority of us found ourselves in a vice-like grip of love, admiration and pure, undiluted fear. Frida was God, our maker. Her wrath inspired trembling; a kind word thrown someone's way, tears. When she said that Hettie's Maria had real gusto, the poor girl had to take a moment outside the rehearsal room to stifle her relieved sobs, while Tiff, her alternate, watched on in quiet envy.

That term, the girls were once again asked to share parts. In week two, Frida announced to our small cohort of women that a portion of our final grades would be dependent on us producing a seamless and coherent characterization with our alternate. This felt like an extra hoop to jump through on top of the line-learning and individual labour we were still expected to do. When Victoria raised her hand to point out that none of the boys had to split roles, Frida replied:

'In the industry you are about to enter, there are ten outstanding female performers to every adequate male performer. And to every ten dreary male roles in a play, there is one female: an ingénue, a maid, a mother, or maybe, if you're lucky, a wife. You will have to work twice as hard and your opportunities will be twice as rare. This is a fact. I cannot change it, the school cannot change it. The sooner you accept the reality ahead of you, the sooner you'll know if you're cut out for this profession.'

I was to share the role of Viola with Lola Aguillard, a willowy French girl who divided her weekends between Paris and London and did modelling in her spare time. She had long straight blonde hair and dark shadows beneath her eyes. I never really understood why people thought she was pretty, but her dad was a respected screenwriter and her mum had received an Oscar nomination in the eighties, so there was that. Lola was a detached sort who seemed to survive exclusively on black coffee, sesame crackers and salted kale. After graduation, she went on to land a string of high-profile modelling contracts and a large-ish role in a new film adaptation of *Grimms' Fairy Tales*.

I didn't particularly want to spend any more time with Lola than I had to. The girl creeped me out, never saying anything, just peeling her split ends and sucking on her hair. But I was glad not to be sharing a role with Victoria. Every day I watched her in rehearsals, the way she commanded the stage as much as she did the room. I watched her laugh and fling her arms around Obi's shoulders, the easy jokes she made with Stefano and Jolly, the warm smiles and kind words she bestowed upon other members of the class. I watched her and I studied her, peering out from behind my notebook as she sailed across the sprung floors of the rehearsal room, her very existence lighting up an otherwise dreary day. I thought back to New Year's, to Victoria's sleeping form on the sofa, curled up like a question mark. I thought about the day after, when she and the others had left, the smell when I brought her used sheets to my nose, the soft cotton still warmed with the memory of her.

'Why are you always watching this girl?' Lola asked me one afternoon.

'What?' I said, distracted. Victoria was helping the group choreograph a movement piece. They were attempting to block out a storm for the shipwreck opener using just their bodies and a length of silk.

'Victoria. You watch her all day long. Are you a lesbian?'

I spun around. 'What are you talking about?'

'It's OK.' She shrugged. 'I don't judge.'

'I am *not* a lesbian.'

'But you are in love with her, no?'

'Keep your voice down,' I hissed. 'I don't *love* Victoria. I'm just watching her – *them* – rehearse. I'm just, just supporting my classmates.'

Lola shrugged and resumed picking at a limp strand of hair. 'Whatever. It doesn't bother me.'

I slammed my notebook shut.

'I need to go over my lines,' I snapped, before picking up my bag and moving to the other end of the room.

IN CRITS THAT TERM, I was given a fail for my final performance. Malcolm said I looked lost onstage, Casper claimed my vocals were strained, and Frida said she'd forgotten the finer points of my performance almost immediately, that I'd disappeared, swallowed up by the enormity of the text. Frida advised me to pair up with another actress for my retake. She said I needed to step up my game soon or this would be my last term at the school. I hated her then. Frida, that is. I really hated her.

VICTORIA AGREED TO HELP me pass the resit.

'There's no shame in having to do it again, you know,' Victoria said, scooping her long hair up into a bun.

'I know.'

'If anything, it's an opportunity to show them you can take direction.'

'Sure.'

'You seem pissed off.'

'I'm not pissed off. I'm just exhausted and tired of being here all the time.'

It was 7 p.m. The lights of the rehearsal room were too bright. We'd been at the school since eight that morning. It was the last week of term before Easter, and I wanted nothing more than to throw my copy of *Twelfth Night* into the fire.

'I'm sick of this play.'

'Come here,' Victoria said, pulling me into a hug. 'You are brave. You are talented. You can do this.' She took a step back and placed her hands on my shoulders. 'So, Act One, Scene Five?'

'Yes.' I rolled my eyes. 'For the billionth time.'

'Right, Viola,' Victoria said, consulting the script. 'Let's go from *Good madam*.'

'OK.' I tucked my T-shirt into my leggings and positioned myself upstage. '*Good madam, let me see your face*.' I dropped to my knee.

'*Have you any commission from your lord to negotiate with my face? You are now out of your text. But we will draw the curtain and show you the picture*.' Victoria, miming, lifted her veil. '*Look you, sir, such a one I was this present. Is't not well done?*'

I gazed at the loose wisps of hair escaping at the nape of her neck, at her dark eyebrows and sharp jawline, her pale cheeks and rosy lips. '*Excellently done, if God did all*.'

'Sorry, can I stop you?' Victoria asked.

'OK,' I muttered, trying to hide my irritation at the interruption, at her well-meaning smile.

'It feels like you're missing something.'

'What?' I said, getting to my feet.

'You're a fake, right?'

'I – err, excuse me?' I said. My heart jumped inside my chest.

'Cesario is a fake. He's just Viola dressed up, pretending to be a boy.'

'Right, yes, of course,' I replied, crossing my arms and avoiding her gaze.

'And so here he is – here *she* is – having to deliver this message and pretend to be a guy, as well as being respectful towards this mad cow who's falling in love with her.'

Victoria placed her hands on her hips. 'Not to mention that she's totally in love with her master *and* she was shipwrecked in a storm, like, yesterday. And on top of all that, she's having to bury this maelstrom of feelings about her dead twin. It just seems like it would be a lot, you know?' She stopped and grimaced. 'And *now*, you're looking at me like you want to shoot me.'

I gave her a small smile. 'I don't want to shoot you.'

'You know I'm only trying to help,'

'I know. Go on. You can be honest.'

'OK, so, like, I guess, right now, it just feels like you haven't layered all those things in. It's just a bit 2D.'

'Yeah . . . you're probably right.'

'Viola's got so much going on inside her. She *is* the storm.' Victoria stood up and came over to me. 'You're close, sweetie. Your Viola's very nearly there.'

'I'm so tired.'

'I know you are.' She tucked a strand of hair behind my ear. 'But why not use that? Put all that exhaustion and frustration into *being* Viola. Imagine you've got all these secrets and lies swirling around you which are bursting at the seams, and you just have to hold them all in somehow.' She tilted her head to one side. 'Does that make sense?'

'Yes,' I said. 'That makes sense.'

I passed the resit.

TWO

'THE SCOTTISH PLAY,' MALCOLM bellowed, clapping his hands together in front of him. 'Jealousy. Greed. Murder. Ambition.'

It was our final term of first year and we were moving from Shakespearean comedy to tragedy: *Macbeth*. Malcolm Hurst was assigned to direct us. After eight weeks of Frida, this came as a relief. Malcolm, despite his lingering gaze, was a soft touch by comparison.

'A robust, bloody text, a masterpiece of gore and wisdom.'

We sat at his feet, pads open, pens poised, waiting for him to finish proselytizing and move on to the thing we actually cared about: casting.

'Now, I don't want to split parts this term, so – sorry, girls – some of you will be playing men this time around, I'm afraid.'

Murmurs, whispers.

'Right, let's get started.' He glanced down at his small brown leather notebook. 'We shall begin with our Scottish hero. Obi, you will be playing Macbeth.'

Obi ran a hand over his head. 'Thanks, sir.'

Everyone sat up a little straighter.

'Stefano, I'd like you to take the role of Banquo.'

Stefano made a fist and muttered something in Italian while the shoulders of the boys around him slumped.

Malcolm continued listing names. 'Macduff, Matthew. King Duncan, Tiff. Lady Macduff, Poppy . . .'

I bit my lip.

'The Doctor, Archie. Donalbain, Seamus. Lola, you'll be playing Fleance . . .'

He still hadn't said my name.

'Victoria, Jolly and Hettie, I'd like you to play The Witches. And Shannon, I'd like you to take the role of Lady Macbeth, please.'

I stared at the floor. My skin felt hot.

'Please familiarize yourselves with your individual characters when you read the play tonight, and yes, I do expect you to all read the play *again* tonight. I want it fresh in your minds. Tomorrow' – he tittered to himself – 'and tomorrow, and tomorrow we'll start exploring super-objectives. Righto.' Malcolm stood from his chair. 'I'll see you all at 9 a.m. sharp. Adieu.'

People started getting up from the floor and gathering their things. I jumped to my feet and chased Malcolm from the room.

'Malcolm?' I said, catching up with him in the corridor, unsure of what I was doing or even what I planned to say. 'I . . . I was just wondering if you'd made a mistake?'

Malcolm folded his arms across his crumpled tweed jacket and narrowed his eyes at me. His glasses slipped down his nose, a greasy smudge gathered in the half-moon lens. 'A mistake?' he said wearily.

'With the casting, I mean. You said you wanted me to play Lady Macbeth. But maybe – I don't know – maybe someone else in the group would play her better, like – I don't know – Victoria or—'

'A lot of thought goes into these casting decisions, you know. We don't just make them up on the spot.' He readjusted his glasses. 'And besides, I consulted with the other tutors, and Frida insisted that you and you alone should take the role.'

'Oh.' I didn't know what to say to that. I bit the inside of my cheek. 'But I don't know if I'm a natural fit or not.'

'A natural fit?' Malcolm tilted his head to one side. 'But my dear, are you not an actress?'

'Yes, but—'

'So *act*,' he said, chuckling, his teeth shining plaque-yellow. He patted my shoulder. 'Get some rest, Shannon.' He turned on his heel and continued down the corridor. 'You've got a busy term ahead of you.'

I watched him go, unsure of what had just transpired. Why did I say all that crap? What had I been thinking? Victoria didn't need my help. She already had everything all worked out: an agent, money, connections. The role was mine. Frida had given it to me, not her.

The door opened. Jolly and Victoria emerged.

'There you are,' Jolly said. 'You ran out pretty quickly.' He handed me my rucksack. 'Here.'

'Thanks,' I said, slinging it over my shoulder.

'I guess congratulations are in order,' Victoria said, nudging my shoulder with more force than I expected. 'Well done, Shan.'

'On what?' I said, suddenly fascinated by a freckle on my wrist.

Victoria scoffed and rolled her eyes. 'OK, so it's like that.' She linked arms with Jolly and led him away. 'I guess we'll see you later, *Big Shot*,' she trilled, waggling her fingers behind her.

I watched them disappear around the corner and down the stairs, their heads bowed, a coven of two already.

'AND WHAT ARE YOU experiencing in this moment?' Malcolm whispered.

Obi and I stood facing one another. My hands rested limply in his. I could feel Victoria staring at me from the other end of the room. I tried to appear nonchalant, to let my attention drift from Obi, but Malcolm caught me.

'Ah-ah-ah, Shannon. Eyes on your husband, please.'

'Sorry.'

'Obi, please continue.'

'I guess Macbeth is experiencing—'

'First person, please.'

'I guess I'm experiencing . . . shame,' Obi responded. 'I feel ashamed, like I'm losing control of the situation or something.'

'Yes, yes, exactly,' Malcolm said, bouncing from one foot to the other. 'You're trapped in a web of your own making.'

Obi caught my eye at Malcolm's little dance. He smirked and gave my hands a light squeeze. I stifled the urge to smile back, conscious of Victoria's supervisory gaze.

We'd been rehearsing the play for six weeks now. Although our assessment was a little less than two weeks away, it didn't feel like we'd made much progress. Malcolm's manner was slow. He tended to get stuck on the early scenes, looping them endlessly until he found whatever nugget of gold he'd been looking for. We'd barely touched my soliloquy.

'Shannon?'

'Hmm?'

Malcolm's eyes glinted from behind his spectacles. 'Daydreaming again, are we?'

'Sorry, sir.'

'Maybe we'll move on from this. Obi, take a seat. I'd like to work with Shannon alone for a minute.' He came closer. 'Let's interrogate your guilt, *Lady M*,' he said, grinning and leading me towards the other end of the room. 'So,' he said, his voice no louder than a whisper, the smell of tuna on his breath, 'how much are you manipulating the situation?'

I glanced across at my classmates, scribbling in their notebooks, actioning their texts, too far away to hear us. 'I don't know. I'm not sure I see her – I'm not sure I see myself as a manipulator.'

'Interesting. And why is that?'

'I don't think I'm conscious of what I want.'

'Continue.'

'I, I think I'm moving towards these things – riches, titles, acclaim – because it's innate, because it's natural for me to do so.'

'Like a moth climbing towards the light.'

'Yes.'

He raised his eyebrows. 'Carry on.'

'I'm nothing without my husband. Probably, before I was married, my only value was in my dowry or my appearance. And then I found myself stuck with this guy, this unambitious nobody.'

'Unambitious?'

'Well, by my standards.'

'Go on.'

'And if my only way to grow, if my only way to expand myself, my horizons, is through him, I think it would only be natural for me to encourage him in whatever way I could.'

'So you see yourself as your husband's champion rather than his manipulator?'

'Maybe. I'm not a cheerleader though. I'm still selfish. And I still don't like that word, *manipulator*. I don't think I can see some perfect end-goal where I get everything I want.' I looked down at my feet. 'I think I have this thing inside me that will always want more, to *become* more, and if I can't achieve that on my own, I suppose my only option is to find a way through someone else.'

'An interesting take. And what of your madness?'

'I think it's the madness of getting what you want,' I said, looking up.

'How do you mean?'

'Well, who ever really gets exactly what they want?'

'Not many people, I suppose.'

'Yes, and I think that must do something to you. I mean, where can you go from there? Especially if your ambitions are tainted by blood.'

'Where indeed.'

VICTORIA CORNERED ME AFTER rehearsals. 'How's it going then?'

'How's what going?'

Victoria put her hands on her hips. 'You don't have to do that, you know. I *don't care* that you're playing Lady Macbeth. They share roles around. We'll all get the chance to play good parts at some point.'

Hettie walked past us and smiled. Victoria grinned back and lowered her voice. 'Well, some of us will, at least.' She returned her gaze to mine. 'Look, I'm thinking of having a few people over on Saturday – nothing too big – just the good people.' Again her eyes flicked towards Hettie.

'At your dad's place?'

She nodded. 'Promise me you'll come?'

I smiled. 'Of course.'

'Perfect.' She looped her arm through mine. 'I think we all need to let off some steam before performance week.'

THREE

I ARRIVED AT HALF ten. I'd not been to the house since our first week of term. Was this the right one? I looked at the engraved slate. *Lamia*. I lowered my face to the intercom and announced myself. After a moment, the gate clunked to life, sliding open to reveal the Parker family pile in all its glory. I gazed up at the house. Despite its obvious charm, the higgledy-piggledy Victorian red-brick and climbing cirrus of ivy, the place had a fuck-you solidity to it, a sort of insouciant confidence that it would outlast the trivial lives of those that dwelled within. I crunched along the gravel path and climbed the steps. Moths fluttered about the porch lantern. Before I could ring the bell, the door swung open to reveal Victoria standing in the hall, wearing a white shirt dress, her hair trying to escape from a messy braid down one shoulder.

'Sweetheart, you made it.' She kissed me once on each cheek and pulled me inside.

The house was much the same: high ceilings, cream panelled walls, a bowl of blue lilies and tastefully arranged *objets* to draw the eye. Victoria led me through into the kitchen where Obi, Stefano and Jolly were already gathered. The three of them laughed as Stefano delivered the punchline to some lewd joke. Jolly caught my eye just as a man in his mid-thirties emerged from the pantry cradling a bag of Doritos.

'Darling, this is Terrence. Terrence, Shannon.'

He was wearing a rumpled pinstripe suit, like he'd come straight from the office. I smiled and the man raised his beer. He had grey hollows beneath his eyes, a pattern of stubble along his jawline, and an obvious nick from where he'd cut himself shaving.

'Terrence got fired yesterday and has been drinking for twenty-four hours straight,' Jolly said, announcing this to the room like it was the funniest thing in the world.

'It's true.' The man pulled Jolly into a headlock and kissed him on the temple. 'I'm fucked.'

I smiled uncertainly.

'Drink, Shan?' Victoria asked.

I glanced around at the discarded bottles of Peroni.

'A beer, please.'

Victoria opened the fridge, briefly revealing two pristine rows of champagne, their foil tips gleaming like the pistons of an organ. She handed me the beer and I sat down at the marble kitchen island.

A bell chimed.

'One sec.' She hurried away, her feet slapping the rustic stone floor. I heard a chorus of voices. More people.

'So, Terrence,' I said, 'what is it you do?'

'Jesus, Shannon,' Jolly said, tearing into the crisps. 'He got fired *yesterday*.'

'No, right, of course,' I stammered, blushing. 'I meant, what did you do before – before you got—?'

'Recruitment,' the man barked. 'Boring as hell. Don't try it. You lot are right to stick to the stage.' Jolly smiled and nuzzled the man's stubble. 'I should never have quit,' he added.

'You were an actor, then?' Obi said.

'Yep. For ten years. Tough fucking business.'

'Where did you train?'

'The Reading Conservatoire. Had the time of my life. They were a good bunch. Not the teachers mind, the students. The faculty were clinically insane.'

'So, why did you quit?' Stefano asked.

'Because there was no work and I had bills to pay.' He took another swig of his drink and swilled the contents around his mouth. 'And then, well, I suppose I got into a bit of a sticky situation in Northampton. *Uncle Vanya*. Assistant director took a dislike to me. Closeted little fuck. Started spreading muck around. Anyway, shit sticks. My agent dropped me. They said they were offloading some clients, but I knew. I suppose you'd say I was blacklisted or something like that. Whatever happened, the work dried up at least.' He blinked rapidly and knocked back the last of his beer. 'Anyway, all that? It's a young man's game.' He cleared his throat. 'Frankly, I don't have the energy.'

'Well, I'll never quit. I'll be a star for the *both* of us,' Jolly said, circling his arms around Terrence's neck and planting a kiss on his lips.

'Guys, this is Emi, Sebastian and Kit,' Victoria said, leading more people inside. She gestured in our direction. 'Jolly, Obi, Stefano, Terrence and Shannon.'

The new people said their hellos, mixed themselves drinks, then wandered through the French doors and out onto the lawn.

The bell chimed again. Victoria hopped to her feet.

'Jesus, V,' Jolly said. 'I thought you said it was just us. How many people have you invited to this thing?'

Victoria bit her lip and smiled. 'Oh, just a few.'

FOUR

I LOST COUNT OF how many people turned up. Tiff, Archie and Matt had been invited too, but otherwise I was adrift among a sea of unfamiliar faces. Although not completely unfamiliar. I did recognize a model who'd been seen on the arm of Prince Harry in the gossip rags, as well as a guy I could've sworn was the Young Vic's most recent Hamlet wiping coke from his nose as he emerged from the bathroom. There was also a man I recognized from my well-thumbed RLSDA prospectus, a recent graduate of the school who was hotly tipped to play Heathcliff in a new movie adaptation of *Wuthering Heights*.

Victoria sat on the graduate's lap, one arm across his shoulder. Obi and I stood huddled in a small group around them. We listened to the young man talk about his time at the school, about how much fun he was having out in the industry and all the auditions his agent was getting him. He talked and he talked, and we listened with razor-sharp focus, as if some of his shine might rub off on us, giving us the edge over the competition when our time eventually came.

'It's not difficult. If you're a good actor, you'll get work. It's as simple as that. It's not about what you look like or who you know. It's about talent. Those who've got it, rise to the top. Those who don't? Well . . .' He shrugged and veered off into another story.

I glanced at the clock on the wall. He'd been talking non-stop for the last twenty minutes. 'Shall we go outside?' I whispered to Obi, but he waved his hand to shush me. I stifled a yawn. I was tired of listening to the guy drone on and on, of exclaiming surprise at yet another anecdote that cast him as the hero. I looked at him, really looked at him. What was it? Why was he doing well while others got nowhere? What magical star quality did he possess? He was handsome, I suppose. Although if you stared at him long enough, his features seemed to rearrange themselves until he took on a snub-nosed, almost puggish quality.

'I think the key thing is confidence. Every time I turn up for an audition, I walk in already knowing I've got the job.'

The more he talked, the more I noticed the self-conscious way he raked his floppy fringe from his eyes, the damp sweat along his hairline, the way he yammered on, name-dropping this actor, that director, the way he fashioned thin rollies beneath his dry fingers, spilling shreds of Amber Leaf onto his jeans, and the way he smoked them, with a Brando-esque squint, as if pained to have such an achingly cool habit.

'Of course, I'm excited to be getting seen for more TV and film, but really, theatre's my first love. There's an honesty to theatre, a grit, a reality that it's impossible to capture on film.'

I fought the urge to roll my eyes.

'But yeah, if you ever need any tips on Tabitha or, like, literally any other casting directors, then just let me know,' he said.

'Wow, that's so generous,' Victoria replied. 'My agent says she's going to try and get me seen for Cathy.'

'Oh yeah?'

'Yeah.'

'Well, I can't really discuss specific casting,' he replied, smirking. 'NDAs and all that.'

'So you *are* playing Heathcliff then?' she purred.

He laughed. 'I never said that.'

'But you've signed an NDA?'

'*Yes*. But that could just mean I've seen the script.'

Victoria pouted. 'I think you've got it in the bag but you just don't want to tell me.'

'Leave it, V,' Obi warned her. 'If the man can't say, then the man can't say.'

'I didn't ask you,' Victoria replied tersely, not looking up.

Obi's nostrils flared. He took another swig of his drink, but the bottle was empty.

'Would you like me to be your wild woman?' Victoria whispered in the graduate's ear.

'I might go get another drink,' Obi said. 'Anyone want anything?'

The man, not taking his eyes from her, shook his head. Victoria rubbed the back of his neck like she hadn't heard the question.

Obi lingered a moment, then headed towards the fridge. He slid a beer from the shelf and charged into the garden. I grabbed one too and followed him.

The air was heavy with the smell of jasmine, the sky bleached with streaks of purple. I found Obi on a bench beneath an oak tree. He was picking the label, wet, from his beer. I sat down next to him. Although we were only a few yards away from the house, it suddenly looked quite distant; the people lit within paper figurines, dolls arranged on a stage.

'You don't have to sit with me, you know. I'm fine out here on my own,' Obi said, his voice flat.

'I know. I want to.'

A blackbird hopped onto the grass nearby and assessed us with its orange eye. A breath of wind rustled the leaves above us. The bird crouched, then flew away.

'She's an idiot.'

I didn't need to ask who he meant.

'She acts like she doesn't care, like everything's just a big laugh. And then she goes and gets herself in trouble. She's an idiot.'

'I know. But she's our friend.'

'Yeah.'

In the distance I could see Jolly and Terrence embracing on the deck, Archie and Tiff making out in the gazebo, and Stefano standing off to one side with a bottle in his hand, gazing up at the night sky.

'Sometimes,' Obi began, 'I wish – I wish that . . .' He trailed off.

'What?' I asked, inching closer to him, feeling almost lightheaded at our proximity. 'What is it?'

He put the beer between his feet and placed his head in his hands. He sighed. 'Never mind.'

'No, tell me.'

'She just thinks I'm this *good guy*, that I'm some fucking saint.' He leaned back. 'She thinks she can do or say anything she wants to me and I'll just take it, that I won't care.'

'You're right. I've seen it,' I said tentatively, daring myself to go further. 'She uses people.'

Obi glanced at me warily. 'No, that's not what I meant. You know what, never mind.'

'You don't have to be with her, you know?' I said, becoming more emboldened by the second.

'Be with her? Look, let's just drop it. I shouldn't have said anything. I've probably just had too much to drink.' He sighed. His shoulders sagged. 'I'm fine. She's fine. Everything's just fine.'

Looking back, maybe that's what made me do it; the hollowness in his voice, the emptiness. I wanted to comfort him, that's all, to let him know he wasn't alone, that I understood him. But somewhere along the way, the signals in my brain became tangled. Somewhere along the way I kissed him. Or tried to.

'Whoa, what are you doing?' he said, jerking away from me.

'I'm sorry, I thought—'

'You thought what?'

'I thought that I could help you,' I stammered. 'That we could, that we could – I don't know – oh God, I'm sorry, I know you and Victoria are – well – we all know that you're—'

'Victoria? What's this got to do with her?'

'Well, because you're *together* and I shouldn't have thought you would want to—'

'Me and Victoria aren't *together*, Shannon. We're nothing.'

'Oh.'

It wasn't because of Victoria that he didn't want me. It was because of me.

He stood up. 'I'm sorry. I just – this? You, me, this? I can't do it, OK?'

'OK,' I said quietly. 'That's OK.'

'It's not that I don't like you, I do, it's just that—'

'Please,' I said, getting up and straightening my skirt. 'You really don't have to explain anything.'

'No, no, I don't want you to think that, like, I don't like you – I do, I do like you, but . . .' He glanced towards the house, the warm lights and cool people gliding effortlessly across floors more expensive than our combined education. 'There are other things I have to think about, other things I need to consider.'

'It's OK, you don't need to explain anything to me, honestly. I'm going to go inside now. I'm so sorry.'

As I left, he said something, but I couldn't make out what. I just kept walking, kept my head down. I needed to get away from him, from my shame, from my own wretched shadow following me across the striped lawn.

FIVE

I LAY IN BED. Victoria's bed? Someone's bed. It was late. Or maybe it was early. I tried shutting my eyes, but every time I did, the room spun like a fairground ride, lurching me awake.

I didn't know where Obi was. Or Victoria. Or anyone.

Once inside, I'd headed straight for the fridge. There was a bottle of champagne already open. I'd lifted it out, slopped a generous helping into a discarded coupe and drunk it in one. Bubbles had fizzed up my nose. I'd coughed, poured myself another.

After that, things got hazy.

I remember seeing the Young Vic guy chatting with some people and marching over to him.

'I know you,' I said. 'You're *The Dane*.'

The small group of people tittered.

'Please can I have some drugs, *The Dane*?'

They laughed again (with me? At me? Who cares?). I remember crossing my arms, waiting, staring the guy down and him raising his eyebrows to his friends, feeling around in his pockets. When he came up empty, one of the women he was with – horsey, skinny, bones jutting from tiers of organza – grabbed my arm and pulled me inside the nearest bathroom.

'What do I do?' I asked, as she divided up two lines of white powder with swift strokes of her American Express card.

She shrugged. 'You just sort of snort it, I guess.'

She handed me a bank note, a pitying expression on her face, and I lowered my head to the counter.

I reared back. My nose felt stuffy, the back of my throat numb. I snorted and a glob of chemical snot hit the back of my gullet. I made a choking sound, and the girl laughed, her too-large teeth reflected a thousand times in the angled mirror.

And then I danced.

And then I kissed someone (I don't remember who).

And then I danced some more.

And then I felt someone's hand scramble up my skirt (I don't remember whose).

And someone cried (maybe me).

And someone puked (definitely me).

And later – despite the huge cloakroom downstairs – I found myself surrounded by bags and coats in what I assume was a guest room.

Someone knocked at the door. I shut my eyes and ignored them. The door opened anyway and a crack of light appeared, slicing the bed and the girl upon it in two.

I felt someone lie down beside me. An arm appeared in my periphery and wrapped around my torso. I mumbled something and the arm retreated.

I was tired. I was so very fucking tired. I wanted a glass of water and for the spinning to stop and for this person to just leave me alone. But the words to explain this got caught in the back of my throat. And so, I said nothing. I did nothing.

We lay like that for a few minutes, me and the stranger. After a while I almost forgot they were there. But then they came closer. I could feel their breath on my neck, their inhales and exhales, excessive, like they were pretending to be asleep. *In. Out.* I breathed in time with them. *In. Out.*

Downstairs there was music and laughter, the noise of people holding tight to the night. *One more drink, one more dance, just one more*. Calmed by this Bacchic lullaby, I felt myself fading, drifting into a dreamless sleep. But then my leg twitched and I jerked awake again.

Taking this bout of sudden movement as an invitation, the stranger nestled closer. I could feel their nose and the soft flutter of their eyelashes against the nape of my neck. I groaned and wriggled away.

'Hey, it's just me.'

I froze.

I opened one eyelid a crack. In the mirror opposite, a face loomed above me.

Stefano.

His hand appeared on my waist. I didn't move. The hand remained there, taut, waiting. And then before I knew what was happening, Stefano's lips were on mine.

He smelled wrong. He felt wrong. His lips were too fleshy, too all-engulfing. Still he continued kissing me. I couldn't breathe. Eventually I managed to roll my head away from his.

'I came in to check on you,' he said, panting. He brushed a hair away from my face. 'I wanted to make sure you were OK.'

'I'm – I'm fine,' I whimpered. I was crying. I don't know when, but at some point I'd started crying.

'Hey, quiet now,' he cooed. He cradled the back of my head, crushing my cheek against his chest. 'It's OK. I'm here now. I'll take care of you.'

I heard the words, I knew their meaning, that they were meant to be reassuring, but still something inside me kicked like a frightened rabbit.

Stefano kissed my forehead, my damp cheeks, my lips. 'I'll take care of you,' he repeated. 'Don't worry. I'm here now.'

SIX

'YOU'RE FULL OF SURPRISES, you know.'

Victoria came up behind me in the canteen while I was queuing for coffee. It was Thursday, the morning of our *Macbeth* examination.

'What are you talking about?'

Victoria looked at me like I was an idiot. 'Stefano?'

'What about Stefano?' I asked, my heart racing.

She raised an eyebrow. 'He said you guys made out.'

'He – he did?' I said, feeling my stomach curl inwards with humiliation.

'Yep. He said you were seeing each other.'

'I'm not – we're not—'

'Come on, Shannon. You said you wouldn't keep secrets from me.'

'I'm not,' I protested.

She leaned in closer and, smirking, whispered, 'Go on then. Are you *in wuv*?'

I wanted to hurt her then, to slap her, to wipe that nasty little smile from her mouth. No, we weren't in love. After Stefano kissed me, we'd both passed out. It was 6 a.m. before I'd come to and, gathering my few belongings, crept from the room. I'd spent the next day in a stupor of shame and regret. Nothing had happened really, but still, I felt embarrassed by the whole situation, reduced, as if something precious had been taken from me.

'I – I don't want to talk about it.'

'You shouldn't be so hard on him you know. Stefano's a good guy.'

I looked at her, searching her face for any traces of mockery. She was being serious.

'You actually like him, don't you?'

'Sure, Stefano's a laugh. And anyway, he really likes you.'

I felt confused. Was that how it worked? A guy liked you, he pursued you and then . . . what? You were just meant to like him back?

'He does?'

'Of course he does. Oh, I can just see you guys together, you'd be such a good couple. Come on, I *know* you, Shannon. You guys would be perfect for each other.'

I could feel the net closing around me, Victoria's coaxing words clinging to me like sticky silk. 'I don't think he's my type.'

Victoria shook her head, disappointed. 'You know you shouldn't be too picky, Shannon. Like don't get me wrong, you're super pretty, but it's not like every guy's going to *get* your vibe.'

'My vibe?' I paid the lady for my coffee.

'Yeah, you know, the whole deadpan thing.'

'Deadpan?'

'Yeah, you know.'

'What are you talking about?'

Victoria sighed and rolled her eyes. 'Never mind.'

Just then Jolly and Stefano cut into the queue behind us.

'Well, hello ladies,' Jolly said. He shared a look with Victoria. 'And how are we today?'

'I'm good,' Victoria replied, 'and Shannon's *very* good, aren't you, Shan?' She nudged my arm.

I could feel Stefano looking at me. I fixed my gaze on the sputtering coffee machine beyond the cashier's shoulder.

'Fantastic,' Jolly said. 'Oh, by the way, Victoria' – he linked his arm through hers – 'can I borrow you a moment? I need to talk to you about . . . *that thing*.' He dragged her from the queue and they went over to the seating area, giggling and squirming like schoolchildren.

The lady slid my coffee towards me. I went to leave, but Stefano grabbed my elbow.

'It's good to see you,' he said, pulling me to one side. 'I've been trying to find a time to talk with you all week, but it's like you keep running away from me.' He laughed, as if the idea of me wanting to run away from him was absurd.

'Yeah, well, I've been busy,' I said, avoiding his eyes. 'You know, preparing for the final performance and everything.'

'I had a great time on Saturday.' He gave me a lopsided smile and waited.

I didn't know what to say to that. His hand was still gripping my elbow. I looked up at his face, so earnest and hopeful. Had I got it wrong? Everything felt jumbled in my mind. That night. Obi. The kiss. He thought this was a love scene, while I didn't know what to think.

'OK,' I finally managed.

'It was nice to be alone together, just the two of us. I guess something was bound to happen eventually.' He laughed again. 'I mean, I really like you, Shannon,' he said, leaning in as if to kiss me.

I flinched and pulled away from him. 'Why did you tell Victoria we were dating?'

'Well, aren't we?' He loosened his grip. 'After what happened on Saturday, I figured . . .' He trailed off and his big dumb smile faded. 'Wait, have I done something to upset you?'

'No – yes – I—'

He was still touching me. I didn't want him to touch me. But . . . but maybe I'd got it wrong? He was acting like I'd got it wrong. Victoria was acting liked I'd got it wrong. The whole damn world was acting like I'd got it wrong.

Obi entered the canteen. Our eyes met. He looked away and made his way over to the others. Victoria gave him a quick peck on the cheek. Whatever had or hadn't happened between them at the weekend was obviously resolved.

'OK,' I said, dragging my gaze away from the two of them.

'OK what?' he replied.

'OK, we can try' – I hesitated – '*dating*, I guess. If you want.'

Stefano's eyes lit up. He grinned and leaned in to kiss me. This time I let him. It was fine, sort of, for a moment. But then his tongue slid inside my mouth, wet, searching and insistent. I squeezed my eyes shut and held my breath. *Maybe this is just how it is*, I thought. *Maybe this is just what love feels like.*

SEVEN

THERE'S THIS MOMENT, ABOUT thirty minutes before the show. They call it 'the half'. Suddenly the day that's gone before you melts away. Lunch, meetings, rehearsals, whatever. It's gone. Now, it's just a countdown, these next 1,800 seconds.

You hear that sound, or maybe the absence of it, roaring in your ears. Your skin turns cold, then hot. Your insides twist. Your mouth feels dry. Your legs shake. *Butterflies*, they say. You don't have butterflies. Your stomach is a swarm of thick hairy moths.

The tannoy. The stage manager. Some discussion, argument. Resolved. The busyness of the theatre, the backstage areas.

Time ticks away.

You should look at your lines. Or not. You don't want to overprepare. It should feel natural. Like you're plucking the words from thin air. Use your breath. Think with your breath.

You can't breathe.

Beginners call. Actors, this is your beginners call.

You exit the dressing room and a calm descends. Is it a calm? You don't feel calm. You feel . . . nothing.

You stand in the wings, inhaling dust from the curtains. Who washes these? Probably no one. You touch the rough fabric. It's tempting. You could just take a peek. They're here to see you, after all. Go on, just beyond the wings, through that crack in the curtains. Not too far though, you don't want them to spot you. Everyone's here, it feels like. *Everyone*. Can you see your parents? There they are. And your grandma too, sitting beside the dead grandad you never met, rotting in his uniform. And look, there's your primary school teacher, the one who said you had far too much energy for a girl. And over there's your middle-school teacher, the one with the halitosis and bushy eyebrows, the one who described you as a little brown mouse at parents' evening while you turned red and sank down in your seat. There's that boy you fancied in Year 8, and he's with his friends. They're not laughing now though. There's the most popular girl in school, the one who developed early. Can you see her blonde crown of hair, just there, above the sea of heads? There's Katie and Amy and Sam and Cassie. There's the girl whose body was found in the canal. There's Sammy and Alex and Holly and Jim. There's your sister, the back of her head, hair floating around her. There's David and Sara and Johnny and Rob. There's the boy who hanged himself in his bedroom. There's Carey and Ross and Melissa and Ben. There's the janitor, the baker, the candlestick maker. They're all here. They're all here to see you.

You step back into the shadows and close your eyes. All around you rings a hubbub of noise. Trolleys trundle back and forth, pushed by weary stagehands. The lighting rig creaks above your head. Standing next to you, the stage manager barks instructions into an earpiece. The audience's chatter rises, filling the auditorium, filling you up, plugging every leaking hole of you with thick excitable noise.

You open your eyes, your glittering bejewelled eyes, heavy with creams and powder. The stage manager whispers in your ear and the lights go down. A hush descends. This is it. The moment you've been waiting for, preparing for all your life.

You take a breath, and step out into the darkness.

*

'*OUT, DAMNED SPOT! OUT, I say.*'

I crouched on the floor of the black-box studio. The rest of the class stood sentry along the perimeter of the curtain. Obi sat on a wooden throne upstage, backlit, casting a long shadow across my actions.

'*What, will these hands ne'er be clean? No more o' that, my lord, no more o' that: you mar all with this starting.*'

A fan whirred above me. The hairs on my arm stood on end. I was wearing an ivory slip. Its static clung to the curves of my body.

'*Here's the smell of the blood still.*'

Frida, Malcolm and Casper were seated behind desks at the far end of the room, scribbling notes.

'*All the perfumes of Arabia will not sweeten this little hand. Oh, oh, oh!*' My voice broke. Frida looked up briefly, then back down at her paper.

Archie, who was playing the Doctor, knelt down beside me and placed his hand on my temple. I stared past him. '*This disease is beyond my practice,*' he said. '*Yet I have known those which have walk'd in their sleep who have died holily in their beds.*'

I pulled away from him and crawled towards an enamel jug and bowl downstage left. '*Wash your hands,*' I said, splashing cold water on my face, '*put on your nightgown; look not so pale. I tell you yet again, Banquo's buried; he cannot come out on's grave.*'

I could feel the eyes of my classmates upon me; Stefano's gaze, roving the surface of my skin.

'*To bed, to bed! There's knocking at the gate: come, come, come, come, give me your hand. What's done cannot be undone. To bed, to bed, to bed!*'

I left the stage, and the play continued without me.

EIGHT

'Tell me, do you believe in magic?'

Frida and I were sitting in her office, crammed knee to knee. Most of our tutors were away for Crits that term, so we were being emailed our feedback. Despite this, Frida had insisted on delivering her critiques in person.

Moments ago, she'd sent Hettie, my scribe, out of the room on some errand, assuring her that the Dictaphone would pick up anything important she might miss.

'Well?' Frida said, staring at me, waiting for a response.

'I don't know,' I said. 'I've never really thought about it.'

She sat back in her chair and turned to face the window. She stayed like that for a moment, the curve of her cheek caught in a sunbeam. Outside the trees rustled, a languid summer sound.

The seconds ticked by. A seam of sweat opened up along my lower back. I fidgeted in my chair, unsure if these were to be my final minutes at the school. *Exit pursued by despair.*

Finally, after what felt like an age, she spoke.

'There are a lot of things we can teach at this school.' She paused. 'But the one thing we cannot teach is *magic*. We have homework, prep, assessments,' she said, listing them on her fingers. 'We have checklists and little grey boxes for feedback. Is this student's diction precise? Are they projecting? But there is no tick box for magic.' She thought for a moment.

'This has always frustrated me.' She sighed. 'We must believe in it. Whatever you call it – magic, inspiration, genius – actors *must* believe in it, Shannon. Otherwise how on earth can we get up onstage each night and *pretend*? How can we dress ourselves up in front of an audience and create worlds without the faith, without the absolute conviction that our audience will come with us, that we will transport them?' She put her hands on her knees and leaned towards me. 'Shannon, yesterday, when you performed – well' – she gave a small shrug – 'it was *magic*.'

'Oh.' *Don't cry*. 'Thank you.'

She sat back again. 'Now, I am not telling you this to inflate your ego. I am telling you this because there are things beyond our understanding and control in this world.' She paused. 'We, my fellow staff and I, cannot teach these things. We can only teach rigor and readiness for when this magic, this inspiration appears.' She shook her head. 'You may never perform like that again. But as your teacher, it is my job to tell you that it's possible, that you captured something yesterday and that, if you work hard, you, one day, may be able to capture it again.' She stopped. Her eyes drifted back to the window. 'In your first term, I asked you why you were here. Do you remember that?'

I nodded and dug my fingernails into the underside of my thigh.

'Words please, Shannon.'

'Yes, sorry,' I stammered. 'Yes, I remember.'

'So,' she said, fixing her gaze on me. 'Why?'

I stared into my lap. For months I'd been racking my brain for an answer to that damned question. For my family? To prove something to the people back home? To prove something to myself? But every time I thought about it I came up short, never knowing *why* I was putting myself through all this, *why* I cared so much.

But then, suddenly, the answer came to me, as cool and clear as day.

I lifted my head and looked at her. 'I'm here to be seen.'

Frida held my gaze for a moment, then got up. She straightened the hem of her shirt and walked towards the door.

'Thank you, Shannon. That will be all.'

NINE

I LAY IN THE grass while summer unspooled before me; endless, aimless and dull. I held a book above my head, trying to blot out the sun.

The Moving Body by Jacques Lecoq.

I had a stack of reading to do before the new term began. I was staying with Grandma for a few nights while my parents visited friends in Scarborough. I figured I could get it done then.

A sparrow wittered from the hedge. An insect scrambled over my foot.

It was hot. Too hot.

I gave up and placed the book over my nose, inhaling my stale breath from within its pages.

I heard Grandma come outside, the clink of glass, the creak of the deckchair as she settled by the pond. I rolled my head to one side and peeked at her while she leafed through the *Morning Star*, pushed her sunglasses up her nose, sipped her drink.

I sighed and returned my attention to the same page I'd been stuck on now for the last fifteen minutes.

There are three masks: the one we think we are, the one we really are, and the one we have in common.

Ice cubes. The pale scent of lemonade.

I shut my eyes.

I'd been having this feeling, this odd sensation that my life, my *real* life, was happening somewhere else. That if I were to return to London now, I'd find another version of myself wandering the corridors, stretching in a rehearsal room or huddled around a picnic bench with my classmates.

On the last day of term, everyone had gathered in the pub to talk and laugh and despair over the travails of the year. I'd tried to join in, to listen and contribute, but my brain was on fire, my mind elsewhere.

Magic.

Frida's words sat like a talisman against my chest. She had *seen* me. Frida had seen me, she knew what I was capable of. From now on, things would be different. No one could hurt or undermine me now. No one. I was a fucking witch.

But that was three weeks ago.

Magic. The word – its edges worn smooth, turned over too many times in my mind – was losing its potency, its power to protect. School felt a long way away. My friends, even further. Victoria had promised she'd stay in touch. She was visiting family in Cape Cod over the summer and travelling the East Coast. She said she'd call me and message whenever she could. She promised me a postcard every week, although I'd long since given up waiting by the door each morning.

I hadn't mentioned my meeting with Frida yet. I didn't know how she'd take it. But in the face of my abandonment, some sly part of me longed to find out.

I thought about sending her an email telling her everything. If I shut my eyes, I could almost picture her reading it, curled up on an oatmeal-coloured sofa in a white clapboard house. There'd be a glass of red wine on the table; pampas grass in a tall jar. She'd be relaxed and sun-tired. Her hair tangled and loose. She'd be wearing a pair of cut-offs and a roll-neck fisherman's jumper. She'd hear a ping and then open her laptop to see my name. She'd click on the email and read everything. She'd see how much better I was than her. She'd see that despite everything she had, everything she was, it was *me* who was the better actress, *me* who could summon magic. Her cheeks would burn. Her neck would flush. She'd feel sick. She'd feel jealous. Maybe she'd cry. Maybe she'd run from the house in a fury, down to the beach, shedding her clothes as she went. Maybe she'd jump in the water, a bitter baptism, her body slipping beneath the waves before emerging slick like a seal, the briny ocean wetting her lips.

'I got a new *Puzzler*, by the way,' Grandma said, startling me from my thoughts. 'Do you fancy doing a crossword?'

'Why?' I replied, flustered.

'Because it's fun.'

'I'm a little busy,' I said, turning onto my front and cracking the spine of the book.

'Not to worry.' She took another sip of her drink. 'Shall we go to the cinema later?'

'I'm all right, thanks.'

'Go on. Just think, air conditioning, ice cream . . .'

'No, thanks.' I flicked a greenfly from my wrist.

'Suit yourself.'

I scowled at the words on the page. I didn't know why I was being so mean, why everything suddenly felt so hopeless. I felt tears well up in my eyes, blurring my vision until the sentences all ran into one another.

Grandma got up. I heard the crunch of gravel and the patio door slide shut behind her.

I dumped the book and wiped my eyes.

I picked up my phone.

There were no new messages.

Why hasn't she messaged?

I checked Facebook. Nothing.

I clicked on Victoria's last response.

Victoria Parker-Tilley posted 11 days ago

Sorry for late reply. Haha yeah that sounds about right. Beach bonfire tonight with cousins, heading into town for provisions, have become addicted to potato chips – SEND HELP. I'll call you next week if I get signal x

The phone buzzed in my hand. My heart leapt. But it was Stefano, not Victoria. A grainy picture. Sunglasses. Chin shot. Standard. He was the only one who stayed in touch. I was so bored I almost didn't mind the distraction. He'd send some dumb observation or joke and I'd reply, parrying inanities back and forth, aware I needed to hold up my end of the 'Girlfriend' contract I'd entered into.

Friday, 30th July at 13:57

Shannon Bell

Looking good 👍

Friday, 30th July at 13:59

Stefano drama school

Guess where I'm heading next week?

Friday, 30th July at 14:01

Shannon Bell

Where

Friday, 30th July at 14:02

Stefano drama school

Rome baby :P

Friday, 30th July at 14:06

Shannon Bell

Cool

Friday, 30th July at 14:07

Stefano drama school

Staying at my uncle's place

Friday, 30th July at 14:21

Shannon Bell

Nice

Friday, 30th July at 14:23

Stefano drama school

You should come

Friday, 30th July at 14:24

Stefano drama school

Keep me company

I locked the screen, ignored it.

No way.
I wouldn't go.
I couldn't.
Could I?

Friday, 30th July at 14:29
Stefano drama school
Got the place to myself, we can see the sights, it'll be fun haha

Rome. I'd never gone further than France on camping holidays with my parents. The summer was getting away from me. All I'd done so far was help Dad paint a fence, eat far too many Cornettos and take an unhealthy number of naps.

The thought of being alone with Stefano for any length of time made my insides squirm, but I was suffocating here.

Friday, 30th July at 14:35
Stefano drama school
Come on, my treat . . . ;)

I rubbed my eyes and tapped out a reply.

TEN

THE APARTMENT WAS DISAPPOINTING. Technically it wasn't even inside the city but sat just outside, hugging the hard shoulder of the motorway, little more than a run-down studio with a kitchen jammed in one corner and a narrow shower room in the other.

We came inside and dropped our bags on the scuffed lino. Stefano jimmied a lever and a bed – nearly colliding with the small sofa – creaked down from the wall.

'It's smaller than I remember,' he said, uncurling the mattress.

I ran my finger along the countertop. It came away smeared with dust. 'When did you say your uncle was last here?'

Stefano thought for a moment. 'I think he died four years ago.'

'He died?'

'Yes.'

'In here?'

I didn't get the chance to probe him any further as, just then, something scuttled past my feet. I screamed and clambered onto a chair.

'Hey, keep it down,' he said. 'The walls are really thin.'

And they were. At night, while Stefano lay curled up on the sofa – *No, little bird, you take the bed, honestly, I insist* – in the next apartment along, a loquacious Don Juan babbled away in Italian to his insatiable yipping mistress.

The daytimes weren't much better. We had to get three buses just to reach any of the major landmarks, and by day two, Stefano's brand of hands-off chivalry was starting to disintegrate.

'Jeez, Shannon, we don't have to go out *all* the time, you know?'

'We're in Rome, I want to see stuff.'

'But it's all tourist shit.'

'I'm only here for a week.'

'What's the hurry? Rome's been here for thousands of years, it'll be here for thousands of years more. Look,' he said, tucking a loose strand of hair behind my ear. 'Why don't we stay inside today? I'll head out and get us some coffee, some pastries, and then we can have some, you know, time *alone* together, get to know each other a bit more . . .'

But I insisted. He could play the gallant all he liked, but I knew what he wanted, the bargain I'd been entered into. He hadn't invited me here out of the goodness of his heart; I knew he expected something in return. But if we were going to have sex, if I was going to relinquish my virginity, I was determined to do so on my own terms.

On the third day, as evening cloaked the city with its inky pall and waiters rolled their tables out into the square, I came upon a violinist playing for coins beside a fountain. I'd left Stefano – becoming increasingly bored by my frigidity – next to a stall selling carnival masks. The musician had a small crowd around him. A half-remembered melody ached from his bow. I moved closer.

A bystander, an old man with leathery skin and bushy eyebrows, stepped forward and offered me his hand. I shook my head, embarrassed. He grinned and gestured again, his hand outstretched. He had trusting eyes and a broken piano of a smile. *Why not?* a small voice inside me said. I gave in and placed my fingers in the crease of his palm.

More people gathered. A woman sang softly in Italian.

The man was a good dancer. He held me close and spun me so my skirt whirled around my knees. I laughed, dizzy, feeling like I was in a movie, the leading lady – the star, finally, of my own life.

But then I saw Stefano, smiling mirthlessly, push through the crowd. The old man, noticing, gave him a nod which Stefano answered by unhooking the man's hands from my shoulder and lower back. Sensing trouble, the old man offered a small bow and melted into the crowd. Stefano took me in his arms and reluctantly continued the dance. I looked over my shoulder, searching for the old man, wishing I could've thanked him or apologized to him somehow.

'Where did he go?' I whispered.

Stefano twirled me like a spinning top then clamped me to his chest.

'Stef—'

'Be quiet,' he hissed, still smiling for the crowd. 'Don't you think you've embarrassed yourself enough for one day?'

THAT NIGHT, STEFANO GLARED at me from across the rickety Formica table.

'You looked ridiculous.'

'I don't care.'

'You showed me up.'

'I was just having fun.'

The oven hummed in the background, warming a cheap frozen pizza into something vaguely palatable.

'Aren't you ashamed of yourself?' he asked. 'Dancing with some *vecchietto* like that.'

'It's not like you were ever going to dance with me.'

'I'm not a sissy.'

'I never said you were.'

'I don't dance.'

'You dance in movement studies.'

'That's different.'

'How?'

'Look, I don't dance.'

'Well, there you go.'

We did this for ten minutes, talking ourselves in circles. When the timer pinged, we ate in silence.

Stefano reached for another slice. 'I didn't think you were like that.'

'Like what?' I said, dropping a crust onto the plate between us.

'Like' – he searched for the words – 'all showy. Today you were different. You acted like Victoria.'

This was news to me. I hadn't been trying to act like Victoria. The square, the old man, the dance was just a spontaneous thing. And what was wrong with that? I'd enjoyed being the centre of attention for a moment. I'd enjoyed strangers applauding me, watching me.

'I didn't act like Victoria—'

'You did,' he said, cutting me off. He swallowed and wiped a string of cheese from his mouth with the back of his hand. 'I thought you were different. I like girls that don't act all . . . These girls who want to talk and show off? They're whores. I didn't think you were like that.'

I dipped my finger in a glob of tomato sauce and swirled it around my plate.

'Are you saying Victoria's a whore?'

I couldn't help myself. I wanted to know what he thought of her, to confirm she was special, to confirm she was trash.

Stefano shrugged. 'Sometimes, maybe, yeah.' He took another bite. 'You know I like her, she's my friend, but she . . . I don't know.' He shrugged again. 'I mean, she sucked that guy's dick at that party—'

'What guy?' I said, my heart beating faster.

'That graduate guy, the Heathcliff guy—'

'She – she wouldn't do that.'

'Obi found them together at the bottom of the garden. It broke his heart, man.' Stefano shook his head and took another bite.

'But they're still together?' I said, my voice pleading and thin.

'Who knows what those guys have got going on,' he muttered, spraying crumbs across the table. 'But that's what I mean.'

'What?'

He sighed, at pains to explain himself. 'Look, I'm a traditional guy. I like girls who act like girls *should*.'

'Like me?'

'Like you.'

I realized I'd been holding my breath. I exhaled and licked the sauce from my finger. We continued eating.

I should've said something, of course I should've said something. I should've defended Victoria or vilified her or, I don't know what, run out of the apartment, called my grandma, got the first flight home or whatever. But right then, I felt exhausted by the situation. I knew that nothing I said or did would change Stefano's opinion of me or Victoria.

'You're a nice girl, Shannon. *My* nice girl.'

He looked up at me with those wet hangdog eyes and, in that moment, I felt something like pity for him. I would leave him – of course I would. The idea was already forming, the words taking shape, buzzing on my tongue like a lick of sherbet. It was so simple. I didn't have to be here. He'd given me a bed, a place to sleep, but that didn't mean I owed him my body. Despite the uneven arrangement of the last few days, I still had a choice. When this trip was over, when I was finally home and away from this awful place, this wretched airless room, I'd end it.

Besides, with one half-baked remark he'd unwittingly lit a fire in my belly.

You acted like Victoria.

Those people – the man in the square, the crowd of smiling onlookers – they'd had no idea who I was. They didn't know I was shy. They didn't know I was unpopular. They didn't know about my northern accent or whether my hair colour was natural or not. They didn't know about the dinky house I'd grown up in. They didn't know about my insecurities, how I felt about my breasts, my skin, my teeth. They hadn't a clue. In front of them, I could be whoever I wanted.

Stefano was saying something, but I wasn't listening. No, I was elsewhere. In the square. *Dancing, dancing, dancing*—

ELEVEN

We got the bus to Gianicolo Park. I sat on a wooden bench and gazed out at the white busts of patriots that lined the grass. I was alone, blissfully so. Stefano had wandered off in a huff to find snacks. That morning we'd done a guided tour of the Colosseum. Stefano had spent the first few minutes of it attempting to lead me into dark corners away from the crowd. But, when a large Spanish-speaking group got between the two of us, I managed to peel off and steal the rest of the hour for myself. I made my way to the highest walkways of the amphitheatre and gazed out over the crumbled grandeur of the Forum. I stood there, grazing my hand along the ancient stone walls, feeling the baked warmth of the city beneath my fingers.

I tilted my head back and stared up through the trees. A pigeon landed by my feet. I scuffed the dust with the toe of my sandal and it waddled away. Park-goers drifted past me: an impossibly beautiful Roman couple, eyes locked and limbs tangled; a harried au pair chasing two infants as they toddled towards the road; a gaggle of American teenagers, hormonal, horny and het up on the promise of who they might be outside school. And then another figure, so familiar, so like V in her manner that I smiled to myself at the comparison. But it wasn't V. Victoria was in the States, a whole world away from me.

The stranger caught my eye and grinned. She began walking towards me. I turned and looked over my shoulder, thinking she must've recognized someone nearby, or else confused me for a friend. I smiled hesitantly, trying to shield the woman from the embarrassment of her mistake. As she came closer, I held my arm up to block out the sun and saw, with a jolt, that it was me who was mistaken.

'*Ciao, bella*,' she said, waggling her fingers as she drew nearer.

It was her. Undoubtedly, unbelievably, her.

'V—' I stood up. 'How did you – what did you—'

She was wearing a cream linen suit and a pair of tortoiseshell Gucci sunglasses which covered half her face. She came closer and pulled me, still stunned, into her arms. 'Hello, sweetie.'

'I just can't – I mean, I can't believe you're here,' I gabbled, gripping her tightly, only then realizing just how much I'd missed her. Her hair smelled citrussy, herbal; it was still damp from the shower. 'What happened to your East Coast road trip?'

'Ugh, I got sick of my family, the States, everything. I just had to get away.' She released me and held my elbows. 'And then I've been texting Jolly, who mentioned you were here, and I had the time to spare, so . . .' She shrugged. 'Voilà! I arrived yesterday. I figured, what's a night or two?'

I thought back to that morning, sitting in the grimy metro station toilet cubicle and messaging Jolly back and forth, telling him about our plans for the day.

Just then, Stefano came around the corner, holding two teetering swirls of pistachio ice cream. 'Victoria?' he said uncertainly. 'What the fuck – no way, man, is that really you?'

He handed me the cone. Victoria flicked the curled tip and sucked her finger. 'It's really me.'

*

WE GOT A TAXI. Victoria insisted on treating us to lunch at a *darling little place* she knew not far from the Spanish Steps. Soon three steaming plates of *cacio e pepe* were placed in front of us, along with a slim carafe of pinot noir. I glanced sideways at Stefano, trying to discern his mood. At first, he'd seemed pissed off at Victoria barrelling in on our plans, which I understood. This wasn't exactly turning out to be the trip of a lifetime for either one of us, but she hadn't been invited, nor even had the decency to warn us of her arrival in advance. But then, as the meal continued and the minutes ticked by, he seemed to soften. Victoria could do that if she wanted to, sprinkle glitter over whatever rancour you were feeling and make you fall in love with her all over again. It wasn't long before the two of them were teasing each other and cracking filthy jokes, as if she'd been there with us the whole time.

'So, what have you lovebirds been up to?' she asked, twirling spaghetti around her fork.

Lovebirds. I cringed inwardly at the word but pretended not to. 'Oh, not much.' I didn't want to mention yesterday, the dance; I didn't want to discuss our conversation back at the flat, Stefano's lewd assessment of Victoria. 'Just seeing all the touristy stuff, right?' I continued, glancing at Stefano for confirmation. He nodded in response, his mouth full.

'Hmm. Funny.' She chewed, swallowed. 'I'd have thought you'd be locked up in your hotel room. I mean, Rome is just so romantic, don't you think?'

'We're not staying at a hote—'

'We've had lots of time together,' Stefano said, cutting me off. 'This one can't keep her hands off me.'

'Oh, *really*?' Victoria said, flashing me a knowing smile and reaching for her glass.

I rolled my eyes, playing along. Stefano and I hadn't slept together and, after last night, I felt certain we never would. But I knew for his pride's sake, and to get through the final two days of the holiday, I should probably keep up the pretence of a rampant shag-fest.

Stefano cupped the base of my neck. 'Yeah. Don't worry about us.' I inched my chair away, but his grip only tightened in response. He grinned at me, the smile never quite reaching his eyes. 'We're having a *great* time.'

'I'm so glad,' Victoria said, tearing off a chunk of bread. 'Where are you staying?'

'On the outskirts,' he answered, enjoying the fantasy. 'This nice little place, out in the sticks, rural.'

'Sounds *divine*.' She thought for a moment. 'Yes, sometimes the smaller places can be so much more charming than these grand hotels.' She gestured airily in the direction of the five-star St. Regis where she was staying. 'You don't get the same experience, you don't feel the actual *heat* of a place, you know?'

'Yes,' I agreed, trying to ignore the tang of bitterness in my mouth. 'Say, where shall we go next?' I asked them both, wanting to change the subject. 'There's still so much of the city I haven't seen yet.'

'Oh wherever, I'm easy,' Victoria said. 'You decide, Shannon.' Then: 'Oh, sweetie.' She tapped her cheek at Stefano. 'You've got a speck of something.'

He wiped his chin with the back of his wrist. 'Did I get it?'

'No. Here, let me.' She licked the corner of her napkin, leaned over me and, placing her palm on my thigh to steady herself, dabbed at the edge of his mouth. When she pulled away, Stefano's gaze darted towards where her hand lingered near my crotch. A glimmer of opportunity flashed behind his eyes.

Victoria threw the napkin onto the table and sank back in her chair.

Stefano cleared his throat. 'So, V, I meant to ask, did you come here alone?'

'Alas, flying solo,' she sighed.

'You know, it's a shame Obi couldn't come,' Stefano continued.

'Yes,' I agreed, longing for his steady presence. 'It would've been great, all being here together. We could've made a real few days of it.'

Victoria placed her hand over mine, a wry smile playing on her lips. 'Oh, I don't know.' She looked at me directly. 'Sometimes three can be more fun.'

'Is that so?' Stefano said, resting his elbows on the table and muscling his shoulders forward.

'Sure,' Victoria replied, her eyes still fixed on mine.

I felt my skin flush, but I forced myself to meet her gaze. I wanted to freeze time, to take a mental picture of the way she was looking at me, the way her thumb was caressing mine. I wanted something to return to, something I could hold up to the light and view from all angles. Proof that she cared.

Her lips parted slightly.

'Well, we should order more wine then,' Stefano said, shattering the moment. He reached for his wallet. 'Let's have fun, the three of us.'

'Honey, no,' she purred, letting go of my hand and gesturing to the waiter. 'Allow me.'

I watched Stefano as Victoria ordered more drinks. I watched him sizing her up, like an animal nosing the ground for its prey. I thought back to our conversation last night.

Are you saying Victoria's a whore?

Sometimes, yeah. I mean, she sucked that guy's dick.

I shrank down in my seat and closed my eyes. I didn't want to think about what was running through Stefano's head, what terrible possibilities might be blooming there.

TWELVE

WE HAD ANOTHER DRINK, and then another. Arms linked, we scaled the Spanish Steps before Stefano chased us back down again, a fearsome ogre. Victoria and I ran ahead of him, giggling, hand in hand; breathless and giddy, *two-at-a-time*, *two-at-a-time*. We threw coins over our shoulders into the Trevi Fountain. One coin for me, although Stefano urged two. *You know the legend, right?* That smirk again. Leaning in for a kiss. And then Victoria, snatching the limelight: *Take my picture. Here, I'll be quick*. There were signs everywhere saying not to, but still she hitched up her trousers and waded in. She got the shot, and we slipped away before the sluggish security detail could stop us.

All day we wandered the cobbled streets, tired and aching, happy and drunk. In the piazza, Stefano bought us each a single red rose from a lady hunched over a bucket. Victoria looped her arms around his neck and gave him a quick peck on the cheek. *You're a doll*. I nodded, fixed my smile in place, tossed him a quiet *thank you*.

We stopped for *supplì*. We stopped for gelato. We stopped for beers in a basement, standing room only. The sun drooped, heavy in the sky; the streets swelled with people; night fell. *One more place*, she begged with increasing desperation. *You can't go home yet*. One more place. Then another one more. Then another: a club. Exposed brick. Blue neon lettering clinging to the wall, a jerky jazz trio clinging to the stage. The black-and-white tiled floor, a game of chess.

The three of us sat crowded around a small table, a red candle burning at its centre.

'Let me get these,' Stefano said, twirling a lock of Victoria's hair between his fingers.

'No, no, *no*,' she protested, swaying slightly. Her eyes were bleary and unfocused. '*I'm* the gate-crasher. *I* buy the drinks.'

Stefano held her gaze, then, quick as a flash, jumped up and made for the bar.

'You're only allowed to pay for *one round*,' she yelled, turning in her seat. 'I mean it, Steffy.'

I heard laughter from down the hallway.

She returned her attention to me and smiled, but sadly, I thought. 'Hello *you*.'

'Hello,' I replied, sandwiching her fingers between mine.

She looked down, then shook her head and guffawed.

'What?' I asked, joining in with her laughter. 'What's so funny?'

'Oh Shannon, oh Shannon, oh Shannon.' She sighed, suddenly serious again. 'Why him?'

'What?' I asked, wondering if I'd misheard her over the music.

'Never mind, never mind,' she mumbled, attempting to catch the straw between her teeth. She took a long sip, which went down the wrong way. She coughed and I thumped her on the back. 'Thank you,' she croaked.

'Tell me about your trip,' I said.

'What trip?'

'The States.'

'Nothing to tell.'

'I don't believe you.' I took her hand again and shook it until her whole body joined in and her head lolled onto her chest. I caught her grinning. 'Come on,' I said, jabbing her middle. 'Tell me. You made out you were having such a lovely time.'

She shrugged, her chin still on her chest, and stared at the scratched table. 'Boy trouble. It's always the same.'

'Which boy?'

'You don't know him. He's a local. A bit older.'

'How much older?'

'We should get nuts. Do they do nuts here?' she asked, suddenly sitting upright and looking over her shoulder. 'Get Stef's attention, I want something salty.'

'V, how much older?'

'It doesn't matter. They're all the same. They all want the same thing.' She paused and scraped a half-moon of dirt out from underneath her fingernail. 'Anyway, what about you?'

'What about me?'

She sniggered. 'What the fuck are you doing here?'

'I'm listening to *jazz, baby*.'

She snorted. 'No, what are you doing *here*, in *Rome*?'

'I'm . . . on holiday, I suppose.'

'Yeah, but . . .' She paused and rolled her head back so she was staring at the ceiling. 'I don't get it . . . why Stefano?'

So I hadn't misheard.

'What do you mean?' I asked nervously. 'I thought you liked him.'

'I do, I do, I *totally* do, but . . .' She sighed, exasperated. 'I mean, you're just *so* . . .' She pulled a face. 'And he's just *so* . . .'

I felt a swell of – I don't know what – anger, betrayal, confusion flare up inside me. 'But you're the one that said we should date each other.'

'I did?'

'Yes. You said we'd be good together, that I shouldn't be too picky.'

She snorted again. 'No. That doesn't sound like something I'd say.'

'But you – but—'

'I would never pressure you into something you didn't want to do,' she said, gazing at me earnestly. 'I mean, does that really sound like me?'

'No. Of course not,' I conceded. Was there any point in arguing with her?

Victoria pushed the candle to one side and slumped forward. She reached for my ponytail and brought me down to the table so our foreheads were touching. I could feel the sweat on her skin; taste her breath, hot and acidic. She looked at me sleepily and blew a hair from her lip. 'Do you want to kiss me?' she mouthed silently.

Do you want to kiss me?

I felt my heart thump against the wood, a dull pressure in my temple.

Is that what she said? Is that what she *meant*? I couldn't be certain, what with the music coming from the band and the blue light casting silhouettes across her face.

Before I could respond, Stefano appeared with our drinks. 'What's going on?' he asked, placing them between us so we were forced to sit up.

'Great timing, Steffy,' Victoria slurred.

'Oh yeah?' he said, sitting down and slinging his arm around her shoulder. 'What's going on then?'

She shrugged him off, visibly irritated. 'Me and your *girlfriend* were just about to have it off.'

I had no idea what Victoria was doing, whether she *had* wanted to kiss me or whether I was just a pawn to her, some foot soldier in a larger war. I glanced sideways at Stefano, watched his expression transform.

He leered at the two of us. 'Is that so?'

'*Yeah.*' Victoria grabbed his chin and jerked his head from side to side. 'But then *you* came and *ruined* things.'

'You can carry on if you want,' he said, escaping her grip. He caught my eye. 'I mean, I won't stop you.'

I felt his leg press against mine beneath the table, and knew with complete certainty he was doing the exact same to Victoria.

'In fact,' he continued, placing his hand on my thigh but looking at her, 'maybe we could all go back to your hotel room, V. The three of us, like you said, continue the fun . . .'

Victoria blinked, processing what he'd just said, then, with a look of horror, shrank away from him. 'Oh my *God*, you cannot be serious.'

Stefano laughed uncertainly.

'Did you hear that, Shannon?' she asked, her eyes wide and indignant. 'He's not seriously suggesting a threesome, is he?'

Stefano's expression hardened.

'Can you actually believe it?' she continued, not even attempting to hide her revulsion. 'Isn't that just the most disgusting thing you've ever heard, Shannon?'

I wished she'd stop addressing me directly, as if I was in on whatever game she was playing.

I looked at Stefano. His ears had turned red. Embarrassed fury blazed in his eyes.

'Oh come on, it was a *joke*,' he scoffed. 'You think I'd want what you're selling?'

'Ha, cute,' she said, narrowing her eyes. 'And now he's backpedalling.'

'Hey, let's just calm down,' I said, attempting to defuse the situation. 'This is all just a miscommunication, a misunderstanding.'

'There's no misunderstanding,' she said, her tone serious. 'Stefano's jealous, aren't you, Steffy?'

'You know what, we're done here. Come on, let's go,' he said.

'See, Shannon. He's jealous of us, Shannon. He's jealous of what we have.'

'Shut up.'

'Look, he's going red, Shannon.'

'Shut up, Victoria.'

'Oh yeah? What are you going to do?'

'I mean it, V. Shut up.' His hand clenched into a fist.

'Please, can you both just calm down.'

'Oooh, big man,' she said, taunting him.

'V,' he warned.

'Is big man going to hit me?'

'*Puttana*,' he barked, kicking the table so our drinks rattled. 'FUCK.' People looked over.

Victoria sank back in her chair and chewed the inside of her cheek.

No one said anything.

Stefano sat, shamefaced, staring at his hands. He reached for his glass, took a sip and placed it down again. He cleared his throat. 'I'm sorry.'

Victoria stared at him, her expression unreadable.

Stefano, unnerved by her silence, continued: 'But you push and you push and you . . .' He clenched and unclenched his fist. 'Look, I said I'm sorry.' Clench, unclench.

But Victoria just stared at him, stared past him, really, as if he wasn't there at all.

'Well, come on then. Fucking say something.' A pause. Then, addressing me: 'You see what happens?' Then, under his breath: '*These bitches*.' A pause. He scraped his chair back and got up. 'You know what, fuck this. We're leaving.' He grabbed my arm and pulled me to my feet.

'Wait – we should make sure she gets back OK,' I protested, as he steered me through the crowd. 'Stefano, stop it. You're hurting me.' I looked over my shoulder.

Victoria was staring into space. It was dark, we were drunk, but still, I could've sworn I saw her smile.

THIRTEEN

STEFANO WAS SILENT THE entire way home. Outside the club, he rang for a taxi which took us all the way to the apartment building's front door. I knew it wasn't for my benefit though. He just wanted to get as far away from Victoria as he could, as quickly as he could. When we got inside, I went straight into the shower room and locked the door. I texted Victoria.

Sunday, 8th August at 02:32
Shannon Bell
Are you back safe? I'm so so sorry, I don't know what happened there xx

She sent me back a picture of her shiny, tanned legs, stretched out along the quilted eiderdown, the hem of a fluffy white robe peeking just out of shot.

Sunday, 8th August at 02:34
Shannon Bell
Good. Such a relief! I was worried! Again I'm so sorry. He's a dick. I don't know what happened xx

And then her reply:

Sunday, 8th August at 02:41

V

Just get some sleep babe x

When I emerged from the shower room, the apartment was empty. I found a hurriedly scribbled note on the Formica table.

Gone for a walk

Don't wait up

I felt exhausted and sick. I thought about deadbolting the door (accidentally) so Stefano wouldn't be able to get in again. But then decided that might be a step too far after all the humiliation of that evening.

I sat down on the bed, and the apartment seemed to sigh. The room was chilly. We'd left the clunky air conditioning unit on all day. I shivered and rubbed the pimpled skin of my arms. Everything was in shadow. A single lamp burned in the corner, casting malevolent tableaus on the walls. I removed my sandals and rubbed the dark welts that had been slowly forming over the past few days, the plump virgin skin cut to ribbons. *Don't wait up*. I took a shower, washed my hair and crawled – the room spinning like a waltzer – beneath the stale sheets.

I HEARD A NOISE. I rolled over and peered at the glowing microwave dial. *4.37 a.m.* It was still dark outside. I rolled back and saw light under the shower room door, movement.

I could hear Stefano in there, the taps gushing, on and off, then something falling to the floor and a grunt as it was kicked against the shower basin.

It shattered; I froze.

I thought back on the night, on the entire week and the eggshells I'd tiptoed across, the fragile casing of Stefano's ego. I wished I'd stayed home. I squeezed my eyes shut and willed myself back into that life: watching Grandma potter around the garden; reclining with Mum and her detective novels on the patio; helping Dad in the garage as he worked on some never-ending project.

The light disappeared from beneath the door.

Shivering, I curled in on myself, making myself as tiny as I could.

Footsteps. The feeling of another person entering the room.

'Shannon . . .'

I didn't answer.

'Shannon, are you awake?'

I waited, my heart pounding in my ears.

I heard a buckle unlatch, a belt slap to the floor.

The mattress sank as Stefano clambered onto the bed. He manoeuvred himself behind me and, with sinking dread, I felt something press against the base of my spine.

His breath was warm and rancid-smelling; his body taut and humming with need. I tried to shift away from him, but his hand gripped my waist, pulling me closer. 'Where do you think you're going?' he whispered playfully.

It was a question that required no answer, only discreet compliance.

So this is how it happens.

'Stef,' I croaked, feigning waking.

'Hey, little bird,' he whispered, nuzzling my neck.

'Please, I'm so tired.'

'Quiet now.'

'Stef, not like this, I don't want to—'

'Shh.'

He lowered his hand and eased my pyjama bottoms down to my knees. I wish he'd pulled them all the way off. Somehow that would've been better, less transactional.

Her face disappears.

A body.

A chest.

Limbs.

Reduced to nothing, to lumps of meat, props.

Your end of the bargain.

'Stef—'

You asked for this.

'Stefano—'

Suddenly his grip tightened. 'Just be quiet, OK? Just – just be quiet now.'

Invited it.

He wrapped his arm around my neck.

'Please, Stef, I don't want to—'

And then he pushed himself inside me.

Like a stranger's finger in your mouth, the familiar made foreign, sticky and unwelcome.

Why didn't you run?

Run where?

I stopped moving, let my limbs go heavy.

Play dead.

The rest I watched from above. Up in the gods. The cheap seats. Observer and participant. Audience and performer.

A mannequin.

He chuckled to himself. 'Fuck, you're so wet.'

A cardboard figurine, bent in half.

'Oh God.'

'Please—' the girl whispered.

A paper doll.

'Stop—' she pleaded.

'Oh fuck . . .'

Someone else, someone else's scene.

I gazed at the girl on the bed. And she stared up at the girl in the sky.

Are you not an actress?

Yes, but—

So act.

FOURTEEN

'I DON'T KNOW.' JOLLY tilted his head to one side and looked me up and down. 'You just seem different. What do you think, V?'

Victoria was in the conservatory, hunched over a book. She'd taken Jolly as her plus-one to a gallery opening in Shoreditch the evening before and stayed the night on the sofa. Her hair was still in a towel from the shower, and she was gripping a mug of tea between her feet like a monkey. She glanced in my direction before returning to the page. 'Definitely.'

'Did you get a tan or do something with your hair?'

'I don't tan.' I scraped burnt pancake from the rim of the frying pan. 'Sorry about this.'

'Don't worry. The first one's always shit.'

It was Sunday morning We were both still in our dressing gowns. Me: fluffy Dalmatian polka-dots. Jolly: a pale blue kimono. My parents had helped move me in two days before. Second year. New digs and a fresh start, that's what I told myself anyway. I was living with Jolly now. Abigail had moved out and Stefano had found somewhere cheaper. I was in Abi's room. It was light and airy and still smelled of Impulse and Versace Red Jeans. A third-year lighting technician had moved into Stefano's room. Whenever I walked past the door, I held my breath. It still smelled of him.

I slid the crispy batter onto Jolly's plate. He tore off a piece.

'Careful,' I said.

'Shit, that's hot.' He fanned his mouth and tipped his head back. 'Oh wait, of course,' he said, his mouth still full. 'It's so obvious. Our darling little Shannon finally got laid! That's it, isn't it? Stefano finally sealed the deal!'

I felt darkness press at the edges of my vision.

Someone else, someone else's scene.

I shook the feeling away and dribbled more batter into the pan. 'Can we not?'

'Oh come on, you've not told me a single thing about Rome. Did it happen there? Was it romantic? Were there cherubs? Or rose petals?' Jolly turned and called over his shoulder. 'Or what about you, V? Were you witness to the act?'

'Not that I recall,' she replied, not looking up.

'So what happened?' Jolly continued, prodding my side.

'We broke up,' I mumbled.

'You broke up?'

'Yes.'

'Oh. Shit.' Jolly patted my shoulder. 'Well, never mind then.'

I could feel Victoria's questioning eyes on me. *Fuck her*, I thought. *Let her stew. She was the one who'd humiliated him, whipped him up into a frenzy.*

'*Although*, now you've broken up with him, you won't mind telling me all the filthy details.'

I sighed. 'Jolly—'

'Come on, Shannon,' he pleaded. 'I've been in fucking Southampton all summer, literally *starved* of gossip. You've got to give me something.'

I poured more batter into the pan and focused on the action of tilting the liquid, of coating the black metal in sweetness. How do you tell someone their friend is a rapist? I tipped the frying pan away from the flame. 'What time's Terrence getting here, by the way?' I said, attempting to change the subject.

'Oh no, you're not getting out of this that easily.'

'Can you please just drop it, Jol.'

'Are we talking Peperami' – Jolly widened his hands – 'or mortadella?'

'For fuck's sake, it's going to be awkward enough on the first day back without you going on about the size of his dick.'

'Fine.' Jolly pulled another piece of pancake off and popped it in his mouth. 'As you are still quite obviously heartbroken over our Italian friend, I will be quiet, *for now*. But mark my words, you *will* tell me all the gory details at some point in the near future. *Capiche?*'

'Fine. Whatever.'

Victoria slammed the book shut, startling the both of us. 'I can't read another fucking word.'

'Lecoq?' Jolly said.

'Yes.' She crawled the length of the sofa and stretched her limbs like a cat. 'Did you honestly get through the entire reading list over the summer?'

'Yes,' Jolly and I replied at the same time.

'Ugh, nerds. Well, they better not test us.'

'They won't.'

'They might,' he said. 'Remember *An Actor Prepares*?'

'Yeah, but that's, like, the acting *bible*. This is just extras.' Victoria got up. 'Like, I seriously feel I learned all I really needed to last year, you know? Actioning, objectives, the *useful* stuff' – she tapped the side of her head – 'it's all in there. But then this' – she shook the book at us – 'this is just them stretching out our tuition fees.'

'Maybe you should've just done a one-year somewhere then,' Jolly said, pulling a questionable tin of golden syrup from the back of the cupboard.

'Yeah, except my agent wanted me to do the whole shebang.'

'Still, we get to do comedy this term,' Jolly replied, licking a rogue sticky patch from the back of his hand. 'That should be fun.'

'I guess.' Victoria padded over to the counter. 'It's all a waste of time though, really, isn't it.'

'What do you mean?' I said, sliding the second pancake, perfect this time, onto Victoria's plate.

'Well, it's kind of like, if you're funny, then *you're funny*, you know? And if you can act, *you can act*. It's like, at what point are they just taking folks for a ride and milking us for profit. I mean, take Hettie, for example—'

'Oh, here we go,' Jolly said, rolling his eyes.

'No, no, I'm not being bitchy, I'm just being honest. Like, really? Is she actually going to get any work when she's out in the industry?'

'I'm not sure that's your decision, V,' Jolly said.

'No, I'm not saying it is, but like, isn't it just a bit cruel making her think she's actually in with a chance? I mean, I actually feel embarrassed for her when she's talking about all the roles she's going to get. It's so fucking tragic.'

'I thought she was good in *Macbeth*,' I said, adding more batter.

'She was *fine*. She was *adequate*. But she's not, like, getting an Olivier any time soon, is she?'

'Maybe not,' Jolly agreed.

'I don't know. Maybe she'll surprise us,' I said.

Victoria snorted. 'No, no. There won't be any more surprises from now on.'

'What do you mean?' I said, pressing the spatula down so hard oil spat from the pan.

I flinched as Victoria came up behind me and wrapped her freckled arms around my waist. I didn't want to, but ever since that night, Stefano's hands . . . Anyway, I don't know if she even noticed. If she did, she didn't say anything. She rested her chin on my shoulder. 'Well, *Shanny-boo*, we're all on our set paths now. You are *you* and I am *me*. We grew up where we grew up, we know who we know, and we are who we are.' She squeezed my middle and I suddenly felt like I was in the grip of a snake. 'And throwing out a few lines in a play or learning a new accent isn't going to change that.'

'Ooh, she's a philosopher now,' Jolly joked. 'So the basic nature versus nurture argument then, yeah, V?'

She let go of me and raised her hands. 'Whatever – you can make fun of me all you want but believe me, I know how things work.' She went up to Jolly and stroked his fringe away from his forehead. 'Like you, for example, my dear. From the day you were born, Jolly McAndrew, you were destined to be a fabulous queen with a tasty little butt and hair the colour of sunshine.'

'Aaaw, V.' He prised the lid from the tin of syrup. 'Can I spread you on my pancakes instead?'

'And what about me?' I said.

'Well, you were destined to be . . . to be . . .' She thought for a moment, scrunching up her nose in a way that made me want to scream, to kiss her, to dash the searing-hot pan against the side of her face. 'You, baby, were destined to be Shannon Bell.'

FIFTEEN

LATER THAT DAY TERRENCE came over, and the four of us squeezed ourselves beneath a quilt on the sofa. After some general squabbling about what to watch, we settled on *Willy Wonka & The Chocolate Factory*. We enjoyed the film for a while, but by the golden-egg-laying geese, Terrence and Jolly had disappeared upstairs and Victoria had dozed off.

Outside, the sky was dark and rain pelted the windows. I reached for the remote and turned the volume down. Victoria remained still beside me. I sank back against the sofa cushions and watched her breathe in and out. Her face was so delicate, so calm while she rested. Gone was the brash confidence, the arched eyebrows and the taunting smirk. Here, now, tucked against my arm, she was a child, and I felt an ache of duty to protect her.

The great glass elevator crashed through the ceiling.

'*But Charlie, don't forget what happened to the man who suddenly got everything he always wanted.*'

'*What happened?*'

'*He lived happily ever after.*'

She stirred. 'Hmm, did I fall asleep?'

I nodded.

She sat up and yawned. 'What time is it?'

'No idea.'

Victoria clicked her neck. She reached for the remote and flicked through the channels.

The BBC title card played. 'And up next, *Countryfile*.'

'Do you mind if I sleep over again?' she asked.

'If you want.'

'I might stay off the sauce tonight though. My mouth tastes like ass.'

I smiled despite myself.

Victoria snuggled closer. She rested her head against my shoulder. I stiffened.

'Are you OK?' she asked. 'You've been acting kind of weird all day.'

'I'm fine,' I said, trying to relax my arms.

'Are you mad at me about something?'

Was I mad at her? I didn't even know any more. She hadn't mentioned her behaviour that night or apologized in any way at all. I wasn't even sure she remembered the extent to which she'd tortured Stefano, she'd been that wasted. But you could never tell with Victoria. *Do you want to kiss me?* She always left you guessing, dangling in thin air as you kicked and scraped and searched for a foothold.

'No,' I replied.

She poked my side. 'You'd tell me if you were though, right?'

'Yes.'

This seemed to satisfy her. She changed the subject. '*Countryfile* reminds me of my dad.'

'Yeah?'

'Yeah.' She paused, perhaps wondering whether to go on. 'He went through a sort of farming stage when I was like four. Bought a load of thoroughbred pigs and a couple of acres in the next village over.' She laughed. 'He didn't have a fucking clue what to do with them though. Ended up selling them at a loss. I think the land went to developers eventually. Mum says it was probably a precursor to his mid-life crisis and the whole *leaving her for his secretary* thing.' She sighed.

'What?'

'No, no. It's silly.'

'Go on.'

She looked at me. 'Well, he had a few employees who handled the pigs, you know, did the *actual* work. But I still remember riding around with him on this big useless tractor. It was a sort of forest green, all shiny and clean. The seat upholstery, the leather, still smelled of the shop he'd bought it from. Ridiculous really. He didn't know what to do with it, he'd just ride it around the fields day after day, waving to the neighbours and dog walkers, people like that. *Wave, Vicky. Smile, Vicky. Look busy, look busy.* God, all the *real* country people must've thought he was an idiot.' She picked at the skin around her thumb. 'Anyway, at the time I thought it was all wonderful. I'd sit in his lap and we'd drive across the fields, doing the rounds and, I don't know, I guess I felt invincible. I thought all those people had turned out to see us, I thought my daddy was respected, that my daddy was *a king*. I felt like I – like we – could do whatever we wanted and things would all turn out fine, that we'd ride around the fields forever. Just me and him. It was a good time.' She sat perfectly still. 'Of course, he walked out pretty soon after that. I didn't see him for a few years then. He tried to get in touch, but Mum was too bitter. I don't think it affected my brothers too much. They already knew him, they were his little pals, they already knew what he was like. But with me? It's like I was just getting to know him.' She stared at the wall, at a spot just above the TV screen. 'I mean, I see him more now, we all do. I'm not trying to make you feel sorry for me or anything.'

'No, I know.'

'I love going to stay with him.'

'Yeah.'

'People have worse childhoods,' she laughed. 'He'd literally do anything for me, absolutely anything.'

I nodded.

'Strange. I've not thought about all that in so long.' She turned her face away so I couldn't read her expression. 'Sundays, eh?'

I pulled her into a hug and we sat quietly for a moment.

I wanted to say something, to offer her some morsel of my own in return. 'If I was at home right now, my mum would be doing a roast,' I murmured into her hair.

'Oh yeah?' came her muffled reply.

'Yeah.'

'What with?'

'Erm, chicken probably, and mash, Yorkshires, peas, roast potatoes—'

'Wait, two types of potato?'

'Yep.'

Victoria laughed. 'My mum would never allow that. She's scared of carbs the way most people are scared of spiders.'

'And then we'd have something like sticky toffee pudding for afters.'

'That sounds good. You must've had a happy childhood.' She winced. 'Sorry, apart from your sister.'

I didn't say anything.

She sat up then, and we watched the television in silence. The presenter was being led around a forest by some schoolchildren.

After a few minutes Victoria said, 'Jolly's right, you know. There is something different about you. I noticed it in Rome. It's like you hold yourself differently or something.'

I remained still, my eyes on the TV screen.

'You can tell me. If you want. Or not. It's up to you.'

I thought back to Frida and me sitting knee to knee, her voice pouring *magic* in my ears; I thought of Stefano's words at the kitchen table: *You acted like Victoria*; I thought of his confused texts when he woke to find me gone the next morning – *I'm sorry. Talk to me, Shannon. What did I do? What did I do?*; I thought back to the violinist and the old man, to the square and my feet on the cobblestones, to that whirling feeling I'd had when I'd danced; the crowd's grinning spinning faces, their features blurring into one as I transformed before their eyes.

'I *feel* different,' I said.

The children led the presenter along the trail, stomping across leaves and twigs, towering oaks and spindly grey saplings bending around their path.

'Why do you think that is?' she asked.

'Well,' I murmured, 'Frida said something to me.'

'Frida?' I felt Victoria's body tense beside me. I glanced sideways. Her face remained impassive, a pleasant mask of indifference. 'What did she say?'

'It was nothing really,' I said, attempting to retreat.

'You can tell me,' she said. 'Go on. What did she say?'

'Erm, well . . .' I hesitated. 'She told me my performance in *Macbeth* was, well – she told me it was magic.'

I knew it was a mistake as soon as I'd said it.

'Oh,' she replied. 'Is that it?'

The wall rose up like a physical thing between us.

'Well, yes, that's what she told me, and I don't know, it's kind of made me feel more—'

'You know she said the same thing to me, right?'

A jab. Something sharp against my side.

'She did?'

'Yes.' Victoria glanced at me, then back towards the screen. 'Oh, don't worry.' She smiled. 'I'm sure she totally meant it with you too.'

When I didn't say anything, she turned and looked at me, her face veiled with concern. 'Oh babe, I'm not trying to shit on you!' Then she laughed – no – she cackled. 'If looks could kill! You're scaring me. You look so serious!'

'She told you the same thing?' I said, trying to keep my voice even, blank, holding off on any tone she might weaponize.

'Mm-hm.' *Liar.* 'Yep.' She threw off the blanket and went and stood in the doorway. The hallway light was on. Her shadow spread like a stain across the wall. 'It's good,' she said. 'It's good that she likes us both the same. It means we're both doing well.'

'Yes.' *Liar, liar, liar.*

She beamed at me. 'Do you want a drink or something? A cup of tea?'

'No.' *She couldn't just let me have this one thing.* 'Thank you.' *Just this one good thing.* 'I'm OK.'

'I'm having cocoa,' she said, her smile frozen in place. She didn't move. But then . . . a moment of hesitation. The mask faltered and a well of absence pooled in her eyes. She saw me notice and her gaze blazed back to life again. 'God, don't you just love Sundays?'

SIXTEEN

AUTUMN BLEW IN AND a new term began. Seeing the White Elephant that first morning, its legs in the air, felt like coming home. When I entered the rehearsal room, Obi and I drew towards each other like magnets. He laughed and gathered me up in his arms. *Shannon*, he sighed into the warm space of my neck. He pulled away and smiled and I had that feeling again, that feeling from the piazza, like I was at the centre of the universe, or at the very least, the centre of someone's universe. But then Victoria entered, and Obi dropped me back down to earth.

After catching up with everyone about their summers, conversation soon turned to the hot gossip of the day: Lena Ogievich.

Lena was in the year above us, a Russian beauty with quick eyes and long dark hair. Apparently, at the end of last year, Lena reported Piers Day, a boy in her class, to Frida and the senior leadership team. Lena told staff that Piers had been stalking her for months. She claimed he'd spiked her drink at a house party whereupon she'd passed out. She said that when she woke up her bra was torn, her skirt hitched up, and that Piers was sleeping next to her.

The school had managed to keep it quiet at the time, but rumours soon took root and spread over the summer months. By the first day back, the entire student body was talking about it.

Jolly said he'd heard from another third-year that the school told

Lena she didn't have any evidence and that it wasn't an RLSDA matter as it had happened off campus. The third-year said that when Lena told Frida she was thinking of going to the police, Frida told her she'd be a fool to do so. Apparently Frida said it sounded like a relationship that had gone wrong and that Lena shouldn't risk disrupting her third year by pursuing a criminal case. She said these things happen when you're young, and that the best thing would be to just get on with things and stay away from the boy. Lena asked how she was meant to do that when she had to see him every day and they'd already been assigned showcase scenes together. To that, Frida replied that there'd be people in the industry who Lena wouldn't get along with but who she'd need to be professional around. She also warned her that news travels fast. Frida said that if Lena insisted on continuing with this witch hunt, she risked getting 'a nasty reputation'.

I couldn't help but glance over at Stefano and the small cabal of boys he'd surrounded himself with. He'd been ignoring me all morning.

Obi said he'd passed Piers in the corridor outside the cafeteria. He said he looked his usual self.

Victoria said she'd seen Lena ordering coffee from the stall outside. She said she didn't look any different and that she certainly didn't look like someone who was dealing with the fallout of a sexual assault.

Jolly said it wasn't fair, that he'd been to loads of house parties but no one had ever bothered to hitch up his skirt.

All morning, in whispered gatherings, we picked and pulled at the story's threads, so much so that by lunch, the whole thing felt rather stale. With not much more to say, we moved on.

'So, Shannon, have you noticed Stefano's new haircut? Drunk barber or a cry for help?'

'Shut up, Jolly.'

Later in the year, Piers got offered the role of Edmund in *King Lear* at the National. Ordinarily, *officially*, students weren't allowed to audition whilst at the school, and they certainly weren't allowed to take jobs. But in third year, if the school got wind of the sniff of acclaim, they usually let the rules slide. This meant Piers was allowed to graduate early and his final grades were awarded based on his professional debut. So a thumbs up for Piers and the school. Lena, not so much.

COMEDY WAS THE ORDER of that eight-week term. Molière's *Tartuffe* was our assigned text alongside a crammed timetable of commedia, music hall and, my favourite, solo comedy.

Every week, a different semi-successful comedian was invited to lead a crash course in their particular discipline. We had classes in stand-up, improv, slapstick and clown. Thursday afternoons became a rollicking four-hour goof-off, a chance to snigger, hoot and howl away from the gaze of our uncompromising tutors.

It turned out I was quite good at comedy. Growing up, I was usually too shy to try and make anyone laugh. But in those Thursday sessions, it wasn't long before I had the whole class in stitches. Not everyone was having fun though. Victoria was right. *If you're funny, then you're funny.* And she was most certainly *not* funny.

Victoria glowered at me whenever I made the class laugh while simultaneously cosying up to whichever minor ex-Perrier-award nominee was teaching us that week. She asked too many questions and tried too hard. Her jokes made no sense, yet after each pregnant silence, she redoubled her efforts. The more she tried, the worse she did, to the point where many of us hid behind our fingers as she took to the stage.

I hated seeing her flail about like that. Her failure was starting to unsettle me. Victoria was meant to be the best. She was meant to shine, to excel. But when she messed up joke after joke, when she confused punchlines, when she laboured weak quips, I felt embarrassed by our friendship and ashamed of my admiration. Victoria was showing me up.

One evening, a few of us stayed late to rehearse after school. Victoria was in a foul mood that day. Casper had berated her in front of the whole class that morning for some slip-up in Voice, and I'd seen her and Obi arguing in the cafeteria at lunch. But we needed to go over some scenes, including the one where Elmire (Victoria) lets herself be seduced by Tartuffe (Jolly). Jolly was unwell that day. He had an ear infection and, after he'd entered the rehearsal room only to lie beneath a pile of coats, we urged him to go to a walk-in and get an appointment. I told him I'd read in for his part.

We began walking through the blocking our director had suggested that afternoon.

'You – well, *Jolly* – should start over there,' Victoria said.

'OK.'

'And then we walk together arm in arm to here.'

'Right.'

'And then you walk and stand there,' she finished.

I paused. 'I thought I was meant to come around the table.'

'No. You stand there.'

'Are you sure?' I asked.

'Yes, I'm sure.' She took my elbow. 'We walk together arm in arm, then you walk on your own and stand there.'

I must've looked sceptical.

Victoria let out an exasperated sigh. 'It's really not that difficult, Shannon. Just walk and stand there. Let's go again.'

'I really think Tartuffe is meant to come around the table—'

'God, Shannon, can you just do as I say?'

Obi looked up from his notebook. He was sitting next to Lola on the floor. 'No, V, I think Shannon's right. Tartuffe's meant to come around the table.'

Lola glanced up from the split end she was peeling. 'Yes, that makes sense,' she added.

Victoria put her hands on her hips. 'No, because then I'm in the wrong place for having my dress lifted.'

'No, because you follow him and then he turns back on you,' Obi continued.

'But then the table's in front of us. That doesn't make any sense,' Victoria countered.

'No, see, you both go around the table in a loop so you're in front of it,' Obi said.

'Then you do the dress lift thingy,' Lola said, returning to her split ends.

Victoria's colour was rising. A muscle pulsed in her jaw. 'I think I'd remember, don't you?' she said. 'I was the one who actually *did* the blocking this afternoon,'

'Whatever,' Lola sighed, not looking up.

'It's OK,' Obi said. 'You've got loads of blocking to remember for this scene. You're bound to forget some things.'

'Yes, I know I've got loads of blocking, Obi. But I'm also not an idiot who forgets something she rehearsed, what, like three hours ago.'

No one said anything.

Victoria glared at Obi, then me. 'Well?'

'I wasn't in the room the whole time,' I said. 'I don't remember.'

Victoria grabbed the script from my hand. 'Brilliant, thank you.' She threw it to the floor and stormed across the room. 'Thank you so much for your help.'

Obi stood. 'Hey, V, what's up? It's not Shannon's fault.'

Lola drew spirals in her notebook.

'Did I say it was anyone's fault?' Victoria said, slinging her bag over one shoulder. 'Did I say a single thing?'

'Look, why don't we just go over the scene again? I can read in instead of Shannon, if you want?'

'No.' I saw her foot twitch, like she wanted to stamp it. 'No, I don't want that.' She swiped an absent strand of hair away from her temple. 'I'm tired and I'm hungry, and I'm going to go home.'

'OK,' Obi said, taking a step back.

She put on her coat and left. The door slammed shut behind her.

No one said anything for a moment.

'She's crazy,' Lola muttered beneath her breath.

'Leave it,' Obi warned her. He grabbed his bag and stuffed the script inside.

Lola started gathering her things too. Apparently the rehearsal was over. I followed the two of them out of the room. We passed the janitor in the corridor. He was chuckling to himself. We ignored him.

After Lola disappeared inside the tube station, Obi and I made our way to the bus stop where we waited, our breath steaming in front of us. I saw his bus in the distance.

'Hey, it's still early,' I said. 'Do you want to go to the pub or something?'

Obi glanced at me, then down at his watch. 'Sure, I could do with a drink.'

*

THE MASONS WAS HUMMING. As we entered, the landlord rushed past us, a quad of glasses splayed between his fingers. One of the ageing regulars drooped from her stool. A swarm of first-years were huddled around the bar. They greeted us starry-eyed and urged us to push in front of them, in awe of our second-year status.

After buying our drinks, Obi and I found an empty table in the corner. He sat down opposite me and we sipped in silence. Although we'd been back a few weeks, this was the first time we'd been alone together since Victoria's house party. I didn't want to mention that night or my bungled attempt at a kiss, but nor did I want to paddle in the shallow waters of small talk with him either. I wanted to talk to him, really *talk* to him. Obi looked over his shoulder and the silence grew. Eventually I gave in and asked him about his summer. Visibly relieved at the break into conversation, he told me about the cushty job he'd found chaperoning at-risk children on day trips out of the city, to beaches, forests and farms.

'It was fun. They were good kids. The money wasn't bad either,' he added.

Like the student union job, Victoria had helped him find this one. Her brother's firm worked with the charity, he knew someone who was in charge of hiring; sure he could get Obi in, no problem.

'So basically I owe V big time.' He gave me a thin smile and played with the silver chain around his neck. 'Anyway, enough about me. I never got to hear about your summer. V mentioned that she gate-crashed Rome.'

I told him about the trip and Victoria's brief visit, doing my best to skirt around her bad behaviour and the fact I'd gone with Stefano. Obi knew we'd been together, of course; everyone knew. The awkwardness between us was still palpable in class, and – despite Victoria and Stefano seemingly having patched things up – we no longer really hung out as a fivesome. But I didn't want to talk about all that, not with Obi. I also left out the part about the violinist in the square. I trusted him, but I still couldn't trust the story not to find its way back to Victoria, who'd no doubt twist the memory into something unsavoury. Instead I told him about how my grandma had loaned me the money for the flight. I said it confused me when I heard people complaining about being completely broke all term, then seeing them living it up on Facebook, travelling the world and taking road trips across New Zealand and America.

Obi grimaced. 'I hear you. Victoria asked me to lend her a fifty last week.'

I nearly spat out my drink. 'She did?'

He nodded.

'Doesn't her dad own like twenty insurance firms?'

'Something like that.' Obi shrugged. 'It's fine. I know she'll pay me back.'

'Wait, you actually gave her the money?'

'Of course I did.'

I stared at the scratched table, careful not to say anything.

'It's OK,' he said. 'She always returns the favour.'

I nodded.

'She's having a hard time at the moment.' I wanted to ask why, but he quickly changed the subject. 'Anyway, it's good to be back in the routine of things – school, rehearsals,' he continued. Then, leaning forward on his elbows and lowering his voice: 'I missed you over the summer, you know.'

The room quietened. It was as if someone had turned the volume down. I swilled the remaining liquid around my glass and stared at my hands, searching for the right words. Obi was looking at me, waiting for an answer. I cleared my throat. 'Nah, I bet you missed everyone.'

He thought for a moment. 'No, not everyone. Just you.'

I glanced up at him. He was smiling at me. I looked away and quickly downed the rest of my drink so I wouldn't open my big stupid mouth and have a repeat of Victoria's garden.

Obi's phone buzzed. He slid it away from me, but not before I saw her name.

Incoming call: Victoria.

He sighed heavily. 'Sorry. I should get this.' He got up from his chair and disappeared around the corner. 'Hey – no, of course I'm free to talk.'

I sat and cradled my empty glass.

I waited five minutes, then ten.

After twenty, I collected my things and left.

SEVENTEEN

I PASSED. I DIDN'T get a special speech or anything this time, but I passed. Frida wasn't available to join the other tutors for Crits that first term of second year but still emailed feedback around. I'll admit, a tiny part of me was disappointed. I clicked on the email.

Voice: Pass.

Movement: Pass.

Solo comedy: Pass.

In *any further comments* she wrote that my listening and awareness had improved but that my eyes appeared hooded onstage and I needed to open them more, that this was something I ought to be aware of.

I frowned. My eyes? Why bother mentioning my eyes? Surely they were *just eyes*, two incontrovertible features of my face. I glanced at myself in the mirror but they looked just the same as they always did. The next day I walked around the house as wide-eyed as possible until Jolly asked me to please stop, I was scaring him.

Victoria passed too, just. Lola had been her scribe. When we met outside the pub after Crits, Jolly asked what Victoria's feedback had been like.

Lola sat back against the wall and took a long draw on her cigarette. 'I think you would say *room for improvement*?'

We asked for details, hungry for any morsel of criticism that might justify our own accomplishments. But then Victoria appeared at the gate and the subject was swiftly dropped.

That Christmas, I checked the Facebook group every day to see if anyone had been asked to leave. It seemed no one had. After scrolling through the mostly dormant page, I'd visit Victoria's profile and cycle through the latest pictures she'd uploaded of herself: slope-side with her family in Vermont; a thick pair of ski goggles pulled down over her beaming face; feet tucked beneath her long legs on a bear-skin rug. *It's a mulled cider kind of night* ✌. Victoria had actually said she'd visit me again in Yorkshire – she'd been promising all year, in fact. But then in November her dad had booked the chalet and, well, that was that. *Next year though, babe. We'll definitely do next year.*

When we returned in January, Victoria had a lot to say about the fact no one had been cut from the course, even though it was obvious that if anyone had struggled, it was her.

'I just don't understand why Hettie is still here?' she said, crossing her legs. We were sitting on a bench in the cafeteria. It was the first day back. 'I mean, she's a nice girl, don't get me wrong. But she's dragging us all down. Honestly, if she's still here for showcase she'll embarrass us all.' She sat up, warming to the topic. 'We'll be tarred with the same brush. *Me-di-o-cre.*' She sipped the foam from her coffee. 'I mean, I don't know if I should even invite my agent to our third-year shows any more.'

Victoria needn't have got so worked up. Hettie dropped out a few days later anyway. We never got a full explanation as to why, but Jolly said he'd seen her ditching her sandwiches at lunch and Obi made a comment about how he was able to fit his thumb and pinkie around her entire wrist in courtly dance.

I thought back on the year and a half I'd known her. It was true that while the rest of the girls wore skin-tight leggings and figure-hugging sweaters, Hettie shrouded herself in shapeless hoodies and sweatpants. She never scraped her hair back either, not after Frida made a passing comment about her head being shaped like a lollipop.

Anorexia. She hid it well.

I thought about reaching out to her. But then things got busy again, and Victoria said it would only make things worse and that the girl probably just wanted to be left alone. So I didn't.

I regret that. I regret a lot of things.

SPRING TERM WAS AMERICAN term. Victoria, a few others and me were grouped together in Arthur Miller's *The Crucible*; the other half of the class did *Death of a Salesman*. Victoria was given the role of Elizabeth, while I played Abigail. Victoria was happier that term. After the complete car crash of solo comedy, she was back on firmer ground.

'Finally, *actual* drama. Serious plays for serious actors.'

The other focus of that term was animal studies. This might've been one of the stranger experiences of my time at drama school. In animal studies, students observe animal behaviours, then make human character choices based on them. In practice, this meant a lot of squawking, grunting and swinging from the rafters of Rehearsal Room Five. To support our research, the school bought us each membership passes for London Zoo. In our second week, Frida announced with great satisfaction that she'd secured us a patch of grass not far from the camel enclosure, where she'd be leading some of our lessons.

The ground was slippery with ice as we approached the zoo. Grey banks of cloud loomed in the distance. Jolly and I trudged arm in arm, still tired from our beds, past the tall fences and netted enclosures of

Regent's Park. As we walked, hundreds of pairs of eyes, glum, alert, doleful, peered up at us from the undergrowth, down from trees, out from behind fibreglass rocks. After taking a wrong turn by the bug house, Jolly and I eventually found our way to the others. They were standing beneath a limp banner. *The Wonders of the Amazon*. Obi beckoned us over and Victoria, leaning against him, gave a small wave. I noticed she was wearing fur, an interesting choice for the zoo.

We'd each been assigned an animal to study. For our final assessment we had to transpose that animal into a human character within a five-minute scene. Obi was given a Transvaal lion. Stefano, a spotted hyena. Jolly, an albino ferret. Victoria was given a Japanese red fox and I, a black witch moth. The teachers never said outright, but it was widely assumed among the students, a rumour passed down from year group to year group, that the animals were based on us as individuals, that our animals were a physical and emotional representation of our true selves, our spirit animals. Jolly pointed out that this might've been what pushed Hettie to quit. Rumour had it she'd been given an elephant.

'Come here, sleepyhead,' Victoria said, pulling me towards her. 'You look freezing.'

I nodded and let myself be tucked in beside her. My hands were stiff, the skin pale and thin. I snuggled against her pelt and we waited, shivering in a tight knot of limbs.

Frida arrived a few minutes later and led us to our designated patch, a puddle-pocked square of slimy grass, where we reluctantly shed our coats and began our daily warm-up. Early-morning tourists and families strolled past, pointing and giggling. We must've looked a sight: a miserable group of students, all dressed in black, stretching on a muddy lawn between the aviary and a block of vending machines on the coldest morning of the year. Frida had to politely shoo away a family of American tourists who asked if they could take pictures.

She gathered us in a circle. 'You, Stefano.' She fixed him with her sharp gaze. 'Tell me about a character from a play you admire.'

'Erm, Stanley Kowalski from *A Streetcar Named Desire*.'

She nodded. 'Now, the character of Stanley. What do we know about him? We know he is driven by lust and power. We know that Blanche describes him as an "ape". We know he is violent, a soldier, an abuser. So, with that knowledge, what animals come to mind when we think of Stanley?'

'An ape?' Stefano replied uncertainly.

Frida clicked her tongue. 'Thank you for that enlightening response, Mr Bianchi. Perhaps the other tutors and I should've assigned you a parrot.'

A few people tittered.

'Anyone else?' she said, training her gaze on the group.

'A tiger.'

'A lion.'

'A bear.'

'Very good.' Frida walked between us. 'So, if you were asked to play Stanley, you could draw upon the qualities of these animals to inform your characterization, yes?'

A few people nodded.

'What form might this take?' Frida asked.

'A roaring voice.'

'A purposeful walk.'

'With a heavy tread.'

'Curled fists.'

'Strength.'

'Power.'

'Good.' She stopped. 'But what if you chose to play against these stereotypes?' She gazed around at our puzzled faces. 'We have already seen a thousand actors strut around in the role like a bear, have we not? What would happen if you chose more unexpected characteristics that played against type?' She paused. 'Name some animals that go against the preconceptions we have about the character of Stanley.'

'Poor Stanley's just a kitten,' Victoria said, earning herself the hint of a smile from Frida.

'A Shetland pony.'

'Butterfly.'

'Puppy.'

'Good, yes,' Frida said. 'Now you're getting it.'

'Worm.'

'Sparrow.'

'Mouse.'

'Excellent. What happens if instead of attributing power and status to Stanley, we imagine he's a Shetland pony who *wishes* he were a tiger, or a sparrow that dreams of being a lion? How would that change the characterization?'

'Well, he'd feel he had something to prove,' Victoria said.

'He'd feel small and pathetic,' I added.

'He might bully others to overcompensate.'

'He would never feel good enough,' Victoria continued.

'Precisely,' Frida said. 'Do you see? No one who goes around being thought of as an ape feels like an ape inside. Human beings are complicated. We are a mix of the past and the present, the future and all we wish to be. We are all tiny vulnerable kittens and puppies who just so happen to have grown into leopards and wolves. We are both predator and prey.

We are never just one thing. Nor should your characters be. To create a fully rounded character you need to inhabit the tiger, the lion *and* the sparrow.'

People nodded; murmurs went around the group.

'With that in mind, today I'd like you to think about your characters from scene studies. Please gather in your groups.'

I shuffled towards *The Crucible* lot.

'Make your way around the zoo and observe the animals but, and this is important, watch out for the unexpected. Seek out animalistic traits you might juxtapose with your roles' more obvious attributes. We'll meet back here in an hour.'

Victoria slipped her arm through mine and propelled me towards the butterfly house.

'Why there?' I asked.

'Because,' she whispered, 'it's warm in there and I'm freezing my tits off.'

INSIDE, VICTORIA FOUND A windowsill to perch on. She unravelled her scarf and removed her fur. I sat beside her. Above us, a canopy of vines crowned the fogged glass. I pulled out my copy of the play. She watched me, her brows knitted together.

'What are you doing?' she asked.

'Well, we're meant to observe the animals, aren't we?' I tucked a pencil behind my ear. 'I thought I could make some notes.'

Victoria threw her head back and groaned. 'God, you never just *exist*, do you?'

I frowned. 'What do you mean?'

'I *mean*, we're *here*' – she gestured at the space – 'surrounded by some of the most beautiful, entrancing, exotic creatures in the world, and you want to stick your beak inside a book and *make notes*?'

I closed it, hurt. 'I just thought we should do some work, that's all. Frida said—'

'*Frida said, Frida said*,' she sang. 'All you ever do is work, Shannon. I don't think I've met anyone who works as hard as you, except maybe Jolly.'

I should've felt proud. But something in Victoria's tone, in the pin-prick sharpness of her words, made me feel ashamed.

'So, what, you think I should just *exist*?'

'Yes,' Victoria said, gazing up at the glass ceiling. 'Exist. Be. Live in the moment.' An intricately patterned green butterfly landed on a leaf beside her. 'There, you see?' She leaned back until her eyes were level with the tip of its wing. 'Isn't she marvellous?'

'How do you know it's a she?'

'She just is. She's a queen. Look, she's beautiful.'

I watched the small creature, the fragile quiver of its wings.

'Isn't she magnificent?'

'Yes,' I replied, wondering what it would be like to pluck its powdery, trembling body apart, piece by piece.

Victoria cooed at the tiny creature as it flew towards another leaf. Her eyes followed it. 'You see? You see?' she said, grabbing my wrist, entranced.

'I see,' I said, my voice flat.

I watched Victoria's eyes dart across the room, hopping from creature to creature, and it suddenly came to me: Victoria and I were different species. I was earthbound, while she could fly. I hid behind rocks, watchful, frightened and alert, while she soared on an invisible jet stream available only to her. Victoria didn't worry. Ever. She had always been comfortable and taken care of. She knew no other existence. The future wasn't a scary place, but one filled with marvellous, curious moments just waiting to be experienced. She didn't need to think about the consequences of not doing the work, of not taking the notes or missing the rehearsal, because failure simply wasn't an option for her. Everything in her life was brilliantly assured, every whim a shining possibility.

'Look at that one,' she said, pointing out a translucent blue butterfly fluttering above us. Her finger tracked it across the room. 'See how delicate it is, how its wings capture the light?'

'Yes,' I said, following it, watching it pulse higher and higher, scattering the other creatures in its wake. 'I see.'

EIGHTEEN

THE DAYS RAN AHEAD of themselves. First year had dragged, but second year sped past in a blur. Assessments followed assessments, rehearsals bled into one another. Before one piece of work was performed, another was being demanded of you. There were parties, cigarettes and sick up the wall. Late walks at night and crack-of-shite starts, piss-yourself laughter and broken hearts. The year spun on its axis, getting faster and faster, until the final weeks of second year approached and third year lay before us, tantalizingly close, the industry, the big wide world, suddenly near enough to touch.

Then, in June, things fell apart.

Grandma had been complaining of a sore throat and shortness of breath for a few months. She was always wheezing and turning away from the receiver to cough when I spoke to her on the phone. I asked Mum what was going on, but she batted my questions away.

'It's nothing, probably bronchitis or something. I'll get her to ring the surgery. You just pick things up at her age. She'll get better soon.'

But she didn't get better. When she finally secured a doctor's appointment, they said her blood oxygen levels were so low they were surprised she'd managed to get herself in. They rushed her to the ICU, stuck tubes down her throat, and pumped her full of God knows what. Dad texted me the news. He told me not to worry, that the hospital said it was pneumonia, and that he and Mum were taking care of it. I remember thinking: *Pneumonia? Who gets pneumonia in June?*

She died a week later.

Jolly knew. We were making a stir-fry and running lines when I got the call. He promised he wouldn't tell anyone, but the next day Victoria sprinted into the rehearsal room and flung her arms around me. She held me for maybe thirty seconds, grasping fistfuls of my hair before stuffing a note inside my palm and turning away.

If you need ANYTHING at all, I've got you. Love you always. X

The funeral was in the penultimate week of second year. We were performing Brecht's *The Caucasian Chalk Circle* on Wednesday. The funeral was on Monday. I caught the train home Sunday night and was back in school for the dress rehearsal at 9 a.m. on Tuesday.

On the morning of the funeral, an extravagant spray of blue lilies arrived at our house. I asked Mum who they were from. She said she didn't know, the sender hadn't left a note. At the local cricket club after, someone had put a hundred quid behind the bar. Sipping their gratis brandies by the buffet, a few of Grandma's circle whispered among themselves, trying to guess who her anonymous benefactor was.

'Well, who's not here?'

'It could be Pat?'

'Surely not, his wife's not been cold two months.'

'Well, what about Lionel?'

'Maybe.'

'A secret admirer! Our Mary's still surprising us even now.'

I picked up a stack of empty plates and took them through to the kitchen. I could've told them about my oh-so-generous friend who conquered every corner with her bounty, flinging her generosity hither and thither. I could've pricked their delight, cut short their gossip, but grief, or maybe just the fat weight of exhaustion, stayed my tongue.

WHEN I RETURNED TO school, Victoria kept her distance. On Thursday, after a Movement class in which I'd excused myself to cry in the bathroom, I saw her speaking in low voices with Frida. I thought they were talking about me, that Victoria was reminding Frida about my recent bereavement. I remember feeling a rush of gratitude, then guilt that made me well up all over again.

Later, after we were kicked out of the rehearsal room by maintenance, I sidled up to her.

'Thank you,' I said, squeezing her hand.

'For what?'

'Everything,' I said, feeling a lump develop in my throat. 'The flowers, the tab, talking to Frida.'

She gave me a queer look. 'Frida?'

'Yes,' I said. 'You spoke to her earlier, didn't you? About why I was upset?'

'Oh, that.' She shook her head. 'No, that was something else.'

Jolly pushed past us. 'Good luck tomorrow, V!' he yelled. 'Sorry, got to run, I'm meeting Terrence.'

'Bye,' Victoria called after him.

We continued down the stairwell in silence. My thoughts ticked. *Good luck, good luck, good luck*. What did he mean? I flexed my fingers, afraid to know, afraid not to know.

'What was that about?' I asked finally. 'I mean, the good luck thing?

'Oh, nothing,' she said, waving the question away. 'Just an audition.'

The words hit me in the gut, winding me. *An audition.* I pushed my fingernail into the centre of my fist and tried to breathe.

'An audition?' I said. We reached the bottom of the stairs. I pushed open the heavy glass door, and Victoria stepped out ahead of me into the warm evening air.

'Yeah, for this TV thing.'

'What is it?' I asked, my fist trembling. 'I mean, what show is it?'

She hesitated, clearly unsure whether to answer. She glanced behind her, then seemed to decide it was safe to do so, that my relative insignificance would shield her from any NDA backlash. 'It's this HBO thing, pretty hush-hush. I can't really say much about it.' She paused, but I could tell she wanted to say more. She smiled to herself and looked sideways, as if some prying interloper might be listening in. 'But if I pull it off,' she whispered, 'it could be, well . . . *significant*.'

'Go on?'

'I shouldn't really say any more, Shan . . .'

'You can trust me. Go on,' I said.

'Well, it's sort of this drama that chronicles the life of Queen Elizabeth the first.'

'And . . .'

'And, well, I'd be playing Queen Elizabeth.'

I felt some part of me flatten.

'The lead,' I said, trying to sound excited, trying to hide the black bile of jealousy rising up inside me. 'That's great,' I said weakly.

'Yeah,' she agreed. 'It's actually a second meeting. I did the first on Monday, so, you know' – she waved her fingers in the air – 'fingers crossed.'

Monday. So, while I was sitting watching my grandmother's body disappear behind a curtain from where it would never return, she was standing in front of some of the biggest TV executives in the world, being praised and fawned over, offered opportunities beyond anything I could ever dream of for myself. While I was drinking her pity booze, she was climbing the ladder, the ladder that would eventually take her up, up and away from me. Her great glass elevator.

'That's so great,' I said again. If she heard the disappointment in my voice, she chose to ignore it.

'I'm trying not to get my hopes up,' she continued. 'But it's a pretty big deal. It'll get me out of this dump, at any rate.' She gestured at the school, *our* school, now behind us.

'You'll – you'll leave?'

'Oh, definitely. I've already discussed it with the tutors. They say my final marks can be based on the TV performance. I can still graduate like everyone else, I can still get my *degree*' – she put the word in air quotes – 'just without having to go through the whole dreary rigmarole of third year.' She glanced across at me. My expression must have faltered. She slipped her arm through mine. 'Oh *Shannypoo*, don't worry,' she said brightly. 'I'll come and see you in all your shows.' But then her attention seemed to drift elsewhere. 'I mean, if my schedule allows.'

NINETEEN

THE NEXT MORNING, VICTORIA wasn't there. The audition wasn't until 3 p.m., but the tutors had given her the day off so she could prepare.

I glowered at Frida as she led the movement warm-up.

I knew I was being irrational, that Frida was our teacher and it was her job to promote everyone on the course, whether she thought they were any good or not, and – despite her comedic shortcomings – Victoria really was very good. I knew it was Frida's duty to prepare students for the industry so that their successes might shine a light back onto the school, sustain its esteemed reputation and nourish its parasitic bio-rhythm. But still, ever since she'd called my performance magic, I'd harboured the stupid belief that *I* was her favourite, that I, for some reason, had been chosen, that I would be the only one to succeed, and everyone else, all my classmates, would eventually become deadweight, driftwood, flotsam in my wake.

Letting Victoria audition in second year hurt, too, because it dispelled the great myth of the school: that our learning was paramount. All throughout our time there, we were reminded of the importance of craft, of our duties as artists, of how success couldn't be measured by the industry, that the industry was fickle, shallow, a changeable beast, that only through creative exploration and rigorous learning could we triumph. These tenets were sacred, immovable. *Bullshit. Lies.* All it took was a little industry flirtation for these lofty principles to crumble. It made me sick, seeing Frida throw her ideals to the wind. We were never allowed to miss rehearsals, never. Funerals were the only exception. Yet here was Frida, allowing Victoria to walk out, to take the whole day for herself, even saying she could graduate without completing her final year if she wanted to. What did it matter? Sure, whatever, take the degree. Wipe your arse with it, in fact. No worries, no bother.

'Shannon?' Frida was clicking her fingers at me. 'Did you hear what I said?'

I blinked, returning to the room. 'I'm sorry.' I shook my head. 'I didn't catch that. I . . . I didn't get much sleep.'

Frida pursed her lips. 'Obi, please partner with Shannon. Perhaps *your* charms will be enough to keep her awake.'

VICTORIA WAS WAITING FOR us after school. She had an iced coffee in one hand and was smoking a roll-up with the other. She looked impossibly cool waiting there, leaning against the iron railings, one foot up off the ground, Ray-Bans balanced on the edge of her nose, hair tumbling over her shoulders, lit like flames in the fading afternoon light.

'Hey V, we're over here!' Jolly hollered.

She glanced over and gave us a tinkling wave.

'How did it go?' Obi yelled.

She shrugged and, holding the cup to her breast, gave an awkward thumbs up. Obi and Jolly jogged over. When I caught up with them, she was already mid-flow.

'There were five of them on the panel. I think two of them had flown in from New York this morning.'

'How were they?' Obi asked.

'Super nice. They just asked me to read the scene a few times, gave me a bit of direction, then asked me to wait. I had like an hour, so I looked around Carnaby Street and when I came back they had the guy in who they've cast as Robert Dudley.'

'Oh my God, I've seen rumours online. Go on, go on, tell us who,' Jolly said.

Victoria flashed us a coy smile. 'I'm not allowed to tell you.' She paused. 'But I will say he was a *really* good kisser.'

Jolly squealed. 'Oh my God, V, you're definitely going to get it. I can feel it in my waters.'

'Don't say that.' She shook her head. 'There were still two or three other girls there, so, you know, I shouldn't get my hopes up.'

'So what? You're *Victoria Parker-Tilley*. You're a star.'

Victoria smirked and nudged Jolly's shoulder. 'Shush now, stop it.' She stubbed out her cigarette. 'OK, OK, enough about me. How was your day?'

Jolly filled her in on what she'd missed, but there wasn't much. As we walked, I stared at the back of her neck, watching her nod and make little noises of interest, watching her pretend to listen, watching her pretend to care.

OUR SONNET ASSESSMENT WAS scheduled for Monday morning. It was our last of the term, of the year in fact. I was doing a vocal warm-up in the corner when Victoria walked in. Her eyes were red and sore, her mascara smudged. Jolly tried to give her a hug, but she shrugged him off. Obi stayed at the far end of the room. No one dared ask. We all already knew.

When Victoria got up to do her sonnet, I found myself willing her to fail. I was sick of watching her drift from assessment to assessment, from rehearsal to rehearsal, never really trying but nearly always succeeding, rolling in each morning late, hungover, still starry-eyed from some premiere or party, while some days I struggled to believe I even deserved a place at the school.

Victoria walked to centre stage. The room quieted. Casper gave her the nod, and she began.

'As an unperfect actor on the stage,
Who with his fear is put beside his part,
Or some fierce thing replete with too much rage,
Whose strength's abundance weakens his own heart,
So I, for fear of trust, forget to say
The perfect ceremony of love's rite,
And in mine own love's strength seem to decay
O'ercharged with burden of mine own love's might.'

And despite it all, she was still magnificent.

After, when we were packing up our stuff, Jolly, Obi and a few other classmates crowded around her. I overheard them say how good she was, that the HBO lot didn't know what they were missing, that she was destined for great things, that this was just a minor blip, that the next big thing would be along soon. She nodded and accepted their condolences, gradually perking up and agreeing with them.

I, meanwhile, went into the girls' bathroom, held my rucksack over my face, and screamed into the lining as hard as I could.

I screamed until my throat was raw—

—until I could taste the metallic tang of blood—

—until I let the violence out.

But then I heard footsteps in the corridor, someone's voice outside the door. 'Hello, is everything OK in there?'

I flushed the loo and ran the tap. When I emerged, I gave the concerned student waiting in the hallway a bland smile. I walked down the corridor, an automaton. I believe I may even have whistled.

TWENTY

I TRIED TO KEEP in touch with Victoria over the summer. I wanted to know what she was doing at all times, who she was meeting, her every action, her every thought. I wanted to climb inside her brain and unlock the glittering mysteries at the heart of her. But it was impossible. She flew to Cape Cod two days after term ended.

Sunday, 3rd July at 12:21

V

I'm so sorry, I'd love to hang out, but you know, it's like a family thing x

Instead, I made do with scrolling through picture after picture of her on Facebook.

Victoria with her arm around a tanned, shirtless youth on the beach at sunset.

Victoria and her nieces squeezed together on the deck of a yacht.

Her grinning face hovering above a foot-long lobster roll.

Playing cards with a group of effortlessly attractive young people I didn't recognize.

Her feet buried, a heart in the sand.

I always liked the pictures, always tried to leave a cute or witty comment for her to return to. Sometimes she responded. Sometimes not.

Then, after a few weeks, the landscape changed. She was in New York. The wholesome all-American pictures were replaced by grainy images of her stumbling out of bars, smoke curling around her face as she sat with friends in Central Park, hip popped in a trendy bathroom, tiled pink, a flash in the mirror, the ghost of her image repeated.

I tried writing to her. I told her about what I was up to, making efforts to embellish, to string out my dull summer into something altogether more enchanting. I described the fields around my home, the waving ears of corn, the rapeseed, its malodorous yellow carpeting the landscape. I told her about the people who populated the estate that wound up the hill, the rusty playground at the top and canisters of laughing gas that littered the ground. I took a picture of myself lying in the long grass. I imagined her seeing it, maybe at night. I imagined her thinking about me, missing me. I invented a summer romance, a boy I'd known in college, a boy who in reality had never looked at me twice. We made love, I told her, over and over and over again. It was wonderful, I said, but I couldn't be held down, my spirit was too restless; she knew, she understood, she was the same. I told her about my grandma, about the sadness I felt going through box after box of bric-a-brac, a life left behind. The porcelain dove with a chipped wing. The sun-bleached packet of courgette seeds. A receipt taped to a box of shoes, like new. Christmas cards, birthday cards, orders of service, kept for years in a wicker hamper beneath the bed. A necklace, the gem missing. Odd socks.

I described the moors above Grandma's house, trying to remind Victoria of the windswept morning we had spent there. I said she should come and visit me if she got the chance, that it would be great to have her here again. Or maybe if not this summer, at New Year's again, like she'd once promised. *Anyway*, I'd say, *stay in touch. I miss you*, I'd say. *I love you, always.*

She never replied – well, not properly. Occasionally she'd respond with a few scratchy lines to my prompts, but there were no insights, no confidences, nothing really but the uneven weight of my devotion. But then, out of the blue, two weeks before term started and long after I'd given up on a surprise visit like in Rome, an email arrived in my inbox.

To: Shannon Bell

Subject: An invitation

Hello darling, sorry for being an absolute horror at replying. Hope you've had a fabulous summer. Wondered if you wanted to finish it with a bang? I'm dying to see you. Come to Godwin.

TWENTY-ONE

I TOOK A TAXI from the station. Jolly and Obi were arriving the next day. Victoria assured me that it would be just the four of us, saying that despite her friendship with Stefano (they'd grown nauseatingly pally again since Rome), she wanted me to be able to fully relax without encountering the spectre of my ex-boyfriend around every corner. 'And the house can be a little scary at night, lots of dark corners and cubby holes. Wouldn't want him jumping out at you now, would we?'

I read out directions to the driver from the scribbled instructions Victoria had hastily relayed down the phone to me that morning. When I met him in the car park and told him we were heading for Godwin House, he glanced at my battered rucksack and stifled a smirk.

The building was hidden down a tree-lined track at least a mile or so from the prying eyes of civilization. As we approached, the house seemed to rear up out of the landscape: commanding, solid and frighteningly magnificent. My stomach dropped. *No*, I thought, as my eyes travelled the length of the imposing building and on to the acreage beyond. This was too much. Victoria had money, I knew that, but this, *this* was too much. As the car pulled onto the gravelled driveway, I suddenly felt sick, small and ugly. I didn't belong here. How had I ever thought I could belong here? All this time I'd been under the illusion that, although not quite equals, there'd been a healthy level of competition between

Victoria and me. But now, seeing Godwin, seeing the building that had borne her, I felt the cold blade of truth slice through me. There was no competition. There never had been. By birthright, she'd already won.

Victoria appeared beneath the stone portico. She was wearing a faded green rugby jersey and denim hotpants. Her feet were bare, and her hair hung loose around her shoulders. She clapped her hands and jumped up and down on the spot as I pulled myself out of the passenger seat.

'Darling,' she said, lassoing her skinny arms around my neck so I stumbled.

The driver handed me my bag, the straps worn thin, and I felt inside my pocket for some cash. But Victoria was quicker. 'Here you go,' she said, handing him a wad of tens. 'For the precious cargo.'

GODWIN HAD BEEN IN the family since the sixties, Victoria explained, as she drew me inside the cavernous entrance hall and up the wide stone staircase. That was when the original occupants went bankrupt, sold all their assets, and Victoria's grandfather swooped in, eager to establish his own dynasty and couch the family in old-world charm.

'But ever since Grandpapa died and Dad left, and then me and my brothers buggered off, well, it's just been Mummy here on her own.' Victoria ran her fingers over an ornate carriage clock, its hands at a standstill. 'Poor thing. She tries her best, but . . .' She trailed off. 'Anyway, here, let me show you to your room.'

I crept behind her, my footsteps echoing off the ceiling. She led me inside a warren of dark, wood-panelled corridors. 'The building's a bit of a hodgepodge, to be honest,' Victoria continued. 'There's still some of the original structure from the 1700s, but a lot was added in the nineteenth century.'

Victoria prattled on while I felt myself shrink smaller at every room we passed, each one grander than the last.

'That's Lawrence's room, I'll put Obi in there. That's Mummy's room – don't go in there, she gets mad if anyone goes in. There's a bathroom here, but there's another one off ours. It's a bit smaller but it's got everything you need. Jolly can go in there. That's the Maple room, the Sycamore, the Larch, and *this* is your room.' The door swung open. I nodded, trying to appear impassive at the quite simply breath-taking space before me. The ceiling was high; the room was broad and stately; four long windows cast soft rectangles of light across the carpet; the walls were flocked with delicately patterned sage-green wallpaper; and the squat queen bed, with plump matching sheets and chevroned panels of fabric ensconcing it, looked almost painfully inviting. 'I hope this will do,' she said, padding across the room. 'The east wing's pretty quiet, and I'm just next door in case you need anything.'

'Thank you,' I said in a small voice. 'Thank you,' I repeated more clearly. 'It's beautiful.'

Victoria shrugged. 'It's home, I suppose. Hey, check this out.' She unlatched what at first appeared to be a recessed wall panel, but was in fact a hidden door. 'I'm just through here.'

I followed her down another slim corridor, to the left of which was an incongruously dated 1970s peach and lime-green bathroom. Just beyond that was another room, a mirror image of my own but burnished in velvety shades of burgundy. 'Apparently the previous owners put Daphne du Maurier in here when she visited,' Victoria said. 'I certainly hope she slept better than I do.'

'You don't sleep well in here?'

'Not recently. Too dark. Too many shadows,' she said, gesturing towards the finger-like branches coming off the tree outside.

After finishing the tour, Victoria encouraged me to take a few moments to freshen up. 'Come meet me and Mummy in the glasshouse when you're done.'

I LAY ON THE bathroom floor, feeling the cool tiles against my skin. Although the day had been oppressively hot, its warmth didn't seem to reach inside the walls of the house. I shut my eyes and cursed my stupidity at ever having come here. How was I meant to approach third year with any sort of confidence now? How was I meant to show my face at drama school again knowing *this* was what I was up against? I let out a groan of frustration and got up. Victoria and her mother would be waiting for me. I splashed water on my face and used an expensive-smelling pat of soap to rub the dirt from my fingers. It was then that I noticed the door to Victoria's room was ajar. I dried my face and hands, and peered inside.

On seeing the room again, I was caught by the strange mix of crumbling nobility and turn-of-the-millennium teenager on display. Gilded aristocrats and muscled horses jostled for wall space beside nineties boybands torn from magazines. Above the bed was a signed poster: *The Sound of Music on tour in venues across the UK and Ireland*. I crept over to the dresser, which was crammed with perfume bottles, old theatre programmes, makeup and framed pictures of her brothers, her parents, a pony, the young Victoria wearing a dirndl with her hair in plaits, then later as a grinning adolescent with her arm around a ruddy-looking girl of a similar age. I brushed my fingers over the frames and opened an ivory jewellery box; a ballerina twirled on her spring to the tinkling chimes of Mozart. Inside there was a laurel brooch, ticket stubs, a bracelet woven with mother-of-pearl petals, and a pair of teardrop earrings inlaid with cornflower-blue opals. I picked the earrings out and held them to my face, where they shimmered like water against my cheek. They were so pretty; they were so *her*. I glanced over my shoulder at the room. *Victoria already has so much.* Without stopping to think, I slipped the earrings down inside the lip of my sock.

At the other end of the room were two walnut armoires. I creaked one open to find the aforementioned dirndl, a rack of winter coats, and the stench of mildew. I rummaged through them like a rat, feeling inside their pockets for treasures: receipts, tissues, buttons, a forgotten pack of gum. I went to the other wardrobe and ran my hands along the curtain of gowns that hung there. I lifted one out, a pale lavender slip dress, and pulled it over my head. To my surprise, it fitted beautifully, clinging to the curves of my body like it was my own. I turned to admire myself in the mirror.

'What are you doing?'

'V – I . . .'

Victoria was standing in the doorway. She narrowed her eyes at me. 'Are you trying on my clothes?'

I laughed nervously. 'Sorry. I couldn't help myself.'

She paused, no doubt weighing up how to use this information, whether to forgive or destroy me. But then her expression changed. She smirked and sauntered over. 'If you *really* want to play dress-up later then we can.' She brushed the silky fabric. 'So, do you like it?' she asked.

'Yes.' I felt the earrings slip further down inside my sock. 'It's lovely.'

'You can have it if you want. I never really liked wearing dresses, not this one anyway.' She pinched the material, and my skin beneath it. 'In fact, my brothers and I used to enjoy dressing up in one another's clothes and putting on silly little plays on the lawn. I'm surprised this one's not been stretched out by Lawrence. When they left home, I raided their wardrobes.' She tugged at the jersey she was wearing. 'Much more comfortable.'

'Me and my sister used to swap clothes too.'

'Oh yeah?'

Without warning, a lump appeared in my throat. I turned to face the mirror. I'd said too much.

'You never talk about her,' Victoria said. When I didn't respond, she prodded my side. 'Shan?'

'No.'

'Why not?'

'It's . . . hard.'

'Were you close?'

'In a way.' I paused, not knowing how much more I dared divulge. I could feel myself floating, drifting. The heat and the shock of Godwin had made me woozy. It had made me bold. 'Mum put bows in our hair. Lavender for her, like this,' I said, stroking the dress, 'and pink for me. We'd swap. It was like a game.'

'How marvellous.'

'Yes.' I allowed myself a small smile at the memory. 'It was fun.' I gazed at my reflection, at my friend standing beside me. 'My sister was more outgoing than me. She liked being the centre of attention. She liked performing for my parents.' I paused, dizzy with the thrill of reanimating her. 'She should've been the actress.'

Victoria put her head on my shoulder. 'I would've liked a sister, growing up,' she said, sighing. 'But I've told you that before.'

'Yes.'

Victoria lifted her head and took a step back. She reached out and touched the strap of the dress. 'Hmm. Yes, that colour suits you.' She glanced up and her gaze met mine. Her expression changed and something dangerous glinted in her eyes. Her hand slid down my arm; she left it there, waiting.

'I should get changed,' I said, half paralysed by her touch. 'We've left your mum alone too long.'

'Never mind her.'

'I'm sorry. She must think I'm so rude. I'll get changed.'

'Does this feel nice?' she asked, stroking my wrist, her voice no louder than a whisper.

I didn't answer, but I didn't pull away from her either.

'You've got goosebumps.' She came closer. 'How about this?' Her fingers continued their journey, snaking along my midriff before coming to rest on my hip. She pulled me towards her. I saw the gap in her smile, smelled mint on her breath, coffee, sleep.

She gazed at me. 'Well?'

I laughed uncertainly.

'You're so pretty. You know that, right, Shannon?'

'Th-thank you,' I stuttered.

'We'll have fun this weekend, yeah?'

'Yes,' I whispered, not daring to breathe.

She dropped her hand abruptly. 'Come on,' she said, turning her back on me. 'Mummy's dying to meet you.'

'AND NOW, NO ONE ever visits.'

'That's not true, Mummy.'

'It is. You'd much rather gad about in London than come and visit poor old me. You were gone all summer and the one before that.'

'What do you want me to say? I was in the States. I only get so much holiday. I can't spend all my spare time out here with you.'

'Nonsense.'

I sipped my iced tea and glanced up at the glasshouse's ceiling, at its rigid metal arbours, its thick tropical tree trunks and lush vines straining against the glass.

Victoria sat forward in her chair. 'You always do this. You always hold me to a higher standard than the boys. When were Lawrence or Rupert last here? Or Henry?'

Victoria's mum waved her hand. 'Psst, that's different. They have jobs, they have families. They can't be expected to drive all the way out here whenever I need them. But you, you pretend you're so busy every weekend. I mean, it's an acting degree, sweetheart. It's not like you're training to be a heart surgeon. When I was at RADA, I went home every weekend to visit your grandmother.'

'I'm not doing this,' Victoria sat back; the wicker chair creaked beneath her weight. 'I'm not going around in circles with you again.' She shot me a look.

'The iced tea is delicious, Mrs Parker,' I interjected.

'Thank you, dear. And you can just call me Helena.'

'Well, Helena, it's delicious. And the whole house, the gardens, they're beautiful.'

'Mmm.' She looked off to one side. Her face took on a glazed expression and she picked up a magazine.

'Mummy,' Victoria hissed, 'you're being rude.'

Helena let out an exasperated sigh and dropped the magazine on the table. 'I suppose I can't even read in my own home now, can I?'

'Not while we have company you can't,' Victoria said, gesturing in my direction.

I shrank down in my seat and fixed my attention on the burbling stone fountain at the structure's centre.

'Fine, we'll *chat.*' Helena's gaze fell on me; she picked up an old Sunday supplement and began fanning herself with it. 'Oh, darling,' she said, addressing Victoria. 'I forgot to mention. That awful girl was here.'

'Which girl?'

'Oh, you know, the dumpy one, brown hair, bad skin. Came around here lots. You used to go riding with her sometimes.'

'Do you mean Cora?'

'That's it. When you were on your run this morning, she came to the front door. Apparently, she'd heard from someone that you were back from London. She was desperate to see you.'

Victoria repressed a shudder. 'And what did you tell her?'

'I said, "I don't know what you've heard, sweetheart, but Victoria's in America all summer."'

'Good. Thank you, Mummy.'

'Who's Cora?' I asked.

'Oh, no one,' Victoria said, with a small wave of her hand.

'She was Victoria's little *friend*, wasn't she, darling?' Helena said, sitting forward and warming to the subject. 'She came from the village. Bit of a *farm girl*. Followed you around like a puppy until you went off to boarding school, if I remember correctly.'

'We don't need to talk about her,' Victoria murmured, an unexpected redness creeping into her cheeks.

'She used to hang around the grounds just trying to catch a glimpse of her,' Helena continued.

'We should go for a walk later,' Victoria said, angling herself towards me. 'There's a wood not far from here which is gorgeous at this time of year.'

'Cora was *in love* with Victoria.'

'Mummy,' Victoria said, exasperated.

'What? She was! Not right in the head, that girl. She was obsessed with you. Always coming around here and trying to inveigle herself into family occasions.'

'I invited her to those family occasions, if you remember.'

'Still, she was a queer one. Couldn't handle it when you went off to school. She still visits every now and again, just to see if you're around. And the mother too. Pair of odd bods, the two of them, if you ask me.'

AFTER A SUPPER OF cold cuts and salad on the veranda – *if you'd prefer something else just tell the kitchen; they can whip up anything you like* – Victoria suggested a walk around the grounds.

'Sorry about Mummy,' Victoria said, tying her hair in a messy bun. 'She's not used to people.'

'She's . . . interesting.'

'That's one word for it,' Victoria scoffed. She unlatched the spiked metal gate that led into Godwin Wood. 'She's a failed actress, a failed businesswoman, a failed mother.' She slipped her arm through mine. 'I only meant to visit for her birthday, but then she just sort of *sucks you in* and it's hard to leave, and then of course the boys never visit and I feel bad for her, and then Dad's stopped ringing and this whole place is falling to pieces on her watch and she can't seem to hold on to staff, and – sorry, I'm ranting.'

'You're fine.'

'But seriously, thank you for coming. It's a nightmare being here on my own.'

'I'm happy to be here.'

'And I wasn't joking earlier. You *can* have that dress, you know. If you really want it.'

I shrugged. 'Lavender's not really my colour.'

'Shut up. You looked gorgeous in it. Take it, please, I insist.'

'OK, well, thank you then.'

We walked in companiable silence for a few moments, the soft brush crunching beneath our feet; birds swooping low for their final feast; the last embers of daylight peeping through the trees.

'I enjoyed your emails, by the way,' she said. 'Sorry I didn't reply much.'

'That's OK.'

'You know what it's like, lots of family running around and parties and beach days. And then New York was just *completely* insane.'

'I understand.'

There was a pause.

'So . . . you're seeing someone.'

'What? No,' I answered, surprised.

'Oh?' She sounded oddly sheepish. 'I thought you said you were seeing some guy over the summer, someone from your old sixth form?'

'Yes, that's right,' I said, stumbling over the lie. 'Of course, yeah, I *was* seeing him, but it was just like a short-term thing.'

'Is he the first guy you've dated since Stefano?'

'Yes.' I walked slightly ahead of her and searched for a way to change the subject. 'This place is beautiful, V. I can't believe all this is on your doorstep.'

'You know, you never did tell me what happened there.'

'Some of these trees must be thousands of years old.'

'Shannon.'

'And the wildlife.'

She caught up with me. 'Come on, please tell me.'

'About what?'

'Tell me about Stefano. I mean, one minute you hate him, the next you're in *fucking Rome* together, and then you go and break up with him. When I said goodbye to you, things were fine. Tell me what happened, what *really* happened.'

'There's not much to say,' I replied, inwardly seething at how conveniently she'd forgotten her part in what had happened that summer.

'Oh come on, I've seen you. All this year, it's like you could barely stand to be in the same room with him.'

'We've been cordial.'

'You've been fucking awkward, is what you've been.'

'Fine. I'm – I'm sorry. I've tried not to be. I've tried not to let him – me – affect you guys.'

'Hey, it's fine,' she said, nudging my arm. 'I'm not having a go at you. I'm just curious, that's all. What happened?'

I hated the way she posed the question, with such perplexed innocence, as if her overbearing presence hadn't been the catalyst for what eventually happened that night. 'He's your friend,' I managed finally. 'I shouldn't say anything.'

'You're *more* my friend though. Come on,' she said, her head on one side. 'What happened?'

Suddenly it was all too much for me. The long day, the heat, Victoria's incessant probing. 'No,' I snapped, pushing past her, the mask slipping. 'I don't want to talk about it.'

'Shannon—'

I stormed ahead.

'What the fuck?' She ran to catch up with me. 'Shannon, are you OK?' She grabbed my arm, bringing me to a standstill. 'I'm sorry if I've said something to upset you. I honestly didn't mean to.'

'It's fine, it's fine,' I said, feeling the corners of my vision darken.

'You can tell me if you want to, you know.' Her voice sounded far away. 'I'll try to understand.'

I gazed at the waving canopy above me.

'Did something happen? Was it that night – that night in Rome?'

I could feel my mind peeling in two—

'Shannon, what happened?'

—the glass descending—

'Talk to me.'

—boxing me in—

'What happened?'

'Stefano's . . . not who you think he is.'

I met Victoria's eyes, watched her expression change as the truth sank in.

'Oh . . .' She trailed off, looking like she might cry. 'OK, sweetie. I think I get it.'

TWENTY-TWO

THE BOYS ARRIVED AT breakfast; we were at the pool by noon. When Victoria said we were going swimming I'd expected a tiled, chlorinated affair, but it wasn't like that at all. The pool was a mossy rectangle with lichen-covered slabs around the perimeter and stone naiads stationed at each corner. There was a thin time-rusted ladder at one end and a shell grotto at the other. Obi and Jolly bobbed in the water while Victoria reclined in the long grass. I sat next to her, hunched over the battered copy of *Jane Eyre* I'd brought with me that weekend.

'Read to me,' Victoria demanded, applying sun cream to the freckly skin of her arms.

'No. I'm too embarrassed.'

'Go on, read to me.' She lay on her front, her chin nestled in the crook of her elbow. 'I like the sound of your voice.'

'You do?'

'Yes, I like your accent, it soothes me.'

'I'll have to restart the chapter.'

'Oh, don't bother with all that. Just read from wherever you are. I wish to be *lulled*.'

'Fine.' I rolled my eyes and cleared my throat theatrically. '*"Because," he said, "I sometimes have a queer feeling with regard to you – especially when you are near me, as now."*'

'Who's speaking?' she asked, lifting her chin.

'Rochester.'

'Who's that?'

'Jane's lover.'

'Grumpy fellow?'

'Yes – sort of.'

'OK, carry on.'

'*It is as if I had a string somewhere under my left ribs, tightly and inextricably knotted to a similar string situated in the corresponding quarter of your little frame.*' I glanced sideways at her. A bead of sweat trickled down her forehead and into her hair. Beneath her brother's smudged Ray-Bans, her eyelids fluttered. '*And if that boisterous Channel, and two hundred miles or so of land come broad between us, I am afraid that cord of communion will be snapt; and then I've a nervous notion I should take to bleeding inwardly.*' I heard a gentle snuffling sound. She rolled onto her side, dozing. '*As for you,—you'd forget me.*'

'Are you two lazy cunts getting in or what?' Jolly yelled, startling us both.

'We will eventually,' Victoria said, with a dismissive wave of her hand.

'Come on. We want to play chicken,' Obi added.

'Who's going on whose shoulders?' Jolly asked. 'I'm not having anyone's thighs around my neck.'

'It's all right, Jol,' I said, placing the book in the grass. 'You can sit on mine.'

'You're not tall enough.'

'I'm five seven, I'll have you know.'

'Fine. But hurry up. My hands are getting all pruney.'

I pushed my sunglasses up my nose and a dragonfly whizzed past me. I watched it dart backwards and forwards, skating across the surface of the pool. But then Obi swam down, trying to grab at Jolly's ankles, and the insect darted away. I lay down beside Victoria, the hairs of my arm touching hers, and stared at the sky, an endless, perfect blue.

Just then, I heard a voice. Not Helena's – who'd gone to bed with a migraine – but a man's. Obi and Jolly craned their necks to see who it was. I sat up and turned around.

'*Ciao amici*,' Stefano called out, barrelling down the hill. 'You miss me?' he asked, removing his T-shirt and shorts.

I nudged Victoria. She remained still.

'V, what the f—?

'Watch out,' Stefano yelled, cutting me off. He sprinted past us and jumped in the water, soaking the four of us. Victoria squealed and, jerking upright, reached for her towel.

'Good to see you,' Obi said as Stefano surfaced for air.

'We weren't expecting you,' Jolly said, swimming over to him and trying to catch my eye.

'Hi Steffy,' Victoria said, dabbing at her hair. 'There are beers in the cooler if you want them.'

'What's he doing here?' I whispered.

'No idea,' she replied, lying flat again. 'The more the merrier though, eh?'

'Hello Shannon,' Stefano said sheepishly, wiping water from his eyes.

'Hello,' I replied, my heart hammering inside my chest.

Stefano ducked his head under the water again and swam to the far end of the pool.

'I thought it would just be us,' I said, lowering my voice. 'You promised it would just be us, V.'

Victoria rolled her head away from me and released a languid sigh. 'I guess Obi invited him.'

I looked at the pool, where Stefano had Obi in a headlock and was trying to push him underwater, then back at Victoria, her face serene beneath the sun's glare. She must have felt me staring at her, because after a moment she got up and tottered over to the pool's edge. I scrambled to my feet and followed her.

'Is it cold?' she asked, her arms crossed around her middle.

'It's fine,' Obi replied.

I went and stood beside her, my body trembling.

'Yeah, come on in,' Jolly added.

Stefano grinned and splashed the edge so that we both reared back.

'I'm scared,' she said.

'You'll be fine,' Obi said. 'Just jump.'

I stared at the murky pool, at our reflections dancing on the surface. The water rippled and sparkled beneath us, distorting our bodies into one greenish monstrosity. But then the right side of me seemed to grow larger; I felt a hand on my shoulder.

Suddenly I was beneath the water, thrashing and twisting, algae wrapping like tentacles around my hands and feet. I could feel myself being pulled under, deeper, drowning. I panicked, reaching for the light and, with a gasp, emerged from the water. My eyes stung. I wiped a lick of slime from my face. I could hear laughter and applause coming from the boys.

'That's one way to do it!' Stefano yelled.

I spun around to find Victoria towering over me, laughing. She caught my eye and, smiling triumphantly, took a bow.

'SHANNON? SHANNON? ARE YOU OK?'

I blinked, slowly. Jolly stood before me. He waved his hand in front of my face.

'*Hellooo?* Anyone there?'

I was sitting on the stone veranda. I'd been out there for an hour. My legs and hands were stiff. The gardens and grounds spread out before me. I was dressed for dinner. Victoria had insisted I wear the lavender gown. She was upstairs getting ready.

My hair was still damp from the pool.

'Hello,' I said evenly.

Jolly sank down into the green-and-burgundy striped deckchair beside me. In my periphery I could see he was wearing a dinner jacket and a white shirt, open at the collar.

'You look nice,' I said.

'Oh, so you *can* see me then,' he said. He picked at his top button. 'It's Henry's. V fished it out of his wardrobe.' He pulled a dickie bow from his pocket and began fiddling with the fastening. 'These people – can you believe we actually have to *dress* for dinner, and in this heat?'

'Hmm.'

'I mean, don't get me wrong, I love the theatricality of it all, but I'm sweating my balls off here.'

'Yes.'

'Also' – he lowered his voice and glanced back at the house – 'I'm completely out of my depth here. I mean, I knew V had money, but *this*' – he gestured at the landscape – 'I feel like I'm in fucking *Brideshead Revisited*, you know? And her mum . . . yikes. I mean, you know me, I can get along with anyone, but the ice queen in there – I don't know, it's like suddenly I don't know how to behave. I guess meeting Helena does explain a lot though.'

'Hmm.'

'And also, what's with our *Italian visitor*? Did you know he was coming? I'm pretty sure V said it would be just us.'

'I didn't know.'

'Are you OK with it?'

'With what?'

'With him.'

'I'm fine.'

'OK.' Jolly paused and ran a hand through his hair. 'And look, well, I'm sorry for laughing earlier, when V pushed you. It was a nasty trick . . .'

I gave a small shrug.

'Shannon?'

I remained still.

'Are you OK?' Jolly asked, leaning forwards.

'I'm fine,' I said, continuing to stare ahead.

'Are you sure? Because you're acting kind of weird.'

A fly landed on my arm, then flew away.

'You can tell me, you know, if something's upset you or if you want to talk. Is it the pool thing? Because again, like, I'm really sorry.'

I narrowed my eyes. 'I'm fine.'

'What's wrong?'

I stared silently at a white tree, thunder-struck and parched in the distance.

'OK.' Jolly cleared his throat and spoke carefully, as if to a madwoman. 'What's going on, Shan?'

He placed a hand on my knee. I looked down at it, then up at him. I opened my mouth, trying to form the words with my tongue, to sound them out with my dry, sunburnt lips. 'I . . . have these moments when I feel like . . . it's like I'm behind glass or underwater. Things feel far away. They don't quite feel like they're real.'

Jolly frowned. 'And does this happen often?'

I shook my head.

'Because it kind of sounds like you're disassociating.'

'Sometimes it feels like I'm someone else . . .'

'My cousin used to disassociate.'

His voice moved further away.

'Sometimes it feels like I'm no one at all . . .'

'You know, there are therapies which can help—'

Like he was in an echo chamber.

'And it's like I'm disappearing—'

'My cousin was given antidepressants as well—'

Like he was a voice in my head.

'And I don't know who I am—'

'She got help.'

Like he was underwater.

'And time moves slowly—'

'With help, she was able to manage it.'

Drowning.

I closed my eyes.

'Shannon?' All of a sudden, Jolly was crouched in front of me, grasping both my forearms and shaking me. 'Look at me.'

I did. The glass shimmered.

'Thank you for telling me,' he said. 'You're OK. I'm here. This is real. It's Saturday, a warm summer's evening. You can smell honeysuckle and jasmine. You can hear birds. You can see trees.'

I stared at him, Jolly, my friend, and gradually the glass began to melt.

He gave my arm a light pinch. 'You can feel me touching you, yes?'

I blinked and nodded my head. I scrunched up my face. I flexed my fingers, pumping blood into them; bringing myself back to life.

TWENTY-THREE

VICTORIA WAS SEATED AT the head of the table. She was wearing a black velvet Bardot dress. Her hair was piled in curls on her head. In the gloom of the dining room, her skin looked pale and vampiric. A hunk of cold veal sat shrivelled and untouched in front of her. She drummed the table with her fingers and surveyed the four of us, the light from the candelabra smouldering in her eyes.

'I can't wait to be a third-year,' Jolly said. 'Remember how impressive we used to think they were when we first joined the school?'

'Yeah, they seemed so much older than us,' Obi added.

'Also, everyone knows Frida goes easier on third-years,' Jolly said. 'Imagine, we might actually get treated like human beings.'

'Don't get your hopes up, man,' Stefano said, laughing.

Victoria sighed.

'You all right there, V?' Obi asked.

She gave a small shrug and looked off to one side. I noticed her leg jiggling beneath the white tablecloth.

'Thanks for dinner, V,' I said, lining up my knife and fork. 'I mean, thank you to the kitchen. It was delicious.'

'Hear, hear,' Jolly added, raising his glass.

'Yes, delicious,' Obi said. 'By the way, have any of you started writing to agents yet?'

'Ugh, don't,' Jolly said, groaning and putting his head in his hands. 'I can't think about all that yet. Did you see Malcolm's email? They want us to start thinking of showcase scenes already.'

'Still,' Obi said, 'it's good to be prepared.'

Victoria sighed again, louder this time.

'V?' Obi said.

'What?'

'You OK?'

'Well, frankly, no.' She reached for the bottle and sloshed a large helping of Barolo into her glass. '*Frankly*, I'm bored out of my brain. You lot have talked about nothing but school for the last hour, while here I was thinking I invited you all here this weekend to have *fun*.'

'You're right.' Stefano banged the table with his fist. 'Let's get this party going.'

Obi held up his hands in surrender. 'OK, OK, fair enough. What do you want to do?'

Victoria took a hearty swig of her drink. She narrowed her eyes and thought for a moment, before grinning at each of us in turn. 'We should all fuck.'

Stefano snorted so wine came out of his nose. Obi smiled politely. I sank back in my chair and Jolly rolled his eyes. 'Ah, finally,' he said. 'She gives us the *real* reason we're here.'

'What?' Victoria said, twirling a loose lock of hair. 'Is that so preposterous? We're young, we're fit. Why not? Shannon, you're up for it, right?'

I smiled weakly and dabbed the corners of my mouth with a napkin. 'Sure, whatever.' I had an uneasy feeling. It was Rome, happening all over again. As Victoria's guests we were at her beck and call, merry players at court, duty-bound to dance whatever jig she demanded of us.

Obviously not having learned his lesson the first time, Stefano loudly proclaimed, 'Count me in.'

'I think she's joking, mate,' Obi said.

'Why do you think that?' Victoria said, resting her chin on her hands and staring at him.

'V,' Jolly cut in, 'don't you think we should maybe wait until your mum is off the premises before we host an orgy?'

'Why? She'd be up for it.'

Stefano tipped his head back and laughed.

'See, *Stefano*'s fun. Why can't you all be more fun like him?'

I peered at Victoria, trying to work out her game, what we were doing here and, after our walk in the woods, why she'd invited Stefano to play along.

She glanced over and caught my eye. Her pupils were so dilated that, in the half-light, her eyes looked black as two coals. I saw her beaded purse, discarded by the door, the slight tremor in her jaw, and knew then that she'd taken something.

'Has everyone got through the reading list for next term?' Obi said.

'Stop trying to change the subject,' Victoria said, brandishing a butter knife at him. 'I didn't invite you here so you could be a boring prude all weekend.'

Obi chewed the inside of his cheek and stared at the portrait above the mantelpiece, a fox pursued by the hunt.

'I got the *Actors' Yearbook* second-hand,' Jolly said. 'It's out of date, but it's probably got all the same information as this year's edition. Obi, you can borrow it if you want.'

'Thanks, mate,' he murmured.

'No, no, no! Stop being boring!' Victoria said petulantly, bashing the knife against her plate. 'I demand that you all stop being boring. It's my house, my rules. Stefano, you go first. Last shag?'

I stared at my plate. My vision darkened.

'Erm, probably like a month ago, this petite girl, real eager to please, a first-year.'

'Which first-year?' Victoria asked, her eyes widening in delight.

'Don't answer that, Stef,' Obi said, a flash of warning in his voice.

'Of course I won't, I'm a gentleman,' Stefano said, holding his hands up and swallowing back a belch. 'But I will say she had *fantastic* breasts, like two ripe beef tomatoes.'

'Beef tomatoes?' Jolly said, pulling a face. 'Jesus Christ. Right, that's it. I am *officially* changing the subject. The riots the other week. Go.'

'My mum wouldn't let me go into central London,' Obi said. 'We just sat there watching it on the news.'

'It's mad what people were doing.'

'Who was your last shag, Jolly?' Victoria asked.

Jolly carried on as if he hadn't heard her. 'I know a guy who stole four boxes of trainers from a Foot Locker on Oxford Street. Perfectly normal guy. I would never have guessed he had it in him.'

Victoria leaned across the table, her breasts skimming the veal platter, until she drew level with his face. 'WHO WAS YOUR LAST SHAG, JACOB MCANDREW?'

Jolly closed his eyes and, gathering his last reserves of patience, answered drily, 'Terrence. As you well know, Victoria.'

'See, that wasn't so difficult now, was it?' She sat back in her chair. Her gaze roamed across Stefano's face before falling on mine. 'And what about you, Shannon? Who was your last shag?'

'I . . .'

'Maybe we should all get some air,' Obi said, loosening his collar.

'Yeah, I'm boiling,' I added quickly.

'Or in fact no, this will be way, way, *waaay* more interesting,' Victoria said, slapping the table with both hands. 'Obi, who was *your* last shag?'

No one said anything.

'V . . .'

'Come on,' she said. 'Tell the group.'

'I'm not going to answer that, V.'

'Who?'

'No.'

'Who?'

'No.'

'WHO?'

'Fuck this,' Obi said, knocking the table and startling us as he stood up. 'I'm going outside.'

We watched him leave in silence.

Jolly gave Victoria a look. 'What the hell is wrong with you?'

'What?' she said. 'What did I say? So the guy can't take a joke. Why is that my problem exactly?'

Jolly turned his gaze on Stefano. 'Was this you?' he asked. 'Did you give her something? What's she taken?'

Stefano held up his hands. 'Hey, man—'

'Is that why you're here? As some sort of mule?'

'This is *my house*, Jolly. You don't get to talk to *my guests* like that.'

'What's she taken?' he repeated, glowering at Stefano.

'I've not *taken* anything!' Victoria yelled, scraping her chair back and standing up. 'And it would be none of your fucking business if I had anyway.' She looked at Stefano, who was staring down into his lap. 'Well, aren't you going to say anything?'

He didn't look up.

'Whatever.' She scoffed. 'You people? You bore me. I don't know why I even bother with you when I actually have *interesting* people in my life who I could be spending my time with. Interesting and *important* people.' She left the room, slamming the door; I flinched. We heard her voice from the corridor: 'Enjoy your fucking stay.'

TWENTY-FOUR

'VICTORIA.' I LEANED MY head against the wood and knocked softly, my breath warming the keyhole. 'V, can you let me in?'

'Go away,' came her muffled reply.

It was 1 a.m. Without Victoria, the party was over. The house was silent; the boys had retreated to their beds. I should've done the same, especially after all she'd put me through that day, but still, some pitiful part of me longed to protect her.

'Please. It's just me. The boys are in their rooms.' I waited, my back slumped against the door. 'Come on, V.'

I heard the floorboards creak and then footsteps. The door opened a fraction, and Victoria's face appeared in the crack above me. 'Just go to bed, Shannon.'

I jammed my arm inside the gap and stood. 'No, let me in.'

'Leave me alone. I've made enough of a fool of myself today,' she said, walking away from me and collapsing face first onto the bed.

I crept inside the room and sat down as lightly as I could beside her. The hem of her dress had ridden up, revealing her underwear. I carefully replaced the fabric.

'V. Talk to me.'

She groaned into her pillow.

'Come on. What was all that about?'

'Everyone hates me.'

'No, they don't.'

'You hate me.'

'I don't.'

'Really?'

'No, I could never—'

'Do you love me?'

'V—'

'Do you?'

'Yes. You know I do.'

She turned her head and peered up at me. Her eyes were black and tear-stained. Her hair, wild and unkempt.

'Sometimes I don't think anyone loves me. Sometimes I think people only want to be around me because of what they think they can get from me.'

I shushed her. 'That's not true. Not for me, at least.'

She gave me a watery smile and sniffed. 'Shannon' – the smile faded – 'I know I'm fucked up right now, but there's something I should tell you, something I should've said a long time ago.'

'Oh.'

'But it – it's hard for me to talk about . . .'

'Well, you don't need to say anything right now,' I said half-heartedly, laying a hand on the small of her back. I paused and waited for her to continue, desperate for her to reveal her secrets to me. But she remained silent. I gave her a tiny nudge. 'I mean – if you want to try though, I'm a good listener . . .'

'I don't want you to think any differently of me,' she whimpered, 'to think any less of me.'

I balled her into my arms. 'I could *never* think any less of you.'

'You're kind.' She took a deep shushing breath in, then out. 'OK.' But then her body tightened and she wriggled free from my grasp. 'Did you say Obi had gone to bed?'

'Err, yes . . .'

Her shoulders slumped. 'He really *does* hate me.'

'He doesn't.'

'He should.'

'Don't be silly.'

'You're not . . . attracted to him, are you?'

'No!' I shot back. 'Why – why would you even ask that?'

'No reason,' she muttered. 'Does he know you're here?'

'No, but V, what did you want to tell me?' I asked, trying to steer her back to her previous admission.

'I don't trust him.'

'Come on, what are you talking about?'

'They're just pretending. Everyone's just pretending to be my friend. But not you. You wouldn't do that. You don't think like that. You're a good person, a good person, Shannon. Everyone uses me. Obi uses me. Stefano, Jolly. Everyone wants a piece of me, but no one wants to help clear up the mess.'

I could see I wasn't about to get anything concrete out of her tonight. She was in a frantic state, babbling and paranoid. I pulled her into my arms again and stroked her hair, trying to calm her racing heart. But she wriggled free again and, kneeling, gripped the straps of my dress. 'You've never been with a girl before, have you?'

'N-no,' I stuttered, taken aback by this sudden swerve in conversation.

'I have,' she said, her eyes wide and unblinking. 'I've done it loads of times. Me and Cora, we used to come up here when the house was empty, when Mummy was away and we were teenagers. I know exactly what to do.' She slipped her hand between my legs.

I gasped and seized her wrist to stop her going any further. 'V – I – are you sure you want to—'

With a mad glint in her eyes, she clambered on top of me. I froze, unsure what was happening, what I was meant to do or if I should stop her.

'I don't want to take advantage of you,' I offered feebly.

She threw her head back and laughed as if the idea was completely absurd. 'Oh sweetie, you could never.'

'But it kind of seems like you've—'

'I've not taken anything,' she said sharply. But then her expression softened. 'Come on.' She leaned over me; her hair tickled my shoulders; I smelled wine on her breath. 'This *is* what you want, isn't it?' she said, worming her fingers inside my underwear.

'Y-yes,' I said.

'So let's just have fun, yeah?'

I looked at her face, searching it for traces of mockery, for evidence that this was all some terrible joke at my expense. Noting my hesitation, she kissed me, gently at first, then with more urgency. That's when I finally gave in, sinking against the pillows, utterly powerless to resist her.

She pulled away for a moment and I took the opportunity to stroke her cheek, her forehead, to check this was real, to check *she* was real. She smiled, showing a row of purple-stained teeth. Her fingers slid inside me.

'V—' I grabbed her neck and pulled her towards me, my body melting beneath her touch. 'I've wanted this, I've wanted this so much—'

She kissed me, a way of shutting me up. I didn't mind. I kissed her back, desperate to consume her, swallow her, make her a part of me. My hands felt their way down the hard ridges of her spine, the soft canvas of her skin, towards her thighs, grabbing fistfuls of her arse, finally, after all this time, allowed to touch her freely. She pulled me tighter and I felt her fingers coax within me, pulsing and insistent.

She released her hand and wiped it on the sheets. She sat back and pulled my underwear all the way past my feet. 'Did Stefano ever go down on you?'

I shook my head.

'And your summer boy?' she asked, raising one eyebrow.

'There – there was no summer boy.'

'Yeah,' she said with a sly smile. 'I figured.' She tossed the flimsy black material onto the floor. 'Lie still,' she whispered, spreading my knees apart.

TWENTY-FIVE

Sunday, 28th August at 11:05

Shannon Bell

On the train now. Thank you for an incredible weekend ;) xx

Sunday, 28th August at 11:09

Shannon Bell

Keep thinking about last night . . . xx

Sunday, 28th August at 11:21

Shannon Bell

Probably a good idea we didn't say anything at breakfast haha xx

Sunday, 28th August at 15:34

Shannon Bell

Back home. Let me know if you want to talk about last night and how we handle things xx

Tuesday, 30th August at 10:01

Shannon Bell

Hey, been a few days now since we've spoken. How are you? xx

Wednesday, 31st August at 13:06

Shannon Bell

Are you going to be in London before term starts? Let me know if you want to grab a coffee and talk xx

Saturday, 3rd September at 10:55

Shannon Bell

Is everything ok? Not heard from you in a while . . . xx

Saturday, 3rd September at 22:13

Shannon Bell

Do you want to talk about last week? No worries if not xx

Sunday, 4th September at 11:32

Shannon Bell

V? xx

TWENTY-SIX

I WAS SITTING ON the tube when I saw it. I was on my way back from a dreary four-hour matinee at the Royal Court Jolly had booked us tickets for, before ditching me to spend time with Terrence. I picked up the discarded *Evening Standard* on the seat beside me and peeled the damp pages apart.

> *Rising star Victoria Parker-Tilley on the arm of director Dexter King, seen emerging from Annabel's in Mayfair.*

With her free hand she was ruching her gown from the gutter. Although her forehead was dipped she was staring down the lens of the camera, almost challenging the viewer to look away. The man beside her, meanwhile, had been captured in a tableau of love-struck awe, his eyes fixed on the beautiful young woman who clung to his side.

I felt my innards crunch in on themselves.

Of course.

Suddenly it all made sense.

At the train station the next morning, Victoria had been convivial but distant. When Jolly and I arrived back in London, I tried not to let slip anything about what had happened that night, careful to nurture mine and Victoria's secret until the moment was right to reveal all. But then there was the silence of the past week; the fact she hadn't responded to any of my texts or emails.

It was never you she wanted.

Victoria had found someone else.

With trembling fingers, I tore the picture from the newspaper and stuffed it inside my bra. When I got home, I flattened the wrinkled photo across my desk and stared at it, her, the two of them. I opened my laptop and typed in his name.

Dexter Mungo King is an English-Dutch actor, model and director. King was born in Camden Town, London, the second son of acclaimed British film director Jeremy King and actress Priscilla MacLean (née Van De Stadt). King was educated at Tower House School and Westminster School before reading English at Cambridge University. At the age of 22, King undertook classical actor training at the Royal Academy of Dramatic Arts . . .

I clicked the link to an article.

I ask King whether he always wanted to direct, to which he laughs and replies, 'I know people won't believe me, but I honestly never even thought about it. Being a director, you have a lot more power than as an actor. And, I don't know.' At this point King blushes. 'I guess I didn't really have the confidence to say, "I've got ideas too, you know?"' King takes a sip of his builder's tea and thinks for a moment. 'But I'm lucky I can talk to my dad about these things.' I ask King whether his father's influence has helped him in his career. 'Not at all,' he replies. 'I didn't receive any help when I was entering the industry as a director, or from my mum when I was focusing on acting.' (King's mother is celebrated actress Priscilla MacLean.) He continues, 'In fact, I think my parents would've preferred it if I'd chosen a "real job", you know? Something steady. I should've been a plumber.' He laughs again, and I notice several female heads turn from the tables surrounding us. King certainly is a young man who commands a lot of attention. He continues, 'I've worked just as hard as any guy off the street to get to where I am today. Directing is tough. And I know that just as much as anyone else.'

When Jolly returned that evening, I appeared in the kitchen and, trying to appear nonchalant, asked him what he knew. He sniffed and said he had no idea she was seeing anyone, that he hadn't spoken to Victoria since Godwin. I asked him whether this Dexter guy and her were in a relationship, how long they'd been together, if Obi knew about the two of them. Jolly got annoyed at me then.

'I'm not her personal secretary, Shannon. If she chooses not to tell me things then there's not much I can do about that.'

Later, he apologized for snapping at me. He said that he and Terrence had had a difficult month and he wasn't sure if things would last much longer between them. I gave him a hug, which he accepted with lukewarm enthusiasm before returning to Victoria.

'Who knows if she'll even turn up on Monday. If she really is banging Dexter King, she probably needn't bother.'

VICTORIA DID TURN UP, and she'd cut her hair. The new style was confident and coquettish, a short bob that curled up and around her sharp cheekbones. On our first morning back, I slunk over to her and the group she was speaking with, desperate to tease out whether she was willing to acknowledge what had happened between us. But when I tried to catch her eye, she tossed me a fleeting *Hiya* and carried on her conversation.

Humiliated, I returned to the other end of the room and continued my warm-up, alone.

Victoria's new hairstyle, coupled with the gossip flying around about her love life, seemed to put a wall around her. She wasn't just *Victoria* any more; she wasn't our classmate, plodding along with the same worries as the rest of us: *Does Frida like me? Will I pass? Will I get an agent?* Victoria had an aura about her. She was different now, an untouchable.

I noticed other people treating her differently too. The teachers gave her a wide berth. The new first-years lowered their eyes when they passed her in the corridor. I saw Poppy sidle up to her at lunch and ask if her boyfriend or anyone from her agency was coming to see our third-year shows.

Victoria shrugged and nibbled on a stick of celery. 'Maybe. We'll see.'

Victoria dipped in and out of school those first weeks back. She was always on the phone, always in demand. We got used to her mobile going off in rehearsals, the low buzz coming from her leather satchel, and then her apologetic whisper as she crept from the room. 'I'm so sorry, I have to get this, it's my *agent*.'

Frida and the other tutors didn't seem to mind the disturbance. When Frida took the register each morning, she barely looked up at the silence that followed Victoria's name.

Things had changed. We'd splintered. It was obvious that after the events of Godwin, Victoria was avoiding me, but she wasn't speaking with Obi any more either. Stefano was always off with his new girlfriend, a moon-faced second-year whose coy smile transformed into a scowl whenever she saw me, and Jolly was spending an increasing amount of time outside the school gates bickering down the phone with Terrence. But Victoria's growing absence wasn't entirely to blame. School was different. Third year had altered the oxygen in the room. Every day the tutors reminded us that the clock was ticking, that the industry was waiting, that you only get one chance to make a good first impression, that it was every man or woman for themselves.

ONE LUNCHTIME, A FEW weeks into our first term of third year, I spied Victoria eating alone in the cafeteria.

In the last few days, she'd begun to acknowledge me a little more. We never spoke about what had happened between us at Godwin – I sensed she'd never allow it, that she was in complete denial about the events of that night – but as long as I continued to behave like her pathetic little friend, her dutiful shadow, she seemed willing to let me near her again. Besides, I had something I needed to ask her.

The question had been eating away at me for weeks. The year already felt like it was slipping through my fingers, and I was desperate to find out what I could do to improve my chances after graduation. That term, we had regular classes on writing to agents, speaking to casting directors and improving our audition technique, but Victoria would often snort and roll her eyes in these sessions. At those moments, everyone in the class looked to her. After all, what did the teachers know? They'd been stuck inside the school for the last twenty years. Some of them hadn't performed since the seventies. Victoria was out there *now*, she was in the field. If she thought a piece of advice was passé, we tended to believe her.

She sighed and skewered a forkful of salad into her mouth. 'OK, so, like I don't really know what you can do to improve *per se*' – she wiped an escaped bead of ranch sauce from the corner of her mouth – 'but there's something you ought to know. Something they won't teach you here.' She looked at me as if to ask, *are you sure you want me to continue?*

I nodded.

'OK, so there's this thing called the graduate glow. Agents and casting directors deny it exists, but it's totally real.'

I frowned. 'Graduate glow?'

'Yeah, so, like, when you graduate, you have this glow. You're like a newborn actor baby, you're pure, fresh, kind of like a virgin, and agents and casting directors, they *love* that. They all want to be the one to discover the next big thing. They all want to find that rough, untouched diamond.' She leaned in close and lowered her voice. 'The thing is, people say there's a ladder, but it's a myth. There is no ladder. If you don't make it in your first year, before the new crop of graduates comes out, all glowing and new and covered in amniotic goodness, then you're fucked. You've either got that glow' – she shrugged – 'or you're nothing.'

I tore off a piece of baguette and put it in my mouth. I focused on the act of chewing, imagining my teeth like a machine grinding the bread down into a pulp.

Victoria picked at her salad. 'I mean, you have to feel sorry sometimes for all the people in our year who aren't going to get agents.' She sighed and scraped her fork along the plate. 'Like, they've gone through the whole three years here, they think they're hot shit, they've learned all this stuff' – she shook her head and smiled dreamily – 'but in reality, they've got no chance.'

Sometimes she'd do that, chat away like she'd forgotten who I was and all that we'd shared. Or maybe she knew exactly what she was doing. Maybe she was twisting the knife on purpose. *You don't have an agent, Shannon. You don't have connections or interest or glow. You're no diamond.*

TWENTY-SEVEN

THE FIRST TERM OF third year was drawing to a close. As we careened wildly from rehearsal room to rehearsal room, the year shut down around us. Crunchy brown leaves dashed along pavements outside the school. Skeletal trees de-robed and, exhausted, surrendered to their final act. Fading seams of daylight pierced the plate-glass windows. Small clusters of students gathered on the wide granite steps, bundled up in jackets and scarves, talk of Christmas, home and family on their lips. But things weren't over for us yet.

One Monday morning, Frida and Malcolm summoned us for a meeting about showcase. Attendance was compulsory, except for Victoria, who'd landed herself a job playing a Cockney shop assistant in a BBC3 comedy pilot. She had two lines: *Pint of milk, is it?* and *I should charge you extra for that*. It wasn't exactly a star vehicle – she'd only miss a day of school for filming – but I still felt sick with jealousy.

'Quiet, please,' Frida said, clapping her hands. 'Leave your coats and bags, and find a space on the floor.'

Malcolm and Frida waited on plastic chairs, notebooks open on their laps while we gathered in front of them.

'I want to begin by saying well done to everyone on your performances last week. You'll receive your individual feedback by this Friday.'

Blood Wedding was the first of our final-year public productions. I'd played the Neighbour during the brief five-night run, not a huge part.

But as Malcolm liked to parrot: '*There are no small parts, only small actors.*'

Frida continued, 'If you haven't done so already, please remember to thank any industry guests who attended. Stefano, I believe you had someone from West Management see the play, didn't you?'

He nodded. 'I've sent them an email.'

'Very good,' Frida replied. 'Malcolm, have you anything to add about last week's performance before we begin?'

Malcolm, startled, looked up. 'Erm, no, no, not really. Erm, it was very good, yes, very good.'

I glanced sideways at Jolly, who rolled his eyes. Waiting for our cues backstage, we'd spied Malcolm happily snoring away in the second row.

'Brilliant play, yes, Lorca, an excellent piece of work.' Malcolm began shuffling through his notes. 'I do feel I should remind you all, though, not to pin your hopes on getting signed merely from the public productions.'

'Yes, and that's what we're here to talk about today: showcase.'

'Yes,' Malcolm continued, 'Showcase is the, err, important one, the big beast, as it were. Of course your public productions matter, but, well, it's showcase that will have the biggest impact on your careers. I was catching up with an old friend of mine, Clarence Briggs, err, from Briggs & Taylor Management, old friend, yes, we did rep together in – when was it? – seventy-eight, I think, wonderful man, quite the wit. Anyway, we were having a drink last week and he, well, we got to talking about showcase, erm, and he said, he said of the public productions' – Malcolm chuckled to himself – 'well, he said he doesn't really bother with them.'

We all sat up a little straighter.

'No, they don't matter so much to agents now, you see. They'd much rather attend a showcase than, err, now, how did he put it? Ah yes, he said, err, he said, "Who wants to sit through a four-hour slog of *Richard III* just to discover one piddly new grad?" So yes, it is, err, showcase where, as it were, the *real* work happens,'

Frida took over. 'Your showcase will take place next term at the Fortune Theatre. You will each have four minutes and twenty-eight seconds of stage time, made up of individual monologues and short scenes.'

Archie raised his hand. 'Who will be there?'

'Everyone, hopefully. The school will invite as many casting directors and agents as we can. You will, however, also be expected to email and write to your own industry guests. We find this two-pronged approach encourages more people to come.' Frida replaced the lid of her pen. 'Each guest will be given a booklet with your headshots and contact details inside. If someone likes what they see, they can get in touch.'

Jolly raised his hand. 'And what if they don't like what they see?'

Frida pursed her lips and glanced sideways at Malcolm, who answered for her. 'Well, err, then let's say you might *struggle* in that first year out.'

I felt the backs of those around me stiffen.

'I've seen, err, seen agents walk into theatre lobbies, flip through a few pages of the showcase booklet and leave.' Malcolm tittered. 'It's a tough business, but if, err, a graduate actor is going to get signed at all, it's probably going to be at showcase. That's just the way it is.'

Frida and Malcolm brought the meeting to a close. We had a five-minute break before our next session (dance prep for next term's production of *As You Like It*). Usually in our breaks, people were boisterous and giddy, chatting and joking around with one another. Not today, though.

Four minutes and twenty-eight seconds to make it count.

I found a corner, lay down and shut my eyes. I thought about

Victoria, on set, hobnobbing with the other actors, making connections. If all this was a race, why did she get to start so close to the finish line? After a minute, I felt someone join me.

'You know, usually if you lie on the floor you're meant to be stretching, not sleeping.' It was Obi.

I kept my eyes shut. 'Animal studies,' I said by way of response. 'I'm being a slug.'

Obi laughed. I felt him inch closer until his arm touched mine. I felt a shiver go through me at the light pressure of his skin, the thin membrane of contact between us. But then an image of Victoria flashed behind my eyes – her forehead buried between my legs – and I felt a twinge of guilt laced with longing.

I moved my arm away.

'Have you thought about what you'll do for showcase yet?' Obi murmured.

'No. I don't want to think about it.'

'Yeah. I know what you mean.' His voice was a comforting well. I could feel it humming through the floorboards, buzzing in my shoulder blades. 'Frida and Malcolm said we should start, though.'

'I know.'

'You scared too?' he asked.

'Terrified.' Behind my lids, the bright lights of the rehearsal room undulated and spread. 'I don't want to think about what comes next.'

'No.'

I'd written to every agent and casting director I could think of, but hadn't received a single reply. As each day ticked by, the realities of the industry loomed ever darker. *You're no diamond*. Soon I'd be belched out onto the streets along with a couple of hundred other promising young graduates. I'd need to find work, to make my degree count for something, to prove all the people who thought me too plain, too forgettable, wrong. *Face disappears.*

I laughed half-heartedly, a pathetic sound. 'I don't know anyone out there. What if no one wants me?'

'They'll want you.'

'But what if they don't?'

Obi didn't respond.

I felt tears gather in my eyes. I rolled my head away so he wouldn't see.

'I was thinking,' Obi began, 'I mean, I don't know, it's up to you, but maybe we could do one of our *Macbeth* scenes?'

'For showcase?'

'Yeah. I thought it went pretty well.' He paused. 'Your performance, Shan – it was magic.'

Lights gathered in the darkness, black skies rearranged themselves into stars, fireworks. *Magic.*

'Maybe.'

'I mean . . .' He paused. 'What's stopping us?'

I wiped the dampness from my lashes and rolled my head towards him. Obi was staring at me, his grey eyes shining. He reached a hand out and brushed my fingertips. The breath caught in my throat.

What's stopping us?

Victoria appeared in my mind's eye again, but this time I pushed her away.

TWENTY-EIGHT

WE DIDN'T TELL ANYONE.

We lived in snatched moments. Our first kiss: brief, lovely, alone in a music practice space in the basement later that day. A feeling of . . . safety. Hands held beneath rolls of costume. Charged looks across the rehearsal room. We had a week until term ended, a week and a half until I was going back up North for Christmas. Looking back, it was short, painfully short.

We took our *Macbeth* scene to Malcolm on Tuesday. He approved it straight away. He said it was a strong choice and one that would show off our casting well. He suggested cutting a few lines to fit the showcase timings and that we should still find a short monologue each, just a paragraph or so of something modern to contrast.

'Shannon, you should look for something northern.'

'Northern – like what?'

'Oh, you know, something working class; the miners' strike, *I can't afford an abortion, they've cut my benefits*, something like that.'

'And what should I look for?'

'Obi, look for something *urban*.'

'. . . Right.'

Victoria had no idea what was going on. We never discussed it, but we both knew she mustn't find out. Despite this, she was suddenly everywhere and seemingly desperate to involve herself in my life again. She had a spare plus-one to a movie premiere, could I join her? She needed to go over some lines, could I help her? She had to choose a dress for the press night of Dexter's mum's new play, could I come over?

I finally agreed to go Christmas shopping with her a week before I was due back up North. I was meant to be having lunch with Obi that day, but I was running out of ways to say no to her. There wasn't much point in me being there. I was skint and had already bought my parents ten-quid gift sets from Boots. I told Victoria this, to which she shrugged and said: 'But darling, you've got such good taste. I need your discerning eye.'

We went to Oxford Street. I walked behind her, panting and trying to keep up as she weaved between slow-moving shoppers. Victoria had an apparently endless list of people to buy for, each requiring something exquisite and one-of-a-kind.

Victoria was spritzing herself with Chanel N°5 in Selfridges when she came out with the real reason I was there.

'I had an audition last week – an important one – and I've got a recall.'

'Oh,' I said, 'good for you.'

'Yes, and I need your help.'

She continued walking, leading me past tubes, pastes and creams promising soft, enduring immortality; elegant gold compacts that snapped shut like clam shells; starched and stanchioned shop assistants; and powders, a billion shades of beige. She turned towards the escalator and hopped on. I followed behind her but hesitated, suddenly afraid of the stairs' sharp, ever-disgorging teeth.

'Hurry up, I've got *loads* to get and not much time. I've got to be at Dexter's by six.'

I stepped on and we rose up past a row of mirrors. Victoria's reflection continued, 'Anyway, it's a new RSC adaptation of *Jane Eyre* and I'm up for Jane.'

I gripped the black belt to steady myself. The store was suddenly too hot, too busy. Warm air blasted down on us. My skin prickled with moisture. I pulled my scarf off, but the feeling of constriction, of sticky wool, clung to my neck. How had this happened? Jane was *my* character. *Me*.

Victoria carried on. 'And at the initial audition, they told me that my accent could use a bit of work, and obviously you're from around there, like up North and stuff, and so I thought you could help.'

'Right,' I said. My voice sounded slow; my tongue felt thick and useless in my mouth.

We reached the top. Ahead of us lay stand after stand of elegant ornaments: impractical, dainty, expensive. Victoria drifted between the displays, lightly grazing her fingers over each item as she passed. I held my coat close to my sides, fearful that I might break something, fearful that I might break.

'And, well, it's not just the accent.' She picked up a crystal flower girl. 'Do you like this?'

'It's fine.'

She placed it back down again. The girl stood askew. She continued, 'The thing is . . .' She threw her head back and sighed, looking faintly embarrassed. 'I know that I'm like *middle class* – upper-middle class or whatever, I don't even know any more. Class is such an outdated concept, don't you think?' she said, glancing over her shoulder.

I said nothing. I didn't know my line.

'But whatever I am, Jane *probably* isn't the same class as me.'

I remained mute, like the flower girl, frozen beneath Victoria's careless touch.

'And so, I thought maybe you could help me get into the mindset of like not having had as much growing up.' Victoria clasped a hand over her mouth and spun around. 'Oh God, *no*, that came out all wrong. Ugh, I'm so sorry, Shannon, I didn't mean it to sound like that.'

'I had plenty growing up,' I said evenly, trying not to betray the nausea curdling in my stomach.

'No, absolutely, *of course* you did, I didn't mean it like that, of course, like I know you weren't *poor*,' she said, whispering the word as if it were catching. 'Obviously both your parents worked, and like you had holidays and food and toys and stuff.' She laughed, a high-pitched needling sound. 'I just meant that' – she tilted her head to one side – 'I just meant that we're from slightly different worlds, right?'

I shrugged. Although I was swaddled in my winter coat, a jumper, jeans and two pairs of socks, I felt exposed, naked beneath my carefully chosen layers.

'So will you help me?' she said, gripping my gloved hands between hers. 'I *need* you, Shannon. This part, well, it's a *big deal* for me.'

I could feel the pressure of her fingers tightening around my own. I could see myself nodding, hear myself saying yes to her demands, over and over and over again.

'Thank you,' she said. Her face broke out into a smile. 'Thank you, thank you, thank you. You know you mean so much to me, Shannon, don't you?'

'You too.'

Victoria gave my hand a quick squeeze and began moving through the stands again. She started telling me about the play she was seeing that evening. 'It's a new piece. A farce, I think. Dex's mum plays this peasant woman who rises through the ranks to become queen. They've been having some problems with the set, though. The revolve keeps malfunctioning.' She stopped before a shelf of jewellery boxes. She reached for a jade leather one. 'This would be perfect for my niece. I wonder if I can get it monogrammed?' She tucked it beneath her arm and, without even glancing at the price, headed for the till.

TWENTY-NINE

On the night before I went back to Yorkshire, Victoria arrived at my front door.

'Happy pre-Christmas!' she said, thrusting a gift bag of corner-shop chocolates and wine at me. 'I thought we could go over some *Jane Eyre* stuff before you head home.'

'V,' I said, barely hiding my alarm as she bundled herself inside.

I was meant to have the house to myself that evening. Jolly and our other housemates had left that morning, and Obi would be arriving soon. I'd shaved my legs. I'd shaved everything.

'Have you got any clean glasses?' she called from the kitchen.

'Yeah, sure, just a second,' I replied, frantically trying to bring up Obi's last message on my phone and abort our date.

But it was too late. The doorbell went just as Victoria was scratching the sticky orange label from the bottle of Blossom Hill.

'Expecting company, Ms Bell?' she asked slyly, her eyebrow raised.

'No – maybe – wait,' I said, scampering down the hallway. 'Let me just see who it is.'

I opened the door. Obi leaned in to kiss me, but I backed away. 'She's here,' I hissed.

'Who's here?' he whispered playfully, trying to peer over my shoulder.

'Victoria.' His face fell. 'She just turned up. You need to go. I'll say you left a package for next door or something.'

'Wait, what? I've been on the train for an hour, Shannon. I'm not just going to leave.'

'Please, I don't want a whole scene, or for her to find out about us, or for you to—'

'Shannon—' Victoria said, appearing round the door. 'Oh.' She stared at Obi. 'This *is* a surprise. I didn't know you two had plans.'

'It's fine, we don't *really*,' I said, tittering nervously. 'We were just going to go over our showcase scene before I head up North. Isn't that right, Obi?'

He nodded slowly, his expression unreadable.

'Oh, well . . .' She trailed off. 'I didn't know.'

No one said anything

'Shannon's helping me prepare for an audition,' Victoria continued, addressing the night sky above Obi's head. She slouched her weight onto her hip. 'I won't need her for long, if you're willing to wait a short while.'

'How long will you be?' he replied evenly.

I glanced down and noticed a prettily wrapped present in the Tesco carrier bag at his feet. I said a silent prayer to myself that Victoria hadn't seen it.

'An hour, maybe.' She slid her arm around my waist. 'No more than two.'

Obi's eyes flicked from Victoria's to mine, then back again. 'No, you're OK. Don't worry.' He gave me a tight smile. 'I suppose we'll catch up again in the New Year, yeah Shan?'

I nodded, trying to appear casual while also telepathically conveying my immense gratitude towards him. 'Yeah. Of course. We've got loads of time until showcase.'

'Sorry you came all this way,' Victoria said airily, reaching for the door handle and bringing the conversation to a close. 'Have a safe journey back, Obi. Oh, and merry Christmas, I guess.'

*

WE STAYED UP UNTIL midnight unpicking the threads of my accent – *butter, cut, slut* – and going over the novel's themes. Victoria had barely touched the thing and seemed vague on major plot points. When I suggested it might be a good idea for her to actually read the book and glean her own interpretation, she reminded me she was dyslexic. After nearly three years spent chasing her shadow, this was news to me.

Once she'd gone, I collapsed on the sofa, exhausted.

I could feel it: a change, a gradual poisoning of my feelings towards her. When had it begun – Rome? Godwin? Or perhaps it was since Obi and I had started seeing one another. Maybe it was the warmth of his affection, shining a harsh light on the few crumbs of endearment she'd ever deigned to throw me. Of course, I still dreamed about her – her soft snuffling snores as she slept against my chest, her smooth, coltish legs twined with mine. Of course, I still pushed thoughts of her from my brain when I was alone with Obi. But now, finally, I could also see a way out, to a life without Victoria, without her lies, without her bullshit, free from her lazy, unending pretending.

And so it was a relief to leave London the next day, even though the pall of death still hung over my parents. Mum had taken to weeping and saying my grandmother's – and occasionally my sister's – name as she loaded the dishwasher, and at other quiet domestic moments when she thought no one would notice. Dad mostly kept to himself, and if he heard Mum coming, he found a task that needed doing. *The tap needs fixing. That bloody light bulb's gone again.* He said he had plans to turn my bedroom into a gym. I wasn't bothered. I knew it would be a nice project for him, one where he could easily lose himself tinkering, shut away from the unpredictable strains of my mother's grief.

That Christmas, I volunteered to help get Grandma's house fixed up. Mum and Dad wanted it on the market by spring, but there was still lots to do. Damp had ripped through the wallpaper in the back bedroom, and the bathroom was a mess of black mould. The kitchen surfaces were sticky with mouse urine, and green spores wreathed the windowsills. In the days leading up to Christmas, I asked Dad to drop me off before he drove to work. It was exhausting, but I soon found I was able to get quite a bit done. I did a room at a time, first clearing and vacuuming the floor, then bleaching the walls and surfaces. Anything I couldn't fix I made a note of, listing materials we might need to make the house new again, reborn, a blank slate for some wholesome starter-family or retirees looking for a downsizer to make their mark on.

Those days in the house were quiet, the only sounds the creaking floorboards and plaintive winter winds howling down the chimney. Often, I'd simply stop what I was doing and stare out of the window, watching my breath fog up the moorland beyond the glass. Sometimes, in those moments, a chill would run through me and I'd suddenly feel like I was being watched, like there was another version of myself, a perfect imitation from moments before, creeping silently from room to room. But the feeling wouldn't last. If I ever became too scared of the hushed spectre in the hallway, I simply twisted the dial on the paint-splattered radio until my fears were banished by noise.

At 6 p.m., I'd hear Dad's car trundling up the lane and run downstairs to fetch my things. In the evenings, we'd sit with trays on our laps in front of the TV. Eating my toad in the hole with the curtains drawn, the tree lights twinkling and the pipes belching warm liquid around the house, I'd pretend, for a moment, that I was a teenager again, that the last three years had never happened, that I was still the same person I'd once been, that my brain wasn't saturated with Frida's pointed praise and devastating criticisms, with Stefano's heat and violence, with Jolly's whooping laughter, our stir-fries and hangovers, with Obi's closeness, his distance, his smile, his fingers stroking the length of my arm; and with Victoria, my dazzling friend Victoria – her eyes, her face, her body, her lips, her tongue, her laugh, her words. Her cruel, unflinching words.

ON BOXING DAY, MUM took the tree down. She said she was sick of pretending to feel merry and bright and she'd be just fine, thank you very much, if she never had to see another effing twinkly star or glittery angel for the rest of her days. Then she burst into tears, sobbing against the arm of the sofa. I didn't know what to say. Neither did Dad. He sighed and rocked on his feet before slowly opening the door and retreating upstairs. I sat in the armchair opposite and picked at the skin around my fingernails until Mum's sobs softened to a whimper. Then, in silence, we set about removing each tin ornament, placing each glass cherub within its nest of tissue paper, unhooking each threadbare limb and bending the rods of unruly green wire back into the box until next year.

We spent the next week, the liminal period between Christmas and January, in a stupor of food and misery, sitting silently in front of the telly, not wanting to speak and upset the saw-toothed quiet my mother had cloaked herself in.

On New Year's Eve, I returned to the moor.

THIRTY

THE ROOMS WERE COMING along. Slowly the layers of decay were being stripped away, peeling back their dirt-encrusted skin to reveal walls and walls of blank possibilities, of a thousand fresh starts. When I entered the house, the air was sharp with ammonia. The smell made my eyes water. But it was good. I felt cleansed by the newly whitened walls, the promise of something different on the horizon, something better.

But there was still one room I avoided, one room I hadn't dared enter. I knew it was silly, that it was two years since Victoria and Obi had slept in there, but the memory refused to dissipate.

I couldn't sleep.

Don't worry.

Come here.

I shook the words away and tried to remind myself that, despite the fact Victoria had very pointedly not chosen me, Obi had. It was me who he rang every evening when he got home from the front-of-house job he'd taken over Christmas at the Theatre Royal Drury Lane; me who he told about his day, babysitting his cousins, drafting showcase invites, playing video games with his brothers; me who he told about his two-bus journey to work and the puffed-up audience members he encountered during the interval, swarming around his tray and barking orders at him for six-pound tubs of ice cream.

'You know some of them pay thousands to sit in the stalls, them and their entire families, and for what? Like two and a half hours of theatre. It's mad.'

'If you were rich though, wouldn't you do the same?'

Obi thought for a moment. The line crackled. 'You know, I don't think I would. I mean, I love theatre and everything, but there are so many things in life I want to do, so many other things I'd rather spend my money on, you know?'

'Yes,' I agreed. 'You can get just as good a view from the gods.'

'Or from onstage,' Obi said. 'Hopefully one day.'

'Yes. One day.'

I enjoyed those conversations; they stole the chill from my nights alone, curled up in bed. But I still couldn't erase the images of Obi and Victoria painted behind my eyes. Surely after her I could only ever be a consolation prize, the wooden spoon on awards day.

Obi and I hadn't slept together yet. There hadn't been time. Victoria had made sure of that. There was one evening when I thought maybe it might happen, but when I started to unbuckle his belt, he put his hands on my shoulders and gently steered me off his lap.

'Slow down, that was a big meal we just ate.'

'I know, but—'

'Have you ever played *Vice City*?'

'Huh?'

'*Grand Theft Auto*.'

'The one where you run over prostitutes?'

'Yeah, but it's more than that. Look.' Obi got up and retrieved the controller from under his bed. 'It's a classic. You're going to love this.'

And later that evening.

'Woah, woah, what's your hurry?'

'I'm not in a hurry – I just like you.'

'I like you too.'

'But you don't want to—?'

'Look, you know what, it's late. Maybe you should think about getting home. There's a night bus that goes from right past here. Mum will box you up some curry.'

I stood outside the room they'd slept in, the room they'd fucked in. I touched the handle and shut my eyes. I'd heard scratching coming from there which I could no longer ignore. Whether it was mice, rats or the pacing figure of Victoria, I needed to be rid of them, ghosts or no ghosts.

I pushed open the door. There were cobwebs in the corners, a layer of dust coating the duvet, a rusted exercise bike, and some mouldering linens shoved under the eaves. The room was just a room. But for the trail of droppings leading under the bed, I was completely alone.

I tied my hair up and crouched down on my hands and knees. I pulled back the frilly valance and peered under the bed. The floor was spotted with tufts of loft insulation and ribbons of newspaper. *Mice.* I stood up and heaved the bed away from the wall. But as I did, I noticed something: writing on the wall.

I squatted between the bedhead and the wall panel to see the felt-tip markings of a child snaking up the plaster.

Wen I grow up I wont to be an actress. I will hav long herr and ware prity dresis and I will stand on the stayj and peepil will clap and frow flowers at me. I will hav lots of muney and everywon will love me very much.

Below, there was a stick figure with curly hair rolling down to her ankles. She was holding a triangular bouquet of flowers. A Mr Happy smile escaped from the pen lines of her face.

I stared at the panel. I had no memory of drawing it. A lump swelled in my throat. What optimism that little girl must have felt. I wanted to unpeel the image, the words, the boundless smile, from the wall and press them like a tattoo against my chest.

Just then I heard a loud bang from downstairs. I stood up, nearly hitting my head against the slanting pitch of the ceiling. I waited, rooted to the spot. Silence, then more banging, and voices, unmistakable voices.

I ran from the room and – trying to avoid the spiked teeth where a new carpet had yet to be installed – thundered down the stairs. I threw open the front door.

'No Bolly this time, I'm afraid,' Victoria said. 'Just us.'

Frustratingly, she looked lovely. Her hair was damp from the cold and her eyes had a smudged, faraway look to them. She pulled me into her arms and air-kissed my cheeks. 'Hello, darling.'

Jolly bounded up the path behind her. 'God, you couldn't have waited two seconds for me, V?' He stepped inside the hallway. 'Roll on 2012, baby! Happy New Year, Shan. Oh no, wait, are we even allowed to say that yet?'

'Not until midnight,' Victoria replied, her cold cheek still pressed against my own.

'Shit, is it bad luck or something?' Jolly asked. 'Have I cursed you with seven years' bad sex?'

'You've haven't cursed Shannon,' she replied. 'You might've damned yourself though.'

'Like I'm not already damned.'

'Just shut up for a minute and come here,' I said, pulling him into the hug. 'What the hell are you both doing here? You should've called ahead.' I meant to sound chastising but couldn't contain my bewildered glee.

'Call ahead?' Victoria pouted. 'When have I *ever* called ahead?'

'I could've got stuff in,' I gabbled, leading them through the house. 'There's loads of food at home, the cupboards are empty here. I can call my dad. Or we can go into town. Oh, but I guess the shops won't be open now, will they? Wait, don't touch the walls. New paint.'

'Chill, Shan. V's got half of Fortnum's in the boot,' Jolly said, rolling his eyes.

'Really?'

'My brother and his wife never know what to get me,' Victoria said, heading into the living room and collapsing onto a plastic-covered armchair. 'So every year: a fucking hamper.'

'Fortnum's?' I said. 'V, no, that's too generous.'

She shrugged. 'I'm on a diet for the role.'

'She wants to be an impoverished waif,' Jolly trilled.

'Really?'

Victoria patted the flat line of her stomach. 'Trust me, Shan, you'll be doing me a favour.'

'I hope you've actually looked inside it,' Jolly said, retrieving a half-drunk bottle of zinfandel from his bag. 'It better not be just *damson chutneys*. I'm starving.' He unscrewed the cap and took a swig. He caught my eye. 'Don't worry, there's more booze in the car.'

Jolly and I went outside. He unlocked the boot. 'She's been insufferable,' he whispered.

'Who, V?'

'Who else? She's not stopped going on about *Dexter* and meeting this person and this person and, oh God, the *Jane Eyre* stuff.' Jolly shook his head. 'I didn't even think she cared about doing theatre. But now she's all like, "Of course, you can't really call yourself a proper actor until you've worked at the RSC." I've no idea how she's getting seen for Jane. She's not right for it *at all*.'

'I don't know, she might be good,' I said unconvincingly.

'Have you heard her accent, Shan? She sounds like an extra in *Kes*, and a piss-poor one at that. It's embarrassing.'

It was true. Her accent was appalling. I'd half-heartedly tried to help, but it was a lost cause. In the end, I let her staccato consonants and pancake-flat vowels slide. I don't know, maybe a small part of me saw it as revenge, payback for the part that should've been mine. Let her make a fool of herself. I wasn't her accent coach and I certainly wasn't her girlfriend. Victoria wasn't my problem.

Jolly hefted the wicker hamper from the boot and I grabbed the opposite handle. 'God, what's in this thing?' he said. 'It's like we're in fucking *Wind in the Willows* or something.' We carried it to the door. 'Anyway, don't mention I said anything,' Jolly whispered. 'I mean, she's a conceited ass, but she's *our* conceited ass.'

'I won't.'

Once the hamper and Londis's finest were inside, I laid an old tablecloth across the bare floorboards of the sitting room and retrieved the white pillar candles Mum had bought from IKEA for when people came to view the house. I lit them in a circle and we arranged our spoils in the centre, our mad picnic for the end of the world. Wine, KP nuts, pork scratchings and Frazzles sat alongside foie gras, oat biscuits, plum jelly and Florentines.

How we feasted that night, talking, laughing and drinking as our gestures cast strange poppets on the walls. I found myself wondering what someone on the outside of this gathering might think, some stranger lost roaming the moor, what they would see if they stumbled across my grandmother's house with its bare curtain poles and misted windows, its flickering candles and ear-splitting cackles.

As the night wore on, the lukewarm chardonnay sloshing around my insides began to feel like the rising waters of a sinking ship. I stuffed handfuls of crackers, crisps and rectangles of cake into my mouth in an effort to soak up the backwash, but I could feel myself losing touch with the scene in front of me, could feel my body pulling further and further away from the others, the guy ropes that tethered my mind and spirit straining at the elastic.

Minutes passed. Or hours.

The clock on the mantelpiece chimed midnight. *Happy 2012, darlings.* Our shadows lengthened, and the year passed on.

I closed my eyes and saw flames burned onto my retinas. I opened them slowly and, through the haze, watched Victoria and Jolly across the circle.

'*Always watching, always watching*,' Victoria sang. 'What are you watching for, little Shannon Bell?'

I smiled in a distant sort of way and Victoria laughed.

Jolly lifted his head. 'Are you behind the glass, Shannon?'

I nodded, registering his concern.

'What does that mean?' Victoria asked, glancing between us. 'What glass?'

'She has these moments . . .' Jolly looked at me for permission to continue. I nodded again. 'She has these moments when she feels trapped, likes she's behind glass, like she's watching things happen but she's not really there.'

Victoria frowned at the explanation. 'I don't understand. You never told me that, Shannon.'

Jolly sipped his wine. 'Never mind.'

'No, no, explain it to me. I want to know.'

'You wouldn't get it. She wouldn't get it, would she, Shan?'

I didn't know how to answer. Jolly's speech, his movements, had taken on a peculiar slowness. I was struggling to piece together the conversation happening in front of me. I looked down at my hands, at the long pale fingers of a stranger that flexed on my command.

'Of course I'd get it, just tell me.'

Jolly shook his head. 'Have you ever felt stuck inside yourself?'

'Stuck how?'

'Like trapped – trapped within your body, within your head, within your existence, so trapped that it hurts you.'

'I'm not following.'

'Like you're in a cage.'

'Wait, what – an actual cage?'

'Never mind. You wouldn't get it.'

'No, come on. Go back to the hurt thing – I've been hurt before, I know pain.'

'Fine.' Jolly held up his hands. 'You've been hurt. You know pain. I shouldn't have said anything.'

There was a pause. Victoria narrowed her eyes at him. 'What is this, Jolly?'

'What? Nothing. Let's talk about something else.'

'If you've got something to say to me, then just say it.'

'I haven't got anything to say.'

Victoria chewed her lip. 'Is this because my agent didn't want to sign you?'

Jolly laughed. 'We were talking about Shannon and now you're bringing up your agent?'

'Tell me the truth, Jolly.'

'You're insane.'

'Am I? Because I feel like the whole journey here you've had some bee in your bonnet, and now you're trying to drag poor Shannon into it.'

'I'm not dragging Shannon into anything, I was just checking she was OK.'

'I knew I shouldn't have introduced you to my agent, I knew it would make you go all weird.'

'Would you please shut up about your fucking agent?'

'Don't swear at me, Jolly.'

'Fine, sorry. But can we not talk about your agent?'

'You're going to get rejected occasionally, Jolly. That's just the way things are. It's not the end of the world. There's no need to turn on me for it.'

'V, just drop it.'

'The three of us are about to enter like *the* hardest industry, Jol. We need to stick together. Rejection affects us all.'

Jolly scoffed. 'And what would you know about rejection?'

'Erm, I actually know quite a lot. I didn't get the *Elizabeth* job, if you remember, and then a bunch of others. You think that was easy for me?'

'Fine, yes. But come on, V. It's not like you're going to be short of golden opportunities, are you?'

'What's that supposed to mean?'

'Nothing. Never mind.'

'Why are you being so spiteful, Jolly? I would never say these things to you.'

'I'm not being spiteful, I'm just being honest. You're going to have a much easier ride in this industry than everyone else.'

'How?'

'Well, for one thing, you're not going to be typecast all the time.'

'I won't be typecast?' She laughed, incredulous. 'Of course I will. I'm going to be playing public-school girls and coked-up Sloanes for the rest of my days.'

'Yes, *but* alongside that you'll play queens, warriors, heroines, and – and' – Jolly threw his hands in the air – 'fucking Brontës!'

'She's not playing a Brontë,' I managed to interject. 'She's playing a *Brontë character.*'

'Whatever,' Jolly said, waving me away. 'The point is—'

'What is the point, Jolly?' Victoria interrupted, clasping her hands together. 'Please, please, *please* tell me the point!'

'I will if you actually let me finish,' Jolly said, a vein pulsing in his temple. 'The point is that you can be whoever you want.'

'Well yes, of course, Jolly, I'm a fucking actress, of course I can be whoever I want, that's the point, that's *acting.*'

'No, you're not listening. *You* can be whoever you want.'

Victoria screwed up her forehead 'What are you talking about?'

'What I said.'

'I don't understand.'

'You think *I* can?' Jolly asked.

'What? You're not making any sense.' She looked at me. 'Is he making any sense?'

'You think *I* can play whoever I want?' Jolly repeated.

'What?' Victoria swigged from the bottle. 'Of course you can.'

'No, V, darling, *darling* V.' Jolly shook his head. 'I'm always, *always* going to be cast as *the gay guy.*'

'That's ridiculous,' Victoria said, swiping her short shock of hair behind her ears.

'It's true. They're never going to let me play *the leader* or *the politician*, or the *boring-ass straight love interest*. I'm always going to be *the gay guy.*'

'But why would you even want to play the boring-ass straight love interest?'

'Because I'm an actor and I want to fucking act.'

'You will!'

'No, I won't!'

'You will!'

'You're not listening, V. I'm *always* going to be cast as the gay guy.'

'Come on, Jol, you don't honestly believe that, do you?' Victoria said, shifting onto her knees. 'You've trained at one of the best drama schools in the country. You're going to have casting directors at your feet, you'll get to play anyone you want.'

'Ha! No, I won't. Malcolm and Frida said as much,' Jolly said, reaching for his glass. 'Oh, and your *oh-so-tactful* agent.'

'I highly doubt that. I think you must've got the wrong end of the stick. What did they say? What did *she* say?'

'That I'm a fucking limp-wristed fairy.'

'No, they didn't.'

'In as many words.'

'Ha! There you go, *in as many words*.'

Jolly looked up, and I caught something hard and unfamiliar flash behind his eyes. He glanced across at me. 'OK, yeah – well, what about *Shannon*?'

'What about Shannon?'

'What about me?' I said, struggling to keep up.

'*She's* always going to be just *the northern girl*.'

'Leave her out of it!'

'I—'

'You are,' Jolly said, rounding on me. 'You are. Because you're normal, because you grew up in a normal house with normal parents, because you're not an ultra-connected millionaire, because your ancestors weren't on the fucking *Mayflower* or whatever. You're always going to have to play up to your one puny little USP.'

'USP?'

'*Unique selling point*. Come on, Shannon, keep up.'

'That's not true,' Victoria said, coming onto all fours. 'Don't listen to him, Shan. You're *super* versatile.'

'It is true, it is! You just don't see it, V, because you're fucking loaded!'

'Jolly!' Victoria yelled.

'Jol—'

'You're fucking loaded and well connected, and you can be whoever you want. But us?' Jolly wrenched himself up to standing. 'Us *little people*, we've got to trade on our differences because that's all we've got. We haven't got town houses and agents and fucking *Dexters*. We've got to, got to . . .' He thought for a moment, grasping for the word. '*Self-fetishize* – that's it – self-fetishize.' Jolly pointed at me and then at himself. '*She's* got to play the plain little northern girl and *I've* got to play the limp-wristed queer because otherwise no one in the industry would ever think to look at us twice.' Jolly's face was twisted, contorted, his words unleashing some hidden anguish I'd not seen before. 'You can drop your Rs and smoke roll-ups and try to sound like you're from Croydon all you like, but you'll never understand what it's like, because you're an *insider*, V. A *fucking insider*. Everywhere you go you're accepted, already at home. You live in a world of open doors. You'll never know what it is to trade on your differences, never. I mean, Jesus, you grew up in a castle, V, a fucking *castle*!'

'It's not a castle, it's a Georgian manor,' Victoria spat back.

Jolly let out a whoop of laughter. 'Are you kidding me?'

'What? Why is that funny?'

'A Georgian manor. OK yeah, fine, *Your Highness*, you win and I'm a fucking pleb.'

'Guys, stop, please—' I tried to interject.

'It's not my fault my family made good investments, Jolly. And why should I feel guilty anyway? I can't help my background.'

'You should feel guilty because all you do is make people feel tiny and pathetic and insignificant.'

'If you feel insignificant, that's got nothing to do with me, Jolly,' Victoria said, cruelty glinting in her eyes.

Jolly looked at her like he'd been slapped. 'You're a real cunt, V, you know that?'

'Whatever,' she snapped, blush lacing her cheeks. 'You're a drunk.'

'And you're a junkie,' he shot back.

Victoria drew a sharp intake of breath. Her lip quivered. She turned away from the two of us, looking like she might cry.

'Yeah, yeah, here come the waterworks.' He drained the last of his glass. 'You'll never get it, V.' He shook his head and sighed. 'You'll never fucking get it.'

THIRTY-ONE

I WOKE TO THE sound of my phone buzzing. I sat up and felt down the side of the sofa cushions. Jolly had left a voicemail. I rubbed my eyes, remembering then that he said he'd sleep in the car, that he didn't like the way the house smelled, that it made his eyes sting, that he thought the fumes had gone to his head. I remember the soft fur of his jaw when I kissed him goodnight, the cautious hug, stolen while Victoria was throwing up in the bathroom, and then watching him trudge outside, alone.

I massaged the pillow marks from my jaw and listened to the message.

'Morning, Shan, and I guess happy New Year. Can you tell V that I've taken the car to look for food. I know nowhere will be open, but I can at least try. I need a fry-up. If I find somewhere, I'll get bread, bacon, beans, sausage. Let me know if there's anything else you want. Do you have oil in the house, or butter? Oh, and tell V I'm using a twenty I found in the glove compartment. She won't mind. I mean, I hope she won't. Who knows, maybe I'm dead to her after last night.'

He chuckled mirthlessly then cleared his throat. The indicator ticked.

'OK, I'm going to try and find an offie. Is there somewhere nearby? Never mind, I'll just drive around for a bit and see. There's bound to be somewhere. Anyway, let me know if you want me to get anything. OK. Bye.'

I dug the sleep from my eyes and peered over the arm of the chair.

Victoria was asleep on the other sofa. Despite Jolly being the one who'd instigated last night's row, I couldn't help but blame her for how it had escalated. I got up, tiptoeing my way through a maze of crisp packets, empty bottles and cellophane wrappers, and went through into the kitchen. The windows were wet. I balled my sleeve and rubbed at a patch of condensation until the morning revealed itself, grey and overcast. Long lines of fog hovered above the landscape. I filled the kettle and inspected the contents of the fridge. Mum and Dad had emptied it a while back. There was just one wrinkled spud of an orange and the mould-frosted remains of a sandwich I'd failed to finish two weeks earlier.

I heard Victoria stir from the other room. Two minutes later she padded through, draped in a blanket, her short hair stuck up on one side and a face like thunder. I felt a stab of resentment. The kettle whistled.

'Morning,' she muttered.

'Happy New Year,' I replied stiffly.

She squinted at me as the memory dawned. 'Oh yeah.' She picked two mugs from the drainer. 'Where's Jolly?'

I told her about the message. She leaned against the sideboard and stared at her fingernails.

'I can call him back if you want. Is there anything you need?' I dropped the teabags into the mugs and lifted the kettle from the stove.

She shrugged. 'Not really.'

So this is how it's going to be. 'I'm sure he feels bad about last night.'

Victoria flicked a granule of sugar from the counter onto the floor.

'It's not like him to talk like that,' I added.

'It's fine.' She cracked a bone in her knuckle. 'I don't care.'

'You know, that's probably why he's gone out so early, to try and say sorry.'

Victoria shrugged again.

'He should be back soon. We'll wait for him and then he'll apologize, and you guys can make up,' I said, hoping I was correct. I didn't think I could handle another second of Victoria's wounded self-importance.

I stirred the teas and slid the sugar bowl towards her, but she was staring out of the window, her eyes vacant, glazed over. She yawned, and I caught the acrid whiff of vomit on her breath. Her gaze fell on me. 'No. Let's go for a walk.'

'What, now?' I asked peevishly, spooning the teabags into the bin. 'No, V, let's wait for Jolly to get back, he won't be long and—'

'No. I want to go now. I don't want to see him yet.'

My stomach gurgled. 'But V,' I said, trying to dampen the irritation in my voice, to sound reasonable, 'I'm sure he's really sorry. And he'll have food.'

'He said shit about you too, Shannon.'

'Well, not really . . .' I hesitated. 'Come on, V . . .'

But she ignored me and slipped out into the hall.

I bit my fist, released it. I picked up my tea. It was Grandma's favourite mug: chipped, familiar, a satirical line drawing of Neil Kinnock printed on the side. I took a sip, but the tea was murky and pond-like. I made a mental note to get Dad to check the pipes. I went to the fridge, a Pavlovian tic. *No milk*. I was about to pick up my phone and text Jolly to ask for some, when I heard rustling coming from the hall. Victoria appeared, holding two coats.

'Here,' she said, handing me a yellow rain mac and slipping her arm inside a blue one. 'We won't go far.'

WE WORE THE COATS over our pyjamas. The air was damp, muggy, far too warm for the time of year. I wished I'd had time to shower. After just a few minutes of trying to keep up with Victoria, I could already feel the residual warmth of last night and my current exertions coupling in sticky synchronicity, the sweat along my lower back, my top lip, the base of my neck.

Victoria clambered over a half-rotted kissing gate. She was going the long way, the wrong way. I stopped and demanded she slow down, but my words flew away from me, lost on the breeze. Victoria walked on, oblivious, her head bowed to the wind.

We continued like that, her leading, me following, for maybe thirty minutes. Finally, Victoria reached the scar and came to a stop. I made a last mad scramble and came alongside her. 'Why didn't you wait for me?' I asked between gasps, bending forward and gripping the tops of my thighs.

'I couldn't hear you,' she replied flatly.

When my breathing returned to normal, I lifted my head and took in the scene in front of me. The valley spread out before us, venerable, industrious and solid. I'd never really appreciated the beauty of where I grew up. It was just a place, the place where I'd been born, where I went to school, where I shopped, where I passed by boarded storefronts and abandoned textile mills, curry houses and cash-and-carries, holding my mother's hand, hiding behind her PVC coat-tails; then it was a place I saw through the lens of glass bottles late at night, from park benches or the fogged windows of a bus, watching, waiting, waiting for my chance to escape. Since moving to London, though, the place sometimes had the ability to capture me unawares, to pull me into a dream and reveal itself as magical, strange and unique. The sun emerged, bathing the morning in bright dew-dripped clarity. In the distance, soot-blackened factories and pump towers slumbered in the mist, Gothic church spires punctured the sky, and terraced windows shone like mirrored ponds, diffracting their double-glazed light heavenward. Home. Impossibly beautiful, painfully so.

A cloud passed over us, and the landscape was once again plunged into gloom. I lowered my gaze. Below us was a steep gully eroded by time. I scraped my heel along the edge. A loose clod of soil detached itself, falling and hitting a strangle of bare roots. I peered over the ledge. The ground was orangey and wet but for some boulders directing the curves of a dribbling brook.

A gust of wind hit the back of my neck. I felt my knees buckle and my stomach lurch. I stepped back from the edge. I was lightheaded. A hangover squatted, dull and threatening behind my eyes. Neither Victoria nor I had eaten a thing since last night, and I'd only managed two limey mouthfuls of burning tea before she was out of the door. I crouched down on my haunches and stared at the grey stone beneath my sneakers. My insides gurgled. I needed carbs, potato, something to stop up the acidic emptiness squirming inside me. I didn't want to walk back down the hill; I felt sure I couldn't, that I'd collapse. The dislocation of last night was still there. *Are you behind the glass, Shannon?* I could feel myself floating. *No.* I stared at the ground, blinking rapidly. Maybe if I could just lie down, maybe then I could get my bearings, return to myself again. I shut my eyes. Stars winked in the darkness.

'Shannon?'

She was saying something.

'Shannon?'

I glanced up and Victoria doubled before my eyes.

'Did you hear what I said?'

'What?'

'I said, when were you going to tell me about Obi?'

The question hit me blunt and square in the chest. How long had she been sitting on that one? And why now? Why the sudden desire for candid conversation? Where had that been when *I'd* needed it? Where had that been in the days, weeks and months since Godwin? I could hear a plane in the distance, the wind spiralling in my ears.

'I didn't know you knew,' I managed.

'I knew,' she said. She gazed out across the valley. 'I always knew that you liked him.'

Then why didn't you say anything. 'Oh.' The plane was coming closer.

'Obi was . . . he was . . .' She searched for the word. '*Good* to me. He was kind.'

'Yes.' No, not a plane, a helicopter.

'Sometimes, that's all you need. Someone who's nice to you.'

'Yes.' Spinning closer.

'I hope he's being nice to you.'

'Yes.' Rotary blades, slicing us both to ribbons. 'He is,' I replied.

'Well' – she paused – 'that's good then.'

The sound grew louder, tongues of steel chopping the air. I waited for the blow, but it never came. The helicopter, red and yellow, reared up then disappeared behind a cloud, its mechanical roar fading to a mosquito whine.

'Shannon . . .'

I managed to stand up. I looked across at her and, from out of nowhere, she flashed me the most achingly pure smile I'd ever seen, one that seemed to light up her eyes, her face, the entire gloomy moor.

'I'm really happy for you guys,' she said. 'You deserve good things, both of you.' She scuffed the toe of her boot against the ground. 'I don't know what I'd do without you, you know. You're my *best friend*, Shannon.'

The words echoed inside my head with gut-wrenching clarity.

B-e-s-t f-r-i-e-n-d.

And that's all you'll ever be.

I shut my eyes and felt the memories of that night hurtle through me. *You've never been with a girl before, have you?* A hand between my legs. *This is what you want, isn't it?* Stroking her cheek. *Yes.* The soft canvas of her skin. *I've wanted this.* A grinning row of purple-stained teeth. *I've wanted this so much.*

I felt in that moment like an explorer, like someone who'd tramped the earth their entire life searching for a single rarefied creature, only to find that it had never existed in the first place, that it was all an illusion. Victoria didn't care about me beyond what I could provide her with. I was an appendage, a tool. Victoria didn't love me. Victoria had never loved me.

All I wanted then was for it to be over, to skewer my bright and brilliant *friend* with a nail, to stick her behind a frame or flatten her within the pages of a book, to conquer, silence and be done with her, and – please God – to move on with my life.

'Shannon?'

'What?'

'Do you forgive me?' she asked.

I frowned, exhausted by her. 'For what?'

A cat-like smile. 'I know I can be a bitch sometimes.'

'No one thinks that.'

'Jolly thinks that.'

'He was drunk. He didn't mean those things,' I said, trying to conceal the irritation bubbling up inside me, the black tickertape behind my eyes.

'He did,' she said. 'But it doesn't matter. I'll be gone soon.'

My head hurt. My body hurt, my mind. What was she saying? What game were we playing now?

'What do you mean?' I managed.

'I didn't want to say anything after last night, but I got the part.'

'What part?'

'Jane Eyre. I had the recall before Christmas.'

'You got the part?'

'Yes. I won't be returning to school.'

'You got the part and you're not coming back.'

She nodded.

I took a step towards her.

She got the part, and I'd helped her do it. I'd given her everything she ever needed so she could take everything I'd ever wanted.

'Well done, V,' I said softly, placing a hand on her shoulder.

She looked at me and squeaked a single word, her last line.

'Don't—'

—Her mouth gaped, locked open in surprise, no – that's not it – in terror. Kind of ugly really, in the end. And then she was falling, her blue coat spread behind her like wings, limbs twisting, hands reaching, grasping, grasping for the bare root, the hold, the branch that wasn't there.

Act Three

ONE

IT'S HERE I COME unstuck, here I can barely type another word. *Victoria.*

Encore! Encore! I wait, applauding her brilliant performance – *you had me there, made me think you were . . .* Waiting for her to emerge from behind the curtain, queuing at the stage door. *I'll stand a few moments more. If I clap hard enough, she's bound to . . .*

What am I meant to tell you now? What am I meant to tell you?

She's gone. *V.* And it's all my fault. *No,* that's not true. *She slipped.* That's what I tell them, the imagined column of jurors who file through my thoughts at night. *My blood sugar levels were low. Hers were low. We were drunk. We were hungover. She startled at my touch, lost her footing. I never pushed her. Just a hand on her shoulder. My hearty congratulations. No, Your Honour. I'm an actress, not a liar. It wasn't me. She slipped . . .*

I reached for my phone. No. I looked around. Sweat, cold on my back. Breathing steady though. In and out. Still breathing. Was she? Still breathing. Down on my hands and knees. An animal. *Meow*, her cat-like smile. Crawled to the edge. There. There she was. *V? Victoria?* Her body slumped awkwardly against the boulder. Neck lolling at a funny angle. Mud splattering her blue coat, like bullet wounds. The blood – lots of blood – pooling behind her ears. Dark, darker than you'd think. *A scratch, a scratch.* Waiting for her to get up, for someone else to appear.

The helicopter. Pre-emptive. An emergency. For her, surely. Limp as a doll. Her brilliant eyes. Staring up at me. Losing their sparkle as the damage set in.

I stood and wiped the dirt from my hands. I could still feel the warmth of her, there on my palm. I looked around, listened for the helicopter again. Had it seen us? Had it seen—?

I threw up. Watery and yellow, like piss. Last night's wine and oh, you simply must have some champagne, *darling*. The morning's emptiness, splattered against my shoe. I retched, strained, blood vessels bursting behind my eyes. *Her eyes*. Her skull, cracked open like an egg. I forgot to ask Jolly for eggs. *No*. Shaking. Shaking myself back to life. Got to go. Before anyone – before the helicopter – need to tell Jolly – tell Jolly what exactly?

I started running, feet tripping down the hill, down and down and away from – had to keep moving – away from – a bad dream – a bad argument – too suspicious? – no, not an argument – she was upset about last night – in a bad mood – *Jolly's* argument – he wasn't there though – it was just me – she was in a bad mood, a really foul one – *we* never argued though – we were *best friends* – that's what she'd said, right? – past tense – no, got to remember – still in the present – she walked on ahead – not a lie – she walked on ahead and I lost sight of her – she went the long way, the wrong way – we never usually go that way – me and my grandma – she passed away – my grandma, that is – I don't know where Victoria is – she walked on ahead – I lost sight of her – I don't know where she is –

I don't know . . .

I . . .

*

'I'M SURE SHE'LL BE fine,' Jolly said airily, sliding a sleeve of bacon inside the fridge. 'It's me I'm worried about. Is she really pissed off?'

'She seemed to be, yeah.'

'I can't believe I said all that to her last night. She must know I didn't mean it. You know I didn't mean it, don't you?'

'Yeah, I know.'

'And she just stormed off?'

'Mm-hm.'

'Ugh, and she accuses *me* of being hot-headed.' Jolly gestured at the bag of food on the counter. 'So what are we meant to do about all this? I'm famished. I don't know how long I can wait for her.'

I knew I wouldn't be able to manage a single bite. I was still in my pyjamas, my back plastered with sweat. I tucked my sleeve inside my fist and shrugged. 'We could have some toast or something. I'm sure she'll find her way back down soon.'

Jolly let out a theatrical sigh. 'Fine. But just one hour, mind.'

THE RAIN BEGAN SOON after. I thought of my vomit, her blood, wet puddles of the stuff, washed away, like new. Thick droplets sliding down the window pane. The bucket in the eaves, a rhythmic patter, fingertips tap, tap, tapping from the attic like a madwoman. I could smell bacon frying, sausages. Oil crackling in the pan. A yelp from Jolly as a bead of fat landed on his forearm. I curled into a ball on the sofa and buried my face in a cushion. The smells from the kitchen, my own sweat, turning my stomach over and over and over.

At two o'clock Jolly quizzed me again.

'I can't believe she'd just run off on her own like that.' He leaned his forehead against the window pane and sipped his coffee. 'She'll be absolutely soaked.'

All I could do was make noises of agreement. I didn't trust myself to say much more. *Keep it simple. Don't say too much. She insisted we go for a walk but she stormed ahead. I saw her take a wrong turn, head off the long way. I tried to catch up with her but I couldn't see her. I searched for a bit, but I was so hungry I came home.*

'I thought we might drive back to London today, but it'll be dark soon.' He turned his gaze on me. 'You're awfully quiet. Is everything OK?'

'I'm tired. I didn't get much sleep.'

'Hmm.' This seemed to satisfy him. He returned to the window. 'You don't mind if we stay another night?'

'Not at all.'

A rumble of thunder sounded in the distance. The rain intensified. Jolly craned his neck to the sky and shuddered. 'I reckon I'll sleep inside the house tonight.'

WHEN THE AFTERNOON GREW DARK, Jolly suggested we call someone.

'Who?'

'I don't know, like the police, search and rescue, the fucking Salvation Army?'

I bit my lip. I didn't want the police here, or search and rescue. What if one of them had been in the helicopter, what if they'd seen . . .?

'I think it's too early,' I said, trying to keep my voice steady, playing the pragmatist, the concerned friend. 'I think it has to be like twenty-four hours or something.'

'But what if she's slipped? You remember how much I fucked my ankle up two years ago, right? She could've fallen over somewhere and be lying, shivering in a ditch for all we know.'

At the mention of a ditch, my stomach tightened. I rubbed my eye with the heel of my palm and let out a groan of frustration. 'So, what do you suggest we do?'

Jolly got up from the windowsill and retrieved his phone from the mantelpiece. He started dialling.

'Who are you calling?'

'999.'

'No, Jol, it's way too soon.'

I didn't know why I was protesting; it wasn't like I wanted to drag the moment out any longer than I had to. But I remember having the feeling – silly, I know – that if we waited, if we just waited a little while longer, she was bound to find her way down from the moor, bound to come back to us – a little worse for wear, of course, but essentially still the same maddening Victoria we knew and loved, hated and adored.

I knew it was stupid, that I was delirious with exhaustion and hunger, guilt and fear, but I simply couldn't face what came next: the search, the torches in the dark, the men barking orders, the dogs barking, slobbering, sniffing the wet ground for her, and then eventually a body, slippery with mud, with blood, zipped tight in plastic, spirited away from us and slid inside some terrible storage unit within the bowels of a hospital; and then what came after, telling everyone, finding the words, my parents, her parents, our friends, the school, everyone, everyone finding out that she wasn't here any more, that she somehow wasn't here.

Jolly looked at me. 'We have to do something, Shannon. She's our *friend*.'

His lip quivered and I felt something break inside me.

I nodded and closed my eyes.

I heard Jolly key in the number, heard the flat dialling tone, and then the woman's voice, cheery and calm on the other end, asking, *please, what's your emergency.*

TWO

I CAN'T TELL YOU how many times I've started writing this story only to place my pen down, shut my notebook and slide the whole wretched thing back inside my desk. Honestly, you'd think the next part would be easy, now that the fall, the difficult part is over. But it isn't. The life I'd led before that day had – I see now – a sort of simplicity to it. There were facts I knew to be true about myself, certain tastes and predilections I could count on with confidence, a history of moments trailing behind me like streamers and a pattern of arrows on the floor pointing me vaguely in the direction of my future. Although I felt myself to be floating half the time in the years leading up to Victoria's death, really I was quite wedded to the ground. But then, one January morning, she was gone, quite suddenly, and everything I thought I knew about myself seemed to go with her, to split like the loose clods of soil that had slid from the ravine's edge that terrible day.

Perhaps I'm finding this retelling difficult because my memory of the weeks that followed are hazy. There was, of course, a search; there was a dead girl; there were grieving relatives; there were short blocks of text in the local press and Harry Gration standing beneath an umbrella on BBC *Look North*; but really, it's hard to remember any of these details with much clarity. They appear in my mind's eye as stills from a dark room, a cabinet of scratched photographs.

I seem to remember that once the emergency services were informed, and due to the intensity of the storm, search and rescue were deployed fairly quickly. When the skies calmed, I remember Jolly and I standing, watching from my grandmother's garden as a red-and-white helicopter circled the hills. It wasn't long before a body was discovered and brought down from the moor. Poor Jolly was beside himself. He was screaming and telling them there had to be some sort of mistake, that they needed to check it was her. *Check it's her!* he kept shouting, like that meant anything. *Just check it's really her before you make any decisions.* But there were no decisions left to make. She was dead.

They took her to the morgue of the nearest hospital, the one where my sister and I were born. I remember that.

Her parents were informed, her brothers.

Terrence drove across the country to retrieve Jolly, and all the problems, all the reasons for their turbulent, protracted near-breakup seemed to disappear for a while.

I, meanwhile, went home to my parents' to wait out the final fortnight before my return to school. That period, I'm afraid, is mostly a blank. I was in shock. That's what Mum said, anyway. Honestly, I couldn't believe she was gone. I woke up every morning bone-tired and crusty-eyed, convinced I'd played witness to some terrible dream. Every day I had to tell myself anew that yes, it was true, Victoria was never coming back. No one accused me of anything. Everyone was very careful to tiptoe around the fact I had been the last person to see her alive. *Accidental death.* There were enquiries from the police. *Drugs found in her system.* Some routine questions. *Suspected suicide.* I remember staring at the wall above the detective's thinning hair. *She insisted we go for a walk.* At a silver thumbtack glinting in my eyeline. *But she stormed ahead.* Dad, sitting beside me. *I saw her take a wrong turn.* My hand held tightly within his own. *We don't usually go that way.* They questioned Jolly, too. *But she was off.* He didn't have much more to add. *I tried to catch up with her.* I told them Victoria and I were best friends. *But I couldn't see her.* That everyone said so. *I searched for a bit.* I told them she was unlucky. *But I was exhausted.* Made myself believe it. *I was so hungry.* That she was troubled. *The wind picked up.* That storm. *So I went home.* It came in from nowhere.

WE WEREN'T TOLD ABOUT the funeral until it was too late. Jolly received a curt email the day after proceedings from her brother, Lawrence, saying that as per Helena's wishes it had been a private funeral, that it was thought that as Victoria had had so many friends from so many walks of life, it would be too difficult and overwhelming for the family to notify and accommodate everyone without missing individuals from the list or causing offence. For this reason, she had thought it best that only close family and friends attend, and she hoped Jolly understood. Lawrence stated that his mother wanted to share her thanks with Jolly and all of Victoria's peers for their friendship and support during her lifetime.

When Jolly told me down the phone, I felt a hard knot I hadn't realized was there loosen slightly. Jolly was torn up, but I didn't want to see Helena again; I didn't want to meet the other Parkers or Tilleys; I didn't want to see Victoria's finely wrought features repeated a hundred times over in the faces of strangers; I didn't want to meet the occasional bit-players of Victoria's anecdotes, her boarding-school chums, her agent, Dexter; I didn't want to nibble on unbearably dainty sandwiches and hear the whispers of guests when they thought my back was turned – *SHE was there; SHE lived*; I didn't want to rake over the dramatic events of her death, or worse, lie about the blameless martyr she'd been in life.

THREE

SOMEHOW TIME PASSED, AND I returned to school.

I texted Obi the night before our first day back, asking if he wanted to enter the gates together, to present some sort of united front, but he never got back to me. His texts (he was always too busy to come to the phone) had been strange ever since an official-looking email had been sent around the student body notifying us of Victoria's death. It was the email that had broken the news to Obi, not me. I did try to contact him, but what could I say? What words existed to explain such horror to him, and how could *my* mouth be the one to form them? Instead, I coated myself in denial and resolved not to let Obi's silence worry me too much. Whatever it was that he and Victoria had been to one another, it was only natural that he should take some time to grieve.

When I entered the rehearsal room, Obi was already there, stretching in the corner. He glanced up at me. 'Shannon.'

I waited, but he didn't elaborate.

'How have you been?' I asked, instantly regretting the female brightness in my voice.

'I've been . . .' He lowered his arms. His brow twitched, a frown. But then he shook his head, unable to connect to the next thought.

'I texted you. Did you see that I texted you?' I said.

'Yes.'

'Cool.' I waited. 'Hey, a new Chinese place has just opened up near mine and Jolly's. Why don't we go there after school and try it out?'

He looked at me oddly. This wasn't working.

'Or not,' I laughed. 'Maybe we could just get a pint at The Masons or something instead.' I could feel it, the wrongness of my behaviour. I was too excited to see him. I'd misread the situation. Obi was upset, he was upset with me. I should've found a way to tell him what had happened.

Just then Stefano and Poppy pushed open the door. Poppy was crying. Stefano guided her inside. His lip trembled as he made eye contact with Obi. They gave each other a restrained nod, then Stefano handed Poppy a tissue. *That's it*, I thought. *That's how I should've entered.*

'We haven't got long,' Obi mumbled. 'I should warm up.'

'Yeah, OK,' I said. 'No worries, we'll catch up later.'

I went to the opposite end of the room, shrugged off my jacket and began stretching. Over the next half-hour, more people trickled in, hugging, whispering, dabbing at their cheeks with crumpled tissues. I watched my classmates, studying their behaviour for instructions on how to act. I'd seen my mum and dad grieve for my sister, for my grandmother, but this was different. Victoria's presence, or lack of, seemed to flood the room. My classmates drifted across it like flotsam, limbs waterlogged, picking through the sharp wreckage of her absence.

At 9 a.m. Frida entered the room. I was relieved to see her. She would know what to do, how to bottle all this mushy, unrestrained grief.

'Actors' – she clapped her hands – 'if you please.' We formed a circle around her. 'By now you should all be aware of the tragedy that took place over the winter break. If you've no idea what I'm talking about then I will assume you haven't been checking your emails, in which case please come and speak to me after class.' She cleared her throat. 'It's very sad news. But I thought it my duty to speak with you all before we get started so you understand the school's expectations of you. Now, we—' She paused, unexpectedly lost for words.

I stared at her, willing her to regain her composure. Her fingers trembled then clenched into a fist.

'We will all, of course, miss Victoria terribly. She was a warm, bright and immensely talented member of the class. I'd like to make clear that the school does not expect you to just switch off your emotions about what has happened, but I would ask that you all please remember this is a *professional* space. You are here to learn. This term will be the most challenging of your time at the school. You have showcase ahead of you and much work to do to prepare yourselves for the industry. Victoria's death was a tragedy, yes, but you must not let it ruin your chances of graduating successfully.' She looked at us. 'Do I make myself clear?'

A ripple of murmurs went around. 'Good. Now, the, err' – she picked up a black Moleskine notebook, her fingers fumbling as she turned its thin pages – 'pastoral care office have asked me to remind you that there's a helpline you can call and that, if needed, two fifteen-minute counselling sessions are available to every student.' She shut the notebook and tossed it aside. 'Right. Get out your scripts and find a partner.'

IT FELT LIKE ALL anyone wanted to talk about was Victoria. Anecdotes were summoned from thin air about her benevolence, her beauty, her humour. *She was the funniest person I knew. Remember comedy term? What talent.* I did everything I could to switch off from the noise. But I could feel my mean-spiritedness, my unwillingness to reminisce about her, transforming me into a pariah. Wherever I went, there was someone glaring at me, their whispers trailing away or else their heads bent low, conveniently shtum. I tried to shake off the looks, the gossip, the rumours going around the school, and train my attention on what was being taught, on our rehearsals, on all the prep that still needed doing. But I found it impossible to focus. *Victoria* made it impossible. The school thrummed with her memory. She was everywhere: a pair of Doc Martens poking out from beneath the heavy curtains of Rehearsal Room Two, a flash of light in the floor-to-ceiling mirrors, the back of her head in the canteen queue at lunch, in the bathroom, a stall door swinging back on its hinges, a laugh, hers maybe, bouncing around the atrium, the soft curve of her cheek glimpsed through a row of books in the library.

When I got home on Friday evening, Jolly was already shut up inside his room. He'd been inconsolable all week and had left school early that day. 'Wuthering Heights' pulsed from behind the door. I considered knocking, but decided against it. Jolly didn't want to see anyone; Jolly didn't want to see *me*. I went to my room instead, where I found a package sitting on the bed.

My heart quickened.

I stared at it, uncertain what to do. It didn't *look* dangerous. I glanced around. Everything was just the same as I'd left it. I took a step closer, whereupon I saw that it wasn't one package, but two, red and gold ribbon binding the whole thing together. There was a strip of card attached. I turned it over in my hand.

Merry Christmas, Shan. (Better late than never.) V xx

I dropped the label, a white-hot thing, and stumbled backwards. My heart pounded in my ears, so much so that I didn't hear the footsteps in the hall.

'She meant to give it to you.'

I gasped and spun around.

'Sorry.' Jolly was leaning in the doorway. 'I didn't mean to startle you,' he said coolly. 'She left it in the car. Lawrence sent it over this morning.' He paused. 'I suppose there's no reason you shouldn't have it.'

The hairs on my neck rose. I looked up, but Jolly was examining his fingernails.

'Do you know what it is?' I asked.

He shrugged. 'You should just open it.' He picked at his nailbed. He looked bored. But I knew Jolly by now; I knew when he was holding back, when he was fighting the urge to say the unsayable – he'd had the same look on his face the night before Victoria's death. *Go on.* My heart pounded, a low and distant drumbeat. *Tell me what I did.*

A jewel of blood emerged from his finger. I saw his lip tremble.

'Jol . . .'

'I did it.'

This surprised me. 'You didn't.'

'I did. I killed her. I'm to blame for all of this.'

'No, Jolly.' I stepped towards him.

'That argument—' He stopped and without warning let out a sound, a terrible, sepulchral cry from the depths of himself. 'That argument – I did this to her.'

'No, Jolly, you didn't—'

'She was upset. Maybe if she hadn't been so upset she wouldn't have . . .' His body started to shake; tears streamed from his eyes. He buried his face in his elbow. 'W-we all knew she had stuff going on, that she wasn't stable, the partying, th-the drugs—'

'You didn't do this to her, Jolly.'

'Then who did, Shannon? Who did this? Because V wouldn't. I mean, why would she do this? V, our V, she wouldn't do this, she couldn't. She had everything to live for. Why would she do this? Why would she do this to us, Shannon?'

Something rose up inside me. I pushed it down. 'I – I don't know.'

'She was good. She was so, so good. She was brilliant and kind and funny and – why? She was generous. God, she was generous. She'd do anything for her friends. She'd do anything for *you*.' He paused, his shoulders heaving, the breath leaving his body in fits and starts. 'I wish I'd been with you that day.'

'There was nothing you could've done.'

'No, maybe not,' he said, his breath slowing. He wiped his cheek with his sleeve. 'But still.'

I couldn't stand it, the guilt and resignation in his voice. I turned around and busied myself, searching through a drawer until I heard him slink out into the hall. Once he was gone, I shut the door and pressed my ear to the grain. When the plaintive wail of Kate Bush started up again, I went towards the bed.

The first package pulled apart easily. A crystal flower girl dropped into my hand, the one from the department store. I stared at it, turning it this way and that so shards of light shone around the room. I placed the girl on the windowsill and reached for the other package. This one was heavier. I pulled back the Sellotape and slid it from its wrapping.

It was a book, faded, the binding a little loose.

Jane Eyre.

I unpeeled the cover; a note slipped out.

'There is no happiness like that of being loved by your fellow-creatures' Love you, bestie. Not a first edition, but old. Handle with care . . . Just like me xx

*

THAT NIGHT, VICTORIA WAS in my room.

She appeared as herself, corporeal, walking, silent.

She wore the same clothes as the first day I'd met her: creamy overalls, the sleeves rolled up halfway. Her feet were bare. Her hair, loose and long again.

She didn't seem aware of me and if she was, she made no indication of registering my presence. She was standing at the far end of the room by the dresser. I watched her, peering over the lip of my duvet as she handled the objects upon it: a notebook, a picture frame, a bottle of nail polish. At the last, a necklace, a cheap trinket I'd picked up in Rome, she shook her head, displeased. She dropped the necklace, sighed, and raked her fingers through her hair before padding over to the window, where she settled herself on the sill.

I watched her from the warmth of my covers, my eyes heavy with sleep. But she never looked over. She just stared out of the window, a small frown etched between her brows, puzzling out some mystery only she could solve.

IN THE MORNING, I woke shivering. I shimmied out of bed and pulled the window closed. It was then that I discovered the crystal girl, lying in pieces on the floor.

FOUR

'*IF WE SHOULD FAIL?*'

'*We fail? But screw your courage to the sticking-place, and we'll not fail.*'

It was late. Obi and I were rehearsing in the school canteen, the only spare room we could find. The chairs were stacked, the shutters pulled down. A miasma of chip fat hung about the place. I'd dragged two tables together where we now sat, our legs dangling from the edge.

'*Bring forth men-children only,*' he said. '*For thy undaunted mettle should compose nothing but males. Will it not be received, when we have marked with blood those sleepy two of his own chamber, and used their very daggers, that they have done 't?*'

I looked at Obi, but he avoided my gaze. '*Who dares receive it other, as we shall make our griefs and clamour roar, upon his death?*' This was the moment when we'd rehearsed me touching his chest. I came forward. But Obi, sensing the impulse, leaned away.

He slapped the script shut and jumped down from the table. 'There.' He stuffed it inside his bag. 'That should do it.'

'Wait, where are you going?'

'Home.'

'But we said we'd rehearse for another twenty minutes.'

'We'll be fine.'

'Showcase is next week, and we've barely touched the scene.'

'My bus leaves in six minutes.'

'We should go over it again.'

'I don't think we need to.'

'Well, I think we *do*.' I said it more forcefully than I'd meant to. It was the first time I'd raised my voice at him, at anyone.

Obi dropped his bag. 'What's this about, Shannon?'

'Excuse me?'

'What do you want from me?'

'What do I want from you? I want – I don't know – I want the scene to be good. I want showcase to go well. I want an agent. I want you to *talk* to me. I want you to *look* at me.' I felt tears prick the corners of my eyes. 'I want, I want you to act like my boyfriend again.'

I regretted the words immediately. *My boyfriend*. God, I was an idiot. Saying it, actually saying it out loud, it was obvious. Of course he wasn't my boyfriend any more, *of course* not. How could he be after everything that had happened?

'You're right,' he said. 'I'm sorry.'

I glanced up, taken aback.

'I've been acting like a monster. And you've been . . .' He trailed off. 'It's just – I've not been coping very well.'

'It's OK,' I said, guilt flooding my veins. Obi had nothing to apologize for. *I* was the one behaving like a monster.

'She was your friend, I know that, but . . .' He paused. 'Look, before Christmas, we—' He frowned. 'We shouldn't have done what we did, Shannon.'

'But she told me she was happy for us,' I said, leaving out the part where she'd tumbled to her death moments later. 'She gave us her blessing.'

'Her *blessing* – what does that even mean? Victoria didn't know what was good for *her*, let alone what was right for other people. Her *blessing*?'

'Obi—'

'She wasn't some goddess, Shannon. She didn't just get to hand out blessings to whoever she wanted.'

'Obi, come on—'

'No, no, I'm sorry, but you always act like everything she said or did mattered more than what anyone else said or did.'

'That's not true.'

'It is!'

'Fine. Whatever.' I tucked a loose strand of hair behind my ear and waited. 'So what do we do now?'

Obi sighed. I wanted to reach out and touch him, to hold his hand, to draw him close. But I couldn't. Everything was different now.

He kicked his bag back under the table. 'We can keep going with the scene. I can stay another fifteen minutes. But—' He stopped. 'We, you know, probably shouldn't . . . any more.'

'OK,' I said. I stared ahead at the window, at the black night beyond the mirrored glass. 'I understand.' In my reflection I could almost see her, I could almost make her out, sitting there, smirking from where she'd been watching me all along.

FIVE

THE TRAIN SCREECHED TO a halt. I climbed the stairs and emerged into Piccadilly Circus, the beating heart of the West End. Turned in circles by taking the wrong exit, I walked towards the fountain to reorientate myself. Chattering tourists swarmed around me, digital cameras swinging from their arms, pushing me from the frame until they found the perfect picture. Eros towered above me, his worn arrow pointed at my heart. I looked out over the sea of heads and spotted the traffic-choked artery I had meant to take, when someone barged past me, knocking my bag to the ground. I knelt down to grab my things and, glancing up, caught a flash of rust-coloured hair melting into the crowd.

Things had got worse. She was everywhere. I'd be in the middle of something, washing up or making a packed lunch and feel the overwhelming certainty of her presence somewhere close behind me. I don't know if she wanted to hurt me, to scare me. I don't even know what she was, if she was a *ghost* or something else, some elective punishment I'd willed into being. Whatever she was, I became more careful. I stopped looking in mirrors, afraid of what might appear behind me. I gripped the banister when I made my way downstairs. I avoided steep walkways. I stopped taking baths.

She'd been there that morning. I'd felt her watching me as I got out of bed and stumbled to the loo; as I showered and picked something out of the laundry basket to wear; as I drank coffee, threw on my coat and caught the tube. There. There. There.

I gathered my things from the pavement, re-entered the crowd, and made my way towards the Fortune Theatre. The school had hired it out for the day because of its proximity to the West End's most important talent management offices. *The Woman in Black* was resident there in the evenings. Archie said he'd seen the play. When Stefano asked him what he thought of it, Archie laughed and said it wasn't exactly *the best* omen for our glittering futures.

I found the stage door and signed my name on the register. Backstage, the theatre was a warren of dark corridors and dead ends. I walked blindly for a few minutes, worried I was lost, before stepping out into the gold-lit auditorium where many of the class were already waiting.

'Shan, over here,' Jolly said.

Ever since that evening in my room, Jolly had been different. It was like some part of him had shut down, like he'd simply decided not to care any more. Now, Jolly rarely spoke about Victoria or what had happened. He had his sights fixed on the future and the brilliant career he felt sure was waiting just around the corner for him.

I slid in next to him and a few others. I looked around. The theatre was smaller than I'd expected, tall rather than wide. The *Woman in Black* set was still there from the night before. A rusty chandelier hung from the rafters. An ornate sofa had been pushed to the back and a rocking chair waited, unnervingly still, downstage left.

'This place gives me the creeps,' Archie murmured.

'What is the creeps?' Lola asked.

'You know' – Archie shrugged – 'ghosts and ghouls, spooky shit.'

I stared ahead, refusing to turn and look at what might be sitting in the row behind me.

'Hey, did you guys see all the stuff out front?' Stefano asked.

'What stuff?' Jolly said. 'I thought we had to come in through the stage door.'

'We did, but I sneaked into the lobby for a look. They've got sandwiches and champagne and . . .' Stefano felt inside his pocket before brandishing a glossy document. '*Showcase booklets*.'

'Ooh, give it here,' Jolly said, pinching it from his grasp and turning to the first page. '*Dear Industry Guests*,' he read aloud. '*We would like to extend a warm welcome to you*, blah blah blah, *please help yourself to champagne and hors d'oeuvres*, blah blah blah, *today's actors represent some of the most talented to have graced the esteemed halls of the Royal London School of Dramatic Farts* – gosh, what an unfortunate typo.'

Lola slapped his chest. 'It does *not* say that!'

Jolly smirked and leafed through the booklet. There we were, one page each: headshot, Spotlight PIN, contact details. He flipped to the back and we all froze.

'Shit,' Stefano said under his breath. 'The school must've got them printed before . . .'

We gazed in silence at the page. I knew the photo well. She'd had it taken over the summer by a hot-shot photographer friend of hers. She'd made me sit with her one evening as she clicked through all five thousand images on her laptop, looking for the three or four that really screamed *Victoria*.

What about this one? Or this one? I like my hair here, but I think my eyes look kind of sleepy. Or this one maybe. My boobs look good in this one, but I guess they'll get cropped out anyway. Never mind. What do you think, Shan?

I'd tried to offer her my objective opinion, to remain neutral. But I wasn't much help. I thought she looked beautiful in all of them.

Stefano took the booklet from Jolly. 'You know, it's weird,' he said, 'but I feel like she's kind of here with us today. Do you know what I mean?'

The others nodded solemnly. I nodded too, trying to ignore the cold stream of air that breathed against my neck.

I FELT SICK. I stood in the wings as the auditorium filled up. I could hear voices, the sound of seats being flipped, colleagues being greeted, laughter and gossip and greedy fingers paging through the brochure, rifling for the next big thing.

Obi and I were opening the show, an honour and a curse.

I closed my eyes and, groaning, buried my face in the black curtain that shielded us from the stage. Was there time to run to the toilet and throw up? I shivered and clutched the pimpled chicken skin of my arms. It would all be over soon. It was just pretending, just a scene, a confluence of moments, words following words following words. It would all be over soon.

I felt someone come up behind me. I flinched and turned around, but it was only Obi.

'Hey, Shan,' he said, putting his hands on my shoulders. He paused and narrowed his eyes at me, concerned. 'Are you OK? You're freezing.'

I nodded, trying to still the trembling in my bones.

'You know we've got this, right?'

I smiled weakly and let him pull me into a hug. He patted my back, a brotherly gesture, a quick reminder not to get any ideas. 'So, have you seen who's out there?'

'Not yet,' I mumbled.

'It's insane. Frida says this is the most industry guests they've ever got in for showcase. Archie says Ivor Callaghan from Precision is in the front row next to Shelley Haart.'

'Who?' I felt black shadows press at the corners of my vision, the glass start its descent.

'You know, the casting director.'

'Oh yeah, right,' I said, grabbing the guardrail to stop myself from swooning.

'And Toby Close is here, Martin Drake, Nigel Burton – oh, and Sarah Hayward-Knight's sitting a few rows back, too.'

'Great.'

'Tiff says she thinks she saw Michael Cahill out there as well. I wrote to him specifically,' he said, grinning with excitement.

'That's great, Obi,' I said, swallowing back the urge to puke.

'Yeah, well, fingers crossed.' He paused. 'Are you sure you're OK, Shannon? You look sort of pale. Have you eaten anything today?'

Jolly brushed past us. 'Good luck, guys, you'll smash it.'

'That's beginners,' someone announced.

'Never mind,' Obi whispered. He jumped up and down on the spot like a boxer about to enter the ring. The lights darkened and the chatter dimmed. 'Break legs.'

THERE'S THIS MOMENT, ABOUT thirty minutes before the show. They call it 'the half'.

No, that's wrong. All wrong.

These things have an order. A beginning, a middle and an end. You know that.

Your skin turns cold, then hot. Your insides twist. Your mouth feels dry. Your legs shake.

You've been here before.

Butterflies, they say. You don't have butterflies. Your stomach is a swarm of thick hairy moths.

Time ticks away.

Your scene partner stares at you.

Use your breath. Think with your breath.

You can't breathe.

He stares at you, panic leaking from his eyes. *Move, speak*, he seems to say.

A calm descends. You don't feel calm. You feel . . . nothing.

Are you behind the glass, Shannon?

You look down at your hands, your knuckles white, gripping the folds of your dress; then at your feet, two blocks of ice, pale and inert.

It's like those dreams, you think. No, not dreams: nightmares. The actor's nightmare. You're standing alone onstage and you don't know your line. Everyone else knows. Everyone else is prepared. They've been preparing their whole lives for this moment, but you, you don't know what to say. Sometimes you're naked in the dream. Sometimes it's the audience who's naked. Usually you wake up in a cold sweat. It was just a dream. But not this time.

You squint out into the auditorium. The house lights are up. The school didn't want to shell out on a technician for the day. Hundreds of faces stare back at you, blank, bored, irritable.

Time starts to slow, to bend like taffy in a machine.

You look at your scene partner. He glares back at you. His mouth moves strangely, twitching. You wonder what he's doing. You realize he's trying to give you the line. You smile at the gesture.

Kind sweet Obi.

Obi loves you.

You are in love.

No, wait. That was before.

He's not being kind. He's trying to save his own skin. Every man for himself. You're messing things up for him too.

Laughter bubbles up inside you, madness. You hide it with a cough.

Your scene partner raises his eyebrows. You notice your classmates in the wings, waving their hands in the air, miming the intricacies of Shakespearean verse in a futile game of charades.

You notice sideways looks in the front row, embarrassed smirks.

Wake up, you say to yourself, pinching your forearm. *Wake up.*

Your scene partner inches towards you. He's openly mouthing the line now. He glowers at you like the mad bitch you are.

Still, you say nothing.

You think about the picture of your friend, the absent beauty on page twelve. You think about how she should be here standing on this stage, not you.

The audience loom at the corner of your vision, a restless squirming mass.

You wish she was here. You shut your eyes and will her to appear.

We're sisters, you and I.

You pray to her, asking her, begging her to tell you what to do, to shake you, to wake you, to take you.

You hear whispers, disgruntled murmurs. You notice someone get up from the front row.

Now would be a good time to wake up.

You think about her, what she would do. You think about her smile, about how she'd shrug off the embarrassment of this moment, somehow making it her strength.

You acted like Victoria.

You close your eyes and become very still. You think about her, every inch of her. You think about her pale skin, the pattern of freckles across her nose; you think about the soft red of her hair, her breath, spearmint and cigarettes. You start to breathe as her, to become her. You let her take control, like a puppeteer untangling threadbare strings, like a sculptor cupping a cold lump of clay; you let her turn you and twist you, shaping you into a better version of yourself; someone more.

Colour bleeds into the scene. Colour and light.

You open your eyes.

You stand up straight.

You look at your scene partner, and you deliver the line.

SIX

I WAITED AT THE edge of the room next to a trestle table loaded with champagne and untouched cucumber and salmon sandwiches. A woman in a purple scarf and headdress drifted past me in a cloud of lavender. I caught her eye and gave her my comeliest grin, but she just pursed her lips at me, the poor unfortunate, and continued moving through the crowd.

Most of the audience left as soon as the curtain fell. I watched those who remained milling around the lobby, brochures tucked beneath their arms, clutching plastic flutes of fizz and fielding frantic interrogations from my classmates.

Lola was in the corner chatting with her agent. He tittered at something she said, then led her towards a casting director he'd been eyeballing from across the room. Archie told a group of guests a joke and the small trio erupted in fits of laughter. Poppy was blocking the door and trying to chat to a man in a fedora who kept looking at his watch. Stefano was talking one-to-one with the purple lady at the far end of the room. Even Obi had found someone to talk to, despite what I'd put him through. I hadn't yet had the chance to apologize to him. I did try to find him after we eventually got through the scene, but he'd already disappeared somewhere backstage.

I looked at the trestle table. Pink and watery green goo oozed from the edges of the as-yet-untouched sandwiches. Maybe it was me. Perhaps

I was putting the guests off their hors d'oeuvres. I glanced at my watch. Ten minutes had passed and still no one had said a word to me. Malcolm had briefly come over and, seemingly about to offer some words of comfort, laid a hand on my lower back. But then he'd recognized an old chum of his from his rep days and veered off to reminisce with him instead.

Jolly sauntered over from where he'd been engaged in an animated five-minute conversation with someone who I recognized from one of the bigger agencies. He grabbed a flute of champagne and leaned against a column, near enough to me to be heard, but not so near as to be tarnished by association.

'So,' he said, 'that was *quite* a performance.'

'Yes.' I reached for a glass. My hands were shaking. 'Everyone did really well.'

'No, not that. I meant your little meltdown out there.' He knocked back his champagne in one gulp and reached for another. 'The words *what the fuck* spring to mind.'

'Jol, please—'

'What the hell happened?'

'Look, if you've come here to gloat then don't bother. I'm not in the mood.'

'Don't be silly, I've not come here to gloat. Who do you think I am? I'm just concerned, that's all. What happened? Did you forget your line?'

I shook my head. 'No.'

'Then what?'

'I don't know. I don't know what happened.'

Jolly raised his eyebrows. 'O-kay.'

'Look, I don't really want to discuss it right now. Can we talk about something else?'

'Fine.'

The crowd was starting to thin. Poppy was going from person to person with a manic look in her eyes, handing out business cards and recounting her skills in tap, ballet and modern jazz, before adding that she was more than happy to do professional nudity if the call came in.

'So, did you speak to anyone yet?' Jolly asked.

'No. No one's been over,' I said, glancing across at Obi. He had a pen lid in his mouth and was taking down an agent's phone number on a napkin.

'But did *you* speak to *them*?'

'No.'

Jolly rolled his eyes. 'God, Shannon.'

'What? I'm not going to throw myself at them after what just happened. Don't you think I've embarrassed myself enough today?'

'Come on, you're overreacting. You only choked for, what, like ten seconds.'

Was that all? It felt like hours. 'I don't want to talk about it.'

Jolly fixed me with a look. 'This is about Victoria, isn't it?'

'Go away, Jolly.'

'You need to let it go.'

'I'm not talking about this. Not now.'

'You do realize there's absolutely no point punishing yourself over what happened to her, right? It's not like if things were the other way round she'd be fucking up her life for you.'

That stung. But he was right. She'd never cared for me as much as I had for her. I took a deep breath in. 'Look, just because you're pretending everything's fine, doesn't mean I have to as well.'

'I'm not pretending anything, Shannon. I just know that we're about to graduate, and I for one don't want the last three years to be all for nothing. This is it for me. I either make it as an actor or I starve.'

'Just leave me alone, Jol.' I stared at the carpet, at its ugly swirling fronds. 'I've got a lot going on.'

'Like what?' he said, prodding my side.

'Like . . .' I hesitated. 'It's not just Victoria. It's Obi too. We were dating.'

'Yeah. I know.'

'You do?'

'Of course, everyone knows.' Jolly looked at me. 'Oh, come on, Shannon. You're hardly the best at keeping secrets.'

I chewed my lip. He had no idea. 'Everyone knows?' I said. 'So – what, is everyone talking about it?'

Jolly shrugged. 'Not really – it only lasted like, what, a couple of weeks? People have moved on. Which reminds me, apparently Archie shagged a second-year in the ground-floor disabled toilets. Lola said people could hear them in Corridor B, and one of the voice teachers had to knock and ask them to stop.'

'Right,' I said, hating the forced levity in his tone, the casual switch from my very real heartache to some random student gossip.

'Anyway, I call bullshit.'

'What?'

'I call bullshit, on you and Obi. You're over it. That' – he gestured towards the auditorium – 'whatever that was, was about Victoria.' He paused. 'You loved her, didn't you?'

I felt my skin flush. 'Don't be ridiculous. I'm not . . . like that.'

'Like what?'

'A *lesbian*,' I whispered.

'I never said you were,' Jolly replied. 'But would that be the worst thing in the world? Who knows, maybe you're a raging bisexual instead, greedy girl.'

'I thought you said bisexuals don't exist.'

'Did I? Hmm, I say a lot of things.' Jolly tossed his head back. 'Look, to be honest, Shan, whatever you *are*, I don't really care—'

'Thanks—'

'But, it's obvious that, whatever did or didn't happen between you and Victoria, her not being here any more is messing with your head.' I tried to protest, but he put his hand up and continued. 'And now I'm telling you this because you're my friend—'

'Can we not?' I said, inching away from him.

He grabbed my shoulder. 'Stop it. Stop trying to walk away from me. Jesus, Shannon, listen to me. I'm trying to give you a lifeline here.'

'I don't need a lifeline, I'm doing just fine.'

Jolly's gaze hardened. 'Really? Is that what you call it? *Fine?* Fine like talking to Victoria in the bathroom mirror when you think no one's home? Fine like waking up in the night screaming her name? Is that what you call *fine*, Shannon?'

'How did you—'

'Listen to me, Shannon. It sucks. It hurts. I hurt every day, but you know what? I'm damned if I'm going to let it ruin my life.' He gestured towards the room. 'Can't you see that this is it? The people in this room? They're the gatekeepers. We might never get the chance to meet these people ever again. Soon we're going to be out of here, *bye-bye* school, we're going to be dumped out into the real world and expected to find work and do auditions and network and suck casting directors' dicks, and if you can't find work you'll run out of money, and if you run out of money then you'll have to go back home to your parents', and I know, I *know* if you go back there then you'll never come back to London again—'

'Jolly—'

'No, seriously, I'm not messing around. You'll find some comforting little job in marketing or as a receptionist or whatever, and you'll quit. And that's fine, that's absolutely fine if that's what you want to do, but I don't think it is. And look, I don't usually say this stuff, but you're too talented to waste what you have and so I'm telling you, I'm fucking telling you, Shannon, get your shit together, get help, get therapy, get drugs, get whatever you need soon, or you'll regret it. Stop feeling guilty about Victoria's shitty, shitty death, and get out of your own fucking way.'

'Are you done?'

'Yes.'

'Good.'

'Are you going to listen to me?'

'Look, Jolly, why don't you worry about your own stuff, yeah? And I'll worry about mine.'

'What's that supposed to mean?'

'Nothing. Just find an agent who knows how *versatile* you are. Be sure to let them know you can play gay *and* gay.'

Jolly's jaw stiffened. 'You're more like her than you know.'

'Thanks.'

He began walking away. 'That's not a good thing.'

SEVEN

WHEN I FIRST HELD the RLSDA acceptance letter in my hand, I thought showcase would be the ending to my story, the grand finale where everything makes sense, the conclusion to my fairy tale. The princess meets her prince, the actress meets her agent, and they all skip off into the sunset to live happily ever after.

But it didn't turn out like that. Not for me, at least. No, instead I had to sit and watch as yet another person from my year *proudly announced* on Facebook that they were now represented by such and such big-shot agency. I had to listen as my classmates filled me in on all the wonderful auditions they were going up for and how their big break was just around the corner.

Things were falling into place for them. Poppy's management company bagged her a job playing a topless whore in the background of an HBO brothel scene; Lola left school a few weeks after showcase to play a courtier in some billion-dollar movie about the life of Anne Boleyn; Jolly got down to the final round for a West End play about a young WWI soldier struggling with his sexuality, and I sunk deeper in on myself.

Frida scheduled a meeting with me to address my recent lack of participation. She said she'd grown concerned that I wasn't taking my studies seriously, that unless I pulled my finger out I'd struggle to graduate. To be honest, I didn't have much to say to her – nothing mattered to me by then, not even her once sought-after approval. After a stilted conversation which didn't really go anywhere, she changed the subject, asking whether anyone from the industry had been in touch after showcase. When I said no, she seemed to lose interest and, looking at the clock on the wall, suggested with a wave of her hand that I *start some projects*. I didn't even bother asking her what that meant. I knew then that she'd filed me away as a failed experiment, not even a has-been but a never-was.

I'd like to tell you that things got better. I'd like to tell you that I was resilient enough to shake off what had happened at showcase and reinvent myself. But I can barely even remember my final term at the school. As the weeks and months flew by, and my last days at RLSDA dwindled to a whimper, I retreated further from the company of my peers. At the time, it felt like I had little choice.

My failure was a poison. It stopped up my veins and blackened my skin. I felt it rise off me, a rancid ordure so that my only defence was to hide myself away from the others, a theatrical leper.

No one seemed to notice my absence. Jolly was busy all the time now anyway. He was back together with Terrence and getting new auditions every week. Obi was still avoiding me too. I couldn't blame him. He had managed to get an agent after showcase, but they weren't getting him seen for much. I heard from Archie that he was still writing to others in the hope of procuring a better one. I didn't speak to Stefano any more either. This, at least, I was fine with. With Victoria gone, I was finally allowed to hate him freely. No, everyone was busy. Even the ghost I'd summoned in my madness was appearing less and less with each passing day. Perhaps she'd grown tired of me. Perhaps in death Victoria had seen me for who I really was: a fake.

In June, our final public performance rolled around and I scuttled through my small role in *Blithe Spirit*, willing it to be over. I didn't care a jot for the important people who might be sitting in the audience and forming an opinion of me, nor even, I'm ashamed to say, my parents, who sat with their overnight bags at their feet, beaming with pride at my lacklustre performance.

That evening, they took me out for dinner at Angus Steakhouse in Leicester Square to celebrate.

'I don't know how you learn all those lines,' Dad said, pouring peppercorn sauce over his slab of sirloin. He looked up. 'Do they teach you that, how to learn lines?'

'Yeah – I don't know – sure.'

Mum leaned over and stole a chip from my plate. 'And those costumes. You all looked ever so lovely.'

'Thanks.'

'I liked your friend, too,' Dad said, his mouth full.

'Which one?'

'You know, your gay friend.'

'Jolly.'

'Yes. He was very funny, wasn't he.'

'We're not really speaking to each other right now.'

'Oh. Well, never mind.'

There was a pause as I watched them both, Dad stabbing meat onto his fork and Mum nibbling on her salad.

'Do you come here much?' Dad asked, his mouth full.

'Where?'

He gestured at our surroundings.

I thought about Victoria and all the glamorous little haunts she was always recommending. I thought about the chef at Godwin. I thought about the food we'd eaten together in Rome, watching the sun set over the city. 'No.' I stared at my plate. 'Not here.'

*

ON THE LAST DAY of school, as was tradition, everyone gathered for a pint at The Masons across the road. Inside, the pub was overflowing with students and teachers alike. I went up to the bar and spied Frida talking to Poppy, Matt and Archie in the corner. I couldn't help but notice how different she seemed. She was softer, more human. She wasn't a god or a monster. She was just a normal woman having a friendly catch-up with her students. I don't know why, but that made me feel more depressed than anything else that had happened that term.

Obi dragged a table over to join Frida. Jolly gathered more stools.

'What can I get you, sweetheart?'

More people arrived.

'Hello?'

They were all so happy, so hopeful.

'I've got people waiting, love.'

Someone told a joke. They all laughed.

'Hello?'

'Oh, sorry. Erm, nothing, thanks.'

I took one last look at them, at Frida, my classmates, my family of three years. And then I turned around and left.

EIGHT

THE LEASE ON OUR digs ended two weeks after term did. I was due to move out the next day, but I hadn't started packing yet. I didn't have the energy. Instead I watched, peering from behind the curtain, as Jolly loaded boxes and bags overflowing with stuff into the back of Terrence's car.

When the boot was full and the pavement empty, Jolly looked back at the house. He put his hand up to shield his eyes from the sun. Was he searching for me? I hesitated and nearly stepped forward, but then Terrence said something and Jolly climbed in beside him. The door slammed shut, the engine roared to life, and the two of them bumped down the road, bound for a new life of coupledom in deepest, darkest Streatham.

The next day I emptied out binbag after binbag of my belongings into an unfamiliar room in Willesden Green. Matt and Archie had invited me to move in with them, but I didn't want to live with anyone I knew, with anyone who knew *me*. I didn't want to hear about the auditions they were getting or them tiptoeing out for early call times; I didn't want to catch them reciting lines through the wall or doing vocal warm-ups in the shower.

I also knew that if I continued orbiting the same old drama school clique, I'd never escape Victoria. She'd always be there, a ready question on their lips. *What happened that day? Did she really kill herself?* So, living with strangers it was.

My room was small, very small – more of a glorified closet than a bedroom, really. Inside, there was a narrow linen wardrobe and a single chest of drawers. The previous tenant had put up shelves, but they never held more than a couple of books before toppling to the floor. Pushed up against the radiator was a single bed. Above that was a window. When I needed to escape the close air of the room, I knelt on the bed and peered out at the house opposite's garden, gazing at the lazy spin of an upturned tricycle wheel, a toddler tamping a mud castle, Spider-Man socks bobbing on the line. The rent was £500 a month. I got a job in a cafe down the road that paid a couple of pence above minimum wage. If I worked my arse off and took any shifts going, I could just about make rent and scrape together enough money to feed myself, although I spent some months hungrier than others.

When my parents found out how much I was paying to live in London without all the various student bursaries and loans I'd grown used to, they begged me to return home. *You've got a room and all your things, it'd be cheaper to get the train down to auditions (if you ever get any) than waste all that money.* I listened to their arguments then changed the subject. I couldn't go back. Jolly's little pep talk had wedged itself like a drawing pin inside my brain. *If you go back there then you'll never come back to London.* So far I'd failed at everything. To return home, back to my childhood bedroom, with nothing to show for myself but a mountain of debt, and a degree not worth the paper it was printed on, was too much to bear.

A few weeks after I moved in, Mum rang me. She said she'd received an envelope in the post with details about graduation, and she was calling to ask which portrait package she should order and what size gown I would need and if she would need a hat, would all the other mums be wearing a hat. I told her not to worry, that I didn't want to go. I told her it was because the whole event was expensive and impersonal, and also because none of my peers would be there so what was the point. Mum said that was fair enough, that I should do whatever made me happy, but I could tell I'd disappointed her. When I put the phone down, I wondered if I should get myself pregnant instead of trying to be an actress. At least then she'd have something to be proud of. At least then she'd have a grandkid, a second chance, another child to replace the complete mess of a daughter she'd reared the first time. At least then there'd be physical proof that I'd Done A Thing, that I'd existed long enough for someone to find me briefly desirable enough to fuck.

But there wasn't much chance to meet anyone, thankfully. My job kept me busy. The cafe where I worked was owned by a Brazilian couple. They were fine. Sometimes the husband would raise an eyebrow to signal the floor needed sweeping or a customer was still waiting for their bill, but mostly they just let me keep to myself.

For me, the cafe was a refuge. It was there, finally, among the napkin dispensers and ketchup bottles, that I learned how to shut off my brain. *Wipe, clear, walk, smile.* Whole shifts would pass in the blink of an eye. *Wipe, clear, walk, smile.* It was there I saw that although life without Victoria was unbearable, it was also, in many ways, much simpler. *Wipe, clear, walk, smile.* As limp and colourless as the greasy French fries we served during the lunchtime rush. *Wipe, clear, walk, smile.* There was no searching for meaning in that too-warm little room, no effort to impress anyone, no having to mould myself into what I thought some other person wanted me to be, to put on a mask and pretend. I was free not to think, free not to yearn. I wouldn't call it happiness, no, but more a dulling of self, a numbing injection for the memories that tormented me. At work I was allowed to sink, like a frog in a pot, deeper, sleepier – *wipe, clear, walk, smile* – hot and shrivelled, my eyes closing, with only the faintest curiosity about whether I'd ever emerge again.

NINE

THAT DECEMBER, I RECEIVED a text from Jolly.

Tuesday, 4th December at 20:11

Jolly

Ugh I miss you . . .

I replied saying I missed him too, that I was sorry for being a bitch at showcase and I hoped we could be friends again. He said it was fine, that he regretted things he'd said in the past and that showcase had been a high-pressure situation for everyone. I rang him then, and he gave me an update on his life. He told me he'd moved out of Terrence's place because the cheating bastard had been visiting saunas, that he was now living with a bunch of artists in a warehouse in Hoxton, working a bar job in the West End, and had bagged himself a walk-on role in a Vodafone advert (only £150 for the day though).

Then he launched into a tirade accusing me of wasting my talents and ordering me to stop being a fucking drama queen and get back out there again. After the call, he sent me a link to a website where actors could sign up for workshops with casting directors. He said he'd been to one recently and found it useful. I clicked the link and scrolled down the page. *Recommend your friends and family for £25 off your next workshop.*

It had been nearly six months since I'd made any attempt to interact with the industry. I didn't know if I could face putting myself out there again. I was comfortable now, finally. I'd found a routine – a fairly boring one, yes, but one where I didn't feel like a complete and utter fraud each day.

Also, the anniversary of Victoria's death was fast approaching. I had planned to retreat from the world, to live out a private vigil for her through December and January. But then I heard Jolly's voice in my head. *It's not like if things were the other way round she'd be fucking up her life for you.* And so I created a login, selected a workshop, entered my details and clicked *Book now.* It wasn't cheap – £61.50 for a two-hour class – but I figured it would be worth it to perform in front of a proper casting director. I knew I shouldn't get my hopes up, that the website made it clear this wasn't an audition, but for the first time in a long while I felt that small blue spark come alive in my belly again. *Tick, tick, tick.*

THE WORKSHOP WAS IN a new-build theatre not far from Warren Street. When I got off the bus, it was raining. Water gushed from the gutters, splashing pedestrians and washing the streets in grey sludge. I took refuge beneath a Korean restaurant's awning. The door opened and a couple emerged. Hot, inviting smells wafted from inside. I pulled out my makeshift map, but the directions had blurred together in my pocket. I gave up and spent the next ten minutes walking in circles, until I eventually saw the theatre's pink neon sign glowing from a side street.

I went to the front desk. 'Hi, my name's Shannon Bell. I'm here for the Pamela Swift workshop.'

The young receptionist – blotchy black eyeliner and a spiral of piercings snaking up her ear – paused the contemporary dance video she was watching on her phone and glowered at me through her spiky fringe. She glanced at the sheet in front of her. 'You're in Omega. First floor.'

Inside there were eight people, already sitting in a circle. I found a chair and draped my dripping coat across the back of it. The girl opposite flashed me a nervous grin. She had shoulder-length hair and grey-blue eyes. Like me. I returned the smile but decided not to speak to or make eye contact with anyone else. I wasn't like these people. These people were desperate.

I pulled out my notebook and wrote *Pamela Swift CD Workshop* at the top of the page. I looked up. It was only then that I noticed a middle-aged woman with long silvery hair sitting hunched in the corner and scrolling through her phone. She was wearing an expensive-looking camel trouser suit with a pair of tortoiseshell glasses perched on the end of her nose. The woman gnawed at the skin around her manicured finger. She looked tired, and bored.

The ceiling light flickered; rain battered the window. A few more girls my age and a handful of men in their early twenties entered. Apart from one guy in his forties, nearly everyone there seemed to be a new graduate. I wondered if coming here had been a mistake.

After another five minutes – ten after the posted start time – the woman in the corner got up and dragged her chair over to join the circle. She pulled out a buttery tan leather notebook and, not looking up, delivered a tepid introduction to the session.

'Hello everyone, and thank you all for coming today.' She was Australian. 'My name is Pamela Swift. I'm a member of the Casting Directors' Guild of Great Britain, and I've been working in the UK and Australia for over sixteen years.' She had an irritating way of hesitating before she began each sentence. 'Err, I've cast for theatre, TV and film, although most of you will probably be more aware of my TV credits. I've assembled casts for shows including *Gary and Sally*, *By Blood*, *Southend's Finest* and *Another One Bites the Dust*.' She looked up from her notes and smiled. She had a poppy seed wedged between her two front teeth. 'Today I'm going to give you a brief introduction to the casting process, what you might face in the room and, if we've got time, I'll take a look at your monologues.'

If we've got time? I slid down in my chair. The chance to perform a monologue for her was the only reason I'd come here today. I looked around and noted the looks of disappointment on other people's faces. They'd obviously thought the same thing.

The woman rattled through her notes – some casting basics, how actors were sourced on Spotlight, how agents were contacted, how to present your idents and profiles to camera, how getting pencilled for a role worked, and then, eventually, job offers. I looked around at the others as she spoke. People were starting to fidget, their eyes beginning to glaze over. The woman had barely acknowledged anyone, barely looked up from her notebook, and most of the information she'd delivered was, so far, blindingly obvious or, at the very least, easy to find online.

A girl two seats to my right put her hand up.

'There'll be time for questions at the end of the session. Just make a note until then, please,' the woman said. 'Oh Jesus, I've lost my train of thought now.'

The girl lowered her hand. Her lip trembled, and I saw her eyes fill with fear. *Have I fucked up? Have I upset the great and powerful casting director? Is my career over?*

The woman flipped through her notes. 'Where was I? Err . . . Oh yes, hmm.' She paused. 'We can probably skip that.' She looked up. 'So, now there's something I'd like to ask you all to do. This is something I often ask actors to go through when I'm casting for a role. Not all casting directors will do this, but I find it's a good way of getting to know people. I'd like you all to think of a memory from childhood or maybe even just from your life now, something significant, and we'll go around the circle and, err, you can tell me that memory.'

The girl raised her hand again. A shot at redemption.

'Yes?'

'What sort of memory would you prefer, Pamela? Like happy, sad, funny, traumatic?'

The woman shrugged. 'I don't care. Whatever you want. It doesn't matter. It's just a way of getting to see the *real you* a little better.' She coughed into her elbow. 'Err, you' – she pointed at the girl to my left – 'we'll start with you then go clockwise around the circle.'

Meaning I was last.

The girl next to me told the story of how her dog, Bailey, got run over by a car when she was nine years old, explaining in great detail how sad she'd been, how she felt like she'd lost her best friend and how, even after all this time, she still felt she hadn't really got over it. Then she burst into tears. The girl beside her put a consoling hand on her knee. The casting director's pen hovered above the leather notepad. She stifled a yawn.

Unfortunately, Bailey's death set the tone for the rest of the session. The next girl told us about her grandad dying at the tragic age of ninety-two. The one after her shared a story about losing her rabbit. The man after her, the one in his forties, told us about his wife miscarrying and how the pain of that, along with his newfound desire to pursue an acting career, had torn them apart.

'She just didn't understand that acting was something I *had* to do. It was a calling, the same as being called to the priesthood or to be a doctor. But she was all like, *what about me, what about my needs, our baby?* She just didn't get it.'

Pamela nodded wearily and pushed her spectacles up her nose. She still hadn't made a single note.

As the man droned on, I glanced around the circle. An air of panic was building in the room. How was anyone going to top divorce and a miscarriage? Most of the people here were barely out of their teens. They'd lived safe, comfortable lives, bouncing from crib to school to uni before eventually finding themselves washed up here. They hadn't lived at all.

I looked at the clock. We were already two thirds of the way through the workshop and we still hadn't got through half the people. It was starting to look unlikely I'd get to say my memory, let alone perform my monologue, the monologue I'd been to the library for, then five different bookstores, then ordered for £16 off Amazon because they didn't have it anywhere else, then spent hours going over, recording myself back, watching myself in the mirror, actioning and learning every beat of the damn thing.

The casting director came to the girl opposite me. 'Err, now you, please.'

'Hello everyone, I'm Octavia.' The girl gave a small wave. 'First, I just want to say a big thank you to Pamela for giving us this opportunity. I've found this session *so* helpful so far, so thank you.'

A couple of people grinned and nodded enthusiastically, no doubt kicking themselves for not thinking to say thank you before their stories.

The girl continued, 'So basically, and I'm sorry if this makes anyone feel uncomfortable, but my story is about the time I was raped.'

The casting director's eyes lit up. She scribbled something in her notebook and a ripple of electricity went around the room.

The girl went on to describe how her brother's friend had raped her at her mum's birthday party when she was fourteen years old. The girl was clear and confident as she spoke, with only the faintest tremble in her voice. She spared no detail, describing what she was wearing, how he'd cornered her in the downstairs bathroom, how he'd pushed her up against the cistern, how she could hear her family, just metres away from where the terrible act was taking place, and the off-key strains of 'Happy Birthday' floating through the open window, how at the time she decided to bury her feelings from that day, to lock them down deep inside herself, but how occasionally, every so often, the pain bubbled up inside her like a well, erupting with anger, grief and unparalleled despair. As she spoke, a single tear slid down her cheek. She wiped it away. I watched the casting director's rapt expression as she listened, her laser-point focus as she absorbed every beat of the girl's story. It was terrible; it was traumatic; it was frustratingly mesmerizing.

The girl finished and dabbed at her mascara with her sleeve.

'Thank you, err . . . what was your name again?' the casting director asked, consulting her notes.

'Octavia,' the girl replied. 'Octavia Lewis.'

'Well, thank you, Octavia. Yes, thank you.' The casting director tucked a stray lock of silvery hair behind her ear. 'Now you, please,' she said, gesturing to the next person.

By the time my turn came, there were only four minutes left until the end of the workshop. The boy to my right had taken a full ten minutes to tell the group about the day he'd crashed his bike into a brick wall outside Waitrose.

'You next, please,' Pamela said, gesturing to me with her fountain pen.

'Right, well, my name is Shannon Bell, and thank you for taking the time to . . .' The casting director's eyes strayed to her watch. 'Well, anyway, thank you for this session. So my story is about . . .' She put the lid on her pen and folded the notebook shut. 'My story is about my best friend. Well, I didn't know – I wasn't totally sure – that we were best friends really until the end . . .' She nodded and slid her notebook inside her bag. 'Because, well, she died and like, it was really unexpected, and we were up on the moors near my grandma's home and . . .' She nodded again; her eyes darted around the room. 'There was a storm and we were hungover – oh, I forgot to say it was New Year's Day, and . . .' Taking their cue from the casting director, a couple of attendees began zipping their belongings into their rucksacks. 'And we'd drunk a lot the night before and not had much to eat, because, well, my friend had a hamper from Fortnum & Mason, but that's not important – the point is . . .' The girl next to me crossed and uncrossed her legs; the girl beside her put on her coat and tiptoed from the room. *Sorry, train*, she mouthed. A handful of people waved. 'The point is that we were really tired and really hungover, and we went for a walk and my friend, she went the wrong way, I lost sight of her and—'

'Err, I'm so sorry, Sharon.'

'Shannon.'

'Shannon, sorry, but I'm going to have to stop you there. Thank you for sharing.' The woman stood and put on her coat. 'I've got to catch a train so I'm going to have to shoot off. Thank you all for coming today. If you have any questions you can always email my team, they'll be happy to answer. You can find all the details on my website, Pamela Swift Casting.' She lifted her laptop bag over her shoulder. 'If you want to leave a review for the organizers, err, Backstage Casting Workshops, then that'd be great. It helps others find out about the sessions. OK, thank you, bye.'

She swept from the room and everyone got up to gather their things. A couple of people hurried after her, probably hoping for a private audience as they oh-so-casually bumped into her on the walk to the tube.

I shut the untouched page of my notebook and dropped it inside my bag. I looked up and accidentally caught the girl opposite – the rape girl's – eye. She wandered over. 'Have we met before?' she asked.

'I don't think so.'

'Didn't you audition for *The Good Person of Szechwan* like a month ago?'

'No. I just have one of those faces.'

She paused. 'Hey, I'm sorry you didn't get to tell your story in full. That sounded awful about your friend.'

'Oh, thanks,' I said. I picked up my still-damp coat. 'Yeah, it was a pretty tough time.' I cleared my throat. 'And you, with your story. I mean, that sounded terrible. I'm so sorry that happened to you.'

The girl shrugged and looked over her shoulder. She watched as the last person exited the room, then leaned in and whispered, 'To be honest, it never happened.'

'What do you mean?'

'My brother's friend never raped me. I made it up.' Her eyes twinkled mischievously. 'I don't even *have* a brother.'

'Oh,' I said, struggling to piece together what she was saying, why she was saying it, why anyone would make up something so awful. 'Why did you—'

'My godmother works at ITV, and she told me Pamela Swift was casting a new drama about this trainee police officer who rapes and murders a young woman, and' – the girl shrugged again – 'I figured if we weren't going to get to do our monologues—'

'So you just . . . made it up?'

'Sure. She's never going to look up if my imaginary brother's friend's a sex pest or not, so who cares?'

I stared at her uncertainly.

'Look,' she said, smiling, 'these people, they've got no imagination. If you really want a role, you literally have to offer it up to them on a plate. I mean, look at you, I'm sure you're a good actor – where did you train?'

'RLSDA.'

'Ah nice, I was LAMDA – but I've been out for two years now and I'm just like *done* with trying to be myself. These people, they don't care. They don't give a shit if you can act or *transform* or whatever. They just want you to turn up as the finished product. So I figured *ta-da*' – the girl did a little flourish with her hands – 'an oven-ready rape victim.'

I swallowed. In a weird way, what she was saying made sense. 'I didn't know,' I replied.

'Well, now you do. *Fake it till you make it*. Isn't that what they say?' She smiled. 'Look, it was nice to meet you – sorry, what was it? Shannon?'

I nodded.

'I'll see you around.'

'Yeah, you too.'

She left and I slowly gathered my things. I didn't want to run into her again outside or on the tube platform. Her naked ambition scared me. It reminded me of V.

A year later, a billboard went up outside the cafe advertising a brand-new ITV crime drama, *Our Little Secret*. Every day I walked past it. Every day I avoided Octavia Lewis's stricken gaze.

TEN

I STAYED IN LONDON for New Year's. As the clocks counted down to 2013 and drunken cackles drifted up through my window, as fireworks erupted across the city and time ran away from me, I lay in bed watching the same reel of moving images play behind my eyes – her blue coat spread behind her like wings, reaching, grasping, grasping. On this most terrible of anniversaries, remembering was the least I could do.

I did the same the next year.

And the year after that.

ALESSANDRO PROMOTED ME TO head waitress among our small team of four. I was paid an extra quid each hour and given my pick of the shifts.

I FOUND AN ARMCHAIR left out on the street. I dragged it home and squeezed it into the only available space in my room.

I VISITED THE LIBRARY every Friday. I read more books.

*

AS EACH YEAR PASSED, my world shrank a little more. Slowly I was disappearing, scraping my presence from other people's lives. Jolly muscled through my solitude occasionally, but he was the only person I really spoke to outside the cafe. We'd meet up every now and again, our conversations following a similar pattern. He'd tell me what he'd been up to, who he was shagging, which auditions he'd gone up for and which bastard had thwarted his chances this time, while I'd sip the grande latte he'd bought me and make small noises of agreement.

'It was this arsehole I see at *every* audition.'

'The one that looks like you?'

'He doesn't look like me, he's just a skinny little twink who seems to get every bloody part I go up for. It's a conspiracy, Shannon, I'm telling you.'

Then he'd tell me about how fucked the industry was and how everything was stacked against him, how it wasn't fair, how he was way more talented than all the other weaselly cunts he'd see at auditions, how they'd never said it would be like this at drama school, that they never told us how hard it would be.

'I mean, I know Frida and Malcolm thought I had zero versatility, but I thought I'd at least get some stuff, you know?'

I responded with the correct interjections, playing the perfect conversationalist, but really, during those conversations I was barely listening. After the Pamela Swift workshop, like amputating a gangrenous limb, I'd cut myself off from the industry entirely. I nodded along, letting Jolly's bitter words wash over me like raw sewage, knowing that ultimately it would all drain away in the end.

I worked in a cafe.

I read books.

I had a chair.

That's who I was now.

THREE YEARS TO THE day after showcase, Obi messaged me asking if I wanted to grab a drink. *It's been too long.* I was so startled to see his name come up on the screen that I texted him yes immediately.

We met in central London, at one of those places that think the more uncomfortable the seating, the better the coffee. I found a thin, roughly hewn bench at the back of the shop and waited for him to arrive.

A bell rang, the crowd shuffled forward, and then suddenly, there he was. I gripped my knees and plastered what I hoped was a friendly smile onto my face. He raised his eyebrows and gestured at the menu board. *Cappuccino*, I mouthed in response. He nodded and, a few minutes later, came over carrying two cups and saucers.

'Hi there.'

'Hi.'

'Thanks,' I said, taking the cup from his hands.

'Good to see you.'

'You too.'

He climbed onto the bench opposite. We smiled at one another. He clicked his neck and ripped open a tab of sugar. I sipped my drink. It was still far too hot.

As he stirred, I stole a glance at him. His arms were thicker. I looked at his wallet open on the table. A gym ID peeked out from the cracked black leather. His head was clean-shaven, his stubble kempt. He looked different, although I suppose to his eyes I must have done too. I wondered what my days of wiping tables and dragging a mop along the floor had done to me, whether he could see the lines of drudgery and sop-water etched into my face.

'How have you been?' he asked, taking a sip and replacing the cup in its saucer.

I answered briefly: cafe, books, chair. Obi frowned as I told him about finding the chair on the street, probably wondering why I was bothering to mention it at all. Still, he listened politely. When I finished, I felt my cheeks colour, suddenly ashamed of the few crumbs of life I had to share with him.

'What about you?' I asked.

His answer was more detailed. He was still living at his mum's. He worked most evenings at a bar in Peckham and occasionally helped out at an after-school youth club. He was still acting. He'd switched agents. His current one had got him a handful of auditions; some commercials, not much theatre, a bit of TV. He told me he had a small part in a historical drama coming up on Channel 4 in the autumn, that he'd been cast as some rich dude's servant. He shrugged as he told me this, his gaze distant.

I told him that was great, that it was great news he was still acting. 'Do you have any lines?' I asked him.

'No.' He shrugged again. His mouth twitched. 'It's fine. It is what it is.'

We spoke about drama school. I asked him if he was still in touch with anyone.

'Yeah, some people. Matt, Archie, Poppy, Jolly occasionally. People come and go. It's hard to keep track of them all sometimes.'

I nodded. 'Yeah, I've only really seen Jolly.'

He told me then that he was still in contact with Frida too, that she sometimes asked him back to assist with the intake auditions. He said he liked helping out, that he enjoyed seeing all the fresh, bright-eyed actors coming through the doors. 'They look so young, though,' he said. 'I look at them and think, were we ever that young?'

'It feels like a lifetime ago.'

'Yeah, we thought we were such big shots, but we were babies. They come in with all these ideas about who they are, what they're going to achieve. But then I guess they get stuck into first term and the real work begins.' He shook his head. 'That's when Frida gets her hands on them and straightens them out.'

I nodded, considering his words. 'Does she need to, though?'

'What?'

'Straighten them out.'

Obi thought for a moment. 'Well, I don't know.'

'Maybe they'd be better off if they were left alone, with that first bit of talent they came in with. Happier.'

'Maybe.'

Obi was silent. I drained my cup and stared at the milky residue around the rim. Obi rubbed his hand across his scalp and glanced at his watch. His eyes seemed to glaze over and I knew then that he thought coming here had been a mistake. Whatever flame he'd hoped to rekindle, of friendship, love or even the thin warmth of nostalgia had long since sputtered out.

I didn't want him to go just yet, to leave things like this. I pulled out my purse, wondering if the fiver I'd brought would stretch to two drinks.

As if reading my mind, Obi got up. 'Same again?' he asked.

I hesitated, then shook my head.

'No worries,' Obi said, noticing the thin fabric purse gripped tight within my fist. 'Do you want a tap water or something?'

I smiled, grateful for his tact. 'Yes, thank you.'

Obi returned and slid the water across the table.

'Thanks,' I said.

'No worries.'

I cradled the glass. 'I think I owe you an apology.'

'What for?' Obi replied, the latte halfway to his lips.

'Showcase.'

Obi took a sip. A line of foam remained along his top lip. 'No need.' He licked it away.

'There is. I messed our scene up and I left you hanging, and I can't really explain why or what happened, but I'm sorry.'

'Look' – Obi shook his head – 'yeah, I was mad at the time. But I'm over it. Honestly, Shannon, it's fine. Sometimes crappy things happen and we can't explain them and we can get mad and curse the sky or whatever, but really, it's pretty pointless.' He sighed. 'I know you didn't do it on purpose, to hurt me, and besides, I'm not sure it even really made much of a difference.'

'Still, you deserved better. I mean, Victoria would never have messed up like that.' The words were out of my mouth before I could stop them.

Obi sighed and bowed his head. 'You're still doing it then?'

'Doing what?'

'Comparing yourself to her,' he said. 'Even after all this time.'

Shame crackled through me. 'I don't know how to stop. I don't know how to forget her.'

Obi brushed a flake of pastry to the floor. 'That's something you just sort of need to work out, I guess,' he muttered, glancing at the door.

I could feel the walls going up again, feel him cloaking himself in some impenetrable fabric, blocking me out. I knew he would leave soon, that he'd make his excuses and it might be months, years even, before I ever got to speak with him again. But I was done with being shut out. I was done with tiptoeing around him and only getting half the story.

'Why wouldn't you sleep with me?'

Obi looked at me, surprised. 'What?'

'You slept with her, I know you did. So, why not me? What's wrong with me?'

'What?' He looked confused. 'Nothing. Nothing's wrong with you.' He sighed and rubbed his face. 'And I never slept with Victoria.'

'I thought you . . .' I felt something compress inside my chest. 'You didn't?'

'No.' Obi picked up a packet of sugar and cleared his throat. He suddenly looked embarrassed. 'I, err, don't believe in *that*, err, before marriage.'

'Oh.'

He tore open the packet and swirled the sugar into his drink. 'I thought you knew,' he mumbled.

'I didn't. You never told me.'

'But you've been round my house,' he said, a defensive tremor in his voice. 'You must've seen all the stuff on the walls, the big cross above the sofa in the sitting room. Or the fact we say grace, go to church. I thought it was obvious.'

'I thought all that was just for your mum.'

Obi, not looking at me, shook his head.

'But you and Victoria—'

'Me and Victoria had *something*, yeah – a relationship, sort of. It's hard to explain without . . .' He trailed off. 'Look, if I tell you something then, like, know I'm telling you to help you move on, so you can stop beating yourself up – forgive yourself, forgive *her*.'

'OK.'

Obi put his head in his hands. 'Early on, not long after we all met, probably the first week of school actually, I found Victoria crying in the library one day. So, anyway, I gave her a hug and asked her what was wrong, and at first she didn't want to tell me, but then, I don't know, something must've broken inside her and she told me about this guy, this piece of work.' Obi paused. 'Remember she was in that BBC period drama, what was it, *Sense and Sensibility*, when she was like sixteen?'

I nodded.

'Well, one of the casting assistants, one of the guys who auditioned her, he asked her out to dinner after the audition and she said yes. They had dinner and it was all fine, but then the guy said he'd drive her home. Anyway, her dad was over. She said she didn't want him knowing she'd been out with an older man, so she told him to drop her at the end of her road. But then the guy, he just kept driving, said his place wasn't far and they should get a nightcap, and, well . . .'

Realization dawned on me. 'He raped her.'

Obi nodded. 'Yes.' He stared at the wall above my head. 'But she got the role. So she never felt certain about what had happened, never felt like she could report it or anything, or whether maybe it was her fault. The guy's worked his way up since then. He's pretty powerful now. I auditioned for him like a year ago. I didn't get the part. I couldn't look him in the eye. I was so angry.' He sighed. 'Anyway, in the end she decided it wasn't worth it, that she should just carry on and pretend it had never happened. You know V. She thought she could just laugh it off, that one day it might soften into some dumb anecdote.' Obi stared at the table. 'But then, that first week at school, he was in the building giving a talk to the third-years, and she saw him and she just froze, she didn't know what to do.' Obi shook his head. 'That's when I found her in the library.' He paused, a look of abject sorrow on his face. 'Shannon, you've never seen anything like it – she was trembling like an animal, like she'd been attacked. I never saw her like that again. She was shaking, sobbing. It was bad, really bad.'

'What happened then?'

Obi's eyes drifted towards the ceiling. 'Well, we didn't really talk about it for a while. But then, I don't know, I guess she felt closer to me or something, like I could *see* her. I think she trusted me. And we started, I don't know if you'd call it *dating*. I never touched her beyond kisses and stuff. I didn't want to. I told her I was a Christian, and she seemed fine with that and so we were close, but not *close* if you know what I mean. She didn't want to go anywhere near sex either, I think. And I was OK with that.' He paused. 'It worked for a while.'

I thought back to Rome, to that night at Godwin and her frenzied desire.

'But she slept with . . .' I paused, choosing my words carefully. 'Loads of guys. What about that party, at her dad's house in Hampstead, with the Heathcliff guy?'

Obi's face darkened. 'That bastard.'

'It was *you* who found her in the garden giving the guy head.'

His eyebrows shot up. 'Who told you that?'

I thought for a second. 'I don't know, maybe Stefano—'

'Stefano's a creep, thinks all women are sluts. Guy lives in a fantasy land, thinks he's some sort of Don Juan.' Obi shook his head, disgusted.

I was suddenly overcome with the memory of Stefano's body pressing down on me, the slap of his belt on the floor, his hot breath in my ear.

'What Stefano said? That never happened,' Obi continued. 'He's a liar. I found Victoria out in the garden, yes. But she was drunk, she'd taken something, she was off her face, and the Heathcliff guy, he was on top of her. She was totally out of it. She didn't know what was happening. Anyway, I dealt with him, then got her inside and put her to bed.'

I closed my eyes. It didn't make sense to me. None of this was making any sense to me. 'Why didn't she tell me?' I asked. 'She always insisted on knowing everything about me.' And then I remembered that night, alone in her room, the words she couldn't quite bring herself to share.

'Don't beat yourself up. Victoria was private in her own way.' He paused. 'We'd pray together sometimes.'

'You'd pray together?'

'She thought it was weird at first. But Victoria had her demons. She told me one time that she felt like she had this shadow, this evil thing following her around, a second self, this darkness that lived inside her, that would kill her one day. Maybe she was just being dramatic, but I don't know. When she died, I figured this bad thing, this thing she'd been running from all her life, finally caught up with her. She was scared a lot of the time, really scared. So, when I didn't know what to suggest, how to help her, we'd pray and that brought her some peace, maybe. I don't know. I think you could spend a lifetime studying Victoria and never really get the full picture, you know?'

I nodded. I knew.

ELEVEN

LEAVE A MESSAGE AFTER *the beep.*

'Hi Shannon, it's Dad. I hope you're all right and your job's going well. Have you got any auditions coming up this week? Me and your mum are doing fine. Anyway it's our twenty-fifth wedding anniversary and we wondered if you wanted to come home – I mean, come back here *to a little party we're thinking of having – nothing big, mind, just a few family and friends.*

'We were thinking we could maybe go for a meal. There's a new tapas place that's opened under the arches which your mum fancies. Anyway, it'd be really good to see you, that's if you think you can make it. We know your job keeps you busy . . . and all the auditions you're getting and that, but we miss you . . . your mum misses you, and it'd be good to see you again. But of course, no pressure. It would just be nice . . . I can text you the details if you'd like. Anyway, your mum's left me in charge of dinner so I'd better go. All right, chuck. Chin up . . . Bye.'

I replayed the message. I thought about Dad, about Mum – ostensibly my parents, although it was Grandma who'd raised me really. She was the one who scooped me up into her arms when my parents rushed to the hospital. She was the one who held my hand at my sister's funeral. She was the one who drove me to the library; who took me to the theatre; who hosted birthday parties, marking the turning of each year with cake and laughter, and always doing her utmost to make sure I felt special, wanted, enough.

My parents tried, I know they did, but after my sister's death I felt them turn away from me, unable to brave the ghost in my image. It was only as I grew, only as my features changed from those of a child to those of a woman, that they learned how to love me again.

It had been three years since I'd been back up North, and I'd only seen my parents a handful of occasions in that time. Sometimes they made excuses to come and visit me in London: *Oh, well, you know, we wanted to see the poppies at the Tower*; *Your mum got a voucher for afternoon tea*; *It was two-for-one on train fares.* I'd take time off work and sit and listen as they filled me in on everything that had been going on back at home, then change the subject when their questions strayed too close to the fiction of my life.

Sometimes I wonder if they knew: that my burgeoning career was a fantasy, that all I did was work in a cafe and fill my head with books. Whatever they knew, I felt bad for them. It wasn't their fault. The cage of lies I'd built around myself kept me from getting too close.

I don't know for certain what finally pushed me to accept their invitation and return home, but ever since Obi's confession on Victoria's behalf, something had shifted within me. For the first time, it felt like Victoria was really gone, like this space had opened up beside me, empty and waiting to be filled. When Victoria was alive, she'd felt so out of reach to me, her life so unattainable. All I'd wanted was to be more like her and less like me. But now, bound by this terrible thing, I finally saw how similar we truly were. *We're sisters, you and I.*

*

I GOT THE TRAIN back. I did my makeup; I put on a smile and braced myself for the bullet-spray of well-meaning questions I knew I'd be subjected to by my parents' nearest and dearest.

Auntie Faye kept touching my hair and remarking on how long it had grown. She asked me if I'd thought about writing to *Coronation Street* and asking for a role, or maybe *EastEnders* if I was set on staying down south. Uncle Tom asked if I had a boyfriend, and Mum's friend Claire wanted to know about the last audition I'd gone up for. The grown-ups sat around the table and waited for an answer, their faces eager and filled with hope. *Go on*, they seemed to say, *tell us it's possible*. I couldn't disappoint them or untangle the mess of lies my parents had unwittingly passed on for the last three years, so I repurposed a recent anecdote of Jolly's, telling them I'd auditioned to play a young heroin addict in Brighton who discovers they're gay while living on the streets. I told them that the casting director said I'd done a really great audition, but that they'd decided to go with someone with a bigger profile for the part. Claire pulled a face. *Well, next time, love*, she said, patting my hand. Then Dad leaned over and brought the conversation back to food, asking if we should get olives and pitta for the table and wondering how many small plates would be enough, and how small was a small plate really?

I WOKE THE NEXT morning in my childhood bedroom from a surprisingly deep and dreamless sleep. My head felt clear, my senses alert. I pulled the powdery-soft covers over my nose and gazed up at the plastic glow-in-the-dark moons and stars stuck to the ceiling. I stared at Dad's gym equipment, now dismantled and crammed at the far end of the room; I stared at the participation rosettes lining my shelves from sports days gone by, at the Victorian dolls, still in their boxes, their springy ringlets pressed against their plastic windows; I stared at the huge volume of Shakespeare plays I'd forgotten to pack for my first term at RLSDA, which sat covered in a fine film of dust, bound within cellophane, pristine, untouched.

A strip of light peeped through the curtain. I reached up and tugged back the fabric so sunlight filled the room. I climbed out of bed. My train back to London was booked for later that day, but there was still one place left I needed to visit.

MY PARENTS HAD SOLD Grandma's house two years prior. They made enough to pay off their mortgage, enjoy a fortnight in Tenerife and put something away in case I ever wanted to, you know, get married, or maybe study for another degree or something, but no pressure.

I didn't want my parents knowing about my plans for the day. I didn't want them thinking I had some morbid fascination with what had happened, so I told them I was meeting an old friend and caught the hourly bus that trundled past the end of our road. I took it to the station, then grabbed a taxi for the final part of my journey.

As I approached, I lowered my gaze. There was no one here to recognize me any more, but still. I crunched up the footpath that led towards the house. There was a silver Kia sitting in the driveway and a green swing set in the garden. The old net curtains were gone, replaced by stylish Roman blinds in Neapolitan pastels. Geraniums spilled from a window box outside the kitchen. An antique trough gurgled serenely by the door. There was a sign clamped to the gatepost: *Moorland Cottage*.

When I drew level with the garden, I spied two little girls, twins, playing by the foot of the swing. One was scooping handfuls of soil with her chubby pink fists into a yellow bucket held by the other. As I passed the fence, the girl holding the bucket picked up a worm between her thumb and forefinger and dangled it in the air for me. She giggled and flashed me a gap-toothed grin. I returned the smile and gave her a small wave before continuing, my eyes fixed on the moor.

I followed the trail up and up, pounding the same path I'd walked a thousand times with my grandmother, with friends and then with her. The way was easier in summer, less treacherous; less frightening. I climbed over the kissing gate. The usually muddy dip on the other side was dry, its tramlines baked hard by the sun.

As I climbed higher, the landscape changed from willowy grasses to carpets of dense, spongy moss. I tripped at one point, nearly falling to my knees, but continued on, a dogged pilgrim. I felt the sun on my shoulders, my arms, long patches of red spreading across my skin. My lower back grew damp, the bone behind my ears, the nape of my neck. Not far now. Nearly there.

When I reached the top, the world was silent. I stood a way back, not yet daring to go near the edge. I shielded my eyes from the sun and stared out at the sloping landscape, past tower blocks in the distance, past toy cars skirting the motorway, to the fields, far, far away, stitched to the contours of the land in quilted squares of brown and green.

I eased myself to the ground and picked at a tuft of grass. I brushed its sharp fingers of hair then rolled onto my back. Clouds drifted across the sky and I closed my eyes.

Minutes passed.

I heard a bird, a buzzard maybe, then a scuffling sound.

I was no longer alone.

I lay still. The wind whistled through me, one straight line from ear to ear. I breathed deeply, inhaling the sweet scent of peat, dirt, an Ice Age's worth of decay. I heard the soft crunch of footsteps moving closer, disturbing the ground with their unearthly tread. *Her.*

A shadow fell across my face and I felt a kind of peace, an emptying, as if the contents of my brain and all the poisonous thoughts that swilled around there were draining out of me; ebbing away; leaching their bitter nutrients into the soil.

The shadow disappeared and light bleached my face again. I lay there a moment, staring at the skin of my eyelids, two red-veined moons.

I clambered to my feet and, with great care, found my way towards the ledge. I half expected to see Victoria there still, but there was nothing, no one. The stream was gone and the dip overgrown, greenery reclaiming its curves.

This was the place. This was the place where I'd pushed her.

A hand on her shoulder – not much, but enough to let gravity do the rest.

I saw her then in my mind's eye: a scratched image, a flash, and then her smile, achingly pure, lighting up the entire gloomy moor.

You're my best friend, Shannon.

Victoria was gone, and I was responsible for that.

I let out a bark of laughter. I felt delirious with relief, with giving myself over, finally, to the truth. She'd rejected me, used me, hurt me. And I'd killed her for it.

When she'd announced the role of Jane Eyre was hers, I'd seen a vision of our shared future, of her, the favourite, forever strutting and fretting in the limelight, climbing the ladder higher and higher, while I watched on from the bottom rung, slowly shrinking from view.

I couldn't let that happen.

I hadn't planned for it to end that day, in that exact moment, but a part of me had always known it had to end somehow. The world hadn't enough space for two creatures such as Victoria and me. There was only so much stage, only so much light, and for someone like me, it would never be enough, living in her shadow – *my best friend* – a mere supporting role.

Was that a good enough reason? the assembly of imagined jurors ask me. *Was it enough to write her out of the story?* I don't know. Love makes us do mad and terrible things. And I did love her. That night at Godwin, I would've done anything she'd asked of me. I would've killed for her. But instead she cast me aside like nothing, less than nothing.

Losing V was hard, but continuing to live alongside her would've been harder.

I heard her voice inside my head then.

Look down.

I crept forward and peered into the abyss.

Look.

The dip was no longer empty. Lying there was one last gift – from Victoria or from the deranged conjuring of my imagination, I don't know. I felt sick, but I forced myself to stare at the terrible image before me: the human remains of Shannon Bell, my eyes staring blankly ahead, my body positioned as Victoria's had once been, at the same broken angle, a perfect imitation.

I stared at the unholy mirage.

My body swayed on the spot, leaning into the emptiness before me, about to fall or take flight.

A tear rolled down my cheek.

I wiped it away. I had no time for tears. The next steps were already forming in my mind. I could see the path before me, illuminated.

It was easy; I'd done it before.

I would leave Shannon behind. She needn't follow. Neither Victoria nor Shannon need ever leave this place. They could be happy up here, and I, whoever *I* was now, could make a life down there. It would be an experiment, no, a *performance*, the next greatest of my life. I stood there as someone better than the girl who'd walked up the hill, better even than the girl who'd died here three years ago. Someone *more*.

TWELVE

I WAS NEVER THE favourite. I knew that early on, as only siblings can.

'Chloe, Shannon,' Mum called from the patio door, 'dinner in ten minutes.'

We were two halves, two peach stones grown within a single fleshy womb. Our parents pinned back our hair with lavender and pink bows so they could tell us apart, so alike were we.

It happened in the garden. I'd been unwell.

'Give it here,' my sister said, trying to yank the lavender bow from my hair. 'You've been sick all day. Now it's my turn.'

I gave in and unclipped it. 'I'm not faking,' I mumbled.

'I know,' she said haughtily, unpinning her own and handing it to me. 'But you've had Mum to yourself *and* had ice cream *and* watched telly all day, and now I want a go.'

I watched her fasten the bow in place; the transformation was immediate. I stifled a mucusy cough. My twin was the sick one now.

'There,' she said, combing her fingers through her hair and kneeling on the rough stone slabs that surrounded the pond. 'Now, come here.'

I obeyed her.

She had an old jam jar. 'Look at this,' she said, rolling up her frilly sleeve and lowering the jar into the pond. 'We did frogspawn today.'

I inched away from her, afraid of the milky, jelly-like globules floating on the surface of the water. A blackbird hopped across the grass.

'Are you scared?' she asked, grinning like a cat and holding the now-full jar up to the light.

The bird flew away. 'No,' I said, trying not to stare directly at the jar and what looked like a thousand swirling eyes.

'You are.' She brandished it at me and I reared back. She laughed. 'Don't be such a baby. They can't hurt you.' She stood up.

I copied her. 'What are they?'

'Eggs. One day they'll turn into frogs.'

'How?'

She shrugged. 'They just decide one day.'

I dared myself to go closer. 'They look yucky.'

I took a step towards her and we both peered inside the jar. She squeezed her hand below the rim and poked the alien substance. But then she gave me a sly look and, without warning, grabbed my wrist. I tried to yank my arm away but she pulled me towards her, hooked a finger into my blouse and poured the contents of the jar down my front. I felt cold pond water gush across my chest and stomach, the slimy, gelatinous eggs sliding down my skin. She laughed and I pulled myself away from her, hot tears burning at the corners of my eyes.

'I HATE YOU!' I screamed. 'I HATE YOU, SHANNON!'

She was still laughing, more now, bent double at the waist.

That was the first time I felt the glass descend, the darkness clouding my vision.

I ran at her.

'GET OFF ME, CHLOE!' she yelled.

We tussled and tumbled in the grass like cubs before she, always the stronger one, managed to pull herself away from me and clamber to her feet. That's when it happened. That's when she tripped.

I heard a crack.

'Shannon . . .' I said, sitting back on my haunches and panting. 'Shannon?'

She was lying on her front, limp like a doll, her face in the pond.

I climbed to my feet and nudged her side with my toe. 'Get up, silly.'

Her head bobbed on the crimson water.

'Shannon,' I said, louder this time, the panic finally starting to build in my chest. 'Stop it now or I'll tell Mum.'

The phone rang inside the house. *'Hiya – yeah no, I'm just doing their tea. What time will you be back?'*

'Shannon,' I hissed, my eyes welling up. 'Shannon, stop it.'

But she didn't move, and slowly it began to dawn on me; my sister was dead.

'Girls, did you hear me? I said your tea's ready,' I heard Mum call. 'And I'd like you to both use the loo and wash your hands this time, please.'

I saw the bow, *my* bow, still attached to her hair, floating on the surface of the water like a lily pad.

'Girls?'

I heard footsteps behind me then, Mum's flip-flops slapping the path.

I remained where I was, frozen to the spot.

'Chloe?' Mum said, her voice trembling.

Slowly, I turned around to face her. But she wasn't looking at me.

'Chloe – *OH GOD OH GOD OH GOD*—'

She fell to her knees and heaved my sister's body from the water.

'CHLOE – *OH GOD OH GOD*. SHANNON' – she looked at me – 'GO INSIDE AND GET THE PHONE, NOW.'

I did as she said, running away as fast as my legs could carry me, never once stopping to correct her. I couldn't bear to tell her the truth, that her favourite child was dead.

But now, looking back on that terrible day, remembering the haunted expression on my mother's face as she wept over the body of my sister while I stood a few paces away, stunned, scared, and hurriedly adjusting my costume, I can't help but wonder if there'd ever been favourites at all.

ONCE I DECIDED I wanted to be someone new, someone other than Shannon Bell, I became like a child again, wobbling around on my new feet, still finding out how to sit up, to roll, to talk. I remember meeting up with Jolly and feeling like a dog who'd learned to stand up on its hind legs – unnatural and faintly ridiculous, but teetering vertically nonetheless – and Jolly asking: *Are you OK? You seem different. Not bad different, but just different.* And later: *I like it. I don't know what's happened to you, but I like it.*

I told him I was thinking of changing my name, that Shannon felt like a sack of shit around my neck, strangling me, a dead weight, that I wanted something different. Jolly thought it was a good idea. He said that people made up stage names all the time. That if I wanted to get back into the industry it might be a good idea, that it might give me a fresh start.

'I like Viola,' I said.

'As in *Twelfth Night*?'

'Yes.'

'It's as good a name as any,' he replied.

VIOLA CUT HER HAIR. Viola dyed it red. Viola quit her job. Viola joined a gym. Viola wore new clothes. One day, a couple of weeks later, a shiny plastic card arrived in the post for her. *Viola Bell.* Equity member.

Viola boxed up the dead; a lavender bow, a pink one; a fragile copy of *Jane Eyre*; a flower girl, in pieces, the separate shards, refracting different-coloured selves.

Viola did everything she could. She attended press nights, she went to workshops, she wrote to directors. Viola was confident. She was smart. People warmed to her. Viola auditioned for a short film. She got the part. She played a ghost, someone who had died long ago, who existed on the edges, afraid to leave. She only appeared in the final scene, but after the modest premiere, chattering audience members in the bar agreed that the actress had made her mark.

The short-film director was impressed. He said she ought to meet his brother. He was producing a play as part of an independent theatre festival. It was a one-woman show and Viola would be perfect for it.

The reviews were good. The writing was patchy in places, *but Viola Bell brought the script to life*. A casting director saw the show. He suggested she audition for a film he was working on. She didn't get the job, but the casting director sent feedback. He said it wasn't a big thing, nothing really, barely worth mentioning at all, but she should soften her accent in future auditions. *Done*. Unless the brief asked for it, Viola never spoke with her natural accent again.

She got more auditions. She attended more press nights. She did more workshops.

She lived in her overdraft.

She climbed out of her overdraft.

Soon there wasn't enough time to fulfil the hours at her temp job. Soon Viola felt less like a *she*, and more like an *I*.

*

WHEN I WOKE UP in the mornings, I couldn't help but marvel at my new reflection, at the play of light across my cheekbones and the familiar stranger in the mirror.

As each month passed, the mental preparation to leave the house, to put on a costume and play my new role, became easier and easier. Just like when I'd transformed from Chloe to Shannon, after a year, moving in Viola's skin was as simple as breathing.

More auditions followed. Another short film. Another play. Jolly wanted to spend more time together. He wanted to know how I was doing it, what my secret was. *I don't have any secrets*, I replied. And I didn't. I was a blank canvas, painting myself anew.

My hair grew. I cut it again. I maintained my appearance with absolute precision. I never let the colour fade from my roots, never let my skin turn grey. I sought out sun and exercise. I went to bars. Vodka and cranberry, but hold the vodka. No one noticed. Everyone was too wrapped up in their own stories, their own irresistible rise and fall.

I met people. I made new friends. One recommended me to their agent. In his cramped office in Chinatown, he signed me on the spot. I got more auditions, more roles, until one day an email landed in my inbox telling me to be at the American Church at 11 a.m. the next day for a meeting with Pamela Swift.

I read the breakdown for the role. The audition was for a BBC drama about a young woman whose father dies, leaving her to run the ailing family farm alone. I was auditioning for the lead.

When I arrived, I followed signs to the staircase.

FIELDS OF HOPE CASTING – THIS WAY

An eager assistant greeted me. She took my name, my agent's details, and handed me four pages of sides.

'Have a read and make sure you're familiar with them. Don't worry, you probably won't read through all of them in there. It's just to get a sense of the character.'

I nodded and took a seat by the window. I flicked through the papers. I could hear voices in the other room, an actress exclaiming wildly, Ms Swift's impassive purr. Footsteps echoed around the stairwell. Another young woman appeared in the waiting room. The assistant repeated the same spiel and handed her the same sides. The girl smiled nervously at me. As she sat down, her eyes darted around the room. *New grad*, I thought.

The door opened and the actress emerged. She swung her bag over her shoulder and dumped the sides on a chair, before clomping out into the corridor and down the stairs. Another assistant, dressed in black, poked her head around the door.

'Viola?'

I stood.

The room was long. At the far end was a trestle table littered with CVs and headshots. Behind it, Pamela Swift sat hunched over a laptop. The assistant smiled anxiously and scurried over to join her.

'Viola, is it?' Ms Swift said, glancing up.

'Yes,' I replied. She didn't recognize me.

'Brilliant. Have you, err, had some time to look through the sides?'

I nodded.

'Excellent.'

I went through the scene with the assistant reading in for the father character, and Pamela Swift staring at her laptop screen. When I finished, she took off her glasses and dug a lump of mascara from the corner of her eye. 'That was great, really great. Err, now, I'm going to ask you to do something. I wonder, please, Viola, if you could tell me a memory – it can be any memory, it doesn't have to be relevant to the script. It's just so I can get a sense of you as a person.'

I heard a high-pitched ringing sound in my ear.

This was it. This was the moment. Viola was ready. *I* was ready. The room suddenly felt smaller, darker. There might as well have been a spotlight above my head. Take a deep breath. *In – out.* All the hurting and twisting, all the contorting myself into something new, pink and wriggling, and here it was. The moment I knew everything was about to change.

'So I guess the memory that first springs to mind is of my dad. When I was a kid, maybe five years old, he went through this farming phase. He bought a load of Jersey cows and a couple of acres.' I smiled to myself. 'He had no idea what to do with them though. In fact, he ended up selling them at a loss and the land went to developers. I guess you'd call it a midlife crisis or something now. Anyway, after all that, he left my mum, moved in with his secretary, started a whole new life, new kids, everything.' I paused. 'But that time, that time when we had the farm, that time was good.' I took a breath. 'I remember he had a tractor, this big useless thing. He'd bought it new from the suppliers. It was green and shiny and didn't have a speck of dirt on it. The seat leather still smelled brand new, not a crease on it. It was ridiculous really. He shouldn't have bought it. I don't think he even knew what to do with it. He'd just climb up and sit in it, then ride around the fields all day. I'd get up into the seat with him and we'd drive around, waving at the neighbours, dog walkers, anyone we saw, and he'd say to me: *Wave, Viola. Smile, Viola. We've got to show them we're busy, that we know what we're doing.*' I shook my head. 'People must've thought he was an idiot.' I paused.

Ms Swift was looking directly at me. She tapped her colleague's wrist, and the assistant began searching through the mess of papers for something.

'Idiot or not, I thought the whole thing was wonderful.' I took a deep breath in, feeling the wind on my face, the sun on my neck, the warmth of this imagined bear-like figure with his big safe arm around me, his great paw resting on my bony knee. 'I remember nestling into his side as we crossed the fields. *Doing the rounds*, he'd call it. We'd check the fences, check the cows, make sure everything was the same as the last time we'd been around.' I stopped and cleared my throat. 'Back then, with his arm around me, high up there on the seat, I felt invincible, like I was at the centre of the universe. When we passed people and they waved, I thought they'd come out to see us especially. I thought my daddy was respected and important. I thought he was *somebody*.' I looked up, my eyes shining. 'Together, I thought we could do whatever we wanted, that he'd always be there to protect me, and that if we were together, everything would turn out fine. I thought we'd drive across those fields together forever. Just me and him.' I clenched my fist and fought back tears. 'He left pretty soon after that. I was still young. I didn't see him for a few years. He had his new family then, you see, his new daughter.' I shrugged. A sigh. 'At least we had that time though.'

Pamela Swift stared at me, transfixed. The assistant tapped her on the shoulder. She blinked, returning to the room. She coughed and picked through some papers. 'That was, err, really magical, Viola – it is Viola, isn't it? Thank you for sharing that with us today.' She touched the assistant's hand, who promptly scribbled something down. 'Can I just double-check we've got your agent's details right, in case we need to get in touch with you again?'

EPILOGUE

I STILL DREAM ABOUT them.

Sometimes I'm Victoria, snorting coke off a coffee table or sitting in a locked cubicle with my head bowed in silent prayer. Sometimes I'm lying in the warm grass of a summer's night, a constellation of glow-in-the-dark stars burning above my head. Other times I'm Shannon, back at the cafe again, my vision blurring as I slide a mop backwards and forwards, backwards and forwards. Sometimes I'm at school, a teenager lurking in the lunch hall with a copy of *Jane Eyre* tucked beneath my arm, staring at a feedback sheet where the words *Face disappears* have been carelessly erased. Sometimes I don't know who I am, but I'm standing in a garden, holding a small girl's hand and watching our reflections double in the water.

One time, I dreamed we were all there, together.

That night I'd been at an awards ceremony, the third or fourth of the season.

And the award for Best Actress goes to . . .

They said my win was irrefutable, glorious, a triumph. Everyone was kissing my cheeks, hugging me close for pictures – *Viola, over here! V, how marvellous to see you!* – buying me drinks, offering me lines. I couldn't very well say no to them, could I? Not on my special night.

Stefano happened to be there too. He'd been involved in the shoot for one of the Best British Film nominees. He wasn't acting any more. He was an intimacy coordinator now. His appearance surprised me. I remember seeing him from across the room and, emboldened by my win, cornering him, saying well done to him, that the scene by the fountain was mesmeric, brutal, terrifying, that he deserved to win. *Well done.* I kept repeating those words, like a curse – *well done, well done, well done* – and marvelling at how he'd managed to coordinate everything to his liking with such utter fucking perfection.

Later his girlfriend, some nepo hanger-on I recognized from the tabloids, toppled my statuette reaching across the table for her purse. Apparently I said something to her about Stefano. I don't remember. Apparently security were called, discreetly, and I was taken to a different part of the hall. I do remember looking over my shoulder though, and seeing him comfort her, his face a picture of baffled innocence.

Not long after, I stumbled and fell on my way to the bathroom. A light flashed. I tried to shield myself. Someone ripped the camera from the man's hand. Then my publicist found me, whispered angry words in my ear – *You do this every time, every fucking time, V* – and before I knew it, I was being bundled into a car.

The housekeeper was gone when I arrived home.

I don't know how – I blacked out – but I somehow found my way to bed. I came to maybe an hour later. My mouth was dry as a birdcage. A bank of lilac feathers sat ruched around my face. I was still wearing my gown, my necklace and my lucky earrings (cornflower-blue teardrops). I groaned and, without warning, puked down myself. I reached for some water, and the ceiling waltzed above me.

That was the night I dreamed of them.

We were in a forest clearing, sitting around a white table. At the centre of the table was a vase of blue lilies like the ones that had greeted me in Lamia, Victoria's house in Hampstead. Apart from a little girl playing in the undergrowth, it was just the three of us: Victoria, the eighteen-year-old Shannon and me. I was still wearing my awards gown, red hair piled on my head, my makeup pristine. Shannon was dressed in drama school black, and Victoria was in her cream overalls.

A crown of branches swung lazily overhead, casting dappled sunlight across the starched linen. The air was sweet with honeysuckle and the soft decay of the forest floor.

Time slowed. Everything slowed.

I turned my head and looked at the two of them.

Shannon was staring ahead, a small frown knitting her brows together, her expression solemn and hard to read. Victoria was smiling at Shannon, but in a blank, lobotomized sort of way, her grin fixed, her eyes gelded of their sparkle.

We talked, slowly – I don't remember about quite what, but I remember the feeling of it, like no time at all had passed, like I was speaking with old friends, which I suppose in a way I was.

We chatted away, the same old nonsense and truth and putting the world to rights. Then evening approached; the air began to turn cooler; creeping shadows appeared on the forest floor. And now this, I do remember. I asked them, both of them, if they were happy to be here. I never specified where *here* was, I didn't even know myself, but they seemed to understand all the same. Shannon stared at the table, then smiled. *I hide and I disappear*, she said. Victoria placed her hand over Shannon's and nodded in agreement.

I heard a child's laughter.

Shannon glanced at Victoria and they shared a look, something private and other. Something I wasn't meant to see or understand.

I opened my mouth to respond. There was something I needed to say to them, something important, urgent. But the light was fading, the crimson curtain of night drawing shut, and suddenly these two young women, my oldest, dearest friends, seemed to me so very far away.

ACKNOWLEDGEMENTS

I'M THAT PERSON WHO flicks to the back to scan the acknowledgments. I like reading the names of all the behind-the-scenes heroes who've helped urge a book into being. I've always dreamed of being able to write one of these pages myself, and now here I am, finally getting to thank all the people who've propped me up and cheered me on over the years.

Thank you to my agent, Rachel Neely. I often return to the first email you ever sent me asking to read my full manuscript just to check that this is all, in fact, real. I'm so lucky to have found an agent who *got* the book straightaway. Thank you for steering me through the choppy waters of debut authordom with persistence, insight and care. I couldn't have done this without you. Thank you also to Juliet Mushens, Catriona Fida, Alba Arnau Prado, Emma Dawson and everyone who's read and championed my book at Mushens Entertainment.

I would also like to say a huge thank you to my editor, Kat Burdon. Your continued hard work, flair and enthusiasm have blown me away. Thank you for your shrewd editorial insight and for all the ways you've helped bring this book to life. Thank you also to Emily Patience, Katy Blott, Ella Horne, Stefanie Bierwerth and everyone at Quercus who's worked tirelessly to get this book into as many readers' hands as possible. And thank you to Claire Gatzen for copyediting the book, and Amber Burlinson for proofreading it.

I also want to thank Bobby Nayyar and the entire team at Spread The Word. Winning the London Writers Award was the boost I needed to take myself and my writing seriously. Thank you for the vote of confidence and for your ongoing support. Thank you also to my critical feedback group and, in particular, Rebecca Lewis and Megan Elliott-Hewson, for your friendship and generous feedback on early drafts.

Next, a huge thank you to two of my closest friends, John Moore and David Fenne. John, thank you for being an early reader and constant cheerleader. And thank you David for being my work-husband in both our writing and performing careers (even flighty freelancers need colleagues they can moan at every now and again). I love you both bucketloads.

I'd also like to thank the members of my reading group – The Porridge Club – Gráinne Clear, Bethan Morgan and John Moore (again) for giving me the nudge I needed to send this manuscript out at the right time.

Thank you to my improv family, Pinch Punch. Thank you David Fenne (again), Sam Martin, Lottie Davies, Angela Eaton, Sophie Warren, Maya-Nika Bewley, Eoin McAndrew, Will Beynon, Duncan Mitchell and Peter Rugman (more on you later). I've genuinely never laughed as much as I do when I'm with you lot. You are all depraved weirdos and I love you very much.

Thank you to Amy Westwood and Rachael Smith. Your tireless years of friendship, love and support continue to mean so much to me. Thank you also to Kate Martin for being my OG writer pal; your lockdown emails helped brighten the dark days of the pandemic.

I also need to say a huge thank you to the friends I've managed to cling onto from when I was at drama school. I hope you recognise the happy memories nestled within the pages of this book, and that you're managing to heal from the bad ones. Thanks in particular to Charlie Hall, Sundi Scott, Matthew Churcher, Bartosz Stanislawek and Gabriele Lombardo (cheers for all the Italian cuss words, buddy). Thank you also to my Gowan Road pals and to Sophie Dessauer-Hall for all the laughter and out-of-work-actor whinges we've shared over the years.

Thank you to my grandmas, Beatrice and Marlene. I am so grateful for your generosity, love and encouragement throughout my life. Thank you also to my brilliant, caring brother, Simon, and to my parents, Colin and Dawn. I am so blessed to be your daughter. Thank you for always loving, encouraging and supporting me, no matter the strange avenues I've ended up pursuing.

And finally, thank you Peter. Where would I be without you? My first reader, my best friend, my love.

RAISING READERS
Books Build Bright Futures

Dear Reader,

We'd love your attention for one more page to tell you about the crisis in children's reading, and what we can all do.

Studies have shown that reading for fun is the **single biggest predictor of a child's future life chances** – more than family circumstance, parents' educational background or income. It improves academic results, mental health, wealth, communication skills, ambition and happiness.[1]

The number of children reading for fun is in rapid decline. Young people have a lot of competition for their time. In 2024, 1 in 10 children and young people in the UK aged 5 to 18 did not own a single book at home.[2]

Hachette works extensively with schools, libraries and literacy charities, but here are some ways we can all raise more readers:

- Reading to children for just 10 minutes a day makes a difference
- Don't give up if children aren't regular readers – there will be books for them!
- Visit bookshops and libraries to get recommendations
- Encourage them to listen to audiobooks
- Support school libraries
- Give books as gifts

There's a lot more information about how to encourage children to read on our website: **www.RaisingReaders.co.uk**

Thank you for reading.

hachette UK

[1] OECD, '21st-Century Readers: Developing Literacy Skills in a Digital World', 2021, https://www.oecd.org/en/publications/21st-century-readers_a83d84cb-en.html

[2] National Literacy Trust, 'Book Ownership in 2024', November 2024, https://literacytrust.org.uk/research-services/research-reports/book-ownership-in-2024